Child of the River

THE FIRST BOOK OF CONFLUENCE

Child of the River

THE FIRST BOOK OF CONFLUENCE

PAUL J. McAULEY

VICTOR GOLLANCZ

LONDON

First published in Great Britain 1997
by Victor Gollancz
An imprint of the Cassell Group
Wellington House, 125 Strand, London WC2R OBB

© Paul J. McAuley 1997

A catalogue record for this book is
available from the British Library.

ISBN 0 575 06427 7

Typeset by SetSystems Ltd, Saffron Walden, Essex
Printed in Great Britain
by St Edmundsbury Press Ltd, Bury St Edmunds, Suffolk

97 98 99   5 4 3 2 1

For Caroline,
shelter from the storm

Praise the Lord! for He hath spoken
Worlds his mighty voice obeyed
Laws, which never shall be broken
For their guidance He hath made.

Kempthorn

1 ~ The White Boat

The Constable of Aeolis was a shrewd, pragmatic man who did not believe in miracles. In his opinion, everything must have an explanation, and simple explanations were best of all. 'The sharpest knife cuts cleanest,' he often told his sons. 'The more a man talks, the more likely it is he's lying.'

But to the end of his days, he could not explain the affair of the white boat.

It happened one midsummer night, when the huge black sky above the Great River was punctuated only by a scattering of dim halo stars and the dull red swirl, no bigger than a man's hand, of the Eye of the Preservers. The heaped lights of the little city of Aeolis and the lights of the carracks riding at anchor outside the harbour entrance were brighter by far than anything in the sky.

The summer heat was oppressive to the people of Aeolis. For most of the day they slept in the relative cool of their seeps and wallows, rising to begin work when the Rim Mountains clawed the setting sun, and retiring again when the sun rose, renewed, above the devouring peaks. In summer, stores and taverns and workshops stayed open from dusk until dawn, fishing boats set out at midnight to trawl the black river for noctilucent polyps and pale shrimp, and the streets of Aeolis were crowded and bustling beneath the flare of cressets and the orange glow of sodium vapour lamps. At night, in summer, the lights of Aeolis shone like a beacon in the midst of the dark shore.

That particular night, the Constable and his two eldest sons were rowing back to Aeolis in their skiff with two vagrant river traders who had been arrested while trying to run bales of cigarettes to the unchanged hill tribes of the wild shore downstream of Aeolis. Part of the traders' contraband cargo, soft bales sealed in plastic wrap and oiled cloth, was

9

stacked in the forward well of the skiff; the traders lay in the stern, tied up like shoats for the slaughter. The skiff's powerful motor had been shot out in the brief skirmish, and the Constable's sons, already as big as their father, sat side by side on the centre thwart, rowing steadily against the current. The Constable was perched on a button cushion in the skiff's high stern, steering for the lights of Aeolis.

The Constable was drinking steadily from a cruse of wine. He was a large man with loose grey skin and gross features, like a figure hastily moulded from clay and abandoned before it was completed. A pair of tusks protruded like daggers from his meaty upper lip. One tusk had been broken when he had fought and killed his father, and the Constable had had it capped with silver; silver chinked against the neck of the cruse each time he took a swig of wine.

The Constable was not in a good temper. He would make a fair profit from his half of the captured cargo (the other half would go to the Aedile, if he could spare an hour or so from his excavations to pronounce sentence on the traders), but the arrest had not gone smoothly. The river traders had hired a pentad of ruffians as an escort, and they had put up a desperate fight before the Constable and his sons had managed to despatch them. The Constable's shoulders had taken a bad cut, cleaving through blubber to the muscle beneath, and his back had been scorched by reflection of the pistol bolt which had damaged the skiff's motor. Fortunately, the weapon, which had probably predated the foundation of Aeolis, had misfired on the second shot and killed the man using it, but the Constable knew that he could not rely on good luck for ever. He was getting old, ponderous and muddled when once he had been quick and strong. He knew that sooner or later one of his sons would challenge him, and he was worried that this night's botched episode was a harbinger of his decline. Like all strong men, he feared his own weakness more than death, for strength was how he measured the worth of his life.

Now and then he turned and looked back at the pyre of the smugglers' boat. It had burnt to the waterline, a flickering dash of light riding its own reflection far out across the river's broad black plain. The Constable's sons had run it aground on a mudbank, so that it would not drift amongst the banyan islands which at this time of year spun in slow circles in the shallow sargasso of the Great River's nearside shoals, tethered only by fine nets of feeder roots.

Of the two river traders, one lay as still as a sated cayman, resigned to his fate, but his mate, a tall, skinny old man naked but for a breechclout and an unravelling turban, was trying to convince the Constable to let him go. Yoked hand to foot, so that his back was bent like a bow, he stared up at the Constable from the well, his insincere frightened smile like a rictus, his eyes so wide that white showed clear around their slitted irises. At first he had tried to gain the Constable's attention with flattery; now he was turning to threats.

'I have many friends, captain, who would be unhappy to see me in your jail,' he said. 'There are no walls strong enough to withstand the force of their friendship, for I am a generous man. I am known for my generosity across the breadth of the river.'

The Constable rapped the top of the trader's turban with the butt of his whip, and for the fourth or fifth time advised him to be quiet. It was clear from the arrowhead tattoos on the man's fingers that he belonged to one of the street gangs which roved the ancient wharves of Ys. Any friends he might have were a hundred leagues upriver, and by dusk tomorrow he and his companion would be dead.

The skinny trader babbled, 'Last year, captain, I took it upon myself to sponsor the wedding of the son of one of my dear friends, who had been struck down in the prime of life. Bad fortune had left his widow with little more than a rented room and nine children to feed. The son was besotted; his bride's family impatient. This poor lady had no one to turn to but myself, and I, captain, remembering the good company of my friend, his wisdom and his friendly laughter, took it upon myself to organize everything. Four hundred people ate and drank at the celebration, and I count them all as my friends. Quails' tongues in aspic we had, captain, and mounds of oysters and fish roe, and baby goats tender as the butter they were seethed in.'

Perhaps there was a grain of truth in the story. Perhaps the man had been one of the guests at such a wedding, but he could not have sponsored it. No one desperate enough to try to smuggle cigarettes to the hill tribes would have been able to lavish that kind of money on an act of charity.

The Constable flicked his whip across the legs of the prisoners. He said, 'You are a dead man, and dead men have no friends. Compose yourself. Our city might be a small place, but it has a shrine, and it was one of the last places along all the river's shore where avatars talked with men, before the heretics silenced them. Pilgrims still come here, for even if the avatars are no longer able to speak, surely they are still listening. We'll let you speak to them after you've been sentenced. I suggest you take the time to think of what account you can give of your life.'

One of the Constable's son's laughed, and the Constable gave their broad backs a touch of his whip. 'Row,' he told them, 'and keep quiet.'

'Quails' tongues,' the talkative trader said. 'Anything you want, captain. You have only to name it and it will be yours. I can make you rich. I can offer you my own home, captain. Like a palace it is, right in the heart of Ys. Far from this stinking hole—'

The boat rocked when the Constable jumped into the well. His sons cursed wearily, and shipped their oars. The Constable knocked off the wretched trader's turban, pulled up the man's head by the greasy knot of hair that sprouted from his crown and, before he could scream, thrust two fingers into his mouth and grasped his writhing tongue. The trader gagged and tried to bite the Constable's fingers, but his teeth scarcely bruised their leathery skin. The Constable drew his knife, sliced the trader's tongue in half and tossed the scrap of flesh over the side of the skiff. The trader gargled blood and thrashed like a landed fish.

At the same moment, one of the Constable's sons cried out. 'Boat ahead! Leastways, there's running lights.'

This was Urthank, a dull-witted brute grown as heavy and muscular as his father. The Constable knew that it would not be long before Urthank roared his challenge, and knew too that the boy would lose. Urthank was too stupid to wait for the right moment; it was not in his nature to suppress an impulse. No, Urthank would not defeat him. It would be one of the others. But Urthank's challenge would be the beginning of the end.

The Constable searched the darkness. For a moment he thought he glimpsed a fugitive glimmer, but only for a moment. It could have been a mote floating in his eye, or a dim star glinting at the edge of the world's level horizon.

'You were dreaming,' he said. 'Set to rowing, or the sun will be up before we get back.'

'I saw it,' Urthank insisted.

The other son, Unthank, laughed.

'There!' Urthank said. 'There it is again! Dead ahead, just like I said.'

This time the Constable saw the flicker of light. His first thought was that perhaps the trader had not been boasting after all. He said quietly, 'Go forward. Feathered oars.'

As the skiff glided against the current, the Constable fumbled a clamshell case from the pouch hung on the belt of his white linen kilt. The trader whose tongue had been cut out was making wet, choking sounds. The Constable kicked him into silence before opening the case and lifting out the spectacles that rested on the waterstained silk lining. The spectacles were the most valuable heirloom of the Constable's family; they had passed from defeated father to victorious son for more than a hundred generations. They were shaped like bladeless scissors, and the Constable unfolded them and carefully pinched them over his bulbous nose.

At once, the hull of the flat skiff and the bales of contraband cigarettes stacked in the forward well seemed to gain a luminous sheen; the bent backs of the Constable's sons and the supine bodies of the two prisoners glowed with furnace light. The Constable scanned the river, ignoring flaws in the old glass of the lenses which warped or smudged the amplified light, and saw, half a league from the skiff, a knot of tiny, intensely brilliant specks dancing above the river's surface.

'Machines,' the Constable breathed. He stepped between the prisoners and pointed out the place to his sons.

The skiff glided forward under the Constable's guidance. As it drew closer, the Constable saw that there were hundreds of machines, a busy cloud swirling around an invisible pivot. He was used to seeing one or two flitting through the sky above Aeolis on their inscrutable business, but he had never before seen so many in one place.

Something knocked against the side of the skiff, and Urthank cursed and feathered his oar. It was a waterlogged coffin. Every day, thousands were launched from Ys. For a moment, a woman's face gazed up at the Constable through a glaze of water, glowing greenly amidst a halo of rotting flowers. Then the coffin turned end for end and was borne away.

The skiff had turned in the current, too. Now it was broadside to the cloud of machines, and for the first time the Constable saw what they attended.

A boat. A white boat riding high on the river's slow current.

The Constable took off his spectacles, and discovered that the boat was glimmering with a spectral luminescence. The water around it glowed too, as if it floated in the centre of one of the shoals of luminous plankton that sometimes rose to the surface of the river on a calm summer night. The glow spread around the skiff; each stroke of the oars broke its pearly light into whirling interlocking spokes, as if the ghost of a machine lived just beneath the river's skin.

The tongue-cut trader groaned and coughed; his partner raised himself up on his elbows to watch as the white boat turned on the river's current, light as a leaf, a dancer barely touching the water.

The boat had a sharp, raised prow, and incurved sides that sealed it shut and swept back in a fan, like the tail of a dove. It was barely larger than an ordinary coffin. It made another turn, seemed to stretch like a cat, and then it was alongside the skiff, pressed right against it without even a bump.

Suddenly, the Constable and his sons were inside the cloud of machines. It was as if they had fallen headfirst into a nebula, for there were hundreds of them, each burning with ferocious white light, none bigger than a rhinoceros beetle. Urthank tried to swat one that hung in front of his snout, and cursed when it stung him with a flare of red light and a crisp sizzle.

'Steady,' the Constable said, and someone else said hoarsely, 'Flee.'

Astonished, the Constable turned from his inspection of the glimmering boat.

'Flee,' the second trader said again. 'Flee, you fools!'

Both of the Constable's sons had shipped their oars and were looking at their father. They were waiting for his lead. The Constable put away his spectacles and shoved the butt end of his whip in his belt. He could not show that he was afraid. He reached through the whirling lights of the machines and touched the white boat.

Its hull was as light and close woven as feathers, and at the Constable's touch, the incurved sides peeled back with a sticky, crackling sound. As a boy, the Constable had been given to wandering the wild shore downriver of Aeolis, and he had once come across a blood orchid growing in the cloven root of a kapok tree. The orchid had made precisely the same noise when, sensing his body heat, it had spread its fleshy lobes wide to reveal the lubricious curves of its creamy pistil. He had fled in terror before the blood orchid's perfume could overwhelm him, and the ghost of that fear stayed his hand now.

The hull vibrated under his fingertips with a quick, eager pulse. Light poured out from the boat's interior, rich and golden and filled with floating motes. A body made a shadow inside this light, and the Constable thought at once that the boat was no more than a coffin set adrift on the river's current. The coffin of some lord or lady no doubt, but in function no different from the shoddy cardboard coffins of the poor or the enamelled wooden coffins of the artisans and traders.

And then the baby started to cry.

The Constable squinted through the light, saw something move within it, and reached out. For a moment he was at the incandescent heart of the machines' intricate dance, and then they were gone, dispersing in flat trajectories into the darkness. The baby, a boy, pale and fat and hairless, squirmed in the Constable's hands.

The golden light was dying back inside the white boat. In moments, only traces remained, iridescent veins and dabs that fitfully illuminated the corpse on which the baby had been lying.

It was the corpse of a woman, naked, flat-breasted and starveling thin, and as hairless as the baby. She had been shot, once through the chest and once in the head, but there was no blood. One hand was three fingered, like the grabs of the cranes of Aeolis's docks; the other was monstrously swollen and bifurcate, like a lobster's claw. Her skin had a silvery-grey cast; her huge eyes, divided into a honeycomb of cells, were like the compound lenses of certain insects, and the colour of blood rubies. Within each facet lived a flickering glint of golden light, and although the Constable knew that these were merely reflections of the white boat's fading light, he had the strange feeling that things, malevolently watchful things, lived behind the dead woman's strange eyes.

'Heresy,' the second trader said. Somehow, he had got up on his knees and was staring wide-eyed at the white boat.

The Constable kicked the trader in the stomach; the man coughed and flopped back into the bilge water alongside his partner. The trader glared up at the Constable and said again, 'Heresy. When they allowed the ship of the Ancients of Days to pass beyond Ys and sail downriver, our benevolent bureaucracies let heresy loose into the world.'

'Let me kill him now,' Urthank said.

'He's already a dead man,' the Constable said.

'Not while he talks treason,' Urthank said stubbornly. He was staring straight at his father.

'Fools,' the trader said. 'You have all seen the argosies and carracks sailing downriver to war with their cannons and siege engines. But there are more terrible weapons let loose in the world.'

'Let me kill him,' Urthank said.

The baby had caught at the Constable's thumb, although he could not close his fingers around it. He grimaced, as if trying to smile, but blew a saliva bubble instead.

The Constable gently disengaged the baby's grip and set him on the button cushion at the stern. He moved carefully, as if through air packed with invisible boxes, aware of Urthank's burning gaze at his back. He turned and said, 'Let the man speak. He might know something.'

The trader said, 'The bureaucrats are trying to wake the Hierarchs from their reveries. Some say by science, some by witchery. The bureaucrats are so frightened of heresy consuming our world that they try anything to prevent it.'

Unthank spat. 'The Hierarchs are all ten thousand years dead. Everyone knows that. They were killed when the Insurrectionists threw down the temples and destroyed most of the aspects.'

'The Hierarchs tried to follow the Preservers,' the trader said. 'They rose higher than any other bloodline, but not so high that they cannot be called back.'

The Constable kicked the man and said roughly, 'Enough theology. Is this one of their servants?'

'Ys is large, and contains a multitude of wonders, but I've never seen anything like this. Most likely it is a foul creature manufactured by the forbidden arts. Those trying to forge such weapons have become more corrupt than the heretics. Destroy it! Return the baby and sink the boat!'

'Why should I believe you?'

'I'm a bad man. I admit it. I'd sell any one of my daughters if I could be sure of a good profit. But I studied for a clerkship when I was a boy, and I was taught well. I remember my lessons, and I know that the existence of this thing is against the word of the Preservers.'

Urthank said slowly, 'We should put the baby back. It isn't our business.'

'All on the river within a day's voyage is my business,' the Constable said.

'You don't know everything,' Urthank said. 'You just think you do.'

The Constable knew then that this was the moment poor Urthank

16

had chosen. So did Unthank, who subtly shifted on the thwart so that he was no longer shoulder to shoulder with his brother. The Constable met Urthank's stare and said, 'Keep your place, boy.'

There was a moment when it seemed that Urthank would not attack. Then he inflated his chest and let out the air with a roar and, roaring, threw himself at his father.

The whip caught around Urthank's neck with a sharp crack that echoed out across the black water. Urthank fell to his knees and grabbed hold of the whip as its loop tightened under the slack flesh of his chin. The Constable gripped the whip's stock with both hands and jerked it sideways as if he held a line which a huge fish had suddenly struck. The skiff tipped wildly and Urthank tumbled headfirst into the glowing water. But the boy did not let go of the whip. He was stupid, but he was also stubborn. The Constable staggered, dropped the whip – it hissed over the side like a snake – and fell overboard too.

The Constable kicked off his loose, knee-high boots as he plunged down through the cold water, kicked out again for the surface. Something grabbed the hem of his kilt, and then Urthank was trying to swarm up his body. Light exploded in the Constable's eye as his son's hard elbow hit his face. They thrashed through glowing water and burst into the air, separated by no more than an arm's length.

The Constable spat a mouthful of water and gasped, 'You're too quick to anger, my son. That was always your weakness.'

He saw the shadow of Urthank's arm sweep through the milky glow, and countered the thrust with his own knife. The blades clashed and slid along each other, locking at their hilts. Urthank growled and pressed down. He was very strong. The Constable felt a terrific pain as his knife was twisted from his grasp and Urthank's blade buried its point in his forearm. He kicked backwards in the water as Urthank slashed at his face; spray flew in a wide fan.

'Old,' Urthank said. 'Old and slow.'

The Constable steadied himself with little circling kicks. He could feel his hot blood pulsing into the water; Urthank had caught a vein. There was a heaviness in his bones; the wound on his shoulder throbbed. He knew that Urthank was right, but he also knew that he was not prepared to die.

He said, 'Come to me, son, and find out who is strongest.'

Urthank grinned, freeing his tusks from his lips. He kicked forward,

17

driving through the water with his knife held out straight, trying for a killing blow. But the water slowed him as the Constable had known it would, and the Constable kicked sideways, always just out of reach, while Urthank stabbed wildly, sobbing curses and uselessly spending his strength. Father and son circled each other. In the periphery of his vision, the Constable was aware that the white boat had separated from the skiff, but he could spare no thought for it as he avoided Urthank's next onslaught.

At last Urthank stopped, paddling to keep in one place and gasping heavily.

'Strength isn't everything,' the Constable observed. 'Come to me, son. I'll grant you a quick release and no shame.'

'Surrender, old man, and I'll give you an honourable burial on land. Or I'll kill you here and let the little fishes strip your bones.'

'O Urthank, how disappointed I am! You're no son of mine after all!'

Urthank lunged with a sudden, desperate fury, and the Constable punched precisely, hitting the boy's elbow where the nerve travelled over the bone. Urthank's fingers opened in reflex and his knife fluttered away through the water. He dove for it without thinking, and the Constable bore down on him with all his weight, enduring increasingly feeble blows to his chest and belly and legs. It took a long time, but at last he let go and Urthank's body floated free, face down in the glowing water.

'You were the strongest of my sons,' the Constable said, when he had his breath back. 'You were faithful after your fashion, but you never had a good thought in your head. If you had killed me and taken my wives, someone else would have killed you in a year.'

Unthank paddled the skiff over and helped his father clamber into the well. The white boat was a dozen oar-lengths off, glimmering against the dark. The skinny trader whose tongue the Constable had cut out lay face-down in the bilgewater, drowned in his own blood. His partner was gone. Unthank shrugged, and said that the man had slipped over the side.

'You should have brought him back. He was bound hand and foot. A big boy like you should have had no trouble.'

Unthank returned the Constable's gaze and said simply, 'I was watching your victory, father.'

'No, you're not ready yet, are you? You're waiting for the right moment. You're a subtle one, Unthank. Not like your brother.'

'He won't have got far. The prisoner, I mean.'

'Did you kill him?'

'Probably drowned by now. Like you said, he was bound hand and foot.'

'Help me with your brother.'

Together, father and son hauled Urthank's body into the skiff. The milky glow was fading out of the water. After the Constable had settled Urthank's body, he turned and saw that the white boat had vanished. The skiff was alone on the wide dark river, beneath the black sky and the smudged red whorl of the Eye of the Preservers. Under the arm of the tiller, on the leather pad of the button cushion, the baby grabbed at black air with pale starfish hands, chuckling at unguessable thoughts.

2 ~ The Anchorite

One evening early in spring, with the wheel of the Galaxy tilted waist-deep at the level horizon of the Great River, Yama eased open the shutters of the window of his room and stepped out on to the broad ledge. Any soldier looking up from the courtyard would have seen, by the Galaxy's blue-white light, a sturdy boy of some seventeen years on the ledge beneath the overhang of the red tile roof, and recognized the long-boned build, pale sharp face and cap of black hair of the Aedile's foundling son. But Yama knew that Sergeant Rhodean had taken most of the garrison of the peel-house on patrol through the winding paths of the City of the Dead, searching for the heretics who last night had tried to firebomb a ship at anchor in the floating harbour. Further, three men were standing guard over the labourers at the Aedile's excavations, leaving only the pack of watchdogs and a pentad of callow youths under the command of old one-legged Rotwang, who by now would have finished his nightly bottle of brandy and be snoring in his chair by the kitchen fire. With the garrison so reduced there was little chance that any of the soldiers would leave the warm fug of the guardroom to patrol the gardens, and Yama knew that he could persuade the watchdogs to allow him to pass unreported.

It was an opportunity for adventure too good to be missed. Yama was going to hunt frogs with the chandler's daughter, Derev, and Ananda, the sizar of the priest of Aeolis's temple. They had agreed on it that afternoon, using mirror talk.

The original walls of the Aedile's peel-house were built of smooth blocks of keelrock fitted together so cunningly that they presented a surface like polished ice, but at some point in the house's history an extra floor had been added, with a wide gutter ledge and gargoyles projecting into the air at intervals to spout water clear of the walls. Yama walked along the ledge as easily as if on a pavement, turned a corner, hooked his rope around the eroded ruff of a basilisk frozen in an agonized howl, and abseiled five storeys to the ground. He would have to leave the rope in place, but it was a small risk.

No one was about. He darted across the wide, mossy lawn, jumped the ha-ha and quickly and silently threaded familiar paths through the dense stands of rhododendrons which had colonized the tumbled ruins of the ramparts of the peel-house's outer defensive wall. Yama had played endless games of soldiers and heretics with the kitchen boys here, and knew every path, every outcrop of ruined wall, all the holes in the ground which had once been guard rooms or stores and the buried passages between them. He stopped beneath a mature cork-oak, looked around, then lifted up a mossy stone to reveal a deep hole lined with stones and sealed with polymer spray. He pulled out a net bag and a long slender trident from this hiding place, then replaced the stone and hung the bag on his belt and laid the trident across his shoulders.

At the edge of the stands of rhododendrons, the ground dropped away steeply in an overgrown demilune breastwork to a barrens of tussock grass and scrub. Beyond was the patchwork of newly flooded paeonin fields on either side of the winding course of the Breas, and then low ranges of hills crowded with monuments and tombs, cairns and cists: league upon league of the City of the Dead stretching to the foothills of the Rim Mountains, its inhabitants outnumbered the living citizens of Aeolis by a thousand to one. The tombs glimmered in the cold light of the Galaxy, as if the hills had been dusted with salt, and little lights flickered here and there, where memorial tablets had been triggered by passing animals.

Yama took out a slim silver whistle twice the length of his forefinger and blew on it. It seemed to make no more than a breathy squeak. Yama blew three more times, then stuck his trident in the deep, soft leaf-mould and squatted on his heels and listened to the peeping chorus of frogs that stitched the night. The frogs had emerged from their mucus cocoons a few weeks ago. They had been frantically feeding ever since, and now they were searching for mates, every male endeavouring to outdo his rivals with passionate froggy arias. Dopey with unrequited lust, they would be easy prey.

Behind Yama, the peel-house reared above the rhododendrons, lifting its freight of turrets against the Galaxy's blue-white wheel. A warm yellow light glowed near the top of the tall watchtower, where the Aedile, who had rarely slept since the news of Telmon's death last summer, would be working on his endless measurements and calculations.

Presently, Yama heard what he had been waiting for, the steady padding tread and faint sibilant breath of a watchdog. He called softly, and the strong, ugly creature trotted out of the bushes and laid its heavy head in his lap. Yama crooned to it, stroking its cropped ears and scratching the ridged line where flesh met the metal of its skullplate, lulling the machine part of the watchdog and, through its link, the rest of the pack. When he was satisfied that it understood it was not to raise the alarm either now or when he returned, Yama stood and wiped the dog's drool from his hands, plucked up his trident, and bounded away down the steep slope of the breastwork towards the barren ruins and the flooded fields beyond.

Ananda and Derev were waiting at the edge of the ruins. Tall, graceful Derev jumped down from her perch halfway up a broken wall cloaked in morning glory, and half-floated, half-ran across overgrown flagstones to embrace Yama. Ananda kept his seat on a fallen stele, eating ghostberries he had picked along the way and pretending to ignore the embracing lovers. He was a plump boy with dark skin and a bare, tubercled scalp, wearing the orange robe of his office.

'I brought the lantern,' Ananda said at last, and held it up. It was a little brass signal lantern, with a slide and a lens to focus the light of its wick. The plan was to use it to mesmerise their prey.

Derev and Yama broke from their embrace and Ananda added, 'I saw your soldiers march out along the old road this noon, brother Yama. Everyone in the town says they're after the heretics who tried to set fire to the floating harbour.'

'If there are heretics within a day's march, Sergeant Rhodean will find them,' Yama said.

'Perhaps they're still hiding here,' Derev said. Her neck seemed to elongate as she turned her head this way and that to peer into the darkness around the ruins. Her feathery hair was brushed back from her shaven forehead and hung to the small of her back. She wore a belted shift that left her long, slim legs bare. A trident was slung over her left shoulder. She hugged Yama and said, 'Suppose we found them! Wouldn't that be exciting?'

Yama said, 'If they are stupid enough to remain near the place they

22

have just attacked, then they would be easy to capture. We would need only to threaten them with our frog-stickers to force their surrender.'

'My father says they make their women lie with animals to create monstrous warriors.'

Ananda spat seeds and said, 'Her father promised to pay a good copper penny for every ten frogs we catch.'

'Derev's father has a price for everything,' Yama said, smiling.

Derev smiled too – Yama felt it against his cheek. She said, 'My father also said I should be back before the Galaxy sets. He only allowed me to come here because I told him that one of the Aedile's soldiers would be guarding us.'

Derev's father was very tall and very thin and habitually dressed in black, and walked with his head hunched into his shoulders and his white hands clasped behind him. From the back he looked like one of the night storks that picked over the city's rubbish pits. He was invariably accompanied by his burly bodyservant; he was scared of footpads and the casual violence of sailors, and of kidnapping. The latter was a real threat, as his family was the only one of its bloodline in Aeolis. He was disliked within the tight-knit trading community because he bought favours rather than earned them, and Yama knew that Derev was allowed to see him only because Derev's father believed it brought him closer to the Aedile.

Ananda said, 'The soldier would be guarding something more important than your life, although, like life, once taken it cannot be given back. But perhaps you no longer have it, which is why the soldier is not here.'

Yama whispered to Derev, 'You should not believe everything your father says,' and told Ananda, 'You dwell too much on things of the flesh. It does no good to brood on that which you cannot have. Give me some berries.'

Ananda held out a handful. 'You only had to ask,' he said mildly.

Yama burst a ghostberry between his tongue and palate: the rough skin shockingly tart, the pulpy seed-rich flesh meltingly sweet. He grinned and said, 'It is spring. We could stay out all night, then go fishing at dawn.'

Derev said, 'My father—'

'Your father would pay more for fresh fish than for frogs.'

'He buys all the fish he can sell from the fisherfolk, and the amount he can buy is limited by the price of salt.'

Ananda said, 'It's traditional to hunt frogs in spring, which is why we're here. Derev's father wouldn't thank you for making her into a fisherman.'

'If I don't get back before midnight he'll lock me up,' Derev said. 'I will never see you again.'

Yama smiled. 'You know that is not true. Otherwise your father would never have let you out in the first place.'

'There should be a soldier here,' Derev said. 'We're none of us armed.'

'The heretics are leagues away. And I will protect you, Derev.'

Derev brandished her trident, as fierce and lovely as a naiad. 'We're equally matched, I think.'

'I cannot stay out all night either,' Ananda said. 'Father Quine rises an hour before sunrise, and before then I must sweep the naos and light the candles in the votary.'

'No one will come,' Yama said. 'No one ever does any more, except on high days.'

'That's not the point. The avatars may have been silenced, but the Preservers are still there.'

'They will be there whether you light the candles or not. Stay with me, Ananda. Forget your duties for once.'

Ananda shrugged. 'I happen to believe in my duties.'

Yama said, 'You are scared of the beating you will get from Father Quine.'

'Well, that's true, too. For a holy man, he has a fearsome temper and a strong arm. You're lucky, Yama. The Aedile is a kindly, scholarly man.'

'If he is angry with me, he has Sergeant Rhodean beat me. And if he learns that I have left the peel-house at night, that is just what will happen. That is why I did not bring a soldier with me.'

'My father says that physical punishment is barbaric,' Derev said.

'It is not so bad,' Yama said. 'And at least you know when it is over.'

'The Aedile sent for Father Quine yesterday,' Ananda said. He crammed the last of the ghostberries into his mouth and got to his feet. Berry juice stained his lips; they looked black in the Galaxy's blue-white light.

Yama said unhappily, 'My father is wondering what to do with me. He has been talking about finding a clerkship for me in a safe corner of the department. I think that is why Dr Dismas went to Ys. But I do not

24

want to be a clerk – I would rather be a priest. At least I would get to see something of the world.'

'You're too old,' Ananda said equitably. 'My parents consecrated me a hundred days after my birth. And besides being too old, you are also too full of sin. You spy on your poor father, and steal.'

'And sneak out after dark,' Derev said.

'So has Ananda.'

'But not to fornicate,' Ananda said. 'Derev's father knows that I'm here, so I'm as much a chaperon as any soldier, although more easily bribed.'

Derev said, 'Oh, Ananda, we really are here to hunt for frogs.'

Ananda added, 'And I will confess my sin tomorrow, before the shrine.'

'As if the Preservers care about your small sins,' Yama said.

'You're too proud to be a priest,' Ananda said. 'Above all, you're too proud. Come and pray with me. Unburden yourself.'

Yama said, 'Well, I would rather be a priest than a clerk, but most of all I would rather be a soldier. I will run away and enlist. I will train as an officer, and lead a company of myrmidons or command a corvette into battle against the heretics.'

Ananda said, 'That's why your father wants you to be a clerk.'

Derev said, 'Listen.'

The two boys turned to look at where she pointed. Far out across the flooded fields, a point of intense turquoise light was moving through the dark air towards the Great River.

'A machine,' Yama said.

'So it is,' Derev said, 'but that isn't what I meant. I heard someone crying out.'

'Frogs fornicating,' Ananda said.

Yama guessed that the machine was half a league off. It seemed to slide at an angle to everything else, twinkling as if stitching a path between the world and its own reality.

He said, 'We should make a wish.'

Ananda smiled, 'I'll pretend you didn't say that, brother Yama. Such superstitions are unworthy of someone as educated as you.'

Derev said, 'Besides, you should never make a wish in case it is answered, like the story of the old man and the fox maiden. I know I heard something. It may be heretics. Or bandits. Quiet! Listen!'

Ananda said, 'I hear nothing, Derev. Perhaps your heart is beating so quickly it cries out for relief. I know I'm a poor priest, Yama, but one thing I know is true. The Preservers see all; there is no need to invoke them by calling upon their servants.'

Yama shrugged. There was no point debating such niceties with Ananda, who had been trained in theology since birth, but why shouldn't machines at least hear the wishes of those they passed by? Wishing was only an informal kind of praying, after all, and surely prayers were heard, and sometimes even answered. For if praying did not bring reward, then people would long ago have abandoned the habit of prayer, as farmers abandon land which no longer yields a crop. The priests taught that the Preservers heard and saw all, yet chose not to act because they did not wish to invalidate the free will of their creations; but machines were as much a part of the world which the Preservers had created as the Shaped bloodlines, although of a higher order. Even if the Preservers had withdrawn their blessing from the world after the affront of the Age of Insurrection, as the divaricationists believed, it was still possible that machines, their epigones, might recognize the justice of answering a particular wish, and intercede. After all, those avatars of the Preservers which had survived the Age of Insurrection had spoken with men as recently as forty years ago, before the heretics had finally silenced them.

In any event, better the chance taken than that lost and later regretted. Yama closed his eyes and offered up the quick wish, hostage to the future, that he be made a soldier and not a clerk.

Ananda said, 'You might as well wish upon a star.'

Derev said, 'Quiet! I heard it again!'

And Yama heard it too, faint but unmistakable above the frogs' incessant chorus. A man's angry wordless yell, and then the sound of jeering voices and coarse laughter.

Yama led the others through the overgrown ruins. Ananda padded right behind him with his robe tucked into his girdle – the better to run away if there was trouble, he said, although Yama knew that he would not run. Derev would not run away either; she held her trident like a javelin.

One of the old roads ran alongside the fields. Its ceramic surface had been stripped and smelted for the metals it had contained thousands of years ago, but the long straight track preserved its geodesic ideal. At the crux between the old road and a footpath that led across the embankment between two of the flooded fields, by a simple shrine set on a wooden post, the Constable's twin sons, Lud and Lob, had ambushed an anchorite.

The man stood with his back to the shrine, brandishing his staff. Its metal-shod point flicked back and forth like a watchful eye. Lud and Lob yelled and threw stones and clods of dirt at the anchorite but stayed out of the staff's striking range. The twins were swaggering bullies who believed that they ruled the children of the town. Most especially, they picked on those few children of bloodlines not their own. Yama had been chased by them a decad ago, when he had been returning to the peel-house after visiting Derev, but he had easily lost them in the ruins outside the town.

'We'll find you later, little fish,' they had shouted cheerfully. They had been drinking, and one of them had slapped his head with the empty bladder and cut a clumsy little dance. 'We always finish our business,' he had shouted. 'Little fish, little fish, come out now. Be like a man.'

Yama had chosen to stay hidden. Lud and Lob had scrawled their sign on a crumbling wall and pissed at its base, but after beating about the bushes in a desultory fashion they had grown bored and wandered off.

Now, crouching with Derev and Ananda in a thicket of chayote vine, Yama wondered what he should do. The anchorite was a tall man with a wild black mane and wilder beard. He was barefoot, and dressed in a crudely stitched robe of metallic-looking cloth. He dodged most of the stones thrown at him, but one had struck him on the head; blood ran down his forehead and he mechanically wiped it from his eyes with his wrist. Sooner or later, he would falter, and Lud and Lob would pounce.

Derev whispered, 'We should fetch the militia.'

'I don't think it's necessary,' Ananda said.

At that moment, a stone struck the anchorite's elbow and the point of his staff dipped. Roaring with glee, Lob and Lud ran in from either side and knocked him to the ground. The anchorite surged up, throwing one of the twins aside, but the other clung to his back and the second knocked the anchorite down again.

Yama said, 'Ananda, come out when I call your name. Derev, you set up a diversion.' And before he could think better of it he stepped out onto the road and shouted the twins' names.

Lob turned. He held the staff in both hands, as if about to break it.

Lud sat on the anchorite's back, grinning as he absorbed the man's blows to his flanks.

Yama said, 'What is this, Lob? Are you and your brother footpads now?'

'Just a bit of fun, little fish,' Lob said. He whirled the staff above his head. It whistled in the dark air.

'We saw him first,' Lud added.

'I think you should leave him alone.'

'Maybe we'll have you instead, little fish.'

'We'll have him all right,' Lud said. 'That's why we're here.' He cuffed the anchorite. 'This culler got in the way of what we set out to do, remember? Grab him, brother, and then we can finish this bit of fun.'

'You will have to deal with me, and with Ananda, too,' Yama said. He did not look around, but by the shift in Lob's gaze he knew that Ananda had stepped out onto the road behind him.

'The priest's runt, eh?' Lob laughed, and farted tremendously.

'Gaw,' his brother said, giggling so hard his triple chins quivered. He waved a hand in front of his face. 'What a stink.'

'Bless me your holiness,' Lob said, leering at Ananda, and farted again.

'Even odds,' Yama said, disgusted.

'Stay there, little fish,' Lob said. 'We'll deal with you when we've finished here.'

'You wetbrain,' Lud said, 'we deal with him first. Remember?'

Yama flung his flimsy trident then, but it bounced uselessly off Lob's hide. Lob yawned, showing his stout, sharp tusks, and swept the staff at Yama's head. Yama ducked, then jumped back from the reverse stroke. The staff's metal tip cut the air a finger's width from his belly. Lob came on, stepping heavily and deliberately and sweeping the staff back and forth, but Yama easily dodged his clumsily aimed blows.

'Fight fair,' Lob said, stopping at last. He was panting heavily. 'Stand and fight fair.'

Ananda was behind Lob now, and jabbed at his legs with his trident. Enraged, Lob turned and swung the staff at Ananda, and Yama stepped forward and kicked him in the kneecap, and then in the wrist. Lob howled and lost his balance, and Yama grabbed the staff when it clattered to the ground. He reversed it and jabbed Lob hard in the gut.

Lob fell to his knees in stages. 'Fight fair,' he gasped, winded. His little eyes blinked and blinked in his corpulent face.

'Fight fair,' Lud echoed, and got off the anchorite and pulled a knife from his belt. It was as black as obsidian, with a narrow, crooked blade. He had stolen it from a drunken sailor, and claimed that it was from the first days of the Age of Enlightenment, nearly as old as the world. 'Fight fair,' Lud said again, and held the knife beside his face and grinned.

Lob threw himself forward then, and wrapped his arms around Yama's thighs. Yama hammered at Lob's back with the staff, but he was too close to get a good swing at his opponent and he tumbled over backwards, his legs pinned beneath Lob's weight.

For a moment, all seemed lost. Then Ananda stepped forward and swung his doubled fist; the stone he held struck the side of Lob's skull with the sound of an axe sinking into wet wood. Lob roared with pain and sprang to his feet, and Lud roared too, and brandished his knife. Behind him, a tree burst into flame.

'It was all I could think of,' Derev said. She flapped her arms about her slim body. She was shaking with excitement. Ananda ran a little way down the road and shouted after the fleeing twins, a high ululant wordless cry.

Yama said, 'It was well done, but we should not mock them.'

'We make a fine crew,' Ananda said, and shouted again.

The burning tree shed sparks upwards into the night, brighter than the Galaxy. Its trunk was a shadow inside a roaring pillar of hot blue flame. Heat and light beat out across the road. It was a young sweetgum tree. Derev had soaked its trunk with kerosene from the lantern's reservoir, and had ignited it with the lantern's flint when Lob had fallen on Yama.

'Even Lob and Lud won't forget this,' Derev said gleefully.

'That is what I mean,' Yama said.

'They'll be too ashamed to try anything. Frightened by a tree. It's too funny, Yama. They'll leave us alone from now on.'

Ananda helped the anchorite sit up. The man dabbed at the blood crusted under his nose, cautiously bent and unbent his knees, then scrambled to his feet. Yama held out the staff, and the man took it and briefly bowed his head in thanks.

Yama bowed back, and the man grinned. Something had seared the left side of his face; a web of silvery scar tissue pulled down his eye and lifted the corner of his mouth. He was so dirty that the grain of his skin looked like embossed leather. The metallic cloth of his robe was filthy, too, but here and there patches and creases reflected the light of the burning tree. His hair was tangled in ropes around his face, and bits of twig were caught in his forked beard. He smelt powerfully of sweat and urine. He fixed Yama with an intense gaze, then made shapes with the fingers of his right hand against the palm of his left.

Ananda said, 'He wants you to know that he has been searching for you.'

'You can understand him?'

'We used hand speech like this in the seminary, to talk to each other during breakfast and supper when we were supposed to be listening to one of the brothers read from the Puranas. Some anchorites were once priests, and perhaps this is such a one.'

The man shook his head violently, and made more shapes with his fingers.

Ananda said uncertainly, 'He says that he is glad that he remembered all this. I think he must mean that he will always remember this.'

'Well,' Derev said, 'so he should. We saved his life.'

The anchorite dug inside his robe and pulled out a ceramic disc. It was attached to a thong looped around his neck, and he lifted the thong over his head and thrust the disc towards Yama, then made more shapes.

'You are the one who is to come,' Ananda translated.

The anchorite shook his head and signed furiously, slamming his fingers against his palm.

'You will come here again. Yama, do you know what he means?'

And Derev said, 'Listen!'

Far off, whistles sounded, calling and answering in the darkness.

The anchorite thrust the ceramic disc into Yama's hand. He stared into Yama's eyes and then he was gone, running out along the footpath between the flooded fields, a shadow dwindling against cold blue light reflected from the water, gone.

The whistles sounded again. 'The militia,' Ananda said, and turned and ran off down the old road.

Derev and Yama chased after him, but he soon outpaced them, and Yama had to stop to catch his breath before they reached the city wall.

Derev said, 'Ananda won't stop running until he's thrown himself into his bed. And even then he'll run in his dreams until morning.'

Yama was bent over, clasping his knees. He had a cramp in his side.

He said, 'We will have to watch out for each other. Lob and Lud will not forgive this easily. How can you run so fast and so far without getting out of breath?'

Derev's pale face glimmered in the Galaxy's light. She gave him a sly look. 'Flying is harder work than running.'

'If you can fly, I would love to see it. But you are teasing me again.'

'This is the wrong place for flying. One day, perhaps, I'll show you the right place, but it's a long way from here.'

'Do you mean the edge of the world? I used to dream that my people lived on the floating islands. I saw one last year—'

Derev suddenly grabbed Yama and pulled him into the long grass beside the track. He fell on top of her, laughing, but she put her hand over his mouth. 'Listen!' she said.

Yama raised his head, but heard only the ordinary noises of the night. He was aware of the heat of Derev's slim body pressing against his. He said, 'I think the militia have given up their search.'

'No. They're coming this way.'

Yama rolled over and parted the long dry grass so that he could watch the track. Presently a pentad of men went past in single file. None of them were of the bloodline of the citizens of Aeolis. They were armed with rifles and arbalests.

'Sailors,' Yama said, when he was sure that they were gone.

Derev pressed the length of her body against his. 'How do you know?'

'They were strangers, and all strangers come to Aeolis by the river, either as sailors or passengers. But there have been no passenger ships since the war began.'

'They are gone now, whoever they are.'

'Perhaps they were looking for the anchorite.'

'He was crazy, that holy man, but we did the right thing. Or you did. I could not have stepped out and challenged those two.'

'I did it knowing you were at my back.'

'I'd be nowhere else.' Derev added thoughtfully, 'He looked like you.'

Yama laughed.

'In the proportion of his limbs, and the shape of his head. And his eyes were halved by folds of skin, just like yours.'

Derev kissed Yama's eyes. He kissed her back. They kissed for a long time, and then Derev broke away.

'You aren't alone in the world, Yama, no matter what you believe. It shouldn't surprise you to find one of your own bloodline.'

But Yama had been looking for too long to believe it would be that easy. 'I think he was crazy. I wonder why he gave me this.'

Yama pulled the ceramic disc from the pocket of his tunic. It seemed no different from the discs the Aedile's workmen turned up by the hundred during their excavations: slick, white, slightly too large to fit comfortably in his palm. He held it up so that it faintly reflected the light of the Galaxy, and saw a distant light in the crooked tower that stood without the old, half-ruined city wall.

Dr Dismas had returned from Ys.

3 ~ Dr Dismas

Dr Dismas's bent-backed, black-clad figure came up the dry, stony hillside with a bustling, crabbed gait. The sun was at the height of its daily leap into the sky, and, like an aspect, he cast no shadow.

The Aedile, standing at the top of the slope by the spoil-heap of his latest excavation site, watched with swelling expectation as the apothecary drew near. The Aedile was tall and stooped and greying, with a diplomat's air of courteous reticence which many mistook for absent-mindedness. He was dressed after the fashion of the citizens of Aeolis, in a loose-fitting white tunic and a linen kilt. His knees were swollen and stiff from the hours he had spent kneeling on a leather pad brushing away dirt, hairfine layer after hairfine layer, from a ceramic disc, freeing it from the cerements of a hundred thousand years of burial. The excavation was not going well and the Aedile had grown bored with it before it was halfway done. Despite the insistence of his geomancer, he was convinced that nothing of interest would be found. The crew of trained diggers, convicts reprieved from army service, had caught their master's mood and worked at a desultory pace amongst the neatly dug trenches and pits, dragging their chains through dry white dust as they carried baskets of soil and limestone chippings to the conical spoil heap. A drill rig taking a core through the reef of land coral which had overgrown the hilltop raised a plume of white dust that feathered off into the blue sky.

So far, the excavation had uncovered only a few potsherds, the corroded traces of what might have been the footings of a watchtower, and the inevitable hoard of ceramic discs. Although the Aedile had no idea what the discs had actually been used for (most scholars of Confluence's early history believed that they were some form of currency, but the Aedile thought that this was too obvious an explanation), he assiduously catalogued every one, and spent hours measuring the faint grooves and pits with which they were decorated. The Aedile believed in measurement. In small things were the gauge of the larger world which contained them, and of worlds without end. He believed that all measurements and constants might be arithmetically derived from a single number, the cypher of the Preservers which could unlock the secrets of the world they had made, and much else.

But here was Dr Dismas, with news that would determine the fate of the Aedile's foundling son. The pinnace on which the apothecary had returned from Ys had anchored beyond the mouth of the bay two days before (and was anchored there still), and Dr Dismas had been rowed ashore last night, but the Aedile had chosen to spend the day at his excavation site rather than wait at the peel-house for Dr Dismas's call. Better that he heard the news, whatever it was, before Yama.

It was the Aedile's hope that Dr Dismas had discovered the truth about the bloodline of his adopted son, but he did not trust the man, and was troubled by speculations about the ways in which Dr Dismas might misuse his findings. It was Dr Dismas, after all, who had proposed that he take the opportunity offered by his summons to Ys to undertake research into the matter of Yama's lineage. That this trip had been forced upon Dr Dismas by his department, and had been entirely funded from the Aedile's purse, would not reduce by one iota the obligation which Dr Dismas would surely expect the Aedile to express.

Dr Dismas disappeared behind the tipped white cube of one of the empty tombs which were scattered beneath the brow of the hill like beads flung from a broken necklace – tombs of the dissolute time after the Age of Insurrection and the last to be built in the City of the Dead, simple boxes set at the edge of the low, rolling hills, crowded with monuments, tombs and statues of the ancient necropolis. Presently, Dr Dismas reappeared almost at the Aedile's feet and laboured up the last hundred paces of the steep, rough path. He was breathing hard. His sharp-featured face, propped amongst the high wings of his black coat's collar and shaded by a black, broad-brimmed hat, was sprinkled with sweat in which, like islands in the slowly shrinking river, the plaques of his addiction stood isolated.

'A warm day,' the Aedile said, by way of greeting.

Dr Dismas took out a lace handkerchief from his sleeve and fastidiously dabbed sweat from his face. 'It *is* hot. Perhaps Confluence tires of circling the sun and is falling into it, like a girl tumbling into the arms of her lover. Perhaps we'll be consumed by the fire of their passion.'

Usually, Dr Dismas's rhetorical asides amused the Aedile, but this wordplay only intensified his sense of foreboding. He said mildly, 'I trust that your business was successful, doctor.'

Dr Dismas dismissed it with a flick of his handkerchief, like a conjuror.

'It was nothing. Routine puffed up with pomp. My department is fond of pomp, for it is, after all, a very old department. I am returned, my Aedile, to serve, if I may, with renewed vigour.'

'I had never thought to withdraw that duty from you, my dear doctor.'

'You are too kind. And more generous than the miserable termagants who nest amongst the dusty ledgers of my department, and do nothing but magnify rumour into fact.'

Dr Dismas had turned to gaze, like a conqueror, across the dry slope of the hill and its scattering of abandoned tombs, the patchwork of flooded fields along the Breas and the tumbled ruins and cluster of roofs of Aeolis at its mouth, the long finger of the new quay pointing across banks of green mud towards the Great River, which stretched away, shining like polished silver, to a misty union of water and air. Now he stuck a cigarette in his holder (carved, he liked to say, from the finger-bone of a multiple murderer; he cultivated a sense of the macabre), lit it and drew deeply, holding his breath for a count of ten before blowing a riffle of smoke through his nostrils with a satisfied sigh.

Dr Dismas was the apothecary of Aeolis, hired a year ago by the same council which regulated the militia. He had been summoned to Ys to account for several lapses since he had taken up his position. He was said to have substituted glass powder for the expensive suspensions of tiny machines which cured river blindness – and certainly there had been more cases of river blindness the previous summer, although the Aedile attributed this to the greater numbers of biting flies which bred in the algae which choked the mud banks of the former harbour. More seriously, Dr Dismas was said to have peddled his treatments amongst the fisherfolk and the hill tribes, making extravagant claims that he could cure cankers, blood cough and mental illness, and halt or even reverse aging. There were rumours, too, that he had made or grown chimeras of

35

children and beasts, and that he had kidnapped a child from one of the hill tribes and used its blood and perfusions of its organs to treat one of the members of the Council for Night and Shrines.

The Aedile had dismissed all of these allegations as fantasies, but then a boy had died after blood-letting, and the parents, mid-caste chandlers, had lodged a formal protest. The Aedile had had to sign it. A field investigator of the Department of Apothecaries and Chirurgeons had arrived a hundred days ago, but quickly left in some confusion. It seemed that Dr Dismas had threatened to kill him when he had tried to force an interview. And then the formal summons had arrived, which the Aedile had had to read out to Dr Dismas in front of the Council of Night and Shrines. The doctor had been commanded to return to Ys for formal admonishment, both for his drug habit and (as the document delicately put it) for certain professional lapses. The Aedile had been informed that Dr Dismas had been placed on probation, although from the doctor's manner he might have won a considerable victory rather than a reprieve.

The apothecary drew deeply on his cigarette and said, 'The river voyage was a trial in itself. It made me so febrile that I had to lay in bed on the pinnace for a day after it anchored before I was strong enough to be taken ashore. I am still not quite recovered.'

'Quite, quite,' the Aedile said. 'I am sure you came here as soon as you could.'

But he did not believe it for a moment. The apothecary was up to something, no doubt about it.

'You have been working with those convicts of yours again. Don't deny it. I see the dirt under your nails. You are too old to be kneeling under the burning sun.'

'I wore my hat, and coated my skin with the unguent you prescribed.' The sticky stuff smelled strongly of menthol, and raised the fine hairs of the Aedile's pelt into stiff peaks, but it seemed uncharitable to complain.

'You should also wear glasses with tinted lenses. Cumulative ultraviolet will damage your corneas, and at your age that can be serious. I believe I see some inflammation there. Your excavations will proceed apace without your help. Day by day, you climb down into the past. I fear you will leave us all behind. Is the boy well? I trust you have taken better care of him than of yourself.'

'I do not think I will learn anything here. There are the footings of a tower, but the structure itself must have been dismantled long ago. A tall tower, too; the foundations are very deep, although quite rusted away. I believe that it might have been made of metal, although that would have been fabulously costly even in the Age of Enlightenment. The geomancer may have been misled by the remains into thinking that a larger structure was once built here. It has happened before. Or perhaps there is something buried deeper. We will see.'

The geomancer had been from one of the hill tribes, a man half the Aedile's age, but made wizened and toothless by his harsh nomadic life, one eye milky with a cataract which Dr Dismas had later removed. This had been in winter, with hoarfrost mantling the ground each morning, but the geomancer had gone about barefoot, and naked under his red wool cloak. He had fasted three days on the hilltop before scrying out the site with a thread weighted with a sliver of lodestone.

Dr Dismas said, 'In Ys, there are buildings which are said to have once been entirely clad in metal.'

'Quite, quite. If it can be found anywhere on Confluence, then it can be found in Ys.'

'So they say, but who would know where to begin to look?'

'If there is any one person, then that would be you, my dear Dr Dismas.'

'I would like to think I have done my best for you.'

'And for the boy. More importantly, the boy.'

Dr Dismas gave the Aedile a quick, piercing look. 'Of course. That goes without saying.'

'It is for the boy,' the Aedile said again. 'His future is constantly in my thoughts.'

With the thumb and forefinger of his left hand, which were as stiffly crooked as the claw of a crayfish, Dr Dismas plucked the stub of his cigarette from the bone holder and crushed its coal. His left hand was almost entirely affected by the drug; although the discrete plaques allowed limited flexure, they had robbed the fingers of all feeling.

The Aedile waited while Dr Dismas went through the ritual of lighting another cigarette. There was something of Dr Dismas's manner that reminded the Aedile of a sly, sleek nocturnal animal, secretive in its habits but always ready to pounce on some scrap or titbit. He was a gossip, and like all gossips knew how to pace his revelations, how to string out a story and tease his audience – but the Aedile knew that like all gossips, Dr Dismas could not hold a secret long. So he waited patiently while Dr Dismas fitted another cigarette in the holder, and lit and drew on it. The Aedile was by nature a patient man, and his training in diplomacy had inured him to waiting on the whims of others.

Dr Dismas blew streams of smoke through his nostrils and said at last, 'It wasn't easy, you know.'

'Oh, quite so. I did not think it would be. The libraries are much debased these days. Since the librarians fell silent, there is a general feeling that there is no longer the need to maintain anything but the most recent records, and so everything older than a thousand years is considerably compromised.'

The Aedile realized that he had said too much. He was nervous, there on the threshold of revelation.

Dr Dismas nodded vigorously. 'And there is the present state of confusion brought about by the current political situation. It is most regrettable.'

'Quite, quite. Well, but we are at war.'

'I meant the confusion in the Palace of the Memory of the People itself, something for which your department, my dear Aedile, must take a considerable part of the blame. All of these difficulties suggest that we are trying to forget the past, as the Committee for Public Safety teaches we should.'

The Aedile was stung by this remark, as Dr Dismas had no doubt intended. The Aedile had been exiled to this tiny backwater city after the triumph of the Committee for Public Safety because he had spoken against the destruction of the records of past ages. It was to his everlasting shame that he had only spoken out, and not fought, as had many of his faction. And now his wife was dead. And his son. Only the Aedile was left, still in exile because of a political squabble mostly long forgotten.

The Aedile said with considerable asperity, 'The past is not so easily lost, my dear Doctor. Each night, we have only to look up at the sky to be reminded of that. In winter, we see the Galaxy, sculpted by unimaginable forces in ages past; in summer, we see the Eye of the Preservers. And here in Aeolis, the past is more important than the present. After all, how much greater are the tombs than the mudbrick houses down by the bay? Even stripped of their ornaments, the tombs are greater, and will endure in ages to come. All that lived in Ys during the Golden Age once came to rest here, and much remains to be discovered.'

Dr Dismas ignored this. He said, 'Despite these difficulties, the library of my department is still well-ordered. Several of the archive units are still completely functional under manual control, and they are amongst the oldest on Confluence. If records of the boy's bloodline could be found anywhere, it is there. But although I searched long and hard, of the boy's bloodline, well, I could find no trace.'

The Aedile thought that he had misheard. 'What is that? None at all?'

'I wish it were otherwise. Truly I do.'

'This is – I mean to say, it is unexpected. Quite unexpected.'

'I was surprised myself. As I say, the records of my department are perhaps the most complete on Confluence. Certainly, I believe that they are the only fully usable set, ever since your own department purged the archivists of the Palace of the Memory of the People.'

The Aedile failed to understand what Dr Dismas had told him. He said weakly, 'There was no correspondence . . .'

'None at all. All Shaped bloodlines possess the universal sequence of genes inserted by the Preservers at the time of the remaking of our ancestors. No matter who we are, no matter the code in which our cellular inheritance is written, the meaning of those satellite sequences are the same. But although tests of the boy's self-awareness and rationality show that he is not an indigen, like them he lacks that which marks the Shaped as the chosen children of the Preservers. And more than that, the boy's genome is quite different from anything on Confluence.'

'But apart from the mark of the Preservers we are all different from each other, Doctor. We are all remade in the image of the Preservers in our various ways.'

'Indeed. But every bloodline shares a genetic inheritance with certain of the beasts and plants and microbes of Confluence. Even the various races of simple indigens, which were not marked by the Preservers and which cannot evolve towards transcendence, have genetic relatives amongst the flora and fauna. The ancestors of the ten thousand bloodlines of Confluence were not brought here all alone; the Preservers also brought something of the home worlds of each of them. It seems that young Yamamanama is more truly a foundling than we first believed, for there is nothing on record, no bloodline, no plant, no beast, nor even any microbe, which has anything in common with him.'

Only Dr Dismas called the boy by his full name. It had been given to him by the wives of the old Constable, Thaw. In their language, the

39

language of the harems, it meant *Child of the River*. The Council for Night and Shrines had met in secret after the baby had been found on the river by Constable Thaw, and it had been decided that he should be killed by exposure, for he might be a creature of the heretics, or some other kind of demon. But the baby had survived for ten days amongst the tombs on the hillside above Aeolis, and the women who had finally rescued him, defying their husbands, had said that bees had brought him pollen and water, proving that he was under the protection of the Preservers. Even so, no family in Aeolis would take in the baby, and so he had come to live in the peel-house, son to the Aedile and brother to poor Telmon.

The Aedile thought of this as he tried to fathom the implications of Dr Dismas's discovery. Insects chirred all around in the dry grasses, insects and grass perhaps from the same long-lost world as the beasts which the Preservers had shaped into the ancestors of his own bloodline. There was a comfort, a continuity, in knowing that you were a part of the intricate tapestry of the wide world. Imagine then what it would be like to grow up alone in a world with no knowledge of your bloodline, and no hope of finding one! For the first time that day, the Aedile remembered his wife, dead more than twenty years now. A hot day then, too, and yet how cold her hands had been. His eyes pricked with the beginnings of tears, but he controlled himself. It would not do to show emotion in front of Dr Dismas, who preyed on weakness like a wolf which follows a herd of antelope.

'All alone,' the Aedile said. 'Is that possible?'

'If he were a plant or an animal, then perhaps.' Dr Dismas pinched out the coal of his second cigarette, dropped the stub and ground it under the heel of his boot. Dr Dismas's black calf-length boots were new, the Aedile noted, hand-tooled leather soft as butter.

'We could imagine him to be a stowaway,' Dr Dismas said. 'A few ships still ply their old courses between Confluence and the mine worlds, and one could imagine something stowing away on one of them. Perhaps the boy is an animal, able to mimic the attributes of intelligence, in the way that certain insects mimic a leaf or a twig. But then we must ask, what is the difference between the reality and the mimic?'

The Aedile was repulsed by this notion. He could not bear to think that his own dear adopted son was an animal imitating a human being. He said, 'Anyone trying to pluck such a leaf would know.'

'Exactly. Even a perfect mimic differs from what it is imitating in that it *is* an imitation, with the ability to dissemble, to appear to be something it is not, to become something else. I know of no creature which is so perfect a mimic that it becomes the thing it is imitating. While there are insects which resemble leaves, they cannot make their food from sunlight. They cling to the plant, but they are not part of it.'

'Quite, quite. But if the boy is not part of our world, then where is he from? The old mine worlds are uninhabited.'

'Wherever he is from, I believe him to be dangerous. Remember how he was found. "In the arms of a dead woman, in a frail craft on the flood of the river." Those, I believe, were your exact words.'

The Aedile remembered old Constable Thaw's story. The man had shamefully confessed the whole story after his wives had delivered the foundling to the peel-house. Constable Thaw had been a coarse and cunning man, but he had taken his duties seriously.

The Aedile said, 'But my dear doctor, you cannot believe that Yama killed the woman – he was just a baby.'

'Someone got rid of him,' Dr Dismas said. 'Someone who could not bear to kill him. Or was not able to kill him.'

'I have always thought that the woman was his mother. She was fleeing from something, no doubt from scandal or from her family's condemnation, and she gave birth to him there on the river, and died. It is the simplest explanation, and surely the most likely.'

'We do not know all the facts of the case,' Dr Dismas said. 'However, I did examine the records left by my predecessor. She performed several neurological tests on Yamamanama soon after he was brought to your house, and continued to perform them for several years afterwards. Counting backwards, and allowing for a good margin of error, I formed the opinion that Yamamanama had been born at least fifty days before he was found on the river. We are all marked by our intelligence. Unlike the beasts of the field, we must all of us continue our development outside the womb, because the womb does not supply sufficient sensory input to stimulate growth of neural pathways. I have no reason to doubt that this is not a universal law for all intelligent races. All the tests indicated that it was no newborn baby that Constable Thaw rescued.'

'Well, no matter where he came from, or why, it seems that we are all he has, doctor.'

Dr Dismas looked around. Although the nearest workers were fifty paces away, chipping in a desultory way at the edge of the neat square of the excavated pit, he stepped closer to the Aedile and said confidingly, 'You overlook one possibility. Since the Preservers abandoned Confluence, one new race has appeared, albeit briefly.'

The Aedile smiled. 'You scoff at my theory, Doctor, but at least it fits with what is known, whereas you make a wild leap into thin air. The ship of the Ancients of Days passed downriver thirty years before Yama was found floating in his cradle, and no members of its crew remained on Confluence.'

'Their heresies live on. We are at war with their ideas. The Ancients of Days were the ancestors of the Preservers, and we cannot guess at their powers.' Dr Dismas looked sideways at the Aedile. 'I believe,' he said, 'that there have been certain portents, certain signs . . . The rumours are vague. Perhaps you know more. Perhaps it would help if you told me about them.'

'I trust you have spoken to no one else,' the Aedile said. 'Talk like this, wild though it is, could put Yama in great danger.'

'I understand why you have not discussed Yamamanama's troublesome origin before, even to your own department. But the signs are there, for those who know how to look. The number of machines that flit at the borders of Aeolis, for instance. You cannot hide these things for ever.'

The machines around the white boat. The woman in the shrine. Yama's silly trick with the watchdogs. The bees which had fed the abandoned baby had probably been machines, too.

The Aedile said carefully, 'We should not talk of such things here. It requires discretion.'

He would never tell Dr Dismas everything. The man presumed too much, and he was not to be trusted.

'I am, and shall continue to be, the soul of discretion.'

Never before had Dr Dismas's dark, sharp-featured face seemed so much like a mask. It was why the man took the drug, the Aedile realized. The drug was a shield from the gaze and the hurts of the world.

The Aedile said sternly, 'I mean it, Dismas. You will say nothing of what you found, and keep your speculations to yourself. I want to see what you found. Perhaps there is something you missed.'

'I will bring the papers tonight, but you will see that I am right in every particular. Now, if I may have permission to leave,' Dr Dismas said, 'I would like to recover from my journey. Think carefully about what I told you. We stand at the threshold of a great mystery.'

When Dr Dismas had gone, the Aedile called for his secretary. While the man was preparing his pens and ink and setting a disc of red wax to soften on a sunwarmed stone, the Aedile composed in his head the letter he needed to write. The letter would undermine Dr Dismas's already blemished reputation and devalue any claims the apothecary might make on Yama, but it would not condemn him outright. It would suggest a suspicion that Dr Dismas, because of his drug habit, might be involved with the heretics who had recently tried to set fire to the floating docks, but it must be the merest of hints hedged round with equivocation, for the Aedile was certain that if Dr Dismas was ever arrested, he would promptly confess all he knew. The Aedile realized then that they were linked by a cat's cradle of secrets that was weighted with the soul of the foundling boy, the stranger, the sacrifice, the gift, the child of the river.

4 ~ Yamamanama

Yama remembered nothing of the circumstances of his birth, or of how he had arrived at Aeolis in a skiff steered by a man with a corpse at his feet and the blood of his own son fresh on his hands. Yama knew only that Aeolis was home, and knew it as intimately as only a child can, especially a child who has been adopted by the city's Aedile and so wears innocently and unknowingly an intangible badge of privilege.

In its glory, before the Age of Insurrection, Aeolis, named for the winter wind that sang through the passes of the hills above the broad valley of the river Breas, had been the disembarkation point for the City of the Dead. Ys had extended far downriver in those days, and then as now it was the law that no one could be buried within its boundaries. Instead, mourners accompanied their dead to Aeolis, where funeral pyres for the lesser castes burned day and night, temples rang with prayers and songs for the preserved bodies of the rich and altars shone with constellations of butter lamps that shimmered amongst heaps of flowers and strings of prayer flags. The ashes of the poor were cast on the waters of the Great River; the preserved bodies of the ruling and mercantile classes, and of scholars and dynasts, were interred in tombs whose ruined, empty shells still riddled the dry hills beyond the town. The Breas, which then had been navigable almost to its source in the foothills of the Rim Mountains, had been crowded with barges bringing slabs of land coral, porphyry, granite, marble and all kinds of precious stones for the construction of the tombs.

An age later, after half the world had been turned to desert during the rebellion of the feral machines, and the Preservers had withdrawn their blessing from Confluence, and Ys had retreated, contracting about its irreducible heart, funeral barges no longer ferried the dead to Aeolis; instead, bodies were launched from the docks and piers of Ys onto the full flood of the Great River, given up to caymans and fish, lammer-geyers and carrion crows. As these creatures consumed the dead, so Aeolis consumed its own past. Tombs were looted of treasures; decorative panels and frescoes were removed from the walls; preserved bodies were stripped of their clothes and jewellery; the hammered bronze facings of doors and tomb furniture were melted down – the old pits of the wind-powered smelters were still visible along the escarpment above the little city.

After most of the tombs had been stripped, Aeolis became no more than a way station, a place where ships put in to replenish their supplies of fresh food on their voyages downriver from Ys. This was the city that Yama knew. There was the new quay which ran across the mudflats and stands of zebra grass of the old, silted harbour to the retreating edge of the Great River, where the fisherfolk of the floating islands gathered in their little coracles to sell strings of oysters and mussels, spongy parcels of red river moss, bundles of riverweed stipes, and shrimp and crabs and fresh fish. There were always people swimming off the new quay or splashing about in coracles and small boats, and men working at the fish traps and the shoals at the mouth of the shallow Breas where razorshell mussels were cultivated, and divers hunting for urchins and abalone amongst the holdfasts of stands of giant kelp whose long blades formed vast brown slicks on the surface of the river. There was the long road at the top of the ruined steps of the old waterfront, where tribesmen from the dry hills of the wild shore downriver of Aeolis squatted at blanket stalls to sell fruit and fresh meat, and dried mushrooms and manna lichen, and bits of lapis lazuli and marble pried from the wrecked facings of ancient tombs. There were ten taverns and two whorehouses; the chandlers' godowns and the farmers' cooperative; straggling streets of mudbrick houses which leaned towards each other over narrow canals; the one surviving temple, its walls white as salt, the gilt of its dome recently renewed by public subscription. And then the ruins of the ancient mortuaries, more extensive than the town, and fields of yams and raffia and yellow peas, and flooded paddies where rice and paeonin were grown. One of the last of Aeolis's mayors had established the paeonin industry in an attempt to revitalize the little city, but when the heretics had silenced the shrines at the beginning of the war there had been a sudden shrinkage in the priesthood and a decline in trade of the pigment which dyed their robes. These days, the mill, built at the downriver point of the bay so that its effluent would not contaminate the silty bay, worked only one day in ten.

Most of the population of Aeolis were of the same bloodline. They called themselves the Amnan, which meant simply *the human beings*; their enemies called them the Mud People. They had bulky but well-muscled bodies and baggy grey or brown skin. Clumsy on land, they were strong swimmers and adept aquatic predators, and had hunted giant otters and manatees almost to extinction along that part of the Great River. They had preyed upon the indigenous fisherfolk, too, before the Aedile had arrived and put a stop to it. More women were born than men, and sons fought their fathers for control of the harem; if they won, they killed their younger brothers or drove them out. The people of Aeolis still talked about the fight between old Constable Thaw and his son. It had lasted five days, and had ranged up and down the waterfront and through the net of canals between the houses until Thaw, his legs paralysed, had been drowned in the shallow stream of the Breas.

It was a barbaric custom, the Aedile said, a sign that the Amnan were reverting to their bestial nature. The Aedile went into the city as little as possible – rarely more than once every hundred days, and then only to the temple to attend the high day service with Yama and Telmon sitting to the right and left side of their father in scratchy robes, on hard, ornately carved chairs, facing the audience throughout the three or four hours of obeisances and offerings, prayer and praise-songs. Yama loved the sturdy square temple, with its clean high spaces, the black disc of its shrine in its ornate gilded frame, and walls glowing with mosaics picturing scenes of the end times, in which the Preservers (shown as clouds of light) ushered the re-created dead into perfect worlds of parklands and immaculate gardens. He loved the pomp and circumstance of the ceremonies, too, although he thought that it was unnecessary. The Preservers, who watched all, did not need ritual praise; to walk and work and play in the world they had made was praise enough. He was happier worshipping at the shrines which stood near the edge of the world on the far side of the Great River, visited every year during the winter festival when the triple spiral of the Home Galaxy first rose in its full glory above the Great River and most of the people of Aeolis migrated to the farside shore in a swarm of boats to set up camps and bonfires and greet the onset of winter with fireworks, and dance and pray and drink and feast for a whole decad.

The Aedile had taken Yama into his household, but he was a remote, scholarly man, busy with his official duties or preoccupied with his excavations and the endless measurements and calculations by which he tried to divide everything into everything else in an attempt to discover the prime which harmonised the world, and perhaps the Universe. It left him with little in the way of small talk. Like many unworldly, learned men, the Aedile treated children as miniature adults, failing to recognize that they were elemental, unfired vessels whose stuff was malleable and fey.

As a consequence of the Aedile's benign neglect, Yama and Telmon spent much of their childhood being passed from one to another of the household servants, or running free amongst the dry hills of the City of the Dead. In summer, the Aedile often left the peel-house for a month at a time, taking most of his household to one or another of his excavation sites in the dry hills of the City of the Dead. When they were not helping with the slow, painstaking work, Yama and Telmon went hunting and exploring amongst desert suburbs of the City of the Dead, Telmon searching for unusual insects for his collection, Yama interrogating aspects – he had a knack for awakening them, and for tormenting and teasing them into revealing details of the lives of the people on whom they were based, and for whom they were both guardians and advocates.

Telmon was the natural leader of the two, five years older, tall and solemn and patient and endlessly inquisitive, with a fine black pelt shot through with chestnut highlights. He was a natural horseman and an excellent shot with bow, arbalest and rifle, and often went off by himself for days at a time, hunting in the high ranges of hills where the Breas ran white and fast through the locks and ponds of the old canal system. He loved Yama like a true brother, and Yama loved him in turn, and was as devastated as the Aedile by news of his death.

Formal education resumed in winter. For two days a week Yama and Telmon were taught fencing, wrestling and horsemanship by Sergeant Rhodean; for the rest, their education was entrusted to the librarian, Zakiel. Zakiel was a slave, the only one in the peel-house; he had once been an archivist, but had committed an unspeakable heresy. Zakiel did not seem to mind being a slave. Before he had been branded, he had worked in the vast stacks of the library of the Palace of the Memory of the People, and now he was librarian of the peel-house. He ate his simple

47

meals amongst dusty tiers of books and scrolls, and slept in a cot in a dark corner under a cliff of quarto-sized ledgers whose thin metal covers, spotted with corrosion, had not been disturbed for centuries. All knowledge could be found in books, Zakiel declared, and if he had a passion (apart from his mysterious heresy, which he had never renounced) it was this. He was perhaps the happiest man in the Aedile's household, for he needed nothing but his work.

'Since the Preservers fully understand the Universe, and hold it whole in their minds, then it follows that all texts, which flow from minds forged by the Preservers, are reflections of their immanence,' Zakiel told Yama and Telmon more than once. 'It is not the world itself we should measure, but the reflections of the world, filtered through the creations of the Preservers and set down in these books. Of course, boys, you must never tell the Aedile I said this. He is happy in his pursuit of the ineffable, and I would not trouble him with these trivial matters.'

Yama and Telmon were supposed to be taught the Summalae Logicales, the Puranas and the Protocols of the Department, but mostly they listened to Zakiel read passages from selected works of natural philosophy before engaging in long, formal discussions. Yama first learned to read upside-down by watching Zakiel's long, ink-stained forefinger tracking glyphs from right to left while listening to the librarian recite in a sing-song voice, and later had to learn to read all over again, this time the right away up, to be able to recite in his turn. Yama and Telmon had most of the major verses of the Puranas by heart, and were guided by Zakiel to read extensively in chrestomathies and incunabulae, but while Telmon dutifully followed the programme Zakiel set out, Yama preferred to idle time away dreaming over bestiaries, prosopographies and maps – most especially maps.

Yama stole many books from the library. Taking them was a way of possessing the ideas and wonders they contained, as if he might, piece by piece, seize the whole world. Zakiel retrieved most of the books from various hiding places in the house or the ruins in its grounds, using a craft more subtle than the tracking skills of either Telmon or Sergeant Rhodean, but one thing Yama managed to retain was a map of the inhabited half of the world. The map's scroll was the width of his hand and almost twice the length of his body, wound on a resin spindle decorated with tiny figures of a thousand bloodlines frozen in represent-ative poses. The map was printed on a material finer than silk and stronger than steel. At one edge were the purple and brown and white ridges of the Rim Mountains; at the other was the blue ribbon of the Great River, with a narrow unmarked margin at its far shore. Yama knew that there were many shrines and monuments to pillar saints on the farside shore – he visited some of them each year, when the whole city crossed the Great River to celebrate with fireworks and feasting the rise of the Galaxy at the beginning of winter – and he wondered why the map did not show them. For there was so much detail crammed into the map elsewhere. Between the Great River and the Rim Mountains was the long strip of inhabited land, marked with green plains and lesser mountain ranges and chains of lakes and ochre deserts. Most cities were scattered along the Great River's nearside shore, a thousand or more which lit up with their names when Yama touched them. The greatest of them all stood below the head of the Great River: Ys, a vast blot spread beyond the braided delta where the river gathered its strength from the glaciers and icefields which buried all but the peaks of the Terminal Mountains. When the map had been made, Ys had been at the height of its glory, and its intricate grids of streets and parks and temples stretched from the shore of the Great River to the foothills and canyons at the edge of the Rim Mountains. A disc of plain glass, attached to the spindle of the map by a reel of wire, revealed details of these streets. By squeezing the edges of the disc, the magnification could be adjusted to show individual buildings, and Yama spent long hours gazing at the crowded rooftops, imagining himself smaller than a speck of dust and able to wander the ancient streets of a more innocent age.

More and more, as he came into manhood, Yama was growing restless. He dreamed of searching for his bloodline. Perhaps they were a high-born and fabulously wealthy clan, or a crew of fierce adventurers who had sailed their ships downstream to the midpoint of the world and the end of the Great River, and fallen from the edge and gone adventuring amongst the floating islands; or perhaps they belonged to a coven of wizards with magic powers, and those same powers lay slumbering within him, waiting to be awakened. Yama elaborated enormously complicated stories around his imagined bloodline, some of which Telmon listened to patiently in the watches of the night, when they were camped amongst the tombs of the City of the Dead.

'Never lose your imagination, Yama,' Telmon told him. 'Whatever you are, wherever you come from, that is your most important gift. But you must observe the world, too, learn how to read and remember its every detail, celebrate its hills and forests and deserts and mountains, the Great River and the thousands of rivers that run into it, the thousand cities and the ten thousand bloodlines. I know how much you love that old map, but you must live in the world as it is to really know it. Do that, and think how rich and wild and strange your stories will become. They will make you famous, I know it.'

This was at the end of the last winter Telmon had spent at home, a few days before he took his muster to war. He and Yama were on the high moors three days' ride inland, chasing the rumour of a dragon. Low clouds raced towards the Great River ahead of a cold wind, and a freezing rain, gritty with flecks of ice, blew in their faces as they walked at point with a straggling line of beaters on either side. The moors stretched away under the racing clouds, hummocky and drenched, grown over with dense stands of waist-high bracken and purple islands of springy heather, slashed with fast-running peaty streams and dotted with stands of windblasted juniper and cypress and bright green domes of bog moss. Yama and Telmon were walking because horses were driven mad by the mere scent of a dragon. They wore canvas trousers and long oilcloth slickers over down-lined jackets, and carried heavy carbon-fibre bows which stuck up behind their heads, and quivers of long arrows with sharply tapered ceramic heads. They were soaked and windblasted and utterly exhilarated.

'I will go with you,' Yama said. 'I will go to war, and fight by your side and write an epic about our adventures that will ring down the ages!'

Telmon laughed. 'I doubt that I will see any fighting at all!'

'Your muster will do the town honour, Tel, I know it.'

'At least they can drill well enough, but I hope that is all they will need to do.'

After the Aedile had received the order to supply a muster of a hundred troops to contribute to the war effort, Telmon had chosen the men himself, mostly younger sons who had little chance of establishing a harem. With the help of Sergeant Rhodean, Telmon had drilled them for sixty days; in three more, the ship would arrive to take them downriver to the war.

Telmon said, 'I want to bring them back safely, Yama. I will lead them into the fighting if I am ordered, but they are set down for working on the supply lines, and I will be content with that. For every man or woman fighting the heretics face to face, there are ten who bring up supplies, and build defences, or tend the wounded or bury the dead. That is why the muster has been raised in every village and town and city. The war needs support troops as desperately as it needs fighting men.'

'I will go as an irregular. We can fight together, Tel.'

'You will look after our father, first of all. And then there is Derev.'

'She would not mind. And it is not as if—'

Telmon understood. He said, 'There are plenty of metic marriages, if it does become that serious.'

'I think it might be, Tel. But I will not get married before you return, and I will not get married before I have had my chance to fight in the war.'

'I'm sure you will get your chance, if that is what you want. But be sure that you really want it.'

'Do you think the heretics really fight with magic?'

'They probably have technology given to them by the Ancients of Days. It might seem like magic, but that is only because we do not understand it. But we have right on our side, Yama. We are fighting with the will of the Preservers in our hearts. It is better than any magic.'

Telmon sprang onto a hummock of sedge and looked left and right to check the progress of the beaters, but it was Yama, staring straight ahead with the rain driving into his face, who saw a little spark of light suddenly blossom far out across the sweep of the moors. He cried out and pointed, and Telmon blew and blew on his silver whistle, and raised both arms above his head to signal that the beaters at the far end of each line should begin to walk towards each other and close the circle. Other whistles sounded as the signal was passed down the lines, and Yama and Telmon broke into a run against the wind and rain, leaping a stream and running on towards the scrap of light, which flickered and grew brighter in the midst of the darkening plain.

It was a juniper set on fire. It was burning so fiercely that it had scorched the grass all around it, snapping and crackling as fire consumed its needle-laden branches and tossed yellow flame and fragrant smoke into the wind and rain. Telmon and Yama gazed at it with wonder, then hugged and pounded each other on the back.

'It is here!' Telmon shouted. 'I know it is here!'

They cast around, and almost at once Telmon found the long scar in a stand of heather. It was thirty paces wide and more than five hundred long, burnt down to the earth and layered with wet black ashes.

It was a lek, Telmon said. 'The male makes it to attract females. The size and regularity of it shows that he is strong and fit.'

'This one must have been very big,' Yama said. The excitement he had felt while running towards the burning tree was gone; he felt a queer kind of relief now. He would not have to face the dragon. Not yet. He paced out the length of the lek while Telmon squatted with the blazing tree at his back and poked through the char.

'Four hundred and twenty-eight,' Yama said, when he came back. 'How big would the dragon be, Tel?'

'Pretty big. I think he was successful, too. Look at the claw marks here. There are two kinds.'

They quartered the area around the lek, moving quickly because the light was going. The tree had mostly burned out when the beaters arrived and helped widen the search. But the dragon was gone.

Three days later, Telmon and the muster from Aeolis boarded a carrack that had anchored at the floating harbour on its way from Ys to the war at the midpoint of the world. Yama did not go to see Telmon off, but stood on the bluff above the Great River and raised his fighting kite into the wind as the little flotilla of skiffs, each with a decad of men, rowed out to the great ship. Yama had painted the kite with a red dragon, its tail curled around its long body and fire pouring from its crocodile jaws, and he flew it high into the snapping wind and then lit the fuses and cut the string. The kite sailed out high above the Great River, and the chain of firecrackers exploded in flame and smoke until the last and biggest of all set fire to the kite's wide diamond, and it fell from the sky.

After the news of the death of Telmon, Yama began to feel an unfocused restlessness. He spent long hours studying the map or sweeping the horizons with the telescope in the tower which housed the heliograph, most often pointing it upriver, where there was always the sense of the teeming vast city, like a thunderstorm, looming beyond the vanishing point.

Ys! When the air was exceptionally clear, Yama could glimpse the slender gleaming towers rooted at the heart of the city. The towers were so tall that they rose beyond the limit of visibility, higher than the bare peaks of the Rimwall Mountains, punching through the atmosphere whose haze hid Ys itself. Ys was three days' journey by river and four times that by road, but even so the ancient city dominated the landscape, and Yama's dreams.

After Telmon's death, Yama began to plan his escape with meticulous care, although at first he did not think of it as escape at all, but merely an extension of the expeditions he had made, first with Telmon, and latterly with Ananda and Derev, in the City of the Dead. Sergeant Rhodean was fond of saying that most unsuccessful campaigns failed not because of the action of the enemy but because of lack of crucial supplies or unforeseeable circumstances, and so Yama made caches of stolen supplies in several hiding-places amongst the ruins in the garden of the peel-house. But he didn't seriously think of carrying out his plans until the night after the encounter with Lud and Lob, when Dr Dismas had an audience with the Aedile.

Dr Dismas arrived at the end of the evening meal. The Aedile and Yama customarily ate together in the Great Hall, sitting at one end of the long, polished table under the high, barrel-vaulted ceiling and its freight of hanging banners, most so ancient that all traces of the devices they had once borne had faded, leaving only a kind of insubstantial, tattered gauze. They were the sigils of the Aedile's ancestors. He had saved them from the great bonfires of the vanities when, after coming to power, the present administration of the Department of Indigenous Affairs had sought to eradicate the past.

Ghosts. Ghosts above, and a ghost unremarked in the empty chair at the Aedile's right hand.

Servants came and went with silent precision, bringing lentil soup, then slivers of mango dusted with ginger, and then a roast marmot dismembered on a bed of watercress. The Aedile said little except to ask after Yama's day.

Yama had spent the morning watching the pinnace which had anchored downriver of the bay three days ago, and now he remarked that he would like to take a boat out to have a closer look at it.

The Aedile said, 'I wonder why it does not anchor at the new quay. It is small enough to enter the mouth of the bay, yet does not. No, I do not think it would be good for you to go out to it, Yama. As well as good, brave men, all sorts of ruffians are recruited to fight the heretics.'

For a moment, they both thought of Telmon.

Ghosts, invisibly packing the air.

The Aedile changed the subject. 'When I first arrived here, ships of all sizes could anchor in the bay, and when the river level began to fall I had the new quay built. But now the bigger ships must use the floating harbour, and soon that will have to be moved further out to accommodate the largest of the argosies. From its present rate of shrinkage I have calculated that in less than five hundred years the river will be completely dry. Aeolis will be a port stranded in a desert plain.'

'There is the Breas.'

'Quite, quite, but where does the water of the Breas come from, except from the snows of the Rim Mountains, which in turn fall from air pregnant with water evaporated from the Great River? I have sometimes thought that it would be good for the town to have the old locks rebuilt. There is still good marble to be quarried in the hills.'

Yama mentioned that Dr Dismas was returned from Ys, but the Aedile only said, 'Quite, quite. I have even talked with him.'

'I suppose he has arranged some filthy little clerkship for me.'

'This is not the time to discuss your future,' the Aedile said, and retreated, as was increasingly his habit, into a book. He made occasional notes in the margins of its pages with one hand while he ate with the other at a slow, deliberate pace that was maddening to Yama. He wanted to go down to the armoury and question Sergeant Rhodean, who had returned from his patrol just before darkness.

The servants had cleared away the great silver salver bearing the marmot's carcass and were bringing in a dish of iced sherbet when the major domo paced down the long hall and announced the arrival of Dr Dismas.

'Bring him directly.' The Aedile shut his book, took off his spectacles, and told Yama, 'Run along, my boy. I know you want to quiz Sergeant Rhodean.'

Yama had used the telescope to spy on the Aedile and Dr Dismas that afternoon, when they had met and talked on the dusty hillside at the edge of the City of the Dead. He was convinced that Dr Dismas had been to Ys to arrange an apprenticeship in some dusty corner of the Aedile's department.

And so, although he set off towards the armoury, Yama quickly doubled back and crept into the gallery just beneath the Great Hall's high ceiling, where, on feast days, musicians hidden from view serenaded the Aedile's guests. Yama thrust his head between the stays of two dusty banners and found that he was looking straight down at the Aedile and Dr Dismas.

The two men were drinking port wine so dark that it was almost black, and Dr Dismas had lit one of his cigarettes. Yama could smell its clove-scented smoke. Dr Dismas sat stiffly in a carved chair, his white hands moving over the polished surface of the table like independently questing animals. Papers were scattered in front of him, and patterns of blue dots and dashes glowed in the air. Yama would have dearly loved to have had a spyglass just then, to find out what was written on the papers, and what the patterns meant.

Yama had expected to hear Dr Dismas and the Aedile discuss his apprenticeship, but instead the Aedile was making a speech about trust. 'When I took Yama into my household, I also took upon myself the responsibility of a parent. I have brought him up as best I could, and I have tried to make a decision about his future with his best interests in my heart. You ask me to overthrow that in an instant, to gamble my duty to the boy against some vague promise.'

'It is more than that,' Dr Dismas said. 'The boy's bloodline—'

Yama's heart beat more quickly, but the Aedile angrily interrupted Dr Dismas. 'That is of no consequence. I know what you told me. It only convinces me that I must see to the boy's future.'

'I understand. But, with respect, you may not be able to protect him from those who might be interested to learn of him, who might believe that they have a use for him. I speak of higher affairs than those of the Department of Indigenous Affairs. I speak of great forces, forces which your few decads of soldiers could not withstand for an instant. You should not put yourself between those powers and that which they may desire.'

The Aedile stood so suddenly that he knocked over his glass of port. High above, Yama thought that for a moment his guardian might strike Dr Dismas, but then the Aedile turned his back on the table and closed his fist under his chin. He said, 'Who did you tell, doctor?'

'As yet, only you.'

Yama knew that Dr Dismas was lying, because the answer sprang so readily to his lips. He wondered if the Aedile knew, too.

'I notice that the pinnace which brought you back from Ys is still anchored off the point of the bay. I wonder why that might be.'

'I suppose I could ask its commander. He is an acquaintance of mine.'

The Aedile turned around. 'I see,' he said coldly. 'Then you threaten—'

'My dear Aedile, I do not come to your house to threaten you. I have better manners than that, I would hope. I make no threats, only predictions. You have heard my thoughts about the boy's bloodline. There is only one explanation. I believe any other man, with the same evidence, would come to the same conclusion as I, but it does not matter if I am right. One need only raise the possibility to understand what danger the boy might be in. We are at war, and you have been concealing him from your own department. You would not wish to have your loyalty put to the question. Not again.'

'Be careful, doctor. I could have you arrested. You are said to be a necromancer, and it is well known that you indulge in drugs.'

Dr Dismas said calmly, 'The first is a only a rumour, and while the second may be true, you have recently demonstrated your faith in me, and your letter is lodged with my department. As, I might add, is a copy of my findings. You could arrest me, but you could not keep me imprisoned for long without appearing foolish or corrupt. But why do we argue? We both have the same interest. We both wish no harm to come to the boy. We merely disagree on how to protect him.'

The Aedile sat down and ran his fingers through the grey pelt which covered his face. He said, 'How much money do you want?'

Dr Dismas laughed. It was like the creaking of old wood giving beneath a weight. 'In one pan of the scales is the golden ingot of the boy; in the other the feather of your worth. I will not even pretend to be insulted.' He stood and plucked his cigarette from the holder and extinguished it in the pool of port spilled from the Aedile's glass, then reached into the glowing patterns. There was a click: the patterns vanished. Dr Dismas tossed the projector cube into the air and made it vanish into one of the pockets of his long black coat. He said, 'If you do not make arrangements, then I must. And believe me, you'll get the poorer part of the bargain if you do.'

When Dr Dismas had gone, the Aedile raked up the papers and clutched them to his chest. His shoulders shook. High above, Yama thought that his guardian might be crying, but surely he was mistaken, for never before, even at the news of Telmon's death, had the Aedile shown any sign of grief.

5 ~ The Siege

Yama lay awake long into the night, his mind racing with speculations about what Dr Dismas might have discovered. Something about his bloodline, he was sure of that at least, and he slowly convinced himself it was something with which Dr Dismas could blackmail the Aedile. Perhaps his real parents were heretics or murderers or pirates ... but who then would have a use for him, and what powers would take an interest? He was well aware that like all orphans he had filled the void of his parents' absence with extreme caricatures. They could be war heroes or colourful villains or dynasts wealthy beyond measure; what they could not be was ordinary, for that would mean that he too was ordinary, abandoned not because of some desperate adventure or deep scandal, but because of the usual small tragedies of the human condition. In his heart he knew these dreams for what they were, but although he had put them away, as he had put aside his childish toys, Dr Dismas's return had awakened them, and all the stories he had elaborated as a child tumbled through his mind in a vivid pageant that ravelled away into confused dreams filled with unspecific longing.

As the sun crept above the ragged blue line of the Rim Mountains, Yama was woken by a commotion below his window. He threw open the shutters and saw that three pentads of the garrison, in black resin armour ridged like the carapaces of sexton beetles and kilts of red leather strips, and with burnished metal caps on their heads, were climbing onto their horses. Squat, shaven-headed Sergeant Rhodean leaned on the pommel of his gelding's saddle as he watched his men settle themselves and their restless mounts. Puffs of vapour rose from the horses' nostrils; harness jingled and hooves clattered on concrete as they stepped about. Other soldiers were stacking ladders, grappling irons, siege rockets and coils of rope on the loadbed of the grimy black steam waggon. Two house servants manoeuvred the Aedile's palanquin, which floated a handspan above the ground, into the centre of the courtyard and then the Aedile himself appeared, clad in his robe of office, black sable trimmed with a collar of white feathers that ruffled in the cold dawn breeze.

The servants helped the Aedile over the flare of the palanquin's skirt and settled him in the backless chair beneath its red and gold canopy. Sergeant Rhodean raised a hand above his head and the procession, two files of mounted soldiers on either side of the palanquin, moved out of the courtyard. Black smoke and sparks shot up from the steam waggon's tall chimney; white vapour jetted from leaking piston sleeves. As the waggon ground forward, its iron-rimmed wheels striking sparks from concrete, Yama threw on his clothes; before it had passed through the arch of the gate in the old wall he was in the armoury, quizzing the stable hands.

'Off to make an arrest,' one of them said. It was the foreman, Torin. A tall man, his shaven bullet-head couched in the hump of muscle at his back, his skin a rich dark brown mapped with paler blotches. He had followed the Aedile into exile from Ys and, after Sergeant Rhodean, was the most senior of his servants. 'Don't be thinking we'll saddle up your horse, young master,' he told Yama. 'We've strict instructions that you're to stay here.'

'I suppose you are not allowed to tell me who they are going to arrest. Well, it does not matter. I know it is Dr Dismas.'

'The master was up all night,' Torin said, 'talking with the soldiers. Roused the cook hours ago to make him early breakfast. There might be a bit of a battle.'

'Who told you that?'

Torin gave Yama an insolent smile. His teeth were needles of white bone. 'Why it's plain to see. There's that ship still waiting offshore. It might try a rescue.'

The party of sailors. What had they been looking for? Yama said, 'Surely it is on our side.'

'There's some that reckon it's for Dr Dismas,' Torin said. 'That's how he came back to town, after all. There'll be blood shed before the end of it. Cook has his boys making bandages, and if you're looking for something to do you should join them.'

Yama ran again, this time to the kitchens. He snatched a sugar roll from a batch fresh from the baking oven, then climbed the back stairs two steps at a time, taking big bites from the warm roll. He waited behind a pillar while the old man who had charge of the Aedile's bedchamber locked the door and pottered off, crumpled towels over one arm, then used his knife to pick the lock, a modern mechanical thing as big as his head. It was easy to snap back the lock's wards one by one and to silence the machines which set up a chorus of protest at his entrance, although it took a whole minute to convince an alembic that his presence would not upset its delicate settings.

Quickly, Yama searched for the papers Dr Dismas had brought, but they were not amongst the litter on the Aedile's desk, nor were they in the sandalwood travelling chest, with its deck of sliding drawers. Perhaps the papers were in the room in the watchtower – but that had an old lock, and Yama had never managed to persuade it to let him pass.

He closed the chest and sat back on his heels. This part of the house was quiet. Narrow beams of early sunlight slanted through the tall, narrow windows, illuminating a patch of the richly patterned carpet, a book splayed upside-down on the little table beside the Aedile's reading chair. Zakiel would be waiting for him in the library, but there were more important things afoot. Yama went back out through the kitchen, cut across the herb garden and, after calming one of the watchdogs, ran down the steep slope of the breastwork and struck off through the ruins towards the city.

Dr Dismas's tower stood just outside the city wall. It was tall and slender, and had once been used to manufacture shot. Molten blackstone had been poured through a screen at the top of the tower, and the droplets, rounding into perfect spheres as they fell, had plummeted into an annealing bath of water at the base. The builders of the tower had sought to advertise its function by adding slit windows and a parapet with a crenellated balustrade in imitation of the watchtower of a castellan, and after the foundry had been razed, the tower had indeed been briefly used as a lookout post. But then the new city wall had been built with the tower outside it, and the tower had fallen into disuse, its stones slowly pried apart by the tendrils of its ivy cloak, the platform where molten stone had been made poured to make shot for the guns of soldiers and hunters becoming the haunt of owls and bats.

Dr Dismas had moved into the tower shortly after taking up his apothecary's post. Once it had been cleaned out and joiners had fitted new stairs and three circular floors within it and raised a tall slender spire above the crenellated balustrade, Dr Dismas had closed its door to the public, preferring to rent a room overlooking the waterfront as his office. There were rumours that he performed all kinds of black arts in the tower, from necromancy to the surgical creation of chimeras and other monsters. It was said that he owned a homunculus he himself had fathered by despoiling a young girl taken from the fisherfolk. The homunculus was kept in a tank of saline water, and could prophesy the future. Everyone in Aeolis would swear to the truth of this, although no one, of course, had actually seen it.

The soldiers had already begun the siege by the time Yama reached the tower, and a crowd had gathered at a respectful distance to watch the fun. Sergeant Rhodean stood at the door at the foot of the tower, his helmet tucked under one arm as he bawled out the warrant. The Aedile sat straight-backed under the canopy of the palanquin, which was grounded amongst the soldiers and a unit of the town's militia, out of range of shot or quarrel. The militiamen were a motley crew in mismatched bits of armour, armed mostly with home-made blunderbusses and rifles but drawn up in two neat ranks as if determined to put on a good show. The soldiers' horses tossed their heads, made nervous by the crowd and the steady hiss of the steam waggon's boiler.

Yama clambered to the top of a stretch of ruined wall near the back of the crowd. It was almost entirely composed of men; wives were not allowed to leave the harems. They stood shoulder to shoulder, grey- and brown-skinned, corpulent and four square on short, muscular legs, barechested in breechclouts or kilts. They stank of sweat and fish and stale riverwater, and nudged each other and jostled for a better view. There was a jocular sense of occasion, as if this were some piece of theatre staged by a travelling mountebank. It was about time the magician got what he deserved, they told each other, and agreed that the Aedile would have a hard time of it winkling him from his nest.

Hawkers were selling sherbet and sweetmeats, fried cakes of riverweed and watermelon slices. A knot of whores of a dozen different bloodlines, clad in abbreviated, brightly coloured nylon chitons, their faces painted dead white under fantastical conical wigs, watched from a little rise at the back of the crowd, passing a slim telescope to and fro. Their panderer, no doubt hoping for brisk business when the show was over, moved amongst the crowd, cracking jokes and handing out clove-flavoured cigarettes. Yama looked for the whore he had lain with the night before Telmon had left for the war, but could not see her, and blushingly looked away when the panderer caught his eye and winked at him.

Sergeant Rhodean bawled out the warrant again, and when there was no reply set his helmet on his scarred, shaven head and limped back to where the Aedile and the other soldiers waited. He leaned on the skirt of the Aedile's palanquin and there was a brief conference.

'Burn him out!' someone in the crowd shouted, and there was a general murmur of agreement.

The steam waggon jetted black smoke and lumbered forward; soldiers dismounted and walked along the edge of the crowd, selecting volunteers from its ranks. Sergeant Rhodean spoke to the bravos and handed out coins; under his supervision, they lifted the ram from the loadbed of the steam waggon and, flanked by soldiers, carried it towards the tower. The soldiers held their round shields above their heads, but nothing stirred in the tower until the bravos applied the ram to its door.

The ram was the trunk of a young pine bound with a spiral of steel, slung in a cradle of leather straps with handholds for eight men and crowned with a steel cap shaped like a caprice, with sturdy, coiled horns. The crowd shouted encouragement as the bravos swung it in steadily increasing arcs. 'One!' they shouted. 'Two!'

At the first stroke of the ram, the door rang like a drum and a cloud of bats burst from the upper window of the tower. The bats stooped low, swirling above the heads of the crowd with a dry rustle of wings, and the men laughed and jumped up, trying to catch them. One of the whores ran down the road screaming, her hands beating at two bats which had tangled in her conical wig. Some in the crowd cheered coarsely. The whore stumbled and fell flat on her face and a militiaman ran forward and slashed at the bats with his knife. One struggled free and took to the air; the man stamped on the other until it was a bloody smear on the dirt. As if blown by a wind, the rest of the bats rose high and scattered into the blue sky.

The ram struck again and again. The bravos had found their rhythm now. The crowd cheered the steady beat. Someone at Yama's shoulder remarked, 'They should burn him out.'

It was Ananda. As usual, he wore his orange robe, with his left breast bare. He carried a small leather satchel containing incense and chrism oil. He told Yama that his master was here to exorcise the tower and, in case things got out of hand, to shrive the dead. He was indecently pleased about Dr Dismas's impending arrest. Dr Dismas was infamous for his belief that chance, not the Preservers, controlled the lives of men. He did not attend any high day services, although he was a frequent visitor to the temple, playing chess with Father Quine and spending hours debating the nature of the Preservers and the world. The priest viewed Dr Dismas as a brilliant mind that might yet be saved; Ananda knew the doctor was too clever and too proud for that.

'He plays games with people,' Ananda told Yama. 'He enjoys making people believe that he's a warlock, although of course he has no such powers. No one has, unless they flow from the Preservers. It's time he was punished. He's been revelling in his notoriety too long.'

'He knows something about me,' Yama said. 'He found it out in Ys. I think that he is trying to blackmail my father with it.'

Yama described what had happened the night before, and Ananda said kindly, 'I shouldn't think that Dismas has found out anything at all, but of course he couldn't return and tell the Aedile that. He was bluffing, and now his bluff has been called. You'll see. The Aedile will put him to question.'

'He should have killed Dr Dismas on the spot,' Yama said. 'Instead, he stayed his hand, and now he has this farce.'

'Your father is a cautious and judicious man.'

'Too cautious. A good general makes a plan and strikes before the enemy has a chance to find a place to make a stand.'

Ananda said, 'He could not strike Dr Dismas dead on the spot, or even arrest him. It would not be seemly. He had to consult the Council for Night and Shrines – Dr Dismas is their man, after all. This way, justice is seen to be done, and all are satisfied. That's why he chose volunteers from the crowd to break down the door. Everyone is involved in this.'

'Perhaps,' Yama said, but he was not convinced. That this whole affair was somehow hinged about his origin was both exciting and shameful. He wanted it over with, and yet a part of him, the wild part that dreamed of pirates and adventurers, exulted in the display of force, and he was more certain than ever that he could never settle into a quiet tenure in some obscure office within the Department of Indigenous Affairs.

The ram struck, and struck again, but the door showed no sign of giving way.

'It is reinforced with iron,' Ananda said, 'and it is not hinged, but slides into a recess. In any case we've a long wait even after they break down the door.'

Yama remarked that Ananda seemed to be an expert on the prosecution of sieges.

'I saw one before,' Ananda said. 'It was in the little town outside the walls of the monastery where I was taught, in the high mountains upriver of Ys. A gang of brigands had sealed themselves in a house. The town had only its militia, and Ys was two days' march away – long before soldiers could arrive, the brigands would have escaped under cover of darkness. The militia decided to capture the brigands themselves, but several were killed trying to break into the place, and at last they burned the house to the ground, and the brigands with it. That's what they should do here; otherwise the soldiers will have to break into every floor of the tower to catch Dismas. He could kill many of them before that – and suppose he has something like the palanquin? He could fly away.'

'Then my father could chase him.' Yama laughed at the vision this conjured up: Dr Dismas fleeing the tower like a black beetle on the wing and the Aedile swooping behind in his richly decorated palanquin like a hungry bird.

The crowd cheered. Yama and Ananda pushed to the front, using their elbows and knees, and saw that the door had split from top to bottom.

Sergeant Rhodean raised a hand and there was an expectant hush. 'One more time, lads,' the sergeant shouted, 'and put some back into it!'

The ram swung and the door shattered and fell away. The crowd surged forward, carrying Ananda and Yama with it, and soldiers pushed them back. One recognized Yama. 'You should not be here, young master,' he said. 'Go back now. Be sensible.'

Yama dodged away before the soldier could grab him and, followed by Ananda, retreated to his original vantage point on the broken bit of wall, where he could see over the heads of the crowd and the line of embattled soldiers. The team of bravos swung the ram with short brisk strokes, knocking away the wreckage of the door; then they stood aside as a pentad of soldiers (the leader of the militia trailing behind) came forward with rifles and arbalests at the ready.

Led by Sergeant Rhodean, this party disappeared into the dark doorway. There was an expectant hush. Yama looked to the Aedile, who sat upright under the canopy of his palanquin, his face set in a grim expression. The white feathers which trimmed the high collar of his sable robe fluttered in the morning breeze.

There was a muffled thump. Thick orange smoke suddenly poured from one of the narrow windows of the tower, round billows swiftly unpacking into the air. The crowd murmured, uncertain if this was part of the attack or a desperate defensive move. More thumps: now smoke poured from every window, and from the smashed doorway. The soldiers stumbled out under a wing of orange smoke. Sergeant Rhodean brought up the rear, hauling the leader of the militia with him.

Flames mingled with the smoke that poured from the windows, which was slowly changing from orange to deep red. Some of the crowd were kneeling, their fists curled against their foreheads to make the sign of the Eye.

Ananda said to Yama, 'This is demon work.'

'I thought you did not believe in magic.'

'No, but I believe in demons. After all, demons tried to overthrow the order of the Preservers an age ago. Perhaps Dismas is one, disguised as a man.'

'Demons are machines, not supernatural creatures,' Yama said, but Ananda had turned to look at the burning tower, and did not seem to have heard him.

The flames licked higher; there was a ring of flames around the false spire that crowned the top of the tower. Red smoke hazed the air. Fat flakes of white ash fell through it. There was a stink of sulphur and something sickly sweet. Then there was another muffled thump and a tongue of flame shot out of the doorway. The tower's spire blew to flinders. Burning strips of plastic foil rained down on the heads of the crowd and men yelled and ran in every direction.

Yama and Ananda were separated by the sudden panic as the front ranks of the crowd tried to flee through the press of those behind and dozens of men clambered over the broken wall. A horse reared up, striking with its hooves at a man who had grabbed hold of its bridle.

The steam waggon was alight from one end to the other. The driver jumped from its burning cab, rolled over and over to smother his smouldering clothes, and staggered to his feet just as the charges on its loadbed exploded and blew him to red ruin.

Siege rockets flew in crisscross trajectories, trailing burning lengths of rope. A cask of napalm burst in a ball of oily flame, sending a mushroom of smoke boiling into the air. Flecks of fire spattered in a wide circle. Men dived towards whatever cover they could find. Yama dropped to the ground, his arms crossed over his head, as burning debris pattered around.

There was a moment of intense quiet. As Yama climbed to his feet, his ears ringing, a heavy hand fell on his shoulder and spun him around.

'We've unfinished business, small fry,' Lob said. Behind his brother, Lud grinned around his tusks.

6 ~ The House of Ghost Lanterns

Lud took Yama's knife and stuck it in his belt beside his own crooked blade. 'Don't go shouting for help,' he said, 'or we'll tear out your tongue.'

People were making a hasty retreat towards the gate in the city wall. Lob and Lud gripped Yama's arms and carried him along with them. The tower was burning furiously, a roaring chimney belching thick red fumes that, with the smoke of the burning waggon and countless lesser fires, veiled the sun. Several horses had thrown their riders and were galloping about wildly. Sergeant Rhodean strode amidst the flames and smoke, organizing countermeasures; already, soldiers and militiamen were beating at small grass fires with wet blankets.

The fleeing crowd split around Ananda and the priest. They were kneeling over a man and anointing his bloody head with oil while reciting the last rites. Yama turned to try and catch Ananda's eye, but Lud snarled and cuffed his head and forced him on.

The fumes of the burning tower hung over the crowded flat roofs of the little city. Along the old waterfront, peddlers were bundling wares into their blankets. Chandlers, tavern owners and their employees were locking shutters over windows and standing guard at doors, armed with rifles and axes. Men were already looting the building where Dr Dismas had his office. They dragged furniture onto the second floor veranda and threw it into the street; books rained down like broken-backed birds; jars of simples smashed on the concrete, strewing arcs of coloured powder. A man was methodically smashing all the windows with a heavy iron hammer.

Lob and Lud bundled Yama through the riot and turned down a sidestreet that was little more than a paved walkway above the green water of a wide, stagnant canal. The single-storey houses which stood

66

shoulder to shoulder along the canal had been built with stone looted from older, grander buildings, and their tall, narrow windows were framed by collages of worn carvings and broken tablets incised with texts in long-forgotten scripts. Chutes led down into the scummy water; this part of the city was where the bachelor field labourers lived, and they could not afford private bathing places.

For a moment, Yama thought that the two brothers had dragged him to this shabby, unremarked sidestreet so that they could punish him for interfering with their fun with the anchorite. He braced himself, but was merely pushed forward. With Lud leading and Lob crowding behind, he was hustled through the street doorway of a tavern, under a cluster of ancient ghost lanterns that squealed and rustled in the foetid breeze.

A square plunge pool lit by green underwater lanterns took up half the echoing space. Worn stone steps led down into the slop of glowing water. An immensely fat man floated on his back in the middle of the pool; his shadow loomed across the galleries that ran around three sides of the room. As Lob and Lud hustled Yama past the pool, the man snorted and stirred, expelling a mist of oily vapour from his nostrils and opening one eye. Lob threw a coin. The fat man caught it in the mobile, blubbery lips of his horseshoe-shaped mouth. His lower lip inverted and the coin vanished into his maw. He snorted again and his eye closed.

Lud jabbed Yama with the point of his knife and marched him around a rack of barrels and along a narrow passage which opened into a tiny courtyard. The space, roofed with glass speckled and stained by green algae and black mould, contained a kind of cage of woven wire that fitted inside the whitewashed walls with only a handsbreadth to spare on either side. Inside the cage, beneath its wire ceiling, Dr Dismas was hunched at a rickety table, reading a book and smoking a clove-scented cigarette stuck in his bone cigarette holder.

'Here he is,' Lud said. 'We have him, doctor!'

'Bring him inside,' the apothecary said, and closed his book with an impatient snap.

Yama's fear had turned to paralysing astonishment. Lob roughly pinioned his arms behind his back while Lud unlocked a door in the cage; then Yama was thrust through and the door was closed and locked behind him.

'No,' Dr Dismas said, 'I am far from dead, although I have paid a

67

heavy price for this venture. Close your mouth, boy. You look like one of the frogs you are so fond of hunting late at night.'

Outside the cage, Lud and Lob nudged each other. 'Go on,' one muttered, and the other, 'You do it!' At last, Lud said to Dr Dismas, 'You'll pay us. We done what you asked.'

'You failed the first time,' Dr Dismas said, 'and I haven't forgotten. There's work still to be done, and if I pay you now you'll turn any money I give you into drink. Go now. We'll start on the second part of this an hour after sunset.'

After more nudging, Lob said, 'We thought maybe we get paid for the one thing, and then we do the other.'

'I told you that I would pay you to bring the boy here. And I will. And there will be more money when you help me take him to the man who has commissioned me. But there will be no money at all unless everything is done as I asked.'

'Maybe we only do the one thing,' Lob said, 'and not the other.'

'I would suggest it is dangerous to leave something unfinished,' Dr Dismas said.

'I don't know if this is right,' Lud said. 'We did what you asked—'

Dr Dismas said sharply, 'When did I ask you to begin the second part of your work?'

'Sunset,' Lob said in a sullen mumble.

'An hour after. Remember that. You will suffer as much as I if the work is done badly. You failed the first time. Don't fail again.'

Lud said sulkily, 'We got him for you, didn't we?'

Lob added, 'We would have got him the other night, if this old culler with a stick hadn't got in the way.'

Yama stared at the brothers through the mesh of the cage. They would not meet his eyes. He said, 'You should allow me to go. I will say you rescued me from the mob. I do not know what Dr Dismas promised, but my father will pay double to have me safe.'

Lud and Lob grinned, nudging each other in the ribs.

'Ain't he a corker,' Lud said. 'Like a proper little gentleman.'

Lob belched, and his brother sniggered.

Yama turned to Dr Dismas. 'The same applies to you, doctor.'

'My dear boy, I don't think the Aedile can afford my price,' Dr Dismas said. 'I was happy in my home, with my research and my books.'

68

He put a hand on his narrow chest and sighed. He had six fingers, with long nails filed to points. 'All gone now, thanks to you. You owe me a great deal, Yamamanama, and I intend to have my price in full. I don't need the Aedile's charity.'

Yama felt a queer mixture of excitement and fear. He was convinced that Dr Dismas had found his bloodline, if not his family. 'Then you really have found where I came from! You have found my family – that is, my real family—'

'O, far better than that,' Dr Dismas said, 'but this is not the time to talk about it.'

Yama said, 'I would know it now, whatever it is. I deserve to know it.'

Dr Dismas said with sudden anger, 'I'm no house servant, boy,' and his hand flashed out and pinched a nerve in Yama's elbow. Yama's head was filled with pain as pure as light. He fell to his knees on the mesh floor of the cage, and Dr Dismas came around the table and caught Yama's chin between long, stiff, cold fingers.

'You are mine now,' he said, 'and don't forget it.' He turned to the twins. 'Why are you two still here? You have your orders.'

'We'll be back tonight,' Lud said. 'See you pay us then.'

'Of course, of course.' Once the twins had gone, Dr Dismas said to Yama in a confiding tone, 'Frankly, I would rather work alone, but I could hardly move amongst the crowd while everyone thought I was in the tower.' He got his hands under Yama's arms and hauled him up. 'Please, do sit. We are civilized men. There, that's better.'

Yama, perched on the edge of the flimsy metal chair, simply breathed for a while until the pain had retreated to a warm throb in the muscles of his shoulder. At last he said, 'You knew the Aedile was going to arrest you.'

Dr Dismas resumed his seat on the other side of the little table. As he screwed a cigarette into his bone holder, he said, 'Your father is a man who takes his responsibilities seriously. Very properly, he confided his intentions to the Council for Night and Shrines. One of them owed me a favour.'

'If there is any problem between you and my father, I am sure it can be worked out, but not while you hold me captive. Once the fire in the tower burns out, they will look for a body. When they do not find one, they will look for you. And this is a small city.'

69

Dr Dismas blew a riffle of smoke towards the mesh ceiling of the cage. 'How well Zakiel has taught you logic. It would be a persuasive argument, except that they will find a body.'

'Then you planned to burn your tower all along, and you should not blame me. I expect you removed your books before you left.'

Dr Dismas did not deny this. He said, 'How did you like the display, by the way?'

'Some are convinced that you are a magician.'

'There are no such creatures. Those who claim to be magicians delude themselves as much as their clients. My little pyrotechnic display was simply a few judiciously mixed salts ignited by electric detonators when the circuit was closed by some oaf stepping on a plate I'd hidden under a rug. No more than a jape which any apprentice apothecary worthy of the trade could produce, although perhaps not on such a grand scale.' Dr Dismas pointed a long forefinger at Yama, who stifled the impulse to flinch. 'All this for you. You do owe me, Yamamanama. The Child of the River, yes, but which river, I wonder. Not our own Great River, I'm certain.'

'You know about my family.' Yama could not keep the eagerness from his voice. It was rising and bubbling inside him – he wanted to laugh, to sing, to dance. 'You know about my bloodline.'

Dr Dismas reached into a pocket of his long coat and drew out a handful of plastic straws. He rattled them together in his long pale hands and cast them on the table. He was making a decision by appealing to their random pattern; Yama had heard of this habit from Ananda, who had reported it in scandalized tones.

Yama said, 'Are you deciding whether to tell me or not, doctor?'

'You're a brave boy to ask after forbidden knowledge, so you deserve some sort of answer.' Dr Dismas tapped ash from his cigarette. 'Oxen and camels, nilgai, ratites and horses – all of them work under the lash, watched by boys no older than you, or even younger, who are armed with no more than fresh-cut withes to restrain their charges. How is this? Because the part in those animals which yearns for freedom has been broken and replaced by habit. No more than a twitch of a stick is required to reinforce that habit; even if those beasts were freed of their harness and their burden, they would be too broken to realize that they could escape their masters. Most men are no different from beasts of burden, their spirits broken by fear of the phantoms of religion invoked by priests and bureaucrats. I work hard to avoid habits. To be unpredictable – that is how you cheat those who would be the masters of men.'

'I thought you did not believe in the Preservers, doctor.'

'I don't question their existence. Certainly they once existed. This world is evidence; the Eye of the Preservers and all the ordered Galaxy is evidence. But I do question the great lie with which the priests hypnotize the population, that the Preservers watch over us all, and that we must satisfy them so that we can win redemption and live for ever after death. As if creatures who juggled stars in their courses would care about whether or not a man beats his wife, or the little torments one child visits upon another! It is a sop to keep men in their places, to ensure that so-called civilization can run on its own momentum. I spit on it.'

And here Dr Dismas did spit, as delicately as a cat, but nevertheless startling Yama.

The apothecary fitted his cigarette holder back between his large, flat-topped teeth. When he smiled around the holder, the plaques over his cheekbones stood out in relief, their sharp edges pressing through brown skin with the coarse, soft grain of wood-pulp.

Dr Dismas said, 'The Preservers created us, but they are gone. They are dead, and by their own hand. They created the Eye, and fell through its event horizon with all their worlds. And why? Because they despaired. They remade the Galaxy, and could have remade the Universe, but their nerve failed. They were cowardly fools, and anyone who believes that they watch us still, yet do not interfere in the terrible suffering of the world, is a worse fool.'

Yama had no answer to this. There was no answer. Ananda was right. The apothecary was a monster who refused to serve anyone or anything except his own swollen pride.

Dr Dismas said, 'The Preservers are gone, but machines still watch us, and regulate the world according to out-of-date precepts. Of course, the machines can't watch everything at once, so they build up patterns and predict the behaviour of men, and watch only for deviation from the norm. It works most of the time for most of the people, but there are a few men like me who defy their predictions by basing important decisions on chance. The machines cannot track our random paths from moment to moment, and so we become invisible. Of course, a cage such as the one in which we sit also helps hide us from them. It screens out the

71

probing of the machines. I wear a hat for the same reason – it is lined with silver foil.'

Yama laughed, because Dr Dismas confessed this ridiculous habit with complete solemnity. 'So you are afraid of machines.'

'Not at all. But I am deeply interested in them. I have a small collection of parts of dead machines excavated from ruins in the deserts beyond the midpoint of the world – one is almost intact, a treasure beyond price.' Dr Dismas suddenly clutched his head and shook it violently for a moment, then winked at Yama. 'But that's not to be spoken of. Not here! They might hear, even in this cage. One reason I came here is because machine activity is higher than anywhere else on Confluence – yes, even Ys. And so, my dear Yamamanama, I found you.'

Yama pointed at the straws scattered on the table. They were hexagonal in cross-section, with red and green glyphs of some unknown language incised along their faces. He said, 'You refuse to acknowledge the authority of the Preservers over men, yet you follow the guidance of these bits of plastic.'

Dr Dismas looked crafty. 'Ah, but I choose which question to ask them.'

Yama had only one question in his mind. 'You found something about my bloodline in Ys, and told my father what you had learned. If you will not tell me everything, will you at least tell me what you told him? Did you perhaps find my family there?'

'You will have to look further than Ys to find your family, my boy, and you may be given the opportunity to do so. The Aedile is a good enough man in his way, I suppose, but that is to say he is no more than a petty official barely capable of ruling a moribund little region of no interest to anyone. Into his hands has fallen a prize which could determine the fate of all the peoples of Confluence – even the world itself – and he does nothing about it. A man like that deserves to be punished, Yamamanama. And as for you, you are very dangerous. For you do not know what you are.'

'I would like very much to know.' Yama had not understood half of what Dr Dismas had said. With a sinking heart, he was beginning to believe that the man was mad.

'Innocence is no excuse,' Dr Dismas said, but he appeared to be speaking to himself. He moved the plastic straws about the tabletop with a long, bony forefinger, as if seeking to rearrange his fate. He lit another cigarette and stared at Yama until Yama grew uncomfortable and looked away.

Dr Dismas laughed, and with sudden energy took out a little leather case and opened it out on the table. Inside, held by elastic loops, were a glass syringe, an alcohol lamp, a bent silver spoon, its bowl blackened and tarnished, a small pestle and mortar, and several glass bottles with rubber stoppers. From one bottle Dr Dismas shook out a single dried beetle into the mortar; from another he added a few drops of a clear liquid that filled the room with the smell of apricots. Dr Dismas ground the beetle into a paste with finicky care and scraped the paste into the bowl of the spoon.

'Cantharides,' he said, as if that explained everything. 'You are young, and will not understand, but sometimes the world becomes too much to bear for someone of my sensibilities.'

'My father said this got you into trouble with your department. He said—'

'That I had sworn to stop using it? Oh yes, of course I said that. If I had not said that, they would not have let me return to Aeolis.'

Dr Dismas lit the wick of the alcohol lamp with a flint and steel and held the spoon over the blue flame until the brown paste liquified and began to bubble. The smell of apricots intensified, sharpened by a metallic tang. Dr Dismas drew the liquid into the hypodermic and tapped the barrel with a long thumbnail to loosen the bubbles which clung to the glass. 'Don't think to escape,' he said. 'I have no key.'

He spread his left hand on the tabletop and probed the web of skin between thumb and forefinger until he hit a vein. He teased back the syringe's plunger until a wisp of red swirled in the thin brown solution, then pressed the plunger home.

He drew in a sharp breath and stretched in his chair like a bow. The hypodermic dropped to the table. For a moment, his heels drummed an irregular tattoo on the mesh floor, and then he relaxed, and looked at Yama with half-closed eyes. His pupils, smeary crosses on yellow balls, contracted and expanded independently. He giggled. 'If I had you long enough . . . ah, what I'd teach you . . .'

'Doctor?'

But Dr Dismas would say no more. His gaze wandered around the cage and at last fixed on the spattered glass which roofed the courtyard. Yama tested the cage's wire mesh, but although he could deform its

73

close-woven hexagons, they were all of a piece, and the door was so close-fitting Yama could not get his fingers into the gap between it and its wire frame. The sun crept into view above the little courtyard's glass ceiling, filling it with golden light, and began its slow reversal.

At last, Yama dared to touch the apothecary's outstretched hand. It was clammy, and irregular plates shifted under the loose skin. Dr Dismas did not stir. His head was tipped back, his face bathed by the sunlight.

Yama found only one pocket inside the apothecary's long black coat, and it was empty. Dr Dismas stirred as Yama withdrew his hand, and gripped his wrist and drew him down with unexpected strength. 'Don't doubt,' he murmured. His breath smelt of apricots and iron. 'Sit and wait, boy.'

Yama sat and waited. Presently the immensely fat man he had seen floating in the tavern's communal pool shuffled down the passage. He was naked except for blue rubber sandals on his broad feet, and he carried a tray covered with a white cloth.

'Stand back,' he told Yama. 'No, further back. Behind the doctor.'

'Let me go. I promise you will be rewarded.'

'I've already been paid, young master,' the fat man said. He unlocked the door, set the tray down, and relocked the door. 'Eat, young master. The doctor, he won't want anything. I never seen him eat. He has his drug.'

'Let me go!' Yama banged at the cage's locked door and yelled threats at the fat man's retreating back before giving up and looking under the cloth that covered the tray.

A dish of watery soup with a cluster of whitened fish eyes sunk in the middle and rings of raw onion floating on top; a slab of black bread, as dense as a brick and almost as hard; a glass of small beer the colour of stale urine.

The soup was flavoured with chili oil, making it almost palatable, but the bread was so salty that Yama gagged on the first bite and could eat no more. He drank the sour beer and somehow fell asleep on the rickety chair.

He was woken by Dr Dismas. He had a splitting headache and a foul taste in his mouth. The courtyard and the cage was lit by a hissing alcohol lantern which dangled from the cage's wire ceiling; the air beyond the glass that roofed the courtyard was black.

'Rise up, young man,' Dr Dismas said. He was filled with barely contained energy and hopped from foot to foot and banged his stiff fingers together. His shadow, thrown across the whitewashed walls of the courtyard, aped his movements.

'You drugged me,' Yama said stupidly.

'A little something in the beer, to take away your cares.' Dr Dismas banged on the mesh of the cage and shouted, 'Ho! Ho! Landlord!' and turned back to Yama and said, 'You have been sleeping longer than you know. The little sleep just past is my gift to make you wake into your true self. You don't understand me, but it doesn't matter. Stand up! Stand up! Look lively! Awake, awake awake! You venture forth to meet your destiny! Ho! Landlord!'

7 ~ The Warlord

In the darkness outside the door of the tavern, Dr Dismas clapped a wide-brimmed hat on his head and exchanged a few words with the landlord, who handed something to the apothecary, knuckled his forehead, and shut the heavy street door. The cluster of ghost lanterns above the door creaked in the breeze, glimmering with a wan pallor that illuminated nothing but themselves. The rest of the street was dark, except for blades of light shining between a few of the closed shutters of the houses on the other side of the wide canal. Dr Dismas switched on a penlight and waved its narrow beam at Yama, who blinked stupidly at the light; his wits were still dulled by sleep and the residue of the drugged beer.

'If you are going to be sick,' Dr Dismas said, 'lean over and don't spatter your clothes or your boots. You must be presentable.'

'What will you do with me, doctor?'

'Breathe, my dear boy. Slowly and deeply. Is it not a fine night? There is a curfew, I'm told. No one will be about to wonder at us. Look at this. Do you know what it is?'

Dr Dismas showed Yama what the landlord had given him. It was an energy pistol, silver and streamlined, with a blunt muzzle and a swollen chamber, and a grip of memory plastic that could mould itself to fit the hands of most of the bloodlines of the world. A dot of red light glowed at the side of the chamber, indicating that it was fully charged.

'You could burn for that alone,' Yama said.

'Then you know what it can do.' Dr Dismas pushed the muzzle into Yama's left armpit. 'I have it at its weakest setting, but a single shot will roast your heart. We will walk to the new quay like two old friends.'

Yama did as he was told. He was still too dazed to try to run. Besides, Sergeant Rhodean had taught him that in the event of being kidnapped he should not attempt to escape unless his life was in danger. He thought that the soldiers of the garrison must be searching for him; after all, he had been missing all day. They might turn a corner and find him at any moment.

The dose of cantharides had made Dr Dismas talkative. He did not seem to think that he was in any danger. As they walked, he told Yama that originally the tavern had been a workshop where ghost lanterns had been manufactured in the glory days of Aeolis.

'The lanterns that advertise the tavern are a crude representation of the ideal of the past, being made of nothing more than lacquered paper. Real ghost lanterns were little round boats made of plastic, with a deep weighted keel to keep them upright and a globe of blown nylon infused with luminescent chemicals instead of a sail. Ghost lanterns were floated on the Great River after each funeral to confuse any restless spirits of the dead and make sure that they would not haunt their living relatives. There is, as you will soon see, an analogy to be made with your fate, my dear boy.'

Yama said, 'You traffic with fools, doctor. The owner of the tavern will be burnt for his part in my kidnap – it is the punishment my father reserves for the common people. Lud and Lob too, though their stupidity almost absolves them.'

Dr Dismas laughed. His sickly sweet breath touched Yama's cheek. He said, 'And will I be burnt, too?'

'It is in my father's power. More likely you will be turned over to the mercies of your department. No one will profit from this.'

'That's where you are wrong. First, I do not take you for ransom, but to save you from the pedestrian fate to which your father would consign you. Second, do you see anyone coming to your rescue?'

The long waterfront, lit by the orange glow of sodium vapour lamps, was deserted. The taverns, the chandlers' godowns and the two whore-houses were shuttered and dark. Curfew notices fluttered from doors; slogans in the crude ideograms used by the Amnan had been smeared on walls. Rubbish and driftwood had been piled against the steel doors of the big godown owned by Derev's father and set alight, but the fire had done no more than discolour the metal. Several lesser merchants' offices had been looted, and the building where Dr Dismas had kept his office had been burnt to the ground. Smouldering timbers sent up a sharp stench that made Yama's eyes water.

Dr Dismas marched Yama quite openly along the new quay, which ran out towards the mouth of the bay between meadows of zebra grass and shoals of mud dissected by shallow stagnant channels. The wide bay faced downriver. Framed on one side by the bluff on which the Aedile's house stood, and by the chimneys of the paeolin mill on the other, the triple-armed pinwheel of the Galaxy stood beyond the edge of the world. It was so big that when Yama looked at one edge he could not see the other. The Arm of the Warrior rose high above the arch of the Arm of the Hunter; the Arm of the Archer curved in the opposite direction, below the edge of the world, and would not be seen again until next winter. The structure known as the Blue Diadem, that Yama knew from his readings of the Puranas was a cloud of fifty thousand blue-white stars each forty times the mass of the sun of Confluence, was a brilliant pinprick of light beyond the frayed point of the outflung Arm of the Hunter, like a drop of water flicked from a finger. Smaller star clusters made long chains of concentrated light through the milky haze of the galactic arms. There were lines and threads and globes and clouds of stars, all fading into a general misty radiance notched by dark lanes which barred the arms at regular intervals. The core, bisected by the horizon, was knitted from thin shells of stars in tidy orbits concentrically packed around the great globular clusters of the heart stars, like layers of glittering tissue wrapped around a heap of jewels. Confronted with this ancient grandeur, Yama felt that his fate was as insignificant as that of any of the mosquitoes which danced before his face.

Dr Dismas cupped his free hand to his mouth and called out, his voice shockingly loud in the quiet darkness. 'Time to go!'

There was a distant splash in the shallows beyond the end of the quay's long stone finger. Then a familiar voice said, 'Row with me, you bugger. You're making us go in circles.'

A skiff glided out of the darkness. Lud and Lob shipped their oars as it thumped against the bottom of a broad stone stair. Lob jumped out and held the boat steady as Yama and Dr Dismas climbed in.

'Quick as you like, your honour,' Lud said.

'Haste makes waste,' Dr Dismas said. Slowly and fussily he settled himself on the centre thwart, facing Yama with the energy pistol resting casually in his lap. He told the twins, 'I hope that this time you did exactly as I asked.'

'Sweet as you like,' Lob said. 'They didn't know we were there until

78

the stuff went up.' The skiff barely rocked when he vaulted back into it; he was surprisingly nimble for someone of his bulk. He and his brother settled themselves in the high seat at the stern and they pushed off from the rough stones of the quay.

Yama watched the string of orange lights along the waterfront swiftly recede into the general darkness of the shore. The cold breeze off the river was clearing his head, and for the first time since he had woken from his drugged sleep he was beginning to feel fear.

He said, 'Where are you taking me, doctor?'

Dr Dismas's eyes gleamed with red fire beneath the brim of his hat; his eyes were backed with a reflective membrane, like those of certain nocturnal animals. He said, 'You return to the place of your birth, Yamamanama. Does that frighten you?'

'Little fish,' Lud said mockingly. 'Little fish, little fish.'

'Fish out of water,' Lob added.

They were both breathing heavily as they rowed swiftly towards the open water of the Great River.

'Keep quiet if you want to earn your money,' Dr Dismas said, and told Yama, 'You must forgive them. Good help is so hard to find in backwater places. At times I was tempted to use my master's men instead.'

Lud said, 'We could tip you overboard, doctor. Ever think of that?'

Dr Dismas said, 'This pistol can kill you and your brother just as easily as Yamamanama.'

'If you shoot at us, you'll set fire to the boat, and drown as neat as if we'd thrown you in.'

'I might do it anyway. Like the scorpion who convinced the frog to carry him across the river, but stung his mount before they were halfway across, death is in my nature.'

Lob said, 'He don't mean anything by it, your honour.'

'I just don't like bad-mouthing of our city,' Lud said sullenly.

Dr Dismas laughed. 'I speak only the truth. Both of you agree with me, for why else would you want to leave? It is an understandable impulse, and it raises you above the rest of your kind.'

Lud said, 'Our father is young, that's all it is. We're strong, but he's stronger. He'd kill either of us or both of us, however we tried it, and we can't wait for him to get weak. It would take years and years.'

Dr Dismas said, 'And Yamamanama wants to leave, too. Do not deny it, my boy. Soon you will have your wish. There! Look upriver! You see how much we do for you!'

The skiff heeled as it rounded the point of the shallow, silted bay and entered the choppier waters of the river proper. As it turned into the current, Yama saw with a shock that one of the ships anchored at the floating harbour half a league upstream was ablaze from bow to stern.

The burning ship squatted over its livid reflection, tossing harvests of sparks into the night, as if to rival the serene light of the Galaxy. It was a broad-beamed carrack, one of the fleet of transports which carried troops or bulk supplies to the armies fighting the heretics at the midpoint of the world. Four small boats were rowing away from it, sharply etched shadows crawling over water that shone like molten copper. Even as Yama watched, gape-mouthed, a series of muffled explosions in the ship's hold blew expanding globes of white flame high above the burning mastheads. The ship, broken-backed, settled in the water.

Lud and Lob cheered, and the skiff rocked alarmingly as they stood to get a better view.

'Sit down, you fools,' Dr Dismas said.

Lud whooped, and shouted, 'We did it, your honour! Sweet as you like!'

Dr Dismas said to Yama, 'I devised a method so simple that even these two could carry it out successfully.'

Yama said, 'You tried to burn a ship a few days ago, did you not?'

'Two barrels of palm oil and liquid soap. One at the bow, one at the stern,' Dr Dismas said, ignoring the question, 'armed with clockwork fuses. It makes a fine diversion, don't you think? Your father's soldiers are busy rescuing sailors and saving the rest of the floating harbour while we go about our business.'

'There is a pinnace anchored further out,' Yama said. 'It will investigate.'

'I think not,' Dr Dismas said. 'Its commander is most anxious to make your acquaintance, Yamamanama. He is a cunning warlord, and knows all about the fire. He understands that it is a necessary sacrifice. The heretics will be blamed for the burning of the ship, as will your disappearance. Your father will receive a ransom note tomorrow, but even if he answers it there will, alas, be no reply. You will disappear without trace. Such things happen, in this terrible war.'

'My father will search for me. He will not stop searching.'

'Perhaps you won't want to be found, Yamamanama. You want to run away, and here you are, set on a great adventure.'

Yama knew now who the sailors had been searching for. He said, 'You tried to kidnap me two days ago. Those burning rafts were your work, so my father's soldiers would chase after imaginary heretics. But these two failed to get hold of me, and you had to try again.'

'And here we are,' Dr Dismas said. 'Now please be quiet. We have a rendezvous to keep.'

The skiff drifted on a slow current parallel to the dark shore. The burning ship receded into the night. It had grounded on the river bottom, and only the forecastle and the masts were still burning. The fisherfolk were abroad, and the lanterns they used to attract fish to their lines made scattered constellations across the breast of the Great River, red sparks punctuating the reflected sheen of the Galaxy's light.

Dr Dismas stared intently into the glimmering dark, swearing at Lud and Lob whenever they dipped their oars in the water. 'We got to keep to the current, your honour,' Lud said apologetically, 'or we'll lose track of where we're supposed to be.'

'Quiet! What was that?'

Yama heard a rustle of wings and a faint splash.

'Just a bat,' Lud said. 'They fish out here at night.'

'We catch 'em with glue lines strung across the water,' Lob explained. 'Make good eating, bats do, but not in spring. After winter they're mainly skin and bone. They need to fatten up—'

'Do shut up!' Dr Dismas said in exasperation. 'One more word and I'll fry you both where you sit. You have so much fat on your bodies that you'll go up like candles.'

The current bent away from the shore and the skiff drifted with it, scraping past young banyans that raised small crowns of leaves a handspan above the water. Yama glimpsed the pale violet spark of a machine spinning through the night. It seemed to be moving in short stuttering jerks, as if searching for something. At any other time he would have wondered at it, but now its remote light and unguessable motives only intensified his feeling of despair. The world had suddenly turned strange and treacherous, its wonders traps for the unwary.

At last Dr Dismas said, 'There! Row, you fools!'

Yama saw a red lamp flickering to starboard. Lud and Lob bent to their oars and the skiff flew across the water towards it. Dr Dismas lit an alcohol lantern with flint and steel and held it up by his face. The light, cast through a mask of blue plastic, made his pinched face, misshappen by the plaques beneath its skin, look like that of a corpse.

The red lantern was hung from the stern of a lateen-rigged pinnace which swung at anchor beside a solitary banyan. It was the ship which had returned Dr Dismas to Aeolis. Two sailors had climbed into the branches of the tree, and they watched over the long barrels of their rifles as the skiff came alongside. Lob stood and threw a line up to the stern of the pinnace. A sailor caught the end and made the skiff fast, and someone vaulted the pinnace's rail, landing so suddenly and lightly in the well of the skiff that Yama half rose in alarm.

The man clamped a hand on Yama's shoulder. 'Easy there, lad,' he said, 'or you'll have us in the river.' He was only a few years older than Yama, bare-chested, squat and muscular, with an officer's sash tied at the waist of his tight, white trousers. His broad, pugnacious face, framed by a cloud of loose, red-gold hair, was seamed with scars, like a clay mask someone had broken and badly mended, but his look was frank and appraising, and enlivened by good-humoured intelligence.

The officer steadied the skiff as Dr Dismas unhandily clambered up the short rope ladder dropped down the side of the pinnace, but when it was his turn Yama shook off the officer's hand and sprang up and grabbed the stern rail. His breath was driven from him when his belly and legs slammed against the clinkered planks of the pinnace's hull, and pain shot through his arms and shoulders as they took his weight, but he pulled himself up, got a leg over the rail and rolled over, coming up in a crouch on the deck of the stern platform at the bare feet of an astonished sailor.

The officer laughed and sprang from a standing jump to the rail and then, lightly and easily, to the deck. He said, 'He has spirit, doctor.'

Yama stood up. He had banged his right knee, and it throbbed warmly. Two sailors leaned on the steering bar and a tall man in black stood beside them. The pinnace's single mast was rooted at the edge of the stern platform; below it, three decks of rowers, naked except for breechclouts, sat in two staggered rows. The sharp prow was upswept, with a white stylized hawk's eye painted on the side. A small, swivel-mounted cannon was set in the prow's beak; its gunner had turned to watch Yama come aboard, one arm resting on the cannon's fretted barrel.

Yama looked at the black-clad man and said, 'Where is the warlord who would buy me?'

Dr Dismas said querulously, 'I dislike doing business with guns pointed at me.'

The officer gestured, and the two sailors perched in the banyan branches above the pinnace put up their rifles. 'Just a precaution, Dismas, in case you had brought along uninvited guests. If I had wanted you shot, Dercetas and Diomedes would have picked you off while you were still rowing around the point of the bay. But have no fear of that, my friend, for I need you as much as you need me.'

Yama said again, loudly, 'Where is he, this warlord?'

The barechested officer laughed. 'Why here I am,' he said, and stuck out his hand.

Yama took it. The officer's grip was firm, that of a strong man who is confident of his strength. His fingers were tipped with claws that slid a little from their sheaths and pricked the palm of Yama's hand.

'Well met, Yamamanama,' the officer said. His large eyes were golden, with tawny irises; the only beautiful feature of his broken face. The lid of the left eye was pulled down by a deep, crooked scar that ran from brow to chin.

'This war breeds heroes as ordure breeds flies,' Dr Dismas remarked, 'but Enobarbus is a singular champion. He set sail last summer as a mere lieutenant. He led a picket boat smaller than his present command into the harbour of the enemy and sank four ships and damaged a dozen others before his own boat was sunk under him.'

'It was a lucky venture,' Enobarbus said. 'We had a long swim of it, I can tell you, and a longer walk afterwards.'

Dr Dismas said, 'If Enobarbus has one flaw, it is his humility. After his boat was sunk, he led fifteen men – his entire crew – through twenty leagues of enemy lines, and did not lose one. He was rewarded with command of a division, and he is going downriver to take it up. With your help, Yamamanama, he will soon command much more.'

Enobarbus grinned. 'As for humility, I always have you, Dismas. If I have any failing, you are swift to point it out. How fortunate, Yamamanama, that we both know him.'

'More fortunate for you, I think,' Yama said.

'Every hero must be reminded of his humanity, from time to time,' Dr Dismas said.

'Fortunate for both of us,' Enobarbus told Yama. 'We'll make history, you and I. That is, of course, if you are what Dismas claims. He has been very careful not to bring the proof with him, so that I must keep him alive. He is a most cunning fellow.'

'I've lied many times in my life,' Dr Dismas said, 'but this time I tell the truth. For the truth is so astonishing that any lie would pale before it, like a candle in the sun. I think we should leave. My diversion was splendid while it lasted, but already it is almost burned out, and while the Aedile of that silly little city may be a weak man, he is no fool. His soldiers searched the hills after my men set fire to the first ship, and they will search the water this time.'

'You should have trusted my men, Dismas,' Enobarbus said. 'We could have taken the boy two nights ago.'

'And the game would have been up at once if anyone had seen you. We should move on at once, or the Aedile will wonder why you do not come to the aid of the burning ship.'

'No,' Enobarbus said, 'we'll tarry here a while. I have brought my own physician, and he'll take a look at your lad.'

Enobarbus called the man in black forward. He was of the same bloodline as Enobarbus, but considerably older. Although he moved with the same lithe tread, he had a comfortable swag of a belly and his mane, loose about his face, was streaked with grey. His name was Agnitus.

'Take off your shirt, boy,' the physician said. 'Let's see what you're made of.'

'It's better you do it yourself,' Dr Dismas advised. 'They can tie you down and do it anyway, and it will be more humiliating, I promise you. Be strong, Yamamanama. Be true to your inheritance. All will be well. Soon you will thank me.'

'I do not think so,' Yama said, but pulled his shirt over his head. Now he knew that he was not going to be killed, he felt a shivery excitement. This was the adventure he had dreamed of, but unlike his dreams it was not under his control.

The physician, Agnitus, sat Yama on a stool and took his right arm and turned the joints of his fingers and wrist and elbow, ran cold hard fingers down his ribs and prodded at his backbone. He shone a light in Yama's right eye and gazed closely at it, then fitted a kind of skeletal helmet over Yama's scalp and turned various screws until their blunt ends gripped his skull, and recorded the measurements in a little oilskin-covered notebook.

Dr Dismas said impatiently, 'You'll see that he has a very distinctive bone structure, but the real proof is in his genotype. I hardly think you can conduct that kind of test here.'

Agnitus said to Enobarbus, 'He's right, my lord. I must take a sample of the boy's blood and a scraping of the skin from the inside of his cheek. But I can tell you now that his bloodline is not one I recognize, and I've seen plenty in my time. And he's not a surgical construct, unless our apothecary is more cunning than I am.'

'I would not presume,' Dr Dismas said.

'A proof by elimination is less satisfactory than one by demonstration,' Enobarbus said. 'But unless we storm the library of the Department of Apothecaries and Chirurgeons, we must be content with what we have.'

'It is true,' Dr Dismas said. 'Haven't I sworn it so? And does he not fulfil the prophesy made to you?'

Enobarbus nodded. 'Yamamanama, you've always believed yourself special. Do you have a clear view of your destiny?'

Yama pulled his shirt over his head. He liked Enobarbus's bold candour, but mistrusted him because he was clearly an ally of Dr Dismas. He realized that everyone was looking at him, and he said defiantly, 'I would say that you are a proud and ambitious man, Enobarbus, a leader of men who would seek a prize greater than mere promotion. You believe that I can help you, although I do not know how – unless it is to do with the circumstances of my birth. Dr Dismas knows about that, I think, but he likes to tease.'

Enobarbus laughed. 'Well said! He reads us both as easily as reading a book, Dismas. We must be careful.'

'The Aedile would have made him a clerk,' Dr Dismas said with disgust.

'The Aedile belongs to a part of our department that is not noted for its imagination,' Enobarbus said. 'It is why men like him are entrusted with the administration of unimportant towns. They can be relied upon precisely because they have no imagination. We should not condemn him for what, in his office, is a virtue.

'Yamamanama, listen to me. With my help, the world itself lies within your grasp. Do you understand? You have always considered yourself to be of special birth, I know. Well, Dismas has discovered that you are unique, and he has convinced me that you are a part of my destiny.'

And then this powerful young man did an extraordinary thing. He knelt before Yama and bowed his head until his forehead touched the deck. He looked up through the tangle of his mane and said, 'I will serve you well, Yamamanama. I swear with my life. Together we will save Confluence.'

'Please get up,' Yama said. He was frightened by this gesture, for it marked a solemn moment whose significance he did not fully understand. 'I do not know why I have been brought here, or why you are saying these things, but I did not ask for any of it, and I do not want it.'

'Stand fast,' Dr Dismas hissed, and grasped Yama's upper arm in a cruel pinch.

Enobarbus stood. 'Let him alone, Dismas. My lord . . . Yamamanama . . . we are about to embark upon a hard and perilous journey. I have worked towards it all my life. When I was a cub, I was blessed by a vision. It was in the temple of my bloodline, in Ys. I was praying for my brother, who had died in battle a hundred days before. The news had just reached me. I was praying that I could avenge him, and that I could play my part in saving Confluence from the heretics. I was very young, as you might imagine, and very foolish, but my prayers were answered. The shrine lit and a woman arrayed in white appeared, and told me of my destiny. I accepted, and I have been trying my best to carry it out ever since.

'Yamamanama, to know one's fate is a privilege granted only to a few men, and it is a heavy responsibility. Most men live their lives as they can. I must live my life in pursuit of an ideal. It has stripped me of my humanity as faith strips an eremite of worldly possessions, and honed my life to a single point. Nothing else matters to me. How often have I wished that the obligation be lifted, but it has not, and I have come to accept it. And here we are, as was predicted long ago.'

Enobarbus suddenly smiled. It transformed his wrecked face as a firework, bursting across the dark sky, transforms the night. He clapped his hands. 'I have spoken enough for now. I will speak more, Yamamanama, I promise, but it must wait until we are safe. Pay your men, Dismas. We are at last embarked on our journey.'

Dr Dismas pulled out his pistol. 'It would be well if your boat put some distance between their miserable skiff. I'm not sure of the range of this thing.'

Enobarbus nodded. 'It's probably for the best,' he said. 'They might guess, and they'll certainly talk.'

'You overestimate them,' Dr Dismas said. 'They deserve to die because they endangered my plans by their stupidity. Besides, I cannot stand boorishness, and I have been exiled amongst these uncivilized creatures for an entire year. This will be a catharsis.'

'I'll hear no more. Kill them cleanly, and do not seek to justify yourself.'

Enobarbus turned to give his orders, and at that moment one of the sailors perched in the branches of the banyan to which the pinnace was moored cried out.

'Sail! Sail ahead!'

'Thirty degrees off the starboard bow,' his mate added. 'Half a league and bearing down hard.'

Enobarbus gave his orders without missing a beat. 'Cut the mooring ropes fore and aft. Dercetas and Diomedes, to your posts at once! Ready the rowers, push off on my word! I want thirty beats a minute from you lads, and no slacking or we're dead men.'

In the midst of the sudden rush of activity, as oars were raised and sailors hacked at mooring lines, Yama saw his opportunity. Dr Dismas made a grab for him, but was too slow. Yama vaulted the rail and landed hard in the well of the skiff.

'Row!' Yama yelled to Lob and Lud. 'Row for your lives!'

'Catch hold of him!' Dr Dismas shouted from above. 'Catch him and make sure you don't let go!'

Lud started forward. 'It's for your own good, little fish,' he said.

Yama dodged Lud's clumsy swipe and retreated to the stern of the little skiff. 'He wants to kill you!'

'Get him, you fools,' Dr Dismas said.

Yama grabbed hold of the sides of the skiff and rocked it from side to side, but Lud stood foursquare. He grinned. 'That won't help, little fish. Keep still, and maybe I won't have to hurt you.'

'Hurt him anyway,' Lob said.

Yama picked up the alcohol lantern and dashed it into the well of the skiff. Instantly, translucent blue flames licked up. Lud reared backwards, and the skiff pitched violently. Unbearable heat beat at Yama's face; he took a deep breath and dived into the river.

He swam as far as he could before he came up and drew a gulp of air that burned all the way down the inverted trees of his lungs. He pulled at the fastenings of his heavy boots and kicked them off.

The skiff was drifting away from the side of the pinnace. Flames flickered brightly in its well. Lud and Lob were trying to beat out the fire with their shirts. Sailors threw ropes down the side of the pinnace and shouted to them to give it up and come aboard. A tremendous glow was growing brighter and brighter beyond the pinnace, turning every-thing into a shadow of its own self. The cannon in the prow of the pinnace spoke: a crisp rattling burst, and then another.

Yama swam as hard as he could, and when he finally turned to float on his back, breathing hard, the whole scene was spread before him. The pinnace was sliding away from the banyan tree, leaving the burning skiff behind. A great glowing ship was bearing down towards the pinnace. She was a narrow-hulled frigate, her three masts crowded with square sails, and every part of her shone with cold fire. The pinnace's cannon spoke again, and there was a crackling of rifle fire. And then Dr Dismas fired his pistol, and for an instant a narrow lance of red fire split the night.

8 ~ The Fisherman

Dr Dismas's shot must have missed the glowing frigate, for it bore down on the pinnace relentlessly. The bristling oars of the pinnace set a steady, rapid beat as it left the burning skiff behind and began to turn towards its pursuer. Yama saw that Enobarbus was planning to come around to the near side of the frigate, to pass beneath its cannons and rake its sides with her own guns, but before he could complete his manoeuvre the frigate swung about like a leaf blown by the wind. In a moment, its bow loomed above the stricken pinnace. The pinnace's cannon hammered defiantly, and Yama heard someone cry out.

But at the instant the frigate struck the pinnace, it dissolved into a spreading mist of white light. Yama backstroked in the cold water, watching as the pinnace was engulfed by a globe of white fog that boiled up higher than the outflung arm of the Galaxy. A point of violet light shot up from this spreading bank of luminous fog, rising into the night sky until it had vanished from sight.

Yama did not stop to wonder at this miracle, for he knew that Enobarbus would start searching for him as soon as the pinnace had escaped the fog. He turned in the water and began to swim. Although he aimed for the dark, distant shore, he quickly found himself in a swift current that took him amongst a scattered shoal of banyans. They were rooted in a gravel bank that at times Yama could graze with his toes; if he had been as tall as the Aedile he could have stood with his head clear of the swiftly running water.

At first, the banyans were no more than handfuls of broad, glossy leaves that stood stiffly above the water, but the current carried Yama deeper into a maze of wide channels between stands of bigger trees. Here, they rose in dense thickets above prop roots flexed in low arches. The prop roots were fringed by tangled mats of feeder roots alive with schools of tiny fish that flashed red or green dots of luminescence as they darted away from Yama.

With the last of his strength, Yama swam towards one of the largest of the banyans as he was swept past it. The cold water had stolen all feeling from his limbs and the muscles of his shoulders and arms were tender with exhaustion. He threw himself into floating nets of feeder roots and, scraping past strings of clams and bearded mussels, dragged himself onto a smooth horizontal trunk, and lay gasping like a fish that had just learned the trick of breathing air.

Yama was too cold and wet and scared to sleep, and something in the tangled thickets of the tree had set up a thin, irregular piping, like the fretting of a sick baby. He sat with his back against an arched root and watched the uppermost arm of the Galaxy set beyond the bank of faintly luminescent fog that had spread for leagues across the black river. Somewhere in the fog was Enobarbus's pinnace, lost, blinded. By what strange allies, or stranger coincidence? The top of the wide fog bank seethed like boiling milk; Yama watched the black sky above it for the return of the machine's violet spark. Answered prayers, he thought, and shivered.

He dozed and woke, and dozed again, and jerked awake from a vivid dream of standing on the flying bridge of the ghostly frigate as it bore down on the pinnace. The frigate was crewed neither by men nor even by ghosts or revenants, but by a crowd of restless lights that responded to his unspoken commands with quick unquestioning intelligence. Zakiel had taught him that although dreams were usually stitched from fragments of daily experience, sometimes they were more, portents of the future or riddles whose answers were keys to the conduct of the dreamer's life. Yama did not know if this dream was of the first or second kind, let alone what it might mean, but when he woke it left him with a clinging horror, as if his every action might somehow be magnified, with terrible consequences.

The Galaxy had set, and dawn touched the flood of the river with flat grey light. The bank of fog was gone; there was no sign of the pinnace. Yama dozed again, and woke with sunlight dancing on his face, filtered through the restless leaves of the banyan. He found himself on a wide limb that gently sloped up from the water and ran straight as an old road into the dense leafy tangles of the banyan's heart, crossed by arching roots and lesser branches that dropped prop roots straight down into the water. The banyan's glossy leaves hung everywhere like the endlessly deep folds of a ragged green cloak, and the bark of its limbs, smoothly wrinkled as skin, was colonized by lichens that hung like curtains of grey lace, the green barrels of bromeliads, and the scarlet and gold and pure white blossoms of epiphytic orchids.

Yama ached in every muscle. He drew off his wet shirt and trousers and hung them on a branch, then set to the exercises Sergeant Rhodean had taught him until at last his joints and muscles loosened. He drank handfuls of cold water, startling shoals of fairy shrimp that scattered from his shadow, and splashed water on his face until his skin tingled with racing blood.

Yama had come ashore on the side of the banyan that faced towards the far side of the river. He slung his damp clothes over his shoulder and, naked, set off through the thickets of the tree, at first following the broad limb and then, when it joined another and bent upwards into the high, sunspeckled canopy, scrambling through a tangle of lesser branches. There was always still, black water somewhere beneath the random lattice of branches and prop roots. Tiny hummingbirds, clad in electric blues and emerald greens, as if enamelled by the most skilful of artists, darted from flower to flower. When Yama blundered through curtains of leaves, clouds of blackflies rose up and got in his eyes and mouth. At last, he glimpsed blue sky through a fall of green vines. He parted the soft, jointed stems and stepped through them onto a sloping spit of mossy ground, where a round coracle of the kind used by the fisherfolk was drawn up on the miniature shore.

The blackened, upturned shell of a snapping turtle held the ashes of a small fire, still warm when Yama sifted them through his fingers. Yama drew on his damp shirt and trousers and called out, but no one answered his call. He cast around and quickly found a winding path leading away from the spit. And a moment later found the fisherman, tangled in a crude net of black threads just beyond the second bend.

The threads were the kind that Amnan used to catch bats and birds, resin fibres as strong as steel covered with thousands of tiny blisters that exuded a strong glue at a touch. The threads had partly collapsed when the fisherman had blundered into them, and he hung like a corpse in an unravelling shroud, one arm caught above his head, the other bound tightly to his side.

He did not seem surprised to see Yama. He said, in a quiet, hoarse voice, 'Kill me quick. Have mercy.'

'I was hoping for rescue,' Yama said.

The fisherman stared at him. He wore only a breechclout, and his pale skin was blotched with islands of pale green. Black hair hung in greasy tangles around his broad, chinless froggy face. His wide mouth hung open, showing rows of tiny triangular teeth. He had watery, protuberant eyes, and a transparent membrane flicked over their balls three times before he said, 'You are not one of the Mud People.'

'I come from Aeolis. My father is the Aedile.'

'The Mud People think they know the river. It's true they can swim a bit, but they're greedy, and pollute her waters.'

'One of them seems to have caught you.'

'You're a merchant's son, perhaps. We have dealings with them, for flints and steel. No, don't come close, or you'll be caught too. There is only one way to free me, and I don't think you carry it.'

'I know how the threads work,' Yama said, 'and I am sorry that I do not have what is needed to set you free. I do not even have a knife.'

'Even steel will not cut them. Leave me. I'm a dead man, fit only to fill the bellies of the Mud People. What are you doing?'

Yama had discovered that the surface of the path was a spongy thatch of wiry roots, fallen leaves and the tangled filaments of epiphytic lichens. He lay on his belly and pushed his arm all the way through the thick thatch until his fingers touched water. He looked at the fisherman and said, 'I have seen your people use baited traps to catch fish. Do you have one on your coracle? And I will need some twine or rope, too.'

While Yama worked, the fisherman, whose name was Caphis, told him that he had blundered into the sticky web just after dawn, while searching for the eggs of a species of coot which nested in the hearts of banyan thickets. 'The eggs are good to eat,' Caphis said, 'but not worth dying for.'

Caphis had put into the banyan shoal last night. He had seen a great battle, he explained, and had thought it prudent to take shelter. 'So I am doubly a fool.'

While the fisherman talked, Yama cut away a section of lichenous thatch and lashed the trap upright to a prop root. He had to use the blade of the fisherman's short spear to cut the twine, and several times sliced his palm. He sucked at the shallow cuts before starting to replace the thatch. It was in the sharp bend of the path; anyone hurrying down it would have to step there to make the turn.

He said, 'Did you see much of the battle?'

'A big ship caught fire. And then the small boat which has been lying offshore of the Mud People's city for three days must have found an enemy, because it started firing into the dark.'

'But there was another ship – it was huge and glowing, and melted into fog . . .'

The fisherman considered this, and said at last, 'I turned for shelter once the firing started, as anyone with any sense would. You saw a third ship? Well, perhaps you were closer than I, and I expect that you saw more than you wanted to.'

'Well, that is true enough.' Yama stood, leaning on the stout shaft of the spear.

'The river carries all away, if you let it. That's our view. What's done one day is gone the next, and there's a new start. He might not come today, or even tomorrow. You will not wait that long. You will take the coracle and leave me to the fate I deserve.'

'My father outlawed this.'

'They are a devious people, the Mud People.' Sunlight splashed through the broad leaves of the banyan, shining on the fisherman's face. Caphis squinted and added, 'If you could fetch water, it would be a blessing.'

Yama found a resin mug in the coracle. He was dipping it into the water at the edge of the mossy spit when he saw a little boat making its way towards the island. It was a skiff, rowed by a single man. By the time Yama had climbed into a crotch of the banyan, hidden amongst rustling leaves high above the spit, the skiff was edging through the slick of feeder roots that ringed the banyan.

Yama recognized the man. Grog, or Greg. One of the bachelor labourers who tended the mussel beds at the mouth of the Breas. He was heavy and slow, and wore only a filthy kilt. The grey skin of his shoulders and back was dappled with a purple rash, the precursor of the skin canker which affected those Amnan who worked too long in sunlight.

Yama watched, his mouth dry and his heart beating quickly, as the man tied up his boat and examined the coracle and the cold ashes in the turtle shell. He urinated at the edge of the water for what seemed a very long time, then set off along the path.

A moment later, while Yama was climbing down from his hiding place, made clumsy because he dared not let go of the fisherman's short spear, someone, the man or the fisherman, cried out. It startled two white herons which had been perching amongst the topmost branches of the banyan; the birds rose up into the air and flapped away as Yama crept down the path, clutching the spear with both hands.

There was a tremendous shaking in the leaves at the bend of the path. The man was floundering hip-deep amongst the broken thatch which Yama had used to conceal the trap. The big trap was wide-mouthed and two spans long, tapering to a blunt point. It was woven from pliable young prop roots, and bamboo spikes had been fastened on the inside, pointing downwards, so that when a fish entered to get at the bait it could not back out. These spikes had dug into the flesh of the man's leg when he had tried to pull free, and he was bleeding hard and grunting with pain as he pushed down with his hands like a man trying to work off a particularly tight boot. He did not see Yama until the point of the spear pricked the fat folds of speckled skin at the back of his neck.

After Yama had used the spray which dissolved the threads' glue, Caphis wanted to kill the man who would have killed and eaten him, but Yama kept hold of the spear, and at last Caphis satisfied himself by tying the man's thumbs together behind his back and leaving him there, with his leg still in the trap.

The man started to shout as soon as they were out of sight. 'I gave you the stuff, didn't I? I didn't mean no harm. Let me go, master! Let me go and I'll say nothing! I swear it!'

He was still shouting when Caphis and Yama put out from the banyan.

The fisherman's scrawny shanks were so long that his knees jutted above the crown of his head as he squatted in the coracle. He paddled with slow, deliberate strokes. The threads of the trap had left a hundred red weals across the mottled yellow skin of his chest. He said that once he had warmed up his blood he would take Yama across to the shore.

'That is, if you don't mind helping me with my night lines.'

'You could take me to Aeolis. It is not far.'

Caphis nodded. 'That's true enough, but it would take me all day to haul against the current. Some us go there to trade, and that's where I got that fine spear-point last year. But we never leave our boats when we go there, because it is a wicked town.'

Yama said, 'It is where I live. You have nothing to fear. Even if the man gets free, he would be burnt for trying to murder you.'

'Perhaps. But then his family would make a vendetta against my family. That is how it is.' Caphis studied Yama, and said at last, 'You'll help me with my lines, and I'll take you to the shore. You can walk more quickly to your home than I can row. But you'll need some breakfast before you can work, I reckon.'

They landed at the edge of a solitary grandfather banyan half a league downstream. Caphis built a fire of dried moss in the upturned turtle shell and boiled up tea in the resin mug, using friable strips of the bark of a twiggy bush that grew, he said, high up in the tangled tops of the banyans. When the tea started to boil he threw in some flat seeds that made it froth, and handed Yama the mug.

The tea was bitter, but after the first sip Yama felt it warm his blood, and he quickly drained the mug. He sat by the fire, chewing on a strip of dried fish, while Caphis moved about the hummocky moss of the little clearing where they had landed. With his long legs and short barrel of a body, and his slow, deliberate, flatfooted steps, the fisherman looked something like a heron. The toes of his feet were webbed, and the hooked claws on his big toes and spurs on his heels helped him climb the banyan's smooth, interlaced branches. He collected seeds and lichens and a particular kind of moss, and dug fat beetle grubs from rotten wood and ate them at once, spitting out the heads.

All anyone could want could be found in the banyans, Caphis told Yama. The fisherfolk pounded the leaves to make a fibrous pulp from which they wove their clothes. Their traps and the ribs of their coracles were made from young prop roots, and the hulls were woven from strips of bark varnished with a distillation of the tree's sap. The kernels of banyan fruit, which set all through the year, could be ground into flour. Poison used to stun fish was extracted from the skin of a particular kind of frog that lived in the tiny ponds cupped within the living vases of bromeliads. A hundred kinds of fish swarmed around the feeder roots, and a thousand kinds of plants grew on the branches; all had their uses, and their own tutelary spirits which had to be individually appeased.

'There's hardly anything we lack, except metals and tobacco, which is

95

why we trade with you land folk. Otherwise we're as free as the fish, and always have been. We've never risen above our animal selves since the Preservers gave us the banyans as our province, and that is the excuse the Mud People use when they hunt us. But we're an old folk, and we've seen much, and we have long memories. Everything comes to the river, we say, and generally that's true.'

Caphis had a tattoo on the ball of his left shoulder, a snake done in black and red that curled around so that it could swallow its own tail. He touched the skin beneath this tattoo with the claw of his thumb and said, 'Even the river comes to its own self.'

'What do you mean?'

'Why, where do you think the river goes, when it falls over the edge of the world? It swallows its own self and returns to its beginning, and so renews itself. That's how the Preservers made the world, and we, who were here from the first, remember how it was. Lately, things are changing. Year by year the river grows less. Perhaps the river no longer bites its own tail, but if that is so I cannot say where it goes instead.'

'Do you – your people, do they remember the Preservers?'

Caphis's eyes filmed over. His voice took on a sing-song lilt. 'Before the Preservers, the Universe was a plain of ice. The Preservers brought light that melted the ice and woke the seeds of the banyans which were trapped there. The first men were made of wood, carved from a banyan tree so huge that it was a world in itself, standing in the universe of water and light. But the men of wood showed their backs to the Preservers, and did not respect animals or even themselves, and destroyed so much of the world-tree that the Preservers raised a great flood. It rained for forty days and forty nights, and the waters rose through the roots of the banyan and rose through the branches until only the youngest leaves showed above the flood, and at last even these were submerged. All of the creatures of the world-tree perished in the flood except for a frog and a heron. The frog clung to the last leaf which showed above the flood and called to its own kind, but the lonely heron heard its call and stooped down and ate it.

'Well, the Preservers saw this, and the frog grew within the heron's stomach until it split open its captor, and stepped out, neither frog nor heron but a new creature which had taken something from both its parents. It was the first of our kind, and just as it was neither frog nor heron, neither was it man or woman. At once the flood receded. The new creature lay down on a smooth mudbank and fell asleep. And while it slept, the Preservers dismembered it, and from its ribs fifty others were made, and these were men and women of the first tribe of my people. The Preservers breathed on them and clouded their minds, so that unlike the men of wood they would not challenge or be disrespectful to their creators. But that was long ago, and in another place. You, if you don't mind me saying so, look as if your bloodline climbed down from the trees.'

'I was born on the river, like you.'

Caphis clacked his wide flat lower jaw – it was the way the fisherfolk laughed. 'Sometime I'd like to hear that story. But now we should set to. The day does not grow younger, and there is work to do. It is likely that the Mud Man will escape. We should have killed him. He would bite off his own leg, if he thought that would help him escape. The Mud People are treacherous and full of tricks – that is how they are able to catch us, we who are more clever than they, as long as our blood is warmed. That is why they generally hunt us at night. I was caught because my blood had the night chill, you see. It made me slow and stupid, but now I am warm, and I know what I must do.'

Caphis pissed on the fire to extinguish it, packed away the cup and the turtle shell beneath the narrow bench which circled the rim of the coracle, and declared himself ready.

'You will bring me luck, for it was by luck that you saved yourself from the phantom and then found me.'

With Yama seated on one side and Caphis wielding a leaf-shaped paddle on the other, the coracle was surprisingly stable, although it was so small that Yama's knees pressed against Caphis's bony shins. As the craft swung out into the current, Caphis paddled with one hand and filled a long-stemmed clay pipe with ordinary tobacco with the other, striking a flint against a bit of rough steel for a spark.

It was a bright clear afternoon, with a gentle wind that barely ruffled the surface of the river. There was no sign of the pinnace; no ships at all, only the little coracles of the fisherfolk scattered across the broad river between shore and misty horizon. As Caphis said, the river bore all away. For a while, Yama could believe that none of his adventures had happened, that his life could return to its normal routines.

Caphis squinted at the sun, wet a finger and held it up to the wind, then drove his craft swiftly between the scattered tops of young banyans

97

(Yama thought of the lone frog in Caphis's story, clinging to the single leaf above the universal flood, bravely calling but finding only death, and in death, transfiguration).

As the sun fell towards the distant peaks of the Rim Mountains, Yama and Caphis worked trotlines strung between bending poles anchored in the bottom of the gravel bank. Caphis gave Yama a sticky, odourless ointment to rub on his shoulders and arms to protect his skin from sunburn. Yama soon fell into an unthinking rhythm, hauling up lines, rebaiting hooks with bloodworms and dropping them back. Most of the hooks were empty, but gradually a pile of small silver fish accumulated in the well of the coracle, frantically jinking in the shallow puddle there or lying still, their gill flaps pulsing like blood red flowers as they drowned in air.

Caphis asked forgiveness for each fish he caught. The fisherfolk believed that the world was packed with spirits which controlled everything from the weather to the flowering of the least of the epiphytic plants of the banyan shoals. Their days were spent in endless negotiations with these spirits to ensure that the world continued its seamless untroubled spinning out.

At last Caphis declared himself satisfied with the day's catch. He gutted a pentad of fingerlings, stripped the fillets of pale muscle from their backbones, and gave half to Yama, together with a handful of fleshy leaves.

The fillets of fish were juicy; chewed, the leaves tasted of sweet limes and quenched Yama's thirst. Following Caphis's example, he spat the leaf pulp overboard, and tiny fish promptly swarmed around this prize as it sank through the clear dark water.

Caphis picked up his paddle and the coracle skimmed across the water towards a bend of the stony shore, where cliffs carved and socketed with empty tombs rose from a broad pale beach.

'There's an old road that leads along the shore to Aeolis,' Caphis told Yama. 'It will take you the rest of this day, and a little of the next, I reckon.'

'If you would take me directly to Aeolis, I can promise you a fine reward. It is little enough in return for your life.'

'We do not go there unless we must, and never after nightfall. You saved my life, and so it is always in your care. Would you risk it so quickly, by taking me into the jaws of the Mud People? I do not think you would be so cruel. I have my family to consider. They'll be watching for me this night, and I don't want to worry them further.'

Caphis grounded his frail craft in the shallows a little way from the shore. He had never set foot on land, he said, and he wasn't about to start now. He looked at Yama and said, 'Don't walk after dark, young master. Find shelter before the sun goes down and stick to it until first light. Then you'll be all right. There are ghouls out there, and they like a bit of live meat on occasion.'

Yama knew about the ghouls. He and Telmon had once hidden from a ghoul on one of their expeditions into the foothills of the City of the Dead. He remembered the way the man-shaped creature's pale skin had glimmered in the twilight like wet muscle, and how frightened he had been as it stooped this way and that, and the stench it had left. He said, 'I will be careful.'

Caphis said, 'Take this. No use against ghouls, but I hear tell there are plenty of coneys on the shore. Some of us hunt them, but not me.'

It was a small knife carved from a flake of obsidian. Its hilt was wrapped with twine, and its exfoliated edge was as sharp as a razor.

'I reckon you can look after your own self, young master, but maybe a time will come when you need help. Then my family will remember that you helped me. Do you recall what I said about the river?'

'Everything comes around again.'

Caphis nodded, and touched the tattoo of the self-engulfing snake on his shoulder. 'You had a good teacher. You know how to pay attention.'

Yama slid from the tipping coracle and stood knee-deep in ooze and brown water. 'I will not forget,' he said.

'Choose carefully where you camp this night,' Caphis said. 'Ghouls are bad, but ghosts are worse. We see their lights sometimes, shining softly in the ruins.'

Then he pushed away from the shallows and the coracle waltzed into the current as he dug the water with his leaf-shaped paddle. By the time Yama had waded to shore, the coracle was already far off, a black speck on the shining plane of the river, making a long, curved path towards a raft of banyan islands far from shore.

9 ~ The Knife

The beach was made of deep, soft drifts of white shell fragments; it was not until Yama began to climb the worn stone stair that zigzagged up the face of the carved cliff that he remembered how difficult it was to walk on firm ground, where each step sent a little shock up the ladder of the spine. At the first turn of the stair, a spring welled inside a trough cut from the native stone. Yama knelt on the mossy ground by the trough and drank clear sweet water until his belly sloshed, knowing that there would be little chance of finding any potable water in the City of the Dead. Only when he stood did he notice that someone else had drunk there recently – no, to judge by the overlapping footprints in the soft red moss, it had been two people.

Lud and Lob. They had also escaped Dr Dismas. Yama had tucked the obsidian knife into his belt under the flap of his shirt, snug against the small of his back. He touched the handle for reassurance before he continued his ascent.

An ancient road ran close to the edge of the cliff, its flat pavement, splashed with the yellow and grey blotches of lichens, so wide that twenty men could have ridden abreast along it. Beyond, the alkaline, shaley land shimmered in the level light of the late afternoon sun. Tombs stood everywhere, casting long shadows towards the river. This was the Silent Quarter, which Yama had rarely visited – he and Telmon preferred the ancient tombs of the foothills beyond the Breas, where aspects could be wakened and the flora and fauna was richer. Compared to the sumptuously decorated mausoleums of the older parts of the City of the Dead, the tombs here were poor things, mostly no more than low boxes with domed roofs, although here and there memorial steles and columns rose amongst them, and a few larger tombs stood on artificial stepped mounds, guarded by statues that watched the river with stony eyes. One of these was as big as the peel-house, half hidden by a small wood of yews grown wild and twisted. In all the desiccated landscape nothing stirred except for a lammergeyer high in the deep blue sky, riding a thermal on outspread wings.

When Yama was satisfied that he was not about to be ambushed, he set off down the road towards the distant smudge that must surely be Aeolis, halfway towards the vanishing point where the Rim Mountains and the misty horizon of the farside seemed to converge.

Little grew in the stone gardens of this part of the City of the Dead. The white, sliding rocks weathered to a bitter dust in which only a few plants could root, mostly yuccas and creosote bushes and clumps of prickly pear. Wild roses crept around the smashed doorways of some of the tombs, their blood-red blooms scenting the warm air. The tombs had all been looted long ago, and of their inhabitants scarcely a bone remained. If the cunningly preserved bodies had not been carted away to fuel the smelters of old Aeolis, then wild animals had long ago dismembered and consumed them once they had been disinterred from their caskets. Ancient debris was strewn everywhere, from fragments of smashed funeral urns and shards of broken furniture fossilized on the dry shale, to slates which displayed pictures of the dead, impressed into their surfaces by some forgotten art. Some of these were still active, and as Yama went past scenes from ancient Ys briefly came to life or the faces of men and women turned to watch him, their lips moving soundlessly or shaping into a smile or a coquettish kiss. Unlike the aspects of older tombs, these were mere recordings without intelligence; the slates played the same meaningless loop over and over, whether for the human eye or the uncomprehending gaze of any lizard that flicked over the glazed surfaces in which the pictures were embedded.

Yama was familiar with these animations; the Aedile had an extensive collection of them. They had to be exposed to sunlight before they would work, and Yama had always wondered why, for they were normally found inside the tombs. But although he knew what these mirages were, their unpredictable flicker was still disturbing. He kept looking behind him, fearful that Lud and Lob were stalking him through the quiet solitude of the ruins.

The oppressive feeling of being watched grew as the sun fell towards the ragged blue line of the Rim Mountains and the shadows of the tombs lengthened and mingled across the bone-white ground. To be walking through the City of the Dead in the bright sunshine was one thing, but as the light faded Yama increasingly glanced over his shoulder as he walked, and sometimes turned and walked backwards a few paces, or stopped and slowly scanned the low hills with their freight of empty tombs. He had often camped in the City of the Dead with the Aedile and his retinue of servants and archaeological workers, or with Telmon and two or three soldiers, but never before alone.

The distant peaks of the Rim Mountains bit into the reddened disc of the sun. The lights of Aeolis shimmered in the distance like a heap of tiny diamonds. It was still at least half a day's walk to the city, and would be longer in darkness. Yama left the road and began to search the tombs for one that would give shelter for the night.

It was like a game. Yama knew that the tombs he rejected now would be better than the one he would choose of necessity when the last of the sun's light fled the sky. But he did not want to choose straight away because he still felt that he was being watched and fancied, as he wandered the network of narrow paths between the tombs, that he heard a padding footfall behind him that stopped when he stopped and resumed a moment after he began to move forward again. At last, halfway up a long, gentle slope, he turned and called out Lud and Lob's names, feeling both fearful and defiant as the echoes of his voice died away amongst the tombs spread below him. There was no answer, but when he moved on he heard a faint squealing and splashing beyond the crest of the slope.

Yama drew the obsidian knife and crept forward like a thief. Beyond the crest, the ground fell away in an abrupt drop, as if something had bitten away half the hill. At the foot of the drop, a seep of brackish water gleamed like copper in the sun's last light, and a family of hyraces were sporting in the muddy shallows.

Yama stood and yelled and plunged down the steep slope. The hyraces bolted in every direction and a youngster ran squealing in blind panic into the middle of the shallow pond. It saw Yama charging towards it and stopped so suddenly that it tumbled head over heels. Before it could change direction, he threw himself on its slim, hairy body and wrestled it onto its back and slit its throat with his knife.

Yama built a fire of twisted strands of dried wood picked from the centres of prickly pear clumps and lit it using a friction bow made from two twigs and a sinew from the hyrax's carcass. He cleaned and skinned and jointed the hyrax, roasted its meat in the hot ashes, and ate until his stomach hurt, cracking bones for hot marrow and licking the fatty juices from his fingers. The sky had darkened to reveal a scattering of dim halo stars, and the Galaxy was rising, salting the City of the Dead with a blue-white glow and casting a confusion of shadows.

The tomb Yama chose as a place to sleep was not far from the seep, and as he rested against its granite façade, which still held the day's heat, he heard something splash in the pool – an animal come to drink. Yama laid the remains of the hyrax on a flat stone a hundred paces from the tomb and took the precaution of dragging a screen of rose stems across the tomb's entrance before curling up to sleep on the empty catafalque inside, his head pillowed on his folded shirt, the obsidian knife in his hand.

Yama awoke from bad dreams at first light, stiff and cold. The golden sun stood a handspan above the Rim Mountains. The tomb in which he had slept was one of a row that stretched along the ridge above the pool, each with a gabled false front of rosy granite; they glowed like so many hearths in the sun's early light. Yama warmed himself with a set of exercises before pulling on his shirt and walking down to the pool.

His offering was gone; only a dark stain was left on the flat white stone. There was a confusion of tracks around the water's edge, but he could find no human ones, only the slots of hyraces and antelopes, and what looked like the impress of the pads of some large cat, most likely a spotted panther.

The seep water of the pool was chalky with suspended solids, and so bitter that Yama spat out the first mouthful. He chewed a strip of cold meat and skinned and ate new buds taken from a prickly pear stand, but the cool juices did not entirely quench his thirst. He put a pebble in his mouth to stimulate the flow of saliva and walked back towards the river, thinking that he would climb down the cliff to drink and bathe at the water's edge.

He had wandered further than he had thought when he had been looking for shelter the previous evening. The narrow paths that meandered between the tombs and memorials and up and down the gentle slopes of the low hills were all alike, and not one ran for more than a hundred paces before meeting with another, or splitting into two, but Yama kept the sun at his back, and by midmorning had reached the wide straight road again.

The cliffs there were sheer and high; if the peel-house had stood in the seething water at their bases, its tallest turret would not have reached to their tops. Yama got down on his belly and hung over the edge and looked right and left, but could not see any sign of a path or of stairs, although there were many tombs cut into the cliff faces – there was one directly below him. Birds nested in the openings, and thousands floated on the wind that blew up the face of the cliff, like flakes of restlessly sifting snow. Yama spat out the pebble and watched it bounce from the ledge in front of the tomb directly below and dwindle away; it vanished from sight before it hit the tumbled slabs of rock that were covered and uncovered by the heave of the river's brown water.

Behind him, someone said, 'A hot morning.'

And someone else: 'Watch you don't fall, little fish.'

Yama jumped to his feet. Lud and Lob stood on top of a bank of white shale on the far side of the road. Both wore only kilts. Lob had a coil of rope over his bare shoulder; the skin of Lud's chest was reddened and blistered by a bad burn.

'Don't think of running,' Lud advised. 'It's too hot for you to get far without water, and you know you can't get away.'

Yama said, 'Dr Dismas tried to have you killed. There is no enmity between us.'

'I wouldn't know about that,' Lud said. 'I reckon we've a score to settle.'

'You owe us,' Lob said.

'I do not see it.'

Lud explained patiently, 'Dr Dismas would have paid us for our trouble, and instead we had to swim for our lives when you pulled that trick. I got burnt, too.'

'And he lost his knife,' Lob added. 'He loved that knife, you miserable culler, and you made him lose it.'

Lud said, 'And then there was the boat you put on fire. You owe for that, I reckon.'

'That was not yours.'

Lud scratched at the patch of reddened skin on his chest and said, 'It's the principle of the thing.'

'In any case, I can only pay you when I get home,' Yama said.

'"In any case",' Lud echoed in a mocking voice. 'That's not how we see it. How do we know we can trust you?'

'Of course you can.'

Lud said, 'You haven't even asked how much we want, and then you might just think to tell your father. I don't think he'd pay us then, would he, brother?'

'It's doubtful.'

'Very doubtful, I'd say.'

Yama knew that there was only one chance to escape. He said, 'Then you do not trust me?'

Lud saw Yama's change in posture. He started down the slope, raising a cloud of white dust, and yelled, 'Don't—'

Yama did. He turned and took two steps backwards, and then, before he could have second thoughts, ran forward and jumped over the edge of the cliff.

He fell in a rush of air, and as he fell threw back his head and brought up his knees (Sergeant Rhodean was saying, 'Just let it happen to you. If you learn to trust your body it's all a matter of timing.'). Sky and river revolved around each other, and then he landed on his feet, knees bent to take the shock, on the ledge before the entrance to the tomb.

The ledge was no wider than a bed, and slippery with bird excrement. Yama fell flat on his back at once, filled with a wild fear that he would tumble over the edge – there had been a balustrade once, but it had long ago fallen away. He caught a tuft of wiry grass and held on, although the sharp blades of grass reopened the wounds made by Caphis's spearhead.

As he carefully climbed back to his feet, a stone clipped the ledge and tumbled away towards the heaving water far below. Yama looked up. Lob and Lud capered at the top of the cliff, silhouetted against the blue sky. They shouted down at him, but their words were snatched away by the wind. One of them threw another stone, which smashed to flinders scarcely a span from Yama's feet.

Yama ran forward, darting between the winged figures, their faces blurred by time, which supported the lintel of the gaping entrance to the tomb. Inside, stone blocks fallen from the high ceiling littered the mosaic floor. An empty casket stood on a dais beneath a canopy of stone carved to look like cloth rippling in the wind. Disturbed by Yama's footfalls, bats fell from one of the holes in the ceiling and dashed around and around above his head, chittering in alarm.

The tomb was shaped like a wedge of pie, and behind the dais it narrowed to a passageway. It had once been sealed by a slab of stone, but that had been smashed long ago by robbers who had discovered the path used by the builders of the tomb. Yama grinned. He had guessed that the tombs in the cliffs would have been breached and stripped just like those above. It was his way of escape. He stepped over the sill and, keeping one hand on the cold dry stone of the wall, felt his way through near darkness.

He had not gone far when the passage struck another running at right angles. He tossed an imaginary coin and chose the left-hand way. A hundred heartbeats later, in pitch darkness, he went sprawling over a slump of rubble. He got up cautiously and climbed the spill of stones until his head bumped the ceiling of the passage. It was blocked.

Then Yama heard voices behind him, and knew that Lud and Lob had followed him. He should have expected it. They would lose their lives if he was able to escape and tell the Aedile about the part they had played in Dr Dismas's scheme.

As Yama slid down the rubble, his hand fell on something cold and hard. It was a metal knife, its curved blade as long as his forearm. It was cold to the touch and gave off a faint glow; motes of light seemed to float in the wake of its blade when Yama slashed at the darkness. Emboldened, he felt his way back to the tomb.

The dim light hurt his eyes; it spilled around one of the twins, who stood in the tomb's narrow entrance.

'Little fish, little fish. What are you scared of?'

Yama held up the long knife. 'Not you, Lud.'

'Let me get him,' Lob said, peering over his brother's shoulder.

'Don't block the light, stupid.' Lud pushed Lob out of the way and grinned at Yama. 'There isn't a way out, is there? Or you wouldn't have come back. We can wait. We caught fish this morning, and we have water. I don't think you do, or you would have set out for the city straight away.'

Yama said, 'I killed a hyrax last night. I ate well enough then.'

Lud started forward. 'But I bet you couldn't drink the water in the pool, eh? We couldn't, and we can drink just about anything.'

106

Yama was aware of a faint breath of air at his back. He said, 'How did you get down here?'

'Rope,' Lob said. 'From the boat. I saved it. People say we're stupid, but we're not.'

'Then I can climb back up,' Yama said, and advanced on Lud, making passes with the knife as he came around the raised casket. The knife made a soft hum, and its rusty hilt pricked his palm. He felt a coldness flowing into his wrist and along his arm as the blade brightened with blue light.

Lud retreated. 'You wouldn't,' he said.

Lob pushed at his brother, trying to get past him. He was excited. 'Break his legs,' he shrieked. 'Break his legs! See how he swims then!'

'A knife! He's got a knife!'

Yama swung the knife again. Lud crowded backwards into Lob and they both fell over.

Yama yelled, words that hurt his throat and tongue. He did not know what he yelled and he stumbled, because suddenly his legs seemed too long and bony and his arms hung wrong. Where was his mount and where was the rest of the squad? Why was he standing in the middle of what looked like a ruined tomb? Had he fallen into the keelways? All he could remember was a tremendous crushing pain, and then he had suddenly woken here, with two fat ruffians threatening him. He struck at the nearest and the man scrambled out of the way with jittery haste; the knife hit the wall and spat a shower of sparks. It was screaming now. He jumped onto the casket – yes, a tomb – but his body betrayed him and he lost his balance; before he could recover, the second ruffian caught his ankles and he fell heavily, striking the stone floor with hip and elbow and shoulder. The impact numbed his fingers, and the knife fell from his grasp, clattering on the floor and gouging a smoking rut in the stone.

Lud ran forward and kicked the knife out of the way. Yama scrambled to his feet. He did not remember falling. His right arm was cold and numb, and hung from his shoulder like a piece of meat; he had to pull the obsidian knife from his belt with his left hand as Lud ran at him. They slammed against the wall and Lud gasped and clutched at his chest. Blood welled over his hand and he looked at it dully. 'What?' he said. He stepped away from Yama with a bewildered look and said again, 'What?'

'You killed him!' Lob said.

Yama shook his head. He could not get his breath. The ancient knife lay on the filthy floor exactly between him and Lob, sputtering and sending up a thick smoke that stank of burning metal.

Lud tried to pull the obsidian knife from his chest, but it snapped, leaving a fingerswidth of the blade protruding. He blundered around the tomb, blood all over his hands now, blood running down his chest and soaking into the waistband of his kilt. He didn't seem to understand what had happened to him. He kept saying over and over again, 'What? What?' and pushed past his brother and fell to his knees at the entrance to the tomb. Light spilled over his shoulders. He seemed to be searching the blue sky for something he could not find.

Lob stared at Yama, his grey tongue working between his tusks. At last he said, 'You killed him, you culler. You didn't have to kill him.'

Yama took a deep breath. His hands were shaking. 'You were going to kill me.'

'All we wanted was a bit of money. Just enough to get away. Not much to ask, and now you've gone and killed my brother.'

Lob stepped towards Yama and his foot struck the knife. He picked it up – and screamed. White smoke rose from his hand and then he was not holding the knife but a creature fastened to his arm by clawed hands and feet. Lob staggered backwards and slammed his arm against the wall, but the creature only snarled and tightened its grip. It was the size of a small child, and seemed to be made of sticks. A kind of mane of dry, white hair stood around its starveling face. A horrid stink of burning flesh filled the tomb. Lob beat at the creature with his free hand and it vanished in a sudden flash of blue light.

The ancient knife fell to the floor, ringing on the stone. Yama snatched it up and fled down the passage, barely remembering to turn right into the faint breeze. He banged from wall to wall as he ran, and then the walls fell away and he was tumbling through a rush of black air.

10 ~ The Curators of the City of the Dead

The room was in some high, windy place. It was small and square, with whitewashed stone walls and a ceiling of tongue-and-groove planking painted with a hunting scene. The day after he first woke, Yama managed to raise himself from the thin mattress on the stone slab and stagger to the deep-set slit window. He glimpsed a series of stony ridges stepping away beneath a blank blue sky, and then pain overcame his will and he fainted.

'He is ill and he does not know it,' the old man said. He had half-turned his head to speak to someone else as he leaned over Yama. The tip of his wispy white beard hung a finger's width from Yama's chin. The deeply wrinkled skin of his face was mottled with brown spots, and there was only a fringe of white hair around his bald pate. Glasses with lenses like small mirrors hid his eyes. Deep, old scars cut the left side of his face, drawing up the side of his mouth in a sardonic rictus. He said, 'He does not know how much the knife took from him.'

'He's young,' an old woman's voice said. She added, 'He'll learn by himself, won't he? We can't—'

The old man curled and uncurled the end of his wispy beard around his fingers. At last, he said, 'I cannot remember.'

Yama asked them who they were, and where this cool white room was, but they did not hear him. Perhaps he had not spoken at all. He could not move even a single fingertip, although this did not scare him. He was too tired to be scared. The two old people went away and Yama was left to stare at the painted hunting scene on the ceiling. His thoughts would not fit together. Men in plastic armour over brightly coloured jerkins and hose were chasing a white stag through a forest of leafless tree trunks. The turf between the trees was starred with flowers. It seemed to be night in the painting, for in every direction the slim trunks of the trees faded into darkness. The white stag glimmered amongst them like a fugitive star. The paint had flaked away from the wood in places, and a patch above the window was faded. In the foreground, a young man in a leather jacket was pulling a brace of hunting dogs away from a pool. Yama thought that he knew the names of the dogs, and who their owner was. But he was dead.

Some time later, the old man came back and lifted Yama up so that he could sip thin vegetable soup from an earthenware bowl. Later, he was cold, so cold that he shivered under the thin grey blanket, and then so hot that he would have cast aside the blanket if he had possessed the strength.

Fever, the old man told him. He had a bad fever. Something was wrong with his blood. 'You have been in the tombs,' the old man said, 'and there are many kinds of old sicknesses there.'

Yama sweated into the mattress, thinking that if only he could get up he would quench his thirst with the clear water of the forest pool. Telmon would help him.

But Telmon was dead.

In the middle of the day, sunlight crept a few paces into the little room before shyly retreating. At night, wind hunted at the corners of the deep-set window, making the candle gutter inside its glass sleeve. When Yama's fever broke it was night. He lay still, listening to the wuthering of the wind. He felt very tired but entirely clearheaded, and spent hours piecing together what had happened.

Dr Dismas's tower, burning like a firework. The strange cage, and the burning ship. The leonine young war hero, Enobarbus, his face as ruined as the old man's. The ghost ship, and his escape – more fire. The whole adventure seemed to be punctuated by fire. He remembered the kindness of the fisherman, Caphis, and the adventure amongst the dry tombs of the Silent Quarter, which had ended in Lud's death. He had run from something terrible, and as for what had happened after that, he remembered nothing at all.

'You were carried here,' the old woman told him, when she brought him breakfast. 'It was from a place on the shore somewhere downstream of Aeolis, I'd judge. A fair distance, as the fox said to the hen, when he gave her a head start.'

Her skin was fine-grained, almost translucent, and her white, feathery hair reached to the small of her back. She was of the same bloodline as Derev, but far older than either of Derev's parents.

Yama said, 'How did you know?'

The old man smiled at the woman's shoulder. As always, he wore his mirrored lenses. 'Your trousers and your shirt were freshly stained with river silt. It is quite distinctive. But I believe that you had been wandering in the City of the Dead, too.'

Yama asked why he thought that.

'The knife, dear,' the woman said.

The old man pulled on his scanty white beard and said, 'Many people carry old weapons, for they are often far more potent than those made today.'

Yama nodded, remembering Dr Dismas's energy pistol.

'However, the knife you carried has a patina of corrosion that suggests it had lain undisturbed in some dark, dry place for many years. Perhaps you have carried it around without scrupling to clean it, but I think that you are more responsible than that. I think that you found it only recently, and did not have time to clean it. You landed at the shore and began to walk through the City of the Dead, and at some point found the knife in an old tomb.'

'It's from the Age of Insurrection, if I'm a judge,' the woman said. 'It's a cruel thing.'

'And she has forgotten a good deal more than I ever knew,' the old man said fondly. 'You will have to learn its ways, or it could kill you.'

'Hush!' the old woman said sharply. 'Nothing should be changed!'

'Perhaps nothing can be changed,' the old man said.

'Then I would be a machine,' the old woman said, 'and I don't like that thought.'

'At least you would not need to worry. But I will be careful. Pay no attention to me, youngster. My mind wanders these days, as my wife will surely remind you at every opportunity.'

They had been married a long time. They both wore the same kind of long, layered shifts over woollen trousers, and shared the same set of gestures, as if love were a kind of imitation game in which the best of both participants was mingled. They called themselves Osric and Beatrice, but Yama suspected that these were not their real names. They both had an air of sly caution which suggested that they were withholding much, although Yama felt that Osric wanted to tell him more than he was allowed to know. Beatrice was strict with her husband, but she favoured Yama with fond glances, and while he had been stricken with fever she had spent hours bathing his forehead with wet cloths infused with oil of spikenard, and had fed him infusions of honey and herbs, crooning to him as if he were her child. While Osric was bent by age, his tall, slender wife carried herself like a young dancer.

Later, husband and wife sat side by side on the ledge beneath the narrow window of the little room, watching Yama eat a bowl of boiled maize. It was his first solid food since he had woken. They said that they were members of the Department of the Curators of the City of the Dead, an office of the civil service which had been disbanded centuries ago.

'But my ancestors stayed on, dear,' Beatrice explained. 'They believed that the dead deserved better than abandonment, and fought against dissolution. There was quite a little war. Of course, we're much diminished now. Most would say that we had vanished long ago, if they had heard of us at all, but we still hold some of the more important parts of the city.'

'You might say that I am an honorary member of the department, by marriage,' Osric said. 'Here, I cleaned the knife for you.'

Osric laid the long, curved knife at the foot of the bed. Yama looked at it and discovered that although it had saved his life he feared it; it was as if Osric had set a live snake at his feet. He said, 'I found it in a tomb in the cliffs by the river.'

'Then it came from somewhere else,' Osric said, and laid a bony finger beside his nose. The tip of the finger was missing. He said, 'I used a little white vinegar to take the bloom of age from the metal, and every decad or so you should rub it down with a cloth touched to mineral oil. But it will not need sharpening, and it will repair itself, within limits. It had been imprinted with a copy of the personality of its previous owner, but I have purged that ghost. You should practise with it as often as you can, and handle it at least once a day, and so it will come to know you.'

'Osric—'

'He needs to know,' Osric told his wife. 'It will not hurt. Handle it often, Yama. The more you handle it, the better it will know you. And leave it in the sunlight, or between places of different temperature – placing the point in a fire is good. Otherwise it will take energy from you again. It had lain in the dark a long time – that was why you were hurt by it when you used it. I would guess it belonged to an officer of the cavalry, dead long ages past. They were issued to those fighting in the rain forests two thousand leagues downriver.'

Yama said stupidly, 'But the war started only forty years ago.'

'This was another war, dear,' Beatrice said.

'I found it by the river. In a tomb there. I put out my hand in the dark.'

Yama remembered how the knife had kindled its eldritch glow when he had held it up, wonderingly, before his face. But when Lob had picked it up, the horrible thing had happened. The knife was different things to different people.

Yama had been brought a long way from the river. This was the last retreat of the last of the curators of the City of the Dead, deep in the foothills of the Rim Mountains. He had not realized until then the true extent of the necropolis.

'The dead outnumber the living,' Osric said, 'and this has been the burial place for Ys since the construction of Confluence. Until this last, decadent age, at least.'

Yama gathered that there were not many curators left now, and that most of those were old. This was a place where the past was stronger than the present. The Department of the Curators of the City of the Dead had once been responsible for preparation and arrangement of the deceased, whom they called clients, and for the care and maintenance of the graves, tombs and memorials, the picture slates and aspects of the dead. It had been a solemn and complex task. For instance, Yama learned that there had been four methods of dealing with clients: by interment, including burial or entombment; by cremation, either by fire or by acids; by exposure, either in a byre raised above the ground or by dismemberment; and by water.

'Which I understand is the only method used these days,' Osric said. 'It has its place, but many die a long way from the Great River, and besides, many communities are too close together, so that the corpses of those upriver foul the water of those below them. Consider, Yama. Much of Confluence is desert or mountain. Interment in the soil is rare, for there is little enough land for cultivation. For myriad upon myriad days, our ancestors built tombs for their dead, or burned them on pyres or dissolved them in tanks of acid, or exposed them to the brothers of the air. Building tombs takes much labour and is suitable only for the rich, for the badly constructed tombs of the poor are soon ransacked by wild animals. Firewood is in as short supply as arable land, for the same reasons, and dissolution in acid is usually considered aesthetically displeasing. How much more natural, in the circumstances, to expose the client to the brothers of the air. It is how I wish my body to be disposed, when my time comes. Beatrice has promised it to me. The world will end before I die, of course, but I think there will still be birds...'

'You forgot preservation,' Beatrice said sharply. 'He always does,' she told Yama. 'He disapproves.'

'Ah, but I did not forget. It is merely a variation on interment. Without a tomb, the preserved body is merely fodder for the animals, or a curiosity in a sideshow.'

'Some are turned into stone,' Beatrice said. 'It is mostly done by exposing the client to limy water.'

'And then there is mummification, and desiccation, either by vacuum or by chemical treatment, and treatment by tar, or by ice.' Osric ticked off the variations on his fingers. 'But you know full well that I mean the most common method, and the most decadent. Which is to say, those clients who were preserved while still alive, in the hope of physical resurrection in ages to come. Instead, robbers opened the tombs and took what there was of value, and threw away the bodies for wild animals to devour, or burned them as fuel, or ground them up for fertilizer. The brave cavalry officer who once wielded your knife in battle, young Yama, was in all probability burned in some furnace to melt the alloy stripped from his tomb. Perhaps one of the tomb robbers picked up the knife, and it attacked him. He dropped it where you would find it an age later. We live in impoverished times. I remember that I played amongst the tombs as a child, teasing the aspects who still spoke for those beyond hope of resurrection. There is a lesson in folly. Only the Preservers outrun time. I did not know then that the aspects were bound to oblige my foolishness; the young are needlessly cruel because they know no better.'

Beatrice straightened her back, held up her hand, and recited a verse:

> Let fame, that all hunt after in their lives,
> Live registered upon our brazen tombs,
> And then grace us in the disgrace of death;

When, spite of the cormorant devouring time,
The endeavour of this present breath may buy
That honour which shall bate his scythe's keen edge,
And makes us heirs to all eternity.

Yama guessed that this was from the Puranas, but Beatrice said that it was far older. 'There are too few of us to remember everything left by the dead,' she said, 'but we do what we can, and we are a long-lived race.'

There was much more to the tasks of the curators than preparation of their clients, and in the next two days Yama learned something about care of tombs and the preservation of the artefacts with which clients had been interred, each according to the customs of their bloodline. Osric and Beatrice fed him vegetable broths, baked roots and succulent young okra, corn and green beans fried in airy batter. He was getting better, and was beginning to feel a restless curiosity. He had not broken any bones, but his ribs were badly bruised and muscles in his back and arms had been torn. There were numerous half-healed cuts on his limbs and torso, too, and the fever had left him very weak, as if most of his blood had been drained.

Beatrice cleaned out the worst of his wounds; she explained that the stone dust embedded in them would otherwise leave scars. As soon as he could, Yama started to exercise, using the drills taught him by Sergeant Rhodean. He practised with the knife, too, mastering his instinctive revulsion. He handled it each day, as Osric had suggested, and otherwise left it on the ledge beneath the narrow window, where it would catch the midday sun. To begin with, he had to rest for an hour or more between each set of exercises, but he ate large amounts of the curators' plain food and felt his strength return. At last, he was able to climb the winding stairs to the top of the hollow crag.

He had to stop and rest frequently, but finally stepped out of the door of a little hut into the open air under an achingly blue sky. The air was clean and cold, as heady as wine after the stuffy room in which he had lain for so long.

The hut was set at one end of the top of the crag, which was so flat that it might have been sheared off by someone wielding a gigantic blade. Possibly this was more or less what had been done, for during the construction of Confluence, long before the Preservers had abandoned the ten thousand bloodlines, energies had been deployed to move whole mountains and shape entire landscapes as easily as a gardener might set out a bed of flowers.

The flat top of the crag was no bigger than the Great Hall of the peel-house, and divided into tiny fields by low drystone walls. There were plots of squash and yams, corn and kale and cane fruits. Little paths wandered between these plots, and there was a complicated system of cisterns and gutters to provide a constant supply of water to the crops. At the far end, Beatrice and Osric were feeding doves which fluttered around a round-topped dovecote built of unmortared stone.

The crag stood at the edge of a winding ridge above a gorge so deep that its bottom was lost in shadow. Other flat-topped crags stood along the ridge, their smooth sides fretted with windows and balconies. There was a scattering of tombs on broad ledges cut into the white rock of the gorge's steep sides, huge buildings with blind, whitewashed walls under pitched roofs of red tile that stood amidst manicured lawns and groves of tall trees. Beyond the far side of the gorge, other ridges stepped up towards the sky, and beyond the furthest ridge the peaks of the Rim Mountains seemed to float free above indistinct blue and purple masses, shining in the light of the sun.

Yama threaded the winding paths to the little patch of grass where Beatrice and Osric were scattering grain. Doves rose up in a whir of white wings as he approached. Osric raised a hand in greeting and said, 'This is the valley of the kings of the first days. Some maintain that Preservers are buried here, but if that is true, the location is hidden from us.'

'It must be a lot of work, looking after these tombs.'

The mirror lenses of Osric's spectacles flashed light at Yama. 'They maintain themselves,' the old man said, 'and there are mechanisms which prevent people from approaching too closely. It was once our job to keep people away for their own good, but only those who know this place come here now.'

'Few know of it,' Beatrice added, 'and fewer come.'

She held out a long, skinny arm. A dove immediately perched on her hand, and she drew it to her breast and stroked its head with a bony forefinger until it began to coo.

Yama said, 'I was brought a long way.'

Osric nodded. His wispy beard blew sideways in the wind. 'The Department of the Curators of the City of the Dead once maintained a city that stretched from these mountains to the river, a day's hard ride distant. Whoever brought you here had a good reason.'

Beatrice suddenly flung out her hands. The dove rose into the wind and circled high above the patchwork of tiny fields. She watched it for a minute and then said, 'I think it's time we showed Yama why he was brought here.'

'I would like to know who brought me here, to begin with.'

'As long as you do not know who saved you,' Osric said, 'there is no obligation.'

Yama nodded, remembering that after he had saved Caphis from the trap, the fisherman had said that his life was for ever in Yama's care. He said, 'Perhaps I could at least know the circumstances.'

'Something had taken one of our goats,' Beatrice said. 'It was in a field far below. We went to look for her, and found you. It is better if you see for yourself why you have been brought here. Then you'll understand. Having climbed so high, you must descend. I think that you are strong enough.'

Descending the long spiral of stairs was easier than climbing up, but Yama felt that if not for him, Osric and Beatrice would have bounded away eagerly, although he was so much younger than they. The stairs ended at a balcony that girdled the crag halfway between its flat top and its base. A series of arched doorways opened off the balcony, and Osric immediately disappeared through one. Yama would have followed, but Beatrice took his arm and guided him to a stone bench by the low wall of the balcony. Sunlight drenched the ancient stone; Yama was grateful for its warmth.

'There were a hundred thousand of us, once,' Beatrice said, 'but we are greatly reduced. This is the oldest part of all that still lies within our care, and it will be the last to fall. It will fall eventually, of course. All of Confluence will fall.'

Yama said, 'You sound like those who say that the war at the midpoint of the world may be the war at the end of all things.'

Sergeant Rhodean had taught Yama and Telmon the major battles, scratching the lines of the armies and the routes of their long marches in the red clay floor of the gymnasium.

Beatrice said, 'When there is a war, everyone believes that it will end in a victory that will bring an end to all conflict, but in a series of events there is no way of determining which is to be the last.'

Yama said stoutly, 'The heretics will be defeated because they challenge the word of the Preservers. The Ancients of Days revived much old technology which their followers use against us, but they were lesser creatures than the Preservers because they were the distant ancestors of the Preservers. How can a lesser idea prevail against a greater one?'

'I forget that you are young,' Beatrice said, smiling. 'You still have hope. But Osric has hope, too, and he is a wise man. Not that the world will not end, for that is certain, but that it will end well. The Great River fails day by day, and at last all that my people care for will fall away.'

'With respect, perhaps you and your husband live for the past, yet I live for the future.'

Beatrice smiled. 'Ah, but which future, I wonder? Osric suspects that there might be more than one. As for us, it is our duty to preserve the past to inform the future, and this place is where the past is strongest. There are wonders interred here which could end the war in an instant if wielded by one side, or destroy Confluence, if used by both against each other.

'The living bury the dead and move on, and forget. We remember. Above all, that is our duty. There are record keepers in Ys who claim to be able to trace the bloodlines of Confluence back to their first members. My family preserves the tombs of those ancestors, their bodies and their artefacts. The record keepers would claim that words are stronger than the phenomena they describe, and that only words endure while all else fails, but we know that even words change. Stories are mutable, and in any story each generation finds a different lesson, and with each telling a story changes slightly until it is no longer the thing it was. The king who prevails against the hero who would have brought redeeming light to the world becomes after many tellings of the story a hero saving the world from fire, and the light-bringer becomes a fiend. Only things remain what they are. They are themselves. Words are merely representations of things; but we have the things themselves. How much more powerful they are than their representations!'

Yama thought of the Aedile, who put so much trust in the objects that the soil preserved. He said, 'My father seeks to understand the past by the wreckage it leaves behind. Perhaps it is not the stories that change but the past itself, for all that lives of the past is the meaning we invest in what remains.'

Behind him, Osric said, 'You have been taught by a record keeper. That is just what one of those beetle-browed near-sighted bookworms would say, bless them all, each and every one. Well, there is more of the past than can be found in books. That is a lesson I had to learn over and over, young man. All that is ordinary and human passes away without record, and all that remains are stories of priests and philosophers, heroes and kings. Much is made of the altar stones and sacraria of temples, but nothing of the cloisters where lovers rendezvoused and friends gossiped, and the courtyards where children played. That is the false lesson of history. Still, we can peer into random scenes of the past and wonder at their import. That is what I have brought you.'

Osric carried something square and flat under his arm, covered with a white cloth. He removed the cloth with a flourish, revealing a thin rectangle of milky stone which he laid in a pool of sunlight on the tiled floor of the balcony.

Yama said, 'My father collects these picture slates, but this one appears blank.'

'He collected them for important research, perhaps,' Osric said, 'but I am sorry to hear of it. Their proper resting place is not in a collection, but in the tomb in which they were installed.'

'I have always wondered why they need to drink sunlight to work, when they were buried away in darkness.'

'The tombs drink sunlight, too,' Osric said, 'and distribute it amongst their components according to need. The pictures respond to the heat given off by a living body, and in the darkness of the tomb would waken in the presence of any watcher. Outside the tomb, without their usual power source, the pictures also require sunlight.'

'Be quiet, husband,' Beatrice said. 'It wakens. Watch it, Yama, and learn. This is all we can show you.'

Colours mingled and ran in the slate, seeming to swirl just beneath its surface. At first they were faint and amorphous, little more than pastel flows within the slate's milky depths, but gradually they brightened, running together in a sudden silvery flash.

For a moment, Yama thought that the slate had turned into a mirror, reflecting his own eager face. But when he leaned closer, the face within the slate turned as if to speak to someone beyond the frame of the picture, and he saw that it was the face of someone older than he was, a man with lines at the corners of his eyes and grooves at either side of his mouth. But the shape of the eyes and their round blue irises, and the shape of the face, the pale skin and the mop of wiry black hair: all these were so very like his own that he cried out in astonishment.

The man in the picture was talking now, and suddenly smiled at someone beyond the picture's frame, a frank, eager smile that turned Yama's heart. The man turned away and the view slid from his face to show the night sky. It was not the sky of Confluence, for it was full of stars, scattered like diamond chips carelessly thrown across black velvet. There was a frozen swirl of dull red light in the centre of the picture, and Yama saw that the stars around it seemed to be drawn into lines that curved in towards the red swirl. Stars streaked as the viewpoint of the picture moved, and for a moment it steadied on a flock of splinters of light hung against pure black, and then it faded.

Osric wrapped the white cloth around the slate. Immediately, Yama wanted to strip the cloth away and see the picture blossom within the slate again, wanted to feast on the stranger's face, the stranger who was of his bloodline, wanted to understand the strange skies under which his long-dead ancestor had stood. His blood sang in his ears.

Beatrice handed him a square of lace-trimmed cloth. A handkerchief. Yama realized then that he was weeping.

Osric said, 'This is the place where the oldest tombs on Confluence can be found, but the picture is older than anything on Confluence, for it is older than Confluence itself. It shows the first stage in the construction of the Eye of the Preservers, and it shows the lands which the Preservers walked before they fell into the Eye and vanished into the deep past or the deep future, or perhaps into another universe entirely.'

'I would like to see the tomb. I want to see where you found this picture.'

Osric said, 'The Department of the Curators of the City of the Dead has kept the picture a long time, and if it once rested in a tomb, then it was so long ago that all records of that tomb are lost. Your bloodline walked Confluence at its beginning, and now it walks it again.'

Yama said, 'This is the second time that someone has hinted that I have a mysterious destiny, but no one will explain why or what it is.'

Beatrice told her husband, 'He'll discover it soon enough. We should not tell him more.'

Osric tugged at his beard. 'I do not know everything. What the hollow man said, for instance, or what lies beyond the end of the river. I have tried to remember it all over again, and I cannot!'

Beatrice took her husband's hands in her own and told Yama, 'He was hurt, and sometimes gets confused about what might happen and what has happened. Remember the slate. It's important.'

Yama said, 'I know less than you. Let me see the slate again. Perhaps there is something—'

Beatrice said, 'Perhaps it is your destiny to discover your past, dear. Only by knowing the past can you know yourself.'

Yama smiled, because that was precisely the motto which Zakiel used to justify his long lessons. It seemed to him that the curators of the dead and the librarians and archivists were so similar that they amplified slight differences into a deadly rivalry, just as brothers feuded over nothing at all simply to assert their individuality.

'You have seen all we can show you, Yama,' Osric said. 'We preserve the past as best we can, but we do not pretend to understand everything we preserve.'

Yama said formally, 'I thank you for showing me this wonder.' But he thought that it proved only that others like him had lived long ago – he was more concerned with discovering if they still lived now. Surely they must – he was proof of that – but where? What had Dr Dismas discovered in the archives of his department?

Beatrice stood with a graceful flowing motion. 'You cannot stay, Yama. You are a catalyst, and change is most dangerous here.'

Yama said, 'If you would show me the way, I would go home at once.'

He said it with little hope, for he was convinced that the two curators were holding him prisoner. But Beatrice smiled and said, 'I will do better than that. I will take you.'

Osric said, 'You are stronger than you were when you arrived here, but not, I think, as strong as you can be. Let my wife help you, Yama. And remember us. We have served as best we can, and I feel that we have served well. When you discover your purpose, remember us.'

Beatrice said, 'Don't burden the poor boy, husband. He is too young. It is too early.'

'He is old enough to know his mind, I think. Remember that we are your friends, Yama.'

Yama bowed from the waist, as the Aedile had taught him, and turned to follow Beatrice, leaving her husband sitting in a pool of sunlight, his ravaged face made inscrutable by the mirror lenses of his spectacles, the blue uncharted mountain ridges framed by the pillars behind him, and the picture slate, wrapped in white cloth, on his lap.

Beatrice led Yama down a long helical stair and through chambers where machines as big as houses stood half-buried in the stone floor. Beyond these were the wide, circular mouths of pits in which long narrow tubes, made of a metal as clear as glass, fell into white mists a league or more below. Vast slow lightnings sparked and rippled in the transparent tubes. Yama felt a slow vibration through the soles of his feet, a pulse deeper than sound.

He would have stayed to examine the machines, but Beatrice urged him past and led him down a long hall with black keelrock walls, lit by balls of white fire that spun beneath a high curved ceiling. Parts of the floor were transparent and Yama saw, dimly, huge machines crouched in chambers far below his feet.

'Don't gawp,' Beatrice said. 'You don't want to wake them before their time.'

Many narrow corridors led off the hall. Beatrice ushered Yama down one of them into a small room which, once its door slid shut, began at once to hum and shake. Yama felt for a moment as if he had stepped over a cliff, and clutched at the rail which ran around the curved walls of the room.

'We fall through the keelways,' Beatrice said. 'Most people live on the surface now, but in ancient times the surface was a place where they came to play and meet, while they had their dwelling and working places underground. This is one of the old roads. It will return you to Aeolis in less than an hour.'

'Are these roads everywhere?'

'Once. No more. We have maintained a few beneath the City of the Dead, but many more no longer function, and beyond the limits of our jurisdiction things are worse. Everything fails at last. Even the Universe will fall into itself eventually.'

'The Puranas say that is why the Preservers fled into the Eye. But if the Universe will not end soon, then surely that is not why they fled. Zakiel could never explain that. He said it was not for me to question the Puranas.'

Beatrice laughed. It was like the tinkling of old, fragile bells. 'How like a librarian! But the Puranas contain many riddles, and there is no harm in admitting that not all the answers are obvious. Perhaps they are not even comprehensible to our small minds, but a librarian will never admit that any text in his charge is unfathomable. He must be the master of them all, and is shamed to admit any possible failure.'

'The slate showed the creation of the Eye. There is a sura in the Puranas, the forty-third sura, I think, which says that the Preservers made stars fall together, until their light grew too heavy to escape.'

'Perhaps. There is much we do not know about the past, Yama. Some have said that the Preservers set us here for their own amusement, as certain bloodlines keep caged birds for amusement, but I would not repeat that heresy. All who believed it are safely dead long ago, but it is still a dangerous thought.'

'Perhaps because it is true, or contains some measure of the truth.'

Beatrice regarded him with her bright eyes. She was a head taller than he was. 'Do not be bitter, Yama. You will find what you are looking for, although it might not be where you expect it. Ah, we are almost there.'

The room shuddered violently. Yama fell to his knees. The floor was padded with a kind of quilting, covered in an artificial material as slick and thin as satin.

Beatrice opened the door and Yama followed her into a very long room that had been carved from rock. Its high roof was held up by a forest of slender pillars and wan light fell from narrow slits in the roof. It had once been a stonemasons' workshop, and Beatrice led Yama around half-finished carvings and benches scattered with tools, all abandoned an age ago and muffled by thick dust. At the door, she took out a hood of soft, black cloth and said that she must blindfold him.

'We are a secret people, because we should not exist. Our department was disbanded long ago, and we survive only because we are good at hiding.'

'I understand. My father—'

'We are not frightened of discovery, Yama, but we have stayed hidden for so long that knowledge of where we are is valuable to certain people. I would not ask you to carry that burden. It would expose you to unnecessary danger. If you need to find us again, you will. I can safely promise that, I think. In return, will you promise that you won't mention us to the Aedile?'

'He will want to know where I have been.'

'You were ill. You recovered, and you returned. Perhaps you were nursed by one of the hill tribes. The Aedile will be so pleased to see you that he won't question you too closely. Will you promise?'

'As long as I do not have to lie to him. I think that I am done with lies.'

Beatrice was pleased by this. 'You were honest from the first, dear heart. Tell the Aedile as much of the truth as is good for him, and no more. Now, come with me.'

Blinded by the soft, heavy cloth of the hood, Yama took Beatrice's hot, fine-boned hand, and allowed himself to be led once more. They walked a long way. He trusted this strange old woman, and he was thinking about the man of his bloodline, dead ages past.

At last she told him to stand still. Something cold and heavy was placed in his right hand. After a moment of silence, Yama lifted the hood away and saw that he was in a dark passageway walled with broken stone blocks, with stout tree roots thrust between their courses. A patch of sunlight fell through a narrow doorway at the top of a stair whose stone treads had been worn away in the centre. He was holding the ancient metal knife he had found in the tomb by the river's shore – or which had found him. A skirl of blue sparks flared along the outer edge of its blade and sputtered out one by one.

Yama looked around for Beatrice and thought he saw a patch of white float around the corner of a passageway. But when he ran after it, he found a stone wall blocking his way. He turned back to the sunlight. This place was familiar, but he did not recognize it until he climbed the stair and stepped out into the ruins in the Aedile's garden, with the peel-house looming beyond masses of dark green rhododendrons.

11 ~ Prefect Corin

Lob and the landlord of *The House of Ghost Lanterns* were arrested before Yama had finished telling his story to the Aedile, and the next day were tried and sentenced to death for kidnap and sabotage. The Aedile also issued a warrant for the arrest of Dr Dismas, although he confided to Yama that he did not expect to see the apothecary again.

Although it took a long time to explain his adventures, Yama did not tell the whole story. He suppressed the part about Enobarbus, for he had come to believe that the young warlord had somehow been caught by Dr Dismas's spell. He kept his promise to Beatrice, too, and said that after he had escaped from the skiff and had been helped ashore by one of the fisherfolk, he had fallen ill after being attacked by Lob and Lud amongst the ransacked tombs of the Silent Quarter, and had not been able to return to the peel-house until he had recovered. It was not the whole truth, but the Aedile did not question him closely.

Yama was not allowed to attend the trial; nor was he allowed to leave the grounds of the peel-house, although he very much wanted to see Derev. The Aedile said that it was too dangerous. The families of Lob and the tavern landlord would be looking for revenge, and the city was still on edge after the riots which had followed the failed siege of Dr Dismas's tower. Yama tried to contact Derev using mirror talk, but although he signalled for most of the afternoon there was no answering spark of light from the apartments Derev's father had built on top of his godown by the old waterfront of the city. Sick at heart, Yama went to plead with Sergeant Rhodean, but the Sergeant refused to provide an escort.

'And you're not to confuse the watchdogs and go sneaking out on your own, neither,' Sergeant Rhodean said. 'Oh yes, I know all about that trick, lad. But see here, you can't rely on tricks to keep yourself out of trouble. They're more likely to get you into it instead. I won't risk having any of my men hurt rescuing you from your own foolishness, and think how it would look if we took you down there in the middle of a decad of armed soldiers. You'd start another riot. My men have already spent too much time looking for you when you were lost in the City of the Dead, and they'll have their hands full in a couple of days. The department is sending a clerk to deal with the prisoners, but no extra troops. Pure foolishness on their part, and I'll get blamed if something goes wrong.'

Sergeant Rhodean was much exercised by this. As he talked, he paced in a tight circle on the red clay floor of the gymnasium. He was a small, burly man, almost as wide as he was tall, as he liked to say. As always, his grey tunic and blue trousers were neatly pressed, his black knee-boots were spit-polished, and the scalp of his heavy, ridged skull was close-shaven and burnished with oil. He favoured his right leg, and the thumb and forefinger of his right hand were missing. He had been the Aedile's bodyguard long before the entire household had been exiled from the Palace of the Memory of the People, and had celebrated his hundredth birthday two years ago. He lived quietly with his wife, who was always trying to overfeed Yama because, she said, he needed to put some muscle on his long bones. They had two married daughters, six sons away fighting the heretics, and two more who had been killed in the war; Sergeant Rhodean had mourned Telmon's death almost as bitterly as Yama and the Aedile.

Sergeant Rhodean suddenly stopped pacing and looked at Yama as if for the first time. He said, 'I see you're wearing that knife you found, lad. Let's take a look at it.'

Yama had taken to hanging the knife from his belt by a loop of leather, with its blade tied flat against his thigh by a red ribbon. He undid the ribbon, unhooked the loop and held out the knife, and Sergeant Rhodean put on thick-lensed spectacles, which vastly magnified his yellow eyes, and peered closely at it for a long time. At last, he blew reflectively through his drooping mustache and said, 'It's old, and sentient, or at least partly so. Maybe as smart as one of the watchdogs. A good idea to carry it around. It will bond to you. You said you were ill after using it?'

'It gave out a blue light. And when Lob picked it up, it turned into something horrible.'

'Well now, lad, it had to get its energy from somewhere for tricks like that, especially after all the time in the dark. So it took it from you.'

'I leave it in sunlight,' Yama said.

'Do you?' Sergeant Rhodean gave Yama a shrewd look. 'Then I can't tell you much more. What did you clean it with? White vinegar? As good as anything, I suppose. Well, let's see you make a few passes with it. It will stop you brooding over your true love.'

For the next hour, Sergeant Rhodean instructed Yama on how to make best use of the knife against a variety of imaginary opponents. Yama found himself beginning to enjoy the exercises, and was sorry when Sergeant Rhodean called a halt. He had spent many happy hours in the gymnasium, with its mingled smell of clay and old sweat and rubbing alcohol, its dim underwater light filtered through green-tinted windows high up in the whitewashed walls, the green rubber wrestling mats rolled up like the shed cocoons of giant caterpillars and the rack of parallel bars, the open cases of swords and knives, javelins and padded staves, the straw archery targets stacked behind the vaulting horse, the battered wooden torsos of the tilting dummies, the frames hung with pieces of plastic and resin and metal armour.

'We'll do some more work tomorrow, lad,' Sergeant Rhodean said at last. 'You need to work on your backhand. You aim too low, at the belly instead of the chest, and any opponent worth their salt would spot that in an instant. Of course, a knife like this is really intended for close work by a cavalryman surrounded by the enemy, and you might do better carrying a long sword or a revolver when walking about the city. It's possible that an old weapon like this might be proscribed. But now I have to drill the men. The clerk is coming tomorrow, and I suppose your father will want an honour guard for him.'

But the clerk sent from Ys to oversee the executions slipped unnoticed into the peel-house early the next morning, and the first time Yama saw him was when the Aedile summoned him to an audience that afternoon.

'The townspeople already believe that you have blood on your hands,' the Aedile said. 'I do not wish to see any more trouble. So I have come to a decision.'

Yama felt his heart turn over, although he already knew that this was no ordinary interview. He had been escorted to the Aedile's receiving chamber by one of the soldiers of the house guard. The soldier now stood in front of the tall double doors, resplendent in burnished helmet and corselet and scarlet hose, his pike at parade rest.

Yama perched on an uncomfortable curved backless seat before the central dais on which the Aedile's canopied chair stood. The Aedile did not sit down but paced about restlessly. He was dressed in a tunic embroidered with silver and gold, and his sable robe of office hung on a rack by his chair.

There was a fourth person in the room, standing in the shadows by the small private door which led, via a stairway, to the Aedile's private chambers. It was the clerk who had been sent from Ys to supervise the executions. Yama watched him out of the corner of his eye. He was a tall, slender man of the Aedile's bloodline, bareheaded in a plain homespun tunic and grey leggings. A close-clipped black pelt covered his head and face, with a broad white stripe, like a badger's marking, on the left side of his face.

Yama's breakfast had been brought to his room that morning, and this was the first chance he had to study the man. He had heard from the stable hands that the clerk had disembarked from an ordinary lugger, armed with only a stout ironshod staff and with no more than a rolled blanket on his back, but the Aedile had prostrated himself at the man's feet as if he were a Hierarch risen from the files.

'I don't think he expected someone so high up in the Committee for Public Safety,' the foreman, Torin, had said.

But the clerk did not look like an executioner, or anyone important. He could have been any one of the thousands of ordinary scribes who plied pens in cells deep in the Palace of the Memory of the People, as indistinguishable from each other as ants.

The Aedile stood before one of the four great tapestries that decorated the high, square room. It depicted the seeding of Confluence. Plants and animals rained out of a blaze of light towards a bare plain crossed by silvery loops of water. Birds soared through the air, and little groups of naked men and women of various bloodlines stood on wisps of cloud, hands modestly covering their genitals and breasts.

Yama had always loved this tapestry, but now that he had talked with the curators of the City of the Dead he knew that it was a lie. Since he had returned, everything in the peel-house seemed to have changed. The house was smaller; the gardens cramped and neglected; the people preoccupied with small matters, their backs bent to routine labour so that, like peasants planting a paddy field, they failed to see the great events of the world rushing above their heads.

At last, the Aedile turned and said, 'It was always my plan to apprentice you to my department, Yama, and I have not changed my mind. You are perhaps a little young to begin proper apprenticeship, but I have great hopes of you. Zakiel says that you are the best pupil he has known, and Sergeant Rhodean believes that in a few years you will be able to best him in archery and fencing, although he adds that your horse riding still requires attention.

'I know your determination and ambition, Yama. I think that you will be a great power in the department. You are not of my bloodline, but you are my son, now and always. I would wish that you could have stayed here until you were old enough to be inducted as a full apprentice, but it is clear to me that if you stay here you are in great danger.'

'I am not afraid of anyone in Aeolis.'

But Yama's protest was a formality. Already he was dizzy with the prospect of kicking the dust of this sleepily corrupt little city from his heels. In Ys, there were records which went back to the foundation of Confluence. Beatrice had said as much. She and Osric had shown him a slate which had displayed the likeness of an ancestor of his bloodline; in Ys, he might learn who that man had been. There might even be people of his bloodline! Anything was possible. After all, surely he had come from Ys in the first place, borne downstream on the river's current. For that reason alone he would gladly go to Ys, although more than ever he knew that he could not serve as a clerk. But he could not tell his father that, of course, and it burned in his chest like a coal.

The Aedile said, 'I am proud that you can say that you are unafraid with such conviction, and I think that you truly believe it. But you cannot spend your life looking over your shoulder, Yama, and that is what you would have to do if you stayed here. One day, sooner or later, Lob and Lud's brothers will seek to press their need for revenge. That they are the sons of the Constable of Aeolis makes this more likely, not less, for if any one of them killed you, it would not only satisfy their family's need for revenge, it would also be a triumph over their father.

'It is not the townspeople I fear, however. Dr Dismas has fled, but he may try to revive his scheme, or he may sell his information to others. In

Aeolis you are a wonder; in Ys, which is the fount of all the wonders of the world, less so. Here, I command only three decads of soldiers; there, you will be in the heart of the department.'

'When will I go?'

The Aedile clasped his hands and bowed his head. It was a peculiarly submissive gesture. 'You will leave with Prefect Corin, after he has concluded his business here.'

The man in the shadows caught Yama's gaze. 'In cases like this,' he said in a soft, lilting voice, 'it is not advisable to linger once duty has been done. I will leave tomorrow.'

No, the clerk, Prefect Corin, did not look like an executioner, but he had already visited Lob and the landlord of the tavern, who had been held in the peel-house's oubliette since their trial. They were to be burned that evening outside the town's walls, and their ashes would be scattered on the wind so that their families would have no part of them as a memorial and their souls would never have rest until the Preservers woke all the dead at the end of the Universe. Sergeant Rhodean had been drilling his men ever since the trial. If there was any trouble, he could not rely on the Constable and the city militia for aid. Every bit of armour had been polished, and every weapon cleaned or sharpened. Because the steam waggon had been destroyed in the siege of Dr Dismas's tower, an ordinary waggon had been sequestered to transport the condemned men from the peel-house to the place of execution. It had been painted white, and its axles greased and its wheels balanced, and the two white oxen which would draw it had been brushed until their coats shone. The entire peel-house had been filled with bustle over the affair, but as soon as he had arrived, Prefect Corin had become its still centre.

The Aedile said, 'It is abrupt, I know, but I will see you in Ys, as soon as I can be sure that there will be no more trouble here. In the meantime, I hope you will remember me with affection.'

'Father, you have done more for me than I ever can deserve.' It was a formal sentiment, and sounded trite, but Yama felt a sudden flood of affection for the Aedile then, and would have embraced him if Prefect Corin had not been watching.

The Aedile turned to study the tapestry again. Perhaps Prefect Corin made him uncomfortable, too. He said, 'Quite, quite. You are my son, Yama. No less than Telmon.'

Prefect Corin cleared his throat, a small sound in the large room, but father and son turned to stare at him as if he had shot a pistol at the painted ceiling.

'Your pardon,' he said, 'but it is time to shrive the prisoners.'

Two hours before sunset, Father Quine, the priest of the temple of Aeolis, came in his orange robes, walking barefoot and bareheaded up the winding road from the city to the peel-house. Ananda accompanied him, carrying a chrism of oil. The Aedile greeted them formally and escorted them to the oubliette, where they would hear the final confessions of the prisoners.

Again, Yama had no part in the ceremony. He sat in one corner of the big fireplace in the kitchen, but that had changed, too. He was no longer a part of the kitchen's bustle and banter. The scullions and the kitchen boys and the three cooks politely replied to his remarks, but their manner was subdued. He wanted to tell them that he was still Yama, the boy who had wrestled with most of the kitchen boys, who had received clouts from the cooks when he had tried to steal bits of food, who had cheeked the scullions to make them chase him. But he was no longer that boy.

After a while, oppressed by polite deference, Yama went out to watch the soldiers drilling in the slanting sunlight, and that was where Ananda found him.

Ananda's head was clean-shaven; there was a fresh cut above his right ear, painted with yellow iodine. His eyes were enlarged by clever use of blue paint and gold leaf. He gave off a smell of cloves and cinnamon. It was the scent of the oil with which the prisoners had been anointed.

Ananda knew how to judge Yama's mood. For a while, the two friends stood side by side in companionable silence and watched the soldiers make squares and lines in the dusty sunlight. Sergeant Rhodean barked orders which echoed off the high wall of the peel-house.

At last, Yama said, 'I have to go away tomorrow.'

'I know.'

'With that little badger of a clerk. He is to be my master. He will teach me how to copy records and write up administrative reports. I will be buried, Ananda. Buried in old paper and futile tasks. There is only one consolation.'

'You can look for your bloodline.'

Yama was astonished. 'How did you know?'

'Why, you've always talked about it.' Ananda looked at Yama shrewdly. 'But you've learnt something about it, haven't you? That's why it's on your mind.'

'A clerk, Ananda. I will not serve. I cannot. I have more important things to do.'

'Not only soldiers help fight the war. And don't change the subject.'

'That is what my father would say. I want to be a hero, Ananda. It is my destiny!'

'If it's your destiny, then it will happen.' Ananda pulled a pouch from inside his robe and spilled hulled pistachios into his meaty palm. 'Want some?'

Yama shook his head. He said, 'It has all changed so quickly.'

Ananda put his palm to his lips and said, around a mouthful of pistachios, 'Is there time to tell me all that happened? I'm never going to leave here, you know. My master will die, and I will take his place, and begin to teach the new sizar, who will be a boy just like me. And so on.'

'I am not allowed to go to the execution.'

'Of course not. It would be unseemly.'

'I want to prove that I am brave enough to see it.'

'What did happen, Yama? You couldn't have been lost for so long, and they couldn't have taken you far if you said you escaped on the night you were taken.'

'A lot of things happened after that. I do not understand all of them, but one thing I do understand. I found something ... something important.'

Ananda laughed. 'You mustn't tease your friends, Yama. Share it with me. Perhaps I can help you understand everything.'

'Meet me tonight. After the executions. Bring Derev, too. I tried to send a message to her by mirror talk, but no one replied. I want her to hear my story. I want to ...'

'I know. There will be a service. We have to exculpate Prefect Corin after he sets the torch to ... well, to the prisoners. Then there's a formal meal, but I'm not invited to that, of course. It begins two hours after sunset, and I'll come then. And I'll find a way of bringing Derev.'

'Have you ever seen an execution, Ananda?'

Ananda poured more pistachios into his palm. He looked at them and said, 'No. No, I haven't. Oh, I know everything that will happen, of course, and I know what I have to do, but I'm not sure how I'll act.'

'You will not disgrace your master. I will see you two hours after sunset. And make sure to bring Derev.'

'As if I would forget.' Ananda tipped the pistachios into the dirt and brushed his hands together. 'The landlord of the tavern was an addict of the drug that Dismas used, did you know that? Dismas supplied him with it, and he'd do anything asked of him. It didn't lessen the sentence, of course, but it was how he pleaded.'

Yama remembered Dr Dismas grinding dried beetles and clear, apricot-scented liquid into paste, the sudden relaxation of his face after he had injected himself.

'Cantharides,' he said. 'And Lob and Lud did it for money.'

'Well, Lob had his payment, at least,' Ananda said. 'He was drunk when he was arrested, and I hear he'd been buying the whole town drinks for several days before that. I think he knew that you'd be back.'

Yama remembered that Lob and Lud had not been paid by Dr Dismas. Where then had Lob got the money for his drinking spree? And who had rescued him from the old tomb, and taken him to the tower of Beatrice and Osric? With a cold pang, he realized who it must have been, and how she had known where to find him.

Ananda had turned to watch the soldiers wheel out on the parade square, one line becoming two that marched off side by side towards the main gate, with Sergeant Rhodean loudly counting the pace as he marched at their head. After a while, Ananda said, 'Did you ever think that Lob and Lud were a little bit like you? They wanted to escape this place, too.'

Yama wanted to watch Lob and the landlord of the tavern leave the peel-house for the place of execution, but even that was denied him. Zakiel found him at a window, staring down at the courtyard where soldiers were harnessing the stamping horses to the white waggon, and took him off to the library.

'We have only a little time, master, and there is so much to tell you.'

'Then why begin to try? Are you going to the executions, Zakiel?'

'It is not my place, master.'

'I suppose that my father told you to keep me occupied. I want to see it, Zakiel. They are trying to exclude me from it all. I suppose it is to spare my feelings. But imagining it is worse than knowing.'

'I have taught you something, then. I was beginning to wonder.'

133

Zakiel rarely smiled, but he smiled now. He was a tall, gaunt man, with a long, heavy-browed face and a shaven skull with a bony crest. His black skin shone in the yellow light of the flickering electric sconce, and the muscles of his heavy jaws moved under the skin on either side of the crest when he smiled. As a party piece, on high day feasts, he would crack walnuts between his strong square teeth. As always, he wore a grey tunic and grey leggings, and sandals soled with rubber that squeaked on the polished marquetry of the paths between the library stacks. He wore a slave collar around his neck, but it was made of a light alloy, not iron, and covered with a circlet of handmade lace.

Zakiel said, 'I could tell you what will happen, if you like. I was instructed in it, because it is believed that to tell the prisoner exactly what will happen to him will make it endurable. But it was the cruellest thing they did, far crueller than being put to question.'

Zakiel had been sentenced to death before he had come to work for the Aedile. Yama, who had forgotten that, was mortified. He said, 'I was not thinking. I am sorry. No, do not tell me.'

'You would rather see it. You believe your senses, but not words. Yet the long-dead men and women who wrote all these volumes which stand about us had the same appetites as us, the same fears, the same ambitions. All we know of the world passes through our sensory organs and is reduced to electric impulses in certain sensory nerve fibres. When you open one of these books and read of events that happened before you were born, some of those nerve fibres are stimulated in exactly the same way.'

'I want to see for myself. Reading about it is different.'

Zakiel cracked his knuckles. They were swollen, like all of his joints. His fingers looked like strings of nuts.

'Why, perhaps I have not taught you anything after all. Of course it is different. What books do is allow you to share the perceptions of those who write them. There are certain wizards who claim to be able to read minds, and mountebanks who claim to have discovered ancient machines that print out a person's thoughts, or project them in a sphere of glass or crystal metal, but the wizards and mountebanks lie. Only books allow us to share another's thoughts. By reading them, we see the world not through our senses, but through those of their authors. And if those authors are wiser than us, or more knowing, or more sensitive, then so are we while we read. I will say no more about this. I know you would read the world directly, and tomorrow you will no longer have to listen to old Zakiel. But I would give you something, if I may. A slave owns nothing, not even his own life, so this is in the nature of a loan, but I have the Aedile's permission.'

Zakiel led Yama deeper into the stacks, where books stood two-deep on shelves that bent under their weight. He pulled a ladder from a recess, set its hooked top on the lip of the highest shelf, and climbed up. He fussed there for a minute, blowing dust from one book after another, and finally climbed down with a volume no bigger than his hand.

'I knew I had it,' he said, 'although I have not touched it since I first catalogued the library. Even the Aedile does not know of this. It was left by one of his predecessors; that is the way this library has grown, and why there is so much of little value. Yet some hold that gems are engendered in mud, and this book is such a gem. It is yours.'

It was bound in a black, artificial stuff that, although scuffed at the corners, shone as if newly made when Zakiel wiped away the dust with the hem of his tunic. Yama riffled the pages of the book. They were stiff and slick, and seemed to contain a hidden depth. When he tilted the pages to the light, images came and went in the margins of the crisp double-columned print. He had expected some rare history of Ys, or a bestiary, like those he had loved to read when he was younger, but this was no more than a copy of the Puranas.

Yama said, 'If my father told you to give me this book, then how is it that he does not know he owns it?'

'I asked if I could give you a volume of the Puranas, and so I have. But this edition is very old, and differs in some details from that which I have taught you. It is an edition that has long been suppressed, and perhaps this is the only copy of that edition which now exists.'

'It is different?'

'In some parts. You must read it all to find out, and remember what I have taught you. So perhaps my teachings will continue, in some fashion. Or you could simply look at the pictures. Modern editions do not, of course, have pictures.'

Yama, who had been tilting the pages of the book to the light as he turned them, suddenly felt a shock of recognition. There in the margin of one of the last pages was the view he had glimpsed behind the face of his ancestor, of stars streaming inwards towards a dull glow.

He said, 'I will read it, Zakiel. I promise.'

For a moment Zakiel stared at Yama in silence, his black eyes inscrutable beneath the bony shelf of his brow. Then the librarian smiled and clapped dust from his big, bony hands. 'Very good, master. Very good. Now we will drink some tea, and talk on the history of the department of which, when you reach Ys, you will be the newest and youngest member.'

'With respect, Zakiel, I am sure that the history of the department will be the first thing I will be taught when I arrive in Ys, and no doubt the clerk will have some words on it during our journey.'

'I do not think that Prefect Corin is a man who wastes words,' Zakiel said. 'And he does not see himself as a teacher.'

'My father would have you occupy my mind. I understand. Well then, I would like to hear something of the history of another department. One that was broken up a long time ago. Is that possible?'

12 ~ The Execution

After sunset, Yama climbed to the heliograph platform that circled the top of the tallest of the peel-house's towers. He uncapped the observation telescope and, turning it on the heavy steel gimbals which floated in sealed oil baths, lined up its declination and equatorial axes in a combination he knew as well as his own name.

Beyond the darkening vanishing point, the tops of the towers that rose up from the heart of Ys shone in the last light of the sun like a cluster of fiery needles floating high above the world, higher than the naked peaks of the Rim Mountains. Ys! In his room, Yama had spent a little time gazing at his old map before reluctantly rolling it up and putting it away. He had traced the roads that crossed the barrens of the coastal plains, the passes through the mountains that embraced the city. He vowed now that in a handful of days he would stand at the base of the towers as a free man.

When he put up the telescope and leaned at the rail, with warm air gusting around him, he saw prickles of light flickering in the middle distance. Messages. The air was full of messages, talking of war, of far-away battles and sieges at the midpoint of the world.

Yama walked to the other side of the tower and stared out across the wide shallow valley of the Breas towards Aeolis, and saw with a little shock that the execution pyre had already been kindled. The point of light flickered like a baleful star fallen to the ground outside the wall of the little city.

'They would have killed me,' he said, trying out the words, 'if there was money in it.'

Yama watched for a long time, until the distant fire began to dim and was outshone by the ordinary lights of the city. Lob and the landlord of *The House of Ghost Lanterns* were dead. The Aedile and the colourless man, the clerk, Prefect Corin, would be in grave procession towards the temple, led by Father Quine and flanked by Sergeant Rhodean's men in polished black armour.

His supper had been set out in his room, but he left it and went down to the kitchen and, armoured by his new authority, hacked a wedge from a wheel of cheese and took a melon, a bottle of yellow wine, and one of the heavy date loaves that had been baked that morning. He cut through the kitchen gardens, fooled the watchdogs for the last time, and walked along the high road before plunging down the steep slope of the bluff and following the paths along the tops of the dikes which divided the flooded paeolin fields.

The clear, shallow Breas made a rushing noise in the darkness as it ran swiftly over the flat rocks of its bed. At the waterlift, two oxen plodded side by side around their circle, harnessed to the trimmed trunk of a young pine. This spar turned the shaft that, groaning as if in protest at its eternal torment, lifted a chain of buckets from the river and tipped them in a never-ending cascade into the channels which fed the irrigation system of the paeolin fields. The oxen walked in their circle under a roof of palm fronds, their tails rhythmically slapping their dung-spattered flanks. Now and then they snatched a mouthful of the fodder scattered around the perimeter of their circular path, but mostly they walked with their heads down, from nowhere to nowhere.

No, Yama thought, I will not serve.

He sat on an upturned stone a little distance off the path and ate meltingly sweet slices of melon while he waited. The oxen plodded around and around, turning the groaning shaft. Frogs peeped in the flooded paeolin fields. Beyond the city, at the mouth of the Breas, the misty light of the Arm of the Warrior was lifting above the far horizon. It would rise a little later each night, a little further downriver. Soon it would not rise at all, and the Eye of the Preservers would appear above the upriver vanishing point, and it would be summer. But before then Yama would be in Ys.

Two people were coming along the path, shadows moving through the Galaxy's blue twilight. Yama waited until they had gone past before he whistled sharply.

'We thought you might not be here,' Ananda said as he walked up to where Yama sat.

'Well met,' Derev said, at Ananda's shoulder. The Galaxy put blue shadows in the unbound mass of her white hair and a spark in each of her large, dark eyes. 'O, well met, Yama!'

She rushed forward and hugged him. Her light-boned body, her long slim arms and legs, her heat, her scent. Yama was always surprised to discover that Derev was taller than himself. Despite the cold certainty he had nursed ever since Ananda's remark about Lob's drunken spree, his love rekindled in her embrace. It was an effort not to respond, and he hated himself because it seemed a worse betrayal than anything she might have done.

Derev drew back a little and said, 'What's wrong?'

Yama said, 'I am glad you came. There is something I want to ask you.'

Derev smiled and moved her arms in a graceful circle, making the wide sleeves of her white dress floatingly glimmer in the half-dark. 'Anything! As long, of course, as I can hear your story. All of it, not just the highlights.'

Ananda found the wedge of cheese and began to pare slices from it. 'I've been fasting,' he explained. 'Water for breakfast, water for lunch.'

'And pistachios,' Yama said.

'I never said I would make a good priest. I am supposed to be cleaning out the narthex while Father Quine dines with the Aedile and Prefect Corin. This is a strange place to meet, Yama.'

'There was something Dr Dismas once said to me, about the habits we fall into. I wanted to be reminded of it.'

Derev said, 'But you are all right. You have recovered from your adventures.'

'I learned much from them.'

'And you will tell all,' Ananda said. He handed around slices of bread and cheese, and pried the cork out of the wine bottle with his little knife. 'I think,' he said, 'that you should start at the beginning.'

The story seemed far stranger and more exciting than the actual experience. To tell it concisely, Yama had to miss out the fear and tension he had felt during every moment of his adventures, the long hours of discomfort when he had tried to sleep in wet clothes on the trunk of the banyan, his growing hunger and thirst while wandering the hot shaly land of the Silent Quarter of the City of the Dead.

As he talked, he remembered a dream he had had while sleeping on the catafalque inside the old tomb in the Silent Quarter. He had dreamed that he had been swimming in the Great River, and that a current had suddenly caught him and swept him towards the edge of the world, where the river fell away in thunder and spray. He had tried to swim against the current, but his arms had been trapped at his sides and he had been helplessly swept through swift white water towards the tremendous noise of the river's fall. The oppressive helplessness of the dream had stayed with him all that morning, right up to the moment when Lud and Lob had caught up with him, but he had forgotten about it until now. And now it seemed important, as if dream and reality were, during the telling of his tale, coterminous. He told his two friends about the dream as if it were one more part of his adventures, and then described how Lob and Lud had surprised him, and how he had killed Lud by accident.

'I had found an old knife, and Lob got hold of it, ready to kill me because I had killed his brother. But the knife hurt him. It seemed to turn into something like a ghoul, or a giant spider. I ran, I am ashamed to say. I left him with his dead brother.'

'He would have killed you,' Derev said. 'Of course you should have run.'

Yama said, 'I should have killed him. The knife would have done it for me if I had not taken it, I think. It helped me, like the ghost ship.'

'Lob escaped,' Ananda said. 'He wanted his father to condemn you for the murder of his brother, the fool, but then you came back. Lob had already convicted himself, and Unprac confessed to his part as soon as he was arrested.'

Unprac was the name of the landlord of *The House of Ghost Lanterns*. Yama had not known it until the trial.

'So I killed Lob anyway. I should have killed him then, in the tomb. It would have been a cleaner death. It was a poor bargain he got in the end.'

'That's what they said about the farmer,' Derev said, 'after the girl fox had lain with him and took his baby in payment.'

Suddenly, with a feeling like falling, Yama saw Derev's face as a stranger might. All planes, with large dark eyes and a small mouth and a bump of a nose, framed by a fall of white hair that moved in the slightest breeze as if possessed with an independent life. They had pursued each other all last summer, awakened to the possibilities of each other's bodies. They had lain in the long dry grasses between the tombs and tasted each other's mouths, each other's skin. He had felt the swell of her small

140

breasts, traced the bowl of her pelvis, the elegant length of her arms, her legs. They had not made love; they had sworn that they would not make love together until they were married. Now, he was glad that they had not.

He said, 'Do you keep doves, Derev?'

'You know that my father does. For sacrifice. Some palmers still come here to pray at the temple's shrine. Mostly they don't want doves, though, but flowers or fruit.'

'There were no palmers this year,' Ananda said.

'When the war is over, they'll come again,' Derev said. 'My father clips the wings of the doves. It would be a bad omen if they escaped in the middle of the sacrifice.'

Ananda said, 'You mean that it would be bad for his trade.'

Derev laughed. 'Then the desires of the Preservers are equal to those of my father, and I am glad.'

'There is one more mystery,' Yama said, and explained that he had been knocked unconscious by a fall and had woken elsewhere, in a little room of a hollowed crag far from the Great River's shore, watched by an old man and an old woman who claimed to be curators of the City of the Dead.

'They showed me a marvel. It was a picture slate from a tomb, and it showed someone of my bloodline. It was as if they had been waiting for me, and I have been thinking about what they showed me ever since I was returned here.'

Derev had the bottle of wine. She took a long swallow from it and said, 'But that's good! That's wonderful! In less than a decad you have found two people of your bloodline.'

Yama said, 'The man in the picture was alive before the building of Confluence. I imagine he is long dead. What is interesting is that the curators already knew about me, for they had the picture slate ready, and they also had prepared a route from their hiding place to the very grounds of the peel-house. That was how I returned. One of them, the woman, was of your bloodline, Derev.'

'Well, so are many. We are traders and merchants. We are to be found throughout the length and breadth of Confluence.'

Derev looked coolly at Yama when she said this, and his heart meltingly turned. It was hard to continue, but he had to. He said, 'I did not think much of it for that very reason, and I did not even make very

141

much of the fact that, like you, they had a fund of cautionary sayings and stories concerning magical foxes. But they kept doves. I wonder, if I looked amongst your father's doves, if I would find some that were not clipped. I think you use them to keep in touch with your people.'

Ananda said, 'What is this, Yama? You make a trial here.'

Derev said, 'It's all right, Ananda. Yama, my father said that you might have guessed. That was why he did not allow me to go to the peel-house, or to talk with you using the mirror. But I came here anyway. I wanted to see you. Tell me what you know, and I'll tell you what we know. How did you guess that I helped you?'

'I think that the old woman, Beatrice, had a son, and that he is your father. When Lob returned to Aeolis, you gave him money and got him drunk to learn his story. I know that he had not been paid by Dr Dismas, so he had to get the money from somewhere. You found me, and took me to your grandparents. They made up a story about looking for a lost goat and finding me instead, but they ate only vegetables. As do you and your parents, Derev.'

'They make cheese from goats' milk,' Derev said. 'And they *did* lose one last year, to a leopard. But you more or less have the truth. I'm not sure what scared me more, getting Lob drunk, or climbing down the cliff using the rope he had left behind and picking my way through the dark tomb to find you.'

'Did your family come here because of me? Am I so important, or am I merely foolish to believe it? Why are you interested in me?'

'Because you are of a bloodline which vanished from the world long ago. My family have stayed true to the old department as no others of my bloodline have. We revere the dead, and keep the memory of their lives as best we can, but we do not remember your bloodline, except in legends from the beginning of the world. Beatrice isn't my grandmother, although she and her husband came to live at the tower after my great-grandparents died. My grandparents wanted a normal life, you see. They established a business downriver and my father inherited it, but Beatrice and her husband persuaded him to move here because of you.' She paused. She said, 'I know you are destined for great things, but it doesn't change what I feel for you.'

Yama remembered Beatrice's verse and recited, '*Let fame, that all hunt after in their lives, Live registered upon our brazen tombs.*'

Derev said, 'Yes, it's a favourite verse of Beatrice's. She has always said that it was far older than Confluence. But we keep the memory of all the dead alive, even if no one else will.'

Yama said, 'Am I then of the dead?'

Derev walked about, pumping her elbows in and out as was her habit when agitated. Her white dress glimmered in the light of the outflung arm of the Galaxy. 'You were very ill when I found you. You had been lying there all night. I took you to Beatrice and Osric by the keel road and they saved your life, using old machines. I didn't know what else to do. I thought you might die if I took you to Aeolis, or if I went to fetch the soldiers who were looking for you. Well, it is time you knew that my family have been watching over you. After all, Dr Dismas found out about you and put you in peril. So might others, and you should be ready.'

Ananda said, 'What are you saying, Derev? That you're some kind of spy? On which side?'

Yama laughed. 'Derev is no spy. She is anxious that I should receive my inheritance, such as it is.'

'My father and mother know, too. It isn't just me. At first, I didn't even know why we came here.'

Ananda had drunk most of the wine. He tipped the bottle to get the last swallow, wiped his mouth on his sleeve, and said gravely, 'So you don't want to sell rubbish to sailors and Mud Men, Derev? There's no harm in that. It's good that you want to keep to the old ways of your people.'

'The Department of the Curators of the City of the Dead was disbanded long ago,' Yama said, looking at Derev.

'It was defeated,' Derev said, 'but it endures. There are not many of us now. We mostly live in the mountains, or in Ys.'

'Why are you interested in me?'

'You've seen the picture,' Derev said. She had turned her back to Yama and Ananda, and was looking out across the swampy fields towards the ridge at the far side of the Breas's valley. 'I don't know why you're important. My father thinks that it is to do with the ship of the Ancients of Days. Beatrice and Osric know more, I think, but won't tell even me all they know. They have many secrets.'

Ananda said, 'The ship of the Ancients of Days passed downriver long before Yama was born.'

Derev ignored his interruption. 'The Ancients of Days left to explore

143

the neighbouring galaxy long before the Preservers achieved godhead. They left more than five million years ago, while the stars of the Galaxy were still being moved into their present patterns. It was long before the Puranas were written, or the Eye of the Preservers was made, or Confluence was built.'

'So they claimed,' Ananda said. 'But there is no word of them in the Puranas.'

'They returned to find all that they knew had passed into the Eye of the Preservers, and that they were the last of their kind. They landed at Ys, travelled downriver and sailed away from Confluence for the galaxy they had forsaken so long ago, but they left their ideas behind.'

'They turned innocent unfallen bloodlines against the word of the Preservers,' Ananda said. 'They woke old technologies and created armies of monsters to spread their heresies.'

'And twenty years later you were born, Yama.'

'So were many others,' Ananda said. 'All three of us here were born after the war began. Derev makes a fantasy.'

'Beatrice and Osric think that Yama's bloodline is the one which built Confluence,' Derev told Ananda. 'Perhaps the Preservers raised his bloodline up for just that task and then dispersed it, or perhaps as a reward it passed over with the Preservers when they fell into the Eye and vanished from the Universe. In any event, it disappeared from Confluence long ago. And yet Yama is here now, at a time of great danger.'

Ananda said, 'The Preservers needed no help in creating Confluence. They spoke a word, and it was so.'

'It was a very long word,' Derev said. She lifted her arms above her head, and raised herself up on the points of her toes, as graceful as a dancer. She was remembering something she had learned long ago. She said, 'It was longer than the words in the nuclei of our cells which define what we are. If all the different instructions for all the different bloodlines of Confluence were put together it would not be one hundredth of the length of the word which defined the initial conditions necessary for the creation of Confluence. That word was a set of instructions or rules. Yama's bloodline was part of those instructions.'

Ananda said, 'This is heresy, Derev. I'm a bad priest, but I know the sound of heresy. The Preservers needed no help in making Confluence.'

'Let her explain,' Yama said.

Ananda stood. 'It's lies,' he said flatly. 'Her people deceive themselves

144

that they know more of Confluence and the Preservers than is written in the Puranas. They spin elaborate sophistries, and delude themselves with dreams of hidden power, and they have snared you, Yama. Come with me. Don't listen any more. You leave for Ys tomorrow. Don't be fooled into thinking that you are more than you are.'

Derev said, 'We don't pretend to understand what we remember. It is simply our duty. It was the duty of our bloodline since the foundation of Confluence, and my family are among the last to keep that duty. After the defeat of the department, my bloodline were scattered the length and breadth of the Great River. They became traders and merchants. My grandparents and my father wanted to be like them, but my father was called back.'

Yama said, 'Sit down, Ananda. Please. Help me understand.'

Ananda said, 'I don't think you're fully recovered, Yama. You've been ill. That part I believe. You have always wanted to see yourself as the centre of the world, for you have no centre to your own life. Derev is treating you cruelly, and I'll hear no more. You've even forgotten about the execution. Let me tell you that Unprac died badly, screaming to the Preservers for aid with one breath, and cursing them and all who watched with the next. Lob was stoic. For all his faults, he died a man.'

'That is cruel, Ananda,' Yama said.

'It's the truth. Farewell, friend Yama. If you must dream of glory, dream of being an ordinary soldier and of giving your life for the Preservers. All else is vanity.'

Yama did not try to stop Ananda. He knew how stubborn his friend could be. He watched as Ananda walked away beside the noisy river, a shadow against the blue-white arch of the Galaxy. Yama hoped that the young priest would at least turn and wave farewell.

But he did not.

Derev said, 'You must believe me, Yama. At first I became your friend because it was my duty. But that quickly changed. I would not be here if it had not.'

Yama smiled. He could not stay angry at her; if she had deceived him, it was because she had believed that she was helping him.

They fell into each other's arms and breathlessly kissed and rekissed. He felt her heat pressing through their clothes, the quick patter of her heart like a bird beating at the cage of her ribs. Her hair fell around his face like a trembling veil: he might drown in its dry scent.

After a while, he said, 'If you took me to Beatrice and Osric, and they nursed me back to health, then what of the ghost ship? Do they claim that, too?'

Derev's eyes shone a handspan from his. She said, 'I'd never heard of it before you told me your story. But there are many strange things on the river, Yama. It is always changing.'

'Yet always the same,' Yama said, remembering Caphis's tattoo, the snake swallowing its own tail. He added, 'You thought that the anchorite we saved from Lud and Lob was one of my bloodline.'

'Perhaps he was the first generation, born just after the ship of the Ancients of Days arrived.'

'There may be hundreds of my bloodline by now, Derev. Thousands!'

'That's what I think. I told Beatrice and Osric about the anchorite, but they didn't seem to be very interested. Perhaps I was mistaken about him being of your bloodline, but I do not think I was. He gave you a coin. You should take it with you.'

'So he did. I had forgotten it.'

13 ~ The Palmers

Yama discovered the knife at the bottom of his satchel on the first evening of his journey to Ys in the company of Prefect Corin. Yama had given the knife to Sergeant Rhodean that morning, because Prefect Corin had said that it was not the kind of thing an apprentice should own. The Prefect had been quite specific about what Yama could and could not carry; before they had set off he had looked through Yama's satchel and had removed the knife and the carefully folded map of Ys and the horn-handled pocket-knife which had once belonged to Telmon. Yama had been able to take little with him but a change of clothes and the money given to him by the Aedile. He had the copy of the Puranas and the anchorite's coin, which he wore around his neck, inside his shirt, but because they had been given to him so recently they did not yet seem like proper possessions.

Sergeant Rhodean must have slipped the knife back into the satchel when Yama had been making his farewells. It was sheathed in brown and white goatskin and tucked beneath Yama's spare shirt and trousers. Yama was pleased to see it, even though it still made him uneasy. He knew that all heroes carried weapons with special attributes, and he was determined to be a hero. He was still very young.

Prefect Corin asked him what he had found. Reluctantly, Yama slipped the knife from its sheath and held it up in the firelight. A blue sheen slowly extended from its hilt to the point of its curved blade. It emitted a faint high-pitched buzz, and a sharp smell like discharged electricity.

'I am certain that Sergeant Rhodean meant well,' Prefect Corin said, 'but you will not need that. If we are attacked, it will do nothing but put you in danger. In any case, it is very unlikely that we will be attacked.'

Prefect Corin sat crosslegged on the other side of the small campfire, neat and trim in his homespun tunic and grey leggings. He was smoking a long-stemmed clay pipe which he held clenched between his small even teeth. His ironshod staff was stuck in the ground behind him. They had walked all day at a steady pace, and this was the most he had said to Yama at any one time.

Yama said, 'That is why I gave it away, dominie, but it has come back.'

'It is not regulation.'

'Well, but I am not yet an apprentice,' Yama said. He added, 'Perhaps I could make a gift of it to the Department.'

'That is possible,' Prefect Corin allowed. 'Tributes are not unknown. Weapons like that are generally loyal to their owner, but loyalty can be broken with suitable treatment. Well, we cannot leave it here. You may carry it, but do not think to try to use it.'

But after Prefect Corin had fallen asleep, Yama took out the knife and practised the passes and thrusts that Sergeant Rhodean had taught him, and later slept sweetly and deeply, with the point of the knife thrust into the warm ashes of the campfire.

The next day, as before, Yama dutifully walked three paces behind Prefect Corin along raised paths between the flooded fields that made an intricate green and brown quilt along the margin of the river. It was the planting season, and the fields were being ploughed by teams of water buffalo commanded by small, naked boys who controlled their charges with no more than shouts and vigorous application of long bamboo switches.

A cool wind blew from the Great River, ruffling the brown waters which flooded the fields, stirring the bright green flags of the bamboos and the clumps of elephant grass that grew at the places where the corners of four fields met. Yama and Prefect Corin rose just before dawn and prayed and walked until it was too hot, and sheltered in the shade of a tree until early evening, when, after a brief prayer, they walked again until the Galaxy began to rise above the river.

Ordinarily, Yama would have enjoyed this adventure, but Prefect Corin was an impassive, taciturn companion. He did not comment on anything they saw, but was like a machine moving implacably through the sunlit world, noticing only what was necessary. He responded with no more than a grunt when Yama pointed to a fleet of argosies far out across the glittering waters of the Great River; he ignored the ruins they passed, even a long sandstone cliff-face which had been carved with pillars and friezes and statues of men and beasts around gaping doors; he ignored the little villages which could be glimpsed amongst stands of palms, flowering magnolias and pines on the ridge of the old river bank in the blue distance, or which stood on islands of higher ground amongst the mosaic of flooded fields; he ignored the fishermen who worked the margin of the Great River beyond the weedy gravel banks and mud flats revealed by the river's retreat, fishermen who stood thigh-deep in the shallows and cast circular nets across the water, or who sat in tiny bark boats further out, using black cormorants tethered by one leg to catch fish. (Yama thought of the verse which the old curator, Beatrice, had recited to him. Had its author seen the ancestors of these fishermen? He understood then a little of what Zakiel had tried to teach him, that books were not obdurate thickets of glyphs but transparent windows, looking out through another's eyes on to a familiar world, or on to a world which lived only when the book was read, and vanished when it was set down.)

The mud walls of the straw-thatched huts of the villages often incorporated slates stolen from tombs, so that pictures from the past (as often as not sideways or upside down) flashed with vibrant colours amongst the poverty of the peasants' lives. Chickens and black pigs ran amongst the huts, chased by naked toddlers. Women pounded grain or gutted fish or mended fishing nets, watched by impassive men sitting in the doorways of their huts or beneath shade trees, smoking clay pipes or sipping green tea from chipped glasses.

In one village there was a stone pen with a small dragon coiled on the white sand inside it. The dragon was black, with a double row of diamond-shaped plates along its ridged back, and it slept with its long, scaley snout on its forelegs, like a dog. Flies clustered around its long-lashed eyes; it stank of sulphur and marsh gas. Yama remembered the abortive hunt at the end of last summer, before poor Telmon went away, and would have liked to see more of this wonder, but Prefect Corin strode past without sparing it a single glance.

Sometimes the villagers came out to watch Yama and Prefect Corin go by, and little boys ran up to try and sell them wedges of watermelon or polished quartz pebbles or charms woven of thorny twigs. Prefect Corin ignored the animated crowds of little boys; he did not even trouble to use his staff to clear a way but simply pushed through them as through a thicket. Yama was left behind to apologize and ask for indulgence, saying over and over that they had no money. It was almost true. Yama had the two gold rials which the Aedile had given him, but one of those would buy an entire village, and he had no smaller coins. And Prefect Corin had nothing but his staff and his hat, his leggings and his homespun tunic, his sandals and his blanket, and a few small tools packed inside the leather purse that hung from his belt.

'Be careful of him,' the Aedile had whispered, when he had embraced Yama in farewell. 'Do all he asks of you, but no more than that. Reveal no more than is necessary. He will seize on any weakness, any difference, and use it against you. It is their way.'

The Prefect was a spare, ascetic man. He drank tea made from fragments of dusty bark and ate only dried fruit and the yeasty buds of manna lichen picked from rocks, although he let Yama cook the rabbits and lizards he caught in wire snares set each evening. As he walked, Yama ate ghostberries picked from thickets which grew amongst ruined tombs, but the ghostberries were almost over now and difficult to find under the new leaves of the bushes, and Prefect Corin would not allow Yama to move more than a few paces from the edge of the path. There were traps amongst the tombs, he said, and ghouls and worse things at night. Yama did not argue with him, but apart from the necessities of toilet he was never out of Prefect Corin's sight. There were a hundred moments when he wanted to make a run for it. But not yet. Not yet. He was learning patience, at least.

The stretches of uncultivated country between the villages grew wider. There were fewer flooded fields and more ruined tombs, overgrown with creepers and moss amidst rustling stands of bamboo or clumps of date or oil palms, or copses of dark green swamp cypress. Then they passed the last village and the road widened into a long, straight pavement. It was like the ancient road that ran between the river and the edge of the Silent Quarter downriver of Aeolis, Yama thought, and then he realized that it was the same road.

It was the third day of the journey. They camped that night in a hollow with tall pines leaning above. Wind moved through the doffing branches of the pines. The Great River stretched away towards the Galaxy, which even at this late hour showed only the upper part of the Arm of the Warrior above the horizon, with the Blue Diadem gleaming cold and sharp at the upflung terminus of the lanes of misty starlight. Halo stars were like dimming coals scattered sparsely across the cold hearth of the sky; the smudged specks of distant galaxies could be seen here and there.

Yama lay near the little fire on a soft, deep layer of brown pine needles and thought of the Ancients of Days and wondered what it might be like to plunge through the emptiness between galaxies for longer than Confluence had been in existence. And the Ancients of Days had not possessed one hundredth of the power of their distant children, the Preservers.

Yama asked Prefect Corin if he had ever seen the Ancients of Days after they had arrived at Ys. For a long time, the man did not answer, and Yama began to believe that he had not been heard, or that Prefect Corin had simply ignored the question. But at last the Prefect knocked out his pipe on the heel of his boot and said, 'I saw two of them once. I was a boy, a little older than you, and newly apprenticed. They were both tall, and as alike as brothers, with black hair and faces as white as new paper. We say that some bloodlines have white skin – your own is very pale – but we mean that it has no pigmentation in it, except that it is suffused by the blood in the tissues beneath. But this was a true white, as if their faces had been powdered with chalk. They wore long white shirts that left their arms and legs bare, and little machines hung from their belts. I was in the Day Market with the oldest of the apprentices, carrying the spices he had bought. The two Ancients of Days walked through the aisles at the head of a great crowd and passed by as close to me as you are now.

'They should have been killed, all of them. Unfortunately, it was not a decision the Department could make, although even then, in Ys, it was possible to see that their ideas were dangerous. Confluence survives only because it does not change. The Preservers unite us because it is to them that each department swears its loyalty, and so no department shows particular favour to any of the bloodlines of Confluence. The Ancients of Days have infected their allies with the heresy that each bloodline, indeed every individual, might have an intrinsic worth. They promote the individual above society, change above duty. You should reflect on why this is wrong, Yama.'

'Is it true that there are wars in Ys now? That different departments fight each other, even in the Palace of the Memory of the People?'

Prefect Corin gave him a sharp look across the little fire and said, 'You have been listening to the wrong kind of gossip.'

Yama was thinking of the curators of the City of the Dead, whose resistance had dwindled to a stubborn refusal to yield to the flow of history. Perhaps Derev would be the last of them. He said, trying to draw out the Prefect, 'But surely there are disputes about whether one department or another should carry out a particular duty. I have heard that outmoded departments sometimes resist amalgamation or disbandment, and I have also heard that these disputes are increasing, and that the Department of Indigenous Affairs is training most of its apprentices to be soldiers.'

'You have a lot to learn,' Prefect Corin said. He tamped tobacco into the bowl of his pipe and lit it before adding, 'Apprentices do not choose the way in which they serve the Department, and you are too young to be an apprentice in any case. You have had an odd childhood, with what amounts to three fathers and no mother. You have far too much pride and not enough education, and most of that in odd bits of history and philosophy and cosmology, and far too much in the arts of soldiering. Even before you can be accepted as an apprentice, you will have to catch up in all the areas your education has neglected.'

Yama said, 'I think I might make a good soldier.'

Prefect Corin drew on his pipe and looked at Yama with narrowed eyes. They were small and close together, and gleamed palely in his black-furred face. The white stripe ran past the outer corner of his left eye. Eventually he said, 'I came down here to execute two men because their crimes involved the Aedile's private life. That is the way it is done in the Department. It demonstrates that the Department supports the action of its man, and it ensures that none of the local staff have to do the job. That way, there is no one for the locals to take revenge on, with the exception of the Aedile himself, and no one will do that as long as he commands his garrison, because he has the authority of the Preservers. I agreed to bring you to Ys because it is my duty. It does not mean I owe you anything, especially answers to your questions. Now get some sleep.'

Later, long after the Prefect had rolled himself in his blanket and gone to sleep, Yama cautiously stood and backed away from the fire, which had burnt down to white ash around a dimming core of glowing coals. The road stretched away between hummocks of dry friable stone and clumps of pines. Its paved surface gleamed faintly in the light of the

Galaxy. Yama settled his pack on his shoulders and set off. He wanted to go to Ys, but he was determined not to become an apprentice clerk, and after the final dismissal of his worth he thought that he could not bear Prefect Corin's company a day longer.

He had not gone very far down the road when he heard a dry rattle in the darkness ahead. Yama put his hand on the hilt of his knife, but did not draw it from its sheath in case its light betrayed him. He advanced cautiously, his eyes wide, his whole skin tingling, his blood rustling in his ears. Then a stone smashed onto the paved road behind him! He whirled around, and another stone exploded at his feet. A fragment cut his shin, and he felt blood trickle into his boot.

He gripped the knife tightly and said, 'Who is it? Show yourself.'

Silence, and then Prefect Corin stepped up behind Yama and gripped the wrist of his right hand and said in his ear, 'You have a lot to learn, boy.'

'A clever trick,' Yama said. He felt oddly calm, as if he had expected this all along.

After a moment Prefect Corin released him and said, 'It is lucky for you I played it, and no one else.' Yama had never seen Prefect Corin smile, but in the blue light of the Galaxy he saw the man's lips compress in what might have been the beginning of a smile. 'I promised to look after you, and so I will. Meanwhile, no more games. All right?'

'All right,' Yama said.

'Good. You need to sleep. We still have a long way to go.'

Early the next day, Yama and Prefect Corin passed a group of palmers. They soon left the group behind, but the palmers caught up with them that night and camped a little way off. They numbered more than two decads, men and women in dust-stained orange robes, their heads cleanly shaven and painted with interlocked curves which represented the Eye of the Preservers. They were a slightly built people, with pinched faces under swollen, bicephalic foreheads, and leathery skin mottled with brown and black patches. Like Prefect Corin, they carried only staffs, bedrolls, and little purses hung from their belts. They sang in clear high voices around their campfire, welding close harmonies that carried a long way across the dry stones and the empty tombs of the hillside.

Yama and Prefect Corin had made camp under a group of fig trees beside the road. A little spring rose amongst the trees, a gush of clear water that fell from the gaping mouth of a stone carved with the likeness of a fierce, bearded face into a shallow pool curbed with flat rocks. The road had turned away from the Great River, climbing a switchback of low, gentle hills dotted with creosote scrub and clumps of saw-toothed palmettos as it rose towards the pass.

The priest who was in charge of the palmers came over to talk with Prefect Corin. His group was from a city a thousand leagues downriver. They had been travelling for half a year, first by a merchant ship and then by foot after the ship had been laid up for repairs after having been attacked by water bandits. The palmers were archivists on their way to the Palace of the Memory of the People, to tell into the records the stories of all those who had died in their city in the last ten years, and to ask for guidance from the prognosticators.

The priest was a large smooth-skinned man by the name of Belarius. He had a ready smile and a habit of mopping sweat from his bare scalp and the fat folds of skin at the back of his neck with a square of cloth. His smooth, chrome-yellow skin shone like butter. He offered Prefect Corin a cigarette and was not offended when his offer was refused, and without prompting started to talk about the risks of travelling by foot. He had heard that there were roving bands of deserters abroad in the land, in addition to the usual bandits.

'Near the battlelines, perhaps,' Prefect Corin said. 'Not this far upriver.' He drew on his pipe and stared judiciously at the fat priest. 'Are you armed?'

Belarius smiled – his smile was as wide as a frog's, and Yama thought that he could probably hold a whole watermelon slice in his mouth. The priest said, 'We are palmers, not soldiers.'

'But you have knives to prepare your food, machetes to cut firewood, that kind of thing?'

'Oh yes.'

'A large group like yours need not worry. It is people travelling alone, or by two or by three, who are vulnerable.'

Belarius mopped at his scalp. His smile grew wider. He said eagerly, 'And you have seen nothing?'

'But for the chattering of this boy, it has been a quiet journey.'

Yama smarted at Prefect Corin's remark, but said nothing. Belarius smoked his cigarette – it smelt overpoweringly of cloves – and gave a rambling account of exactly how the ship on which he had hoped to

take his charges all the way to Ys had been ambushed one night by water
bandits in a decad of small skiffs. The bandits had been beaten off when
the ship's captain had ordered pitch spread on the water and set on fire.

'Our ship put every man to the oars and rowed free of the flames,'
Belarius said, 'but the bandits were consumed.'

Prefect Corin listened, but made no comment.

Belarius said, 'The bandits fired chainshot. It damaged the mast and
rigging and struck the hull at the waterline. We were taking on water in
several places, and so we limped to the nearest port. My charges did not
want to wait out the repairs, so we walked on. The ship will meet us at
Ys, when we have finished our business there. A ghoul has been following
us the past week, but that is the only trouble we have had. Such are the
times, when the road is safer than the Great River.'

After Belarius had filled his waterskin from the spring and taken his
leave, Yama said, 'You do not like him.'

Prefect Corin considered this, then said in a measured tone, 'I do not
like veiled insults about the competence of the Department. If the Great
River is no longer safe, it is because of the war, and those who travel on
it should take suitable precautions and travel in convoy. Not only that,
but our well-upholstered priest did not hire any bodyguards as escort on
the road, which would have been prudent, and it would have been more
prudent to have waited until the ship was repaired than to have gone
forward on foot. I rather think that he has told us only half of the story.
Either he does not have the money to hire men or to pay for repairs to
the ship, or he is willing to risk the lives of his charges to make extra
profit. And he put aboard with a bravado captain, which says little for
his judgement. If the ship was able to outdistance the fire it set on the
water, then it could have outdistanced the bandits. Often flight is better
than fight.'

'If less honourable.'

'There is no honour in needless fighting. The captain could have
destroyed his ship as well as the bandits with his trick.'

'Will we stay with these people?'

'Their singing will wake every bandit in a hundred leagues,' Prefect
Corin said. 'And if there are any bandits, then they will be attracted to
the larger group rather than to the lesser.'

14 ~ The Bandits

The next day, Yama and Prefect Corin drew ahead of the group of palmers, but never so far ahead that the dust cloud the palmers raised was lost from sight. That night, the palmers caught up with them and camped nearby, and Belarius came over and talked to Prefect Corin about the day's journey for the length of time it took him to smoke two of his clove-flavoured cigarettes. The palmers' songs sounded clear and strong in the quiet evening.

When Prefect Corin woke Yama from a deep sleep it was past midnight, and the fire was no more than warm ashes. They had camped by a square tomb covered in the scrambling thorny canes of roses, on top of a bluff that overlooked the Great River. He was leaning on his staff. Behind him, the white roses glimmered like ghosts of their own selves. Their strong scent filled the air.

'Something bad nearby,' Prefect Corin said in a quiet voice. Galaxy light put a spark in each of his close-set eyes. 'Take up your knife and come with me.'

Yama whispered, 'What is it?'

'Perhaps nothing. We will see.'

They crossed the road and circled the palmers' camp, which had been pitched in a grove of eucalyptus. Low cliffs loomed above. The openings of tombs carved into the rock were like staggered rows of hollow eyes: a hiding place for an army. Yama heard nothing but the rustle of eucalyptus leaves, and, far off, the screech of a hunting owl. In the camp, one of the palmers groaned in his sleep. Then the wind shifted, and Yama caught a faint, foul odour above the medicinal tang of the eucalyptus.

Prefect Corin pointed towards the camp with his staff and moved forward, dry leaves crackling beneath his feet. Yama saw something scuttle away through the trees, man-sized yet running on all fours with a lurching sideways movement. He drew his knife and gave chase, but Prefect Corin overtook him and sprang onto an outcrop of rock beyond the trees with his staff raised above his head. He held the pose for a moment, then jumped down.

'Gone,' he said. 'Well, the priest is right about one thing. They have a ghoul following them.'

Yama sheathed his knife. His hand was trembling. He was out of breath and his blood sang in his head. He remembered the time he and Telmon had hunted antelope, armed only with stone axes like the men of the hill tribes. He said, 'I saw it.'

'I will tell them to bury their rubbish and to make sure that they hang their food in branches.'

'Ghouls can climb,' Yama said. He added, 'I am sorry. I should not have chased after it.'

'It was bravely done. Perhaps we scared it off.'

Yama and Prefect Corin reached the pass the next day. It was only a little wider than the road, cutting through a high scarp of rough-edged blocks of grey granite which rose abruptly from the gentle slope they had been climbing all morning. A cairn of flat stones stood at the edge of the road near the beginning of the pass, built around a slab engraved with a list of names. Prefect Corin said that it was the memorial of a battle in the Age of Insurrection, when those few men whose names were engraved on the slab had held the pass against overwhelming odds. Every man defending the pass had died, but the army they had fought had been held up long enough for reinforcements from Ys to arrive and drive them back.

Across the road from the shrine was a house-sized platform of red rock split down the middle by a single, straight-edged crack. Prefect Corin sat in the shade of the rock's overhang and said that they would wait for the palmers to catch up before they tried the pass.

'Safety in numbers,' Yama said, to provoke a reaction.

'Quite the reverse, but you do not seem to understand that.' Prefect Corin watched as Yama restlessly poked about, and eventually said, 'There are supposed to be footprints on top of this rock, one either side of the crack. It is said that an aesthetic stood there an age past, and ascended directly to the Eye of the Preservers. The force of his ascent cracked the rock, and left his footprints melted into it.'

'Is it true?'

'Certainly a great deal of energy would be required to accelerate someone so that they could fall beyond the influence of Confluence's gravity fields, more than enough to melt rock. But if the energy was applied all at once a normal body would be flash-heated into a cloud of steam by friction with the air. I do not blame you for not knowing that, Yama. Your education is not what it should be.'

Yama did not see any point replying to this provocation, and continued to wander about in the dry heat, searching for nothing in particular. The alternative was to sit by Prefect Corin. Small lizards flicked over the hot stones; a scarlet and gold hummingbird hung in the air on a blur of wings for a few moments before darting away. At last, Yama found a way up a jumble of boulders to the flat top of the outcrop. The fracture was straight and narrow, and its depths glittered with shards of what looked like melted glass. The fabled prints were just as Prefect Corin had described them, no more than a pair of foot-sized oval hollows, one on either side of the crack.

Yama lay down on warm, gritty rock and looked up at the empty blue sky. His thoughts moved lazily. He started to read his copy of the Puranas, but did not find anything that was different from his rote learning and put the book away. It was too bright and hot to read, and he had already looked long and hard at the pictures; apart from the one which showed the creation of the Eye of the Preservers, they were little different from the scenes of the lost past captured in the slates of tombs – and unlike the pictures in the slates, the pictures in the book did not move.

Yama idly wondered why the ghoul was following the palmers, and wondered why the Preservers had created ghouls in the first place. For if the Preservers had created the world and everything in it, as was written in the Puranas, and had raised up the ten thousand bloodlines from animals of ten thousand worlds, then what were the ghouls, which stood between animals and the humblest of the indigenous races?

According to the argument from design, which Zakiel had taught Yama and Telmon, ghouls existed because they aided the processes of decay, but there were many other scavenger species, and ghouls had a particular appetite for the flesh of men, and would take small children and babies if they could. Others said that ghouls were only imperfectly raised up, their natures partaking of the worst of men and of beasts, or that their bloodline had not advanced like those of other kinds of men, or remained unchanged, like the various indigenous races, but had run backwards until they retained nothing of the gifts of the Preservers but the capacity for evil. Both arguments suggested that the world which the Preservers had created was imperfect, although neither denied the possibility of perfectibility. Some claimed that the Preservers had chosen not to create a perfect world because such a world would be unchanging, and only an imperfect world allowed the possibility of evil and, therefore, of redemption. By their nature, Preservers could do only good, but while they could not create evil, the presence of evil was an inevitable consequence in their creation, just as light casts shadows when material objects are interposed. Others argued that since the light of the Preservers had been everywhere at the construction of the world, where then could any shadows lie? By this argument, evil was the consequence of the rebellion of men and machines against the Preservers, and only by rediscovering the land of lost content which had existed before that rebellion could evil be banished and men win redemption.

Still others argued that evil had its use in a great plan that could not be understood by any but the Preservers themselves. That such a plan might exist, with past, present and future absolutely determined, was one reason why no one should rely on miracles. As Ananda would say, no use praying for intercession if all was determined from the outset. If the Preservers wanted something to be so, then they would have created it already, without waiting to hear prayers asking for intercession, without needing to watch over every soul. Everything was predestined in the single long word which the Preservers had spoken to bring the world into existence.

Yama's mind rebelled against this notion, as a man buried before his death might fight against a winding sheet. If everything was part of a predetermined plan, then why should anyone in it do anything at all, least of all worship the Preservers? Except that too was a part of the plan, and everyone in the world was a wind-up puppet ratcheting from birth to death in a series of preprogrammed gestures.

It was undeniable that the Preservers had set the world in motion, but Yama did not believe that they had abandoned it in disgust or despair, or because, seeing all, they knew every detail of its destiny. No, Yama preferred to think that the Preservers had left the world to grow as it would, as a fond parent must watch a child grow into independence. In this way, the bloodlines which the Preservers had raised up from animals might rise further to become their equals, and that could not occur if the Preservers interfered with destiny, for just as a man cannot make another man, so gods cannot make other gods. For this reason, it was necessary that individuals must be able to choose between good and evil – they must be able to choose, like Dr Dismas, not to serve goodness, but their own appetites. Without the possibility of evil, no bloodline could define its own goodness. The existence of evil allowed blood-lines to fail and fall, or to transcend their animal natures by their own efforts.

Yama wondered if ghouls had chosen to fall, revelling in their bestial nature as Dr Dismas revelled in his rebellion against the society of men. Animals did not choose their natures, of course. A jaguar did not delight in the pain it caused its prey; it merely needed to eat. Cats played with mice, but only because their mothers had taught them to hunt by such play. Only men had free will and could choose to wallow in their base desires or by force of will overcome them. Were men little different from ghouls, then, except they struggled against their dark side, while ghouls swam in it with the innocent unthinking ease of fish in water? By praying to the Preservers, perhaps men were in reality doing no more than praying to their own as yet unrealized higher natures, as an explorer might contemplate the untravelled peaks he must climb to reach his goal.

If the Preservers had left the world to its own devices and there were no miracles, except the existence of free will, what then, of the ghost ship? Yama had not prayed for it, or at least had not known that he had done so, and yet it had come precisely when he had needed a diversion to make good his escape. Was something watching over him? If so, to what purpose? Or perhaps it was no more than a coincidence: some old machinery had been accidentally awakened, and Yama had seized the moment to escape. It was possible that there was another world where the ghost ship had not appeared, or had appeared too early or too late, and Yama had gone with Dr Dismas and the warlord, Enobarbus. He would be travelling downriver on the pinnace even now, a willing or unwilling participant in their plans, perhaps to death, perhaps to a destiny more glorious than the apprenticeship which now lay ahead of him.

Yama's speculations widened and at some point he was no longer in control of them but was carried on their flow, like a twig on the Great River's flood. He slept, and woke to find Prefect Corin standing over him, a black shadow against the dazzling blue of the sky.

'Trouble,' the man said, and pointed down the long gentle slope of the road. A tiny smudge of smoke hung in the middle distance, trembling in the heat haze, and at that moment Yama realized that all along Prefect Corin had been protecting the palmers.

They found the dead first. The bodies had been dragged off the road and stacked and set on fire. Little was left but greasy ash and charred bones, although, bizarrely, a pair of unburnt feet still shod in sandals protruded from the bottom of the gruesome pyre. Prefect Corin poked amongst the hot ashes with his staff and counted fourteen skulls, leaving nine unaccounted for. He cast about in one direction, bending low as he searched the muddle of prints on the ground, and Yama, although not asked, went in the other. It was he, following a trail of blood speckles, who found Belarius hiding inside a tomb. The priest was cradling a dead woman, and his robe was drenched in her blood.

'They shot at us from hiding places amongst the tombs,' Belarius said. 'I think they shot Vril by accident because they did not shoot any of the other women. When all the men had been killed or badly wounded, they came for the women. Small fierce men with bright red skin and long arms and legs, some on foot, some on horse, three or four decads of them. Like spiders. They had sharp teeth, and claws like thorns. I remember they couldn't close their hands around their weapons.'

'I know the bloodline,' Prefect Corin said. 'They are a long way from home.'

'Two came and looked at me, and jeered and went away again,' Belarius said.

'They would not kill a priest,' Prefect Corin said. 'It is bad luck.'

'I tried to stop them despoiling the bodies,' Belarius said. 'They threatened me with their knives or spat on me or laughed, but they didn't stop their work. They stripped the bodies and dismembered them, cut what they wanted from the heads. Some of the men were still alive. When they were finished, they set the bodies on fire. I wanted to shrive the dead, but they pushed me away.'

'And the women?'

Belarius started to cry. He said, 'I meant no harm to anyone. No harm. No harm to anyone.'

'They took the women with them,' Prefect Corin said. 'To despoil or to sell. Stop blubbering, man! Which way did they go?'

'Towards the mountains. You must believe that I meant no harm. If you had stayed with us instead of getting ahead – no, forgive me. That is unworthy.'

'We would have been killed, too,' Prefect Corin said. 'These bandits strike quickly, and without fear. They will attack larger groups better armed than themselves if they think that the surprise and fury of their assault will overcome their opponents. As it is, we may yet save some of your people. Go and shrive your dead, man. After that you must decide whether you want to come with us or stay here.'

When Belarius was out of earshot, Prefect Corin said to Yama, 'Listen carefully, boy. You can come with me, but only if you swear that you will do exactly as I say.'

'Of course,' Yama said at once. He would have promised anything for the chance.

It was not difficult to track the bandits and the captured women across the dry, sandy land. The trail ran parallel to the granite scarp across a series of flat, barren salt pans. Each was higher than the next, like a series of giant steps. Prefect Corin set a relentless pace, but the priest, Belarius, kept up surprisingly well; he was one of those fat men who are also strong, and the shock of the ambush was wearing off. Yama supposed that this was a chance for Belarius to regain face. Already, the priest was beginning to speak of the attack as if it was an accident or natural disaster from which he would rescue the survivors.

'As if he did not invite the lightning,' Prefect Corin said to Yama, when they stopped to rest in the shade of a tomb. 'At the best of times, bringing a party of palmers on the land route to Ys without proper escort is like herding sheep through a country of wolves. And these were archivists, too. Not proper archivists – those are from the Department, and are trained in the art of memory. These use machines to record the lives of the dying. If you had looked closely at the skulls, you would have seen that they had been broken open. Some bandits eat the brains of their victims, but these wanted the machines in their heads.'

Yama laughed in disbelief. 'I have never heard of such a thing!'

Prefect Corin passed a hand over his black-furred face, like a grooming cat. 'It is an abomination, promulgated by a department so corrupt and debased that it seeks to survive by coarse imitation of the tasks properly carried out by its superiors. Proper archivists learn how to manage their memories by training; these people would be archivists in a few days, by swallowing the seeds of machines which migrate to a certain area of the brain and grow a kind of library. It is not without risks. In one in fifty of those who swallow the seeds, the machines grow unchecked and destroy their host's brains.'

'But surely only the unchanged need archivists? Once changed, everyone is remembered by the Preservers.'

'Many no longer believe it, and because the Department will not supply archivists to the cities of the changed, these mountebanks make fortunes by pandering to the gullible. Like real archivists, they listen to the life stories of the dying and promise to transmit them to the shrines of the Palace of the Memory of the People.'

Yama said, 'No wonder the priest is upset. He believes that many more died than we saw.'

'They are all remembered by the Preservers in any event,' Prefect Corin said. 'Saints or sinners, all men marked by the Preservers are remembered, while true archivists remember the stories of as many of the unchanged bloodlines as they can. The priest is upset because his reputation will be blemished, and he will lose trade. Hush. Here he comes.'

Belarius had ripped away the blood-soaked part of his orange robe, leaving only a kind of kilt about his waist. The smooth yellow skin of his shoulders and his fat man's breasts had darkened in the sun to the colour of blood oranges, and he scratched at his sunburnt skin as he told Yama and Prefect Corin that he had found fresh horse droppings.

'They are not more than an hour ahead of us. If we hurry, we can catch them before they reach the foothills.'

Prefect Corin said, 'They make the women walk. It slows them down.'

'Then their cruelty will be their undoing.' Belarius curled his right hand into a fist and ground it into the palm of his left. 'We will catch them and we will crush them.'

Prefect Corin said calmly, 'They are cruel but not stupid. They could tie the women to their horses if they wanted to outpace us, yet they do not. They taunt us, I think. They want sport. We must proceed carefully. We will wait until night, and follow them to their camp.'

'They will leave us behind in the darkness!'

'I know this bloodline. They do not travel by night, for their blood slows as the air cools. Meanwhile we will rest. You will pray for us, Belarius. It will set our minds to the struggle ahead.'

They waited until the sun had fallen behind the Rim Mountains and the Galaxy had begun to rise above the farside horizon before they set off. The tracks left by the bandits ran straight across the flat white land into a tangle of shallow draws which sloped up towards a range of low hills. Yama tried his best to imitate Prefect Corin's ambling gait, and remembered to go flatfooted on loose stones, as Telmon had taught him. Belarius was less nimble, and every now and then would stumble and send stones clattering away downslope. There were tombs scattered at irregular intervals along the sides of the draws, unornamented and squarely built, with tall narrow doors which had been smashed open an age ago. A few had picture slates, and these wakened when the three men went by, so that they had to walk along the tops of the ridges between the draws to avoid being betrayed by the light of the past. Belarius fretted that they would lose the trail, but then Yama saw a flickering dab of light brighten ahead.

It was a dry tree set on fire in the bottom of a deep draw. It burned with a white intensity and a harsh crackling, sending up volumes of acrid white smoke. Its tracery of branches made a web of black shadows within the brightness of its burning. The three men looked down on it, and Prefect Corin said, 'Well, they know that we are following them. Yama, look after Belarius. I will not be long.'

He was gone before Yama could reply, a swift shadow flowing down the slope, circling the burning tree and disappearing into the darkness beyond. Belarius sat down heavily and whispered, 'You two should not die on my account.'

'Let us not talk of death,' Yama said. He had his knife in his hand — he had drawn it upon seeing the burning tree. It showed not a spark, and he sheathed it and said, 'A little while ago, I was taken aboard a pinnace by force, but a white ship appeared, glowing with cold fire. The pinnace attacked the white ship and I was able to escape. Yet the white ship was not real; even as it bore down on the pinnace it began to dissolve. Was this a miracle? And was it for my benefit? What do you think?'

'We shouldn't question the plan of the Preservers. Only they can say what is miraculous.'

It was a rote reply. Belarius was more intent on the darkness beyond the burning tree than on Yama's tale. He was smoking one of his clove-scented cigarettes, cupping it hungrily to his wide mouth. The light of the burning tree beat on him unmercifully; shadows in his deep eye sockets made a skull of his face.

Prefect Corin came back an hour later. The tree had burnt down to a stump of glowing cinders. He appeared out of the darkness and knelt between Belarius and Yama. 'The way is clear,' he said.

Yama said, 'Did you see them?'

Prefect Corin considered this. Yama thought he looked smug, the son-of-a-bitch. At last he said, 'I saw our friend of last night.'

'The ghoul?'

'It is following us. It will feed well tonight, one way or the other. Listen carefully. This ridge rises and leads around to a place above a canyon. There are large tombs at the bottom of the canyon, and that is where the bandits are camped. They have stripped the women and tied them to stakes, but I do not think they have used them.' Prefect Corin looked directly at Belarius. 'These people come into heat like dogs or deer, and it is not their season. They display the women to make us angry, and we will not be angry. They have built a big fire, but away from it the night air will make them sluggish. Yama, you and Belarius will create a diversion, and I will go in and cut the women free and bring them out.'

Belarius said, 'It is not much of a plan.'

'Well, we could leave the women,' Prefect Corin said, with such seriousness that it was plain he would do just that if Belarius refused to help.

'They'll sleep,' the priest said. 'We wait until they sleep, and then we take the women.'

Prefect Corin said, 'No. They never sleep, but simply become less active at night. They will be waiting for us. That is why we must make them come out, preferably away from their fire. I will kill them then. I have a pistol.'

It was like a flat, water-smoothed pebble. It caught the Galaxy's cold blue light and shone in Prefect Corin's palm. Yama was amazed. The Department of Indigenous Affairs was surely greater than he had imagined, if one of them could carry a weapon not only forbidden to most but so valuable, because the secret of its manufacture was lost an age past, that it could ransom a city like Aeolis. Dr Dismas's energy pistol, which merely increased the power of light by making its waves march in step, had been a clumsy imitation of the weapon Prefect Corin held.

Belarius said, 'Those things are evil.'

'It has saved my life before now. It has three shots, and then it must lie in sunlight all day before it will fire again. That is why you must get them into the open, so I have a clear field of fire.'

Yama said, 'How will we make the diversion?'

'I am sure you will think of something when you get there,' Prefect Corin said.

His lips were pressed together as if he was suppressing a smile, and now Yama knew what this was all about.

Prefect Corin said, 'Follow the ridge, and be careful not to show yourself against the sky.'

'What about guards?'

'There are no guards,' Prefect Corin said. 'Not any more.'

And then he was gone.

The canyon was sinuous and narrow, a deeply folded crevice winding back the hills. The ridge rose above it to a tabletop bluff dissected by dry ravines. Lying on his belly, looking over the edge of the drop into the canyon, Yama could see the fire the bandits had lit on the canyon floor far below. Its red glow beat on the white faces of the tombs that were set into the walls of the canyon, and the brushwood corral where a decad of horses milled, and the line of naked women tied to stakes.

Yama said, 'It is like a test.'

Belarius, squatting on his heels a little way from the edge, stared at him.

'I have to show initiative,' Yama said. 'If I do not, Prefect Corin will not try to rescue the women.'

He did not add that it was also a punishment. Because he carried the knife; because he wanted to be a soldier; because he had tried to run away. He knew that he could not allow himself to fail, but he did not know how he could succeed.

'Pride,' Belarius said sulkily. He seemed to have reached a point where

166

nothing much mattered to him. 'He makes himself into a petty god, deciding whether my poor clients live or die.'

'That is up to us, I think. He is a cold man, but he wants to help you.'

Belarius pointed into the darkness behind him. 'There's a dead man over there. I can smell him.'

It was one of the bandits. He was lying on his belly in the middle of a circle of creosote bushes. His neck had been broken and he seemed to be staring over his shoulder at his doom.

Belarius mumbled a brief prayer, then took the dead man's short, stout recurved bow and quiver of unfledged arrows. He seemed to cheer up a little, and Yama asked him if he knew how to use a bow.

'I'm not a man of violence.'

'Do you want to help rescue your clients?'

'Most of them are dead,' Belarius said gravely. 'I will shrive this poor wight now.'

Yama left the priest with the dead man and quartered the ground along the edge of the canyon. Although he was tired, he felt a peculiar clarity, a keen alertness sustained by a mixture of anger and adrenalin. This might be a test, but the women's lives depended on it. That was more important than pleasing Prefect Corin, or proving to himself that he could live up to his dreams.

A round boulder stood at the edge of the drop. It was half Yama's height and bedded in the dirt, but it gave a little when he put his back to it. He tried to get Belarius to help him, but the priest was kneeling as if in prayer and either did not understand or did not want to understand, and he would not stand up even when Yama pulled at his arm. Yama groaned in frustration and went back to the boulder and began to attack the sandy soil around its base with his eating knife. He had not been digging for long when he struck something metallic. The little knife quivered in his hands and when he drew it out he found that the point of the blade had been neatly cut away. He had found a machine.

Yama knelt and whispered to the thing, asking it to come to him. He did it more from reflex than hope, and was amazed when the soil shifted between his knees and the machine slid into the air with a sudden slipping motion, like a squeezed watermelon seed. It bobbed in the air before Yama's face, a shining, silvery oval that would have fitted into his palm, had he dared touch it. It was both metallic and fluid, like a big drop of hydrargyrum. Flecks of light flickered here and there on its surface. It emitted a strong smell of ozone, and a faint crepitating sound.

Yama said, slowly and carefully, shaping the words in his mind as well as his mouth as he did when instructing the peel-house's watchdogs, 'I need to make this part of the edge of the canyon fall. Help me.'

The machine dropped to the ground and a little geyser of dust and small stones spat up as it dug down out of sight. Yama sat on his heels, hardly daring to breathe, but although he waited a long time, nothing else seemed to happen. He had started to dig around the base of the boulder again when Belarius found him.

The priest had uprooted a couple of small creosote bushes. He said, 'We will set these alight and throw them down onto those wicked men.'

'Help me with this boulder.'

Belarius shook his head and sat by the edge and began to tie the bushes together with a strip of cloth torn from remnants of his robe.

'If you set fire to those bushes, you will make yourself a target,' Yama said.

'I expect that you have a flint in your satchel.'

'Yes, but—'

In the canyon below, horses cried to each other. Yama looked over the edge and saw that the horses were running from one corner of the corral to the other. They moved in the firelight like water running before a strong, choppy wind, bunched together and flicking their tails and tossing their heads. At first, Yama thought that they had been disturbed by Prefect Corin, but then he saw something white clinging upside-down to the neck of a black mare in the middle of the panicky herd. The ghoul had found the bandits. Men were running towards the horses with a scampering crabwise gait, casting long crooked shadows because the fire was at their backs, and Yama threw his weight against the boulder, knowing he would not have a better chance.

The ground moved under Yama's feet and he lost his footing and fell backwards, banging the back of his head against the boulder. The blow dazed him, and he was unable to stop Belarius pawing through his satchel and taking the flint. The ground moved again and the boulder stirred and sank a handspan into the soil. Yama realized what was happening and scrambled out of the way just as the edge of the canyon collapsed.

The boulder dropped straight down. A cloud of dust and dirt shot up and there was a crash when the boulder struck the side of the canyon, and then a moment of silence. The ground was still shaking. Yama tried to get to his feet, but it was like trying to stand up in a boat caught in cross-currents. Belarius was kneeling over the bundle of creosote bushes, striking the flint against its stone. Dust puffed up behind him, defining a long crooked line, and a kind of lip opened in the ground. Little lights swarmed in the churning soil. Yama saw them when he snatched up his satchel and jumped the widening gash. He landed on hands and knees and the ground moved again and he fell down. Belarius was standing on the other side of the gash, his feet planted wide apart as he swung two burning bushes around his head. Then the edge of the canyon gave way and fell with a sliding roar into the canyon. A moment later a vast cloud of dust boiled up amidst a noise like a thunderclap, and lightning lit the length of the canyon at spaced intervals. Once, twice, three times.

15 ~ The Magistrate

At first the houses were no more than empty tombs that people had moved into, making improvised villages strung out along low cliff terraces by the old edge of the Great River. The people who lived there went about naked. They were thin and very tall, with small heads and long, glossy black hair, and skin the colour of rust. The chests of the men were welted with spiral patterns of scars; the women stiffened their hair with red clay. They hunted lizards and snakes and coneys, collected the juicy young pads of prickly pear and dug for tuberous roots in the dry tableland above the cliffs, picked samphire and watercress in the marshes by the margin of the river and waded out into the river's shallows and cast circular nets to catch fish, which they smoked on racks above fires built of creosote bush and pine chips. They were cheerful and hospitable, and gave food and shelter freely to Yama and Prefect Corin.

Then there were proper houses amongst the tombs, foursquare and painted yellow or blue or pink, with little gardens planted out on their flat roofs. The houses stepped up the cliffs like piles of boxes, with steep narrow streets between. Shanty villages had been built on stilts over the mudbanks and silty channels left by the river's retreat, and beyond these, sometimes less than half a league from the road, sometimes two or three leagues distant, was the river, and docks made of floating pontoons, and a constant traffic of little cockle-shell sailboats and barges and sleek fore-and-aft rigged cutters and three-masted xebecs hugging the shore. Along the old river road, street merchants sold fresh fish and oysters and mussels from tanks, and freshly steamed lobsters and spiny crabs, samphire and lotus roots and water chestnuts, bamboo and little red bananas and several kinds of kelp, milk from tethered goats, spices, pickled walnuts, fresh fruit and grass juice, ice, jewellery made of polished shells, black seed pearls, caged birds, bolts of brightly patterned cloth, sandals made from the worn rubber tread of steam waggon tyres, cheap plastic toys, tape recordings of popular ballads or prayers, and a thousand other things. The stalls and booths of the merchants formed a kind of ribbon market strung along the dusty margin of land at the shoulder of the old road, noisy with the cries of hawkers and music from tape recorders and itinerant musicians, and the buzz of commerce as people bargained and gossiped. When a warship went past, a league beyond the crowded tarpaper roofs of the shanty villages and the cranes of the floating docks, everyone stopped to watch it. As if in salute, it raised the red and gold blades of its triple-banked oars and fired a charge of white smoke from a cannon, and everyone watching cheered.

That was when Yama realized that he could see, for the first time, the far shore of the Great River, and that the dark line at the horizon, like a storm cloud, were houses and docks. The river here was deep and swift, stained brown along the shore and dark blue further out. He had reached Ys and had not known it; the city had crept up on him like an army in the night, the inhabited tombs like scouts, these painted houses and tumbledown shanty villages like the first ranks of footsoldiers. It was as if, after the fiasco of the attempted rescue of the palmers, he had suddenly woken from a long sleep.

Prefect Corin had said little about the landslide which had killed the bandits, the kidnapped women and their priest, Belarius. 'You did what you could,' he had told Yama. 'If we had not tried, the women would be dead anyway.'

Yama had not told Prefect Corin about the machine. Let him think what he liked. But Yama had not been able to stop himself reliving what had happened as he had trudged behind the Prefect on the long road to Ys. Sometimes he felt a tremendous guilt, for it had been his foolish pride which had prompted him to use the machine, which had led to the deaths of the bandits and the kidnapped women. And sometimes he felt a tremendous anger towards Prefect Corin, for having laid such a responsibility upon him. He had little doubt that the Prefect could have walked into the bandits' camp, killed them all, and freed the women. Instead he had used the situation to test Yama, and Yama had failed, and felt guilt for having failed, and then anger for having been put to an impossible test.

Humiliation or anger. At last, Yama settled for the latter. As he walked behind Prefect Corin, he often imagined drawing his knife and hacking

171

the man's head from his shoulders with a single blow, or picking a stone from the side of the road and using it as a hammer. He dreamed of running fast and far and, until the warship passed, had been lost in his dreams.

Yama and Prefect Corin ate at a roadside stall. Without being asked, the owner of the stall brought them steamed mussels, water lettuce crisply fried in sesame oil with strands of ginger, and tea made from kakava bark; there was a red plastic bowl in the centre of the table into which fragments of bark could be spat. Prefect Corin did not pay for the food – the stall's owner, a tall man with loose, pale skin and rubbery webs between his fingers, simply smiled and bowed when they left.

'He is glad to help someone from the Department,' Prefect Corin explained, when Yama asked.

'Why is that?'

Prefect Corin waved a hand in front of his face, as if at a fly. Yama asked again.

'Because we are at war,' the Prefect said. 'Because the Department fights that war. You saw how they cheered the warship. Must you ask so many questions?'

Yama said, 'How am I to learn, if I do not ask?'

Prefect Corin stopped and leaned on his tall staff and stared at Yama. People stepped around them. It was crowded here, with two- and three-storey houses packed closely together on either side of the road. A string of camels padded past, their loose lips curled in supercilious expressions, little silver bells jingling on their leather harness.

'The first thing to learn is when to ask questions and when to keep silent,' Prefect Corin said, and then he turned and strode off through the crowd.

Without thinking, Yama hurried after him. It was as if this stern, taciturn man had made him into a kind of pet, anxiously trotting at his master's heels. He remembered what Dr Dismas had said about the oxen, trudging endlessly around the water lift because they knew no better, and his resentment rose again, refreshed.

For long stretches, now, the river disappeared behind houses or godowns. Hills rose above the flat roofs of the houses on the landward side of the road, and after a while Yama realized that they were not hills but buildings. In the hazy distance, the towers he had so often glimpsed using the telescope on the peel-house's heliograph platform shone like silver threads linking earth and sky.

For all the long days of travelling, the towers seemed as far away as ever.

There were more and more people on the road, and strings of camels and oxen, and horse-drawn or steam waggons bedecked with pious slogans, and sleds gliding at waist height, their loadbeds decorated with intricately carved wooden rails painted red and gold. There were machines here, too. At first, Yama mistook them for insects or humming-birds as they zipped this way and that above the crowds. No one in Aeolis owned machines, not even the Aedile (the watchdogs were surgically altered animals, and did not count) and if a machine strayed into the little city's streets everyone would get as far away from it as possible. Here, no one took any notice of the many machines that darted or spun through the air on mysterious errands. Indeed, one man was walking towards Yama and Prefect Corin with a decad of tiny machines circling above his head.

The man stopped in front of the Prefect. The Prefect was tall, but this man was taller still – he was the tallest man Yama had ever seen. He wore a scarlet cloak with the hood cast over his head, and a black tunic and black trousers tucked into thigh-high boots of soft black leather. A quirt like those used by ox drivers was tucked into the belt of his trousers; the ends of the quirt's hundred strands were braided with diamond-shaped metal tags. The man squared up to Prefect Corin and said, 'You're a long way from where you should be.'

Prefect Corin leaned on his staff and looked up at the man. Yama stood behind the Prefect. People were beginning to form a loose circle with the red-cloaked man and Prefect Corin in its centre.

The man in the red cloak said, 'If you have business here, I haven't heard of it.'

A machine landed on Prefect Corin's neck, just beneath the angle of his jaw. Prefect Corin ignored it. He said, 'There is no reason why you should.'

'There's every reason.' The man noticed the people watching and slashed the air with his quirt. The tiny, bright machines above his head widened their orbits and one dropped down to hover before the man's lips.

'Move on,' the man said. His voice, amplified by the machine, echoed off the faces of the buildings on either side of the street, but most of the people only stepped back a few paces. The machine rose and the man told Prefect Corin in his ordinary voice, 'You're causing a disturbance.'

Prefect Corin said, 'There was no disturbance until you stopped me. I would ask why.'

'This is the road, not the river.'

Prefect Corin spat in the dust at his feet. 'I had noticed.'

'You are carrying a pistol.'

'By the authority of my Department.'

'We'll see about that. What's your business? Are you spying on us?'

'If you are doing your duty, you have nothing to fear. But do not worry, brother, I am no spy. I am returning from a downriver city where I had a task to perform. It is done, and now I return.'

'Yet you travel by road.'

'I thought I would show this boy something of the countryside. He has led a very sheltered life.'

A machine darted forward and spun in front of Yama's face. There was a flash of red light in the backs of Yama's eyes and he blinked, and the machine flew up to rejoin the spinning dance above the man's head. The man said, 'This is your catamite? The war is going badly if you can't find better. This one has a corpse's skin. And he is carrying a proscribed weapon.'

'Again, by the authority of my Department,' Prefect Corin said.

'I don't know the bloodline, but I'd guess he's too young for an apprenticeship. You had better show your papers to the officer of the day.'

The man snapped his fingers and the machines dropped and settled into a tight orbit around the Prefect's head, circling him like angry silver wasps. The man turned then, slashing the air with his quirt so that those nearest him fell back, pressing against those behind. 'Make way!' the man shouted as he hacked a path through the crowd with his quirt. 'Make way! Make way!'

Yama said to Prefect Corin, as they followed the man, 'Is this the time to ask a question?'

'He is a magistrate. A member of the autonomous civil authority of Ys. There is some bad blood between his department and mine. He will make a point about who is in charge here, and then we will be on our way.'

'How did he know about the pistol and my knife?'

'His machines told him.'

Yama studied the shuttling weave of the little machines around Prefect Corin's head. One still clung to the Prefect's neck, a segmented silver bead with four pairs of wire-like legs and mica wings folded along its back. Yama could feel the simple thoughts of the machines, and wondered if he might be able to make them forget what they had been ordered to do, but he did not trust himself to say the right thing to them, and besides, he was not about to reveal his ability by helping the Prefect.

The road opened onto a square lined with flame trees just coming into leaf. On the far side, a high wall rose above the roofs of the buildings and the tops of the trees. It was built of closely fitted blocks of black, polished granite, with gun platforms and watch-towers along its top. Soldiers lounged by a tall gate in the wall, watching the traffic that jostled through the shadow of the gate's arch. The magistrate led Prefect Corin and Yama across the square and the soldiers snapped to attention as they went through the gate. They climbed a steep stair that wound widdershins inside the wall to a wide walkway at the top. A little way along, the wall turned at a right-angle and ran beside the old bank of the river, and a faceted blister of glass, glittering in the sunlight, clung there.

It was warm and full of light inside the glass blister. Magistrates in red cloaks stood at windows hung in the air, watching aerial views of the road, of ships moored at the docks or passing up and down the river, of red tile rooftops, of a man walking along a crowded street. Machines zipped to and fro in the bright air, or spun in little clouds. At the centre of all this activity, a bareheaded officer sat with his boots up on a clear plastic table, and after the magistrate had talked with him the officer called Prefect Corin over.

'Just a formality,' the officer said languidly, and held out his hand. The eight-legged machine dropped from the Prefect's neck and the officer's fingers briefly closed around it. When they opened again, the machine sprang into the air and began to circle the magistrate's head.

The officer yawned and said, 'Your pass, Prefect Corin, if you please.' He ran a fingernail over the imprinted seal of the resin tablet Prefect

Corin gave him, and said, 'You didn't take return passage by river, as you were ordered.'

'Not ordered. I could have taken the river passage if I chose to, but it was left to my discretion. The boy is to be apprenticed as a clerk. I thought that I would show him something of the country. He has led a sheltered life.'

The officer said, 'It's a long, hard walk.' He was looking at Yama now. Yama met his gaze and the officer winked. He said, 'There's nothing here about this boy, or his weapon. Quite a hanger for a mere apprentice.'

'An heirloom. He is the son of the Aedile of Aeolis.' Prefect Corin's tone implied that there was nothing more to be said about the matter.

The officer set the tablet on the desk and said to the magistrate, 'Nym, fetch a chair for Prefect Corin.'

Prefect Corin said, 'There's no need for delay.'

The officer yawned again. His tongue and teeth were stained red with the narcotic leaf he had wadded between gum and cheek. His tongue was black, long and sharply pointed. 'It'll take a little while to confirm things with your department. Would you like some refreshment?'

The tall, red-cloaked magistrate set a stool beside Prefect Corin. The officer indicated it, and after a moment Prefect Corin sat down. He said, 'I do not need anything from you.'

The officer took out a packet of cigarettes and put one in his mouth and lit it with a match he struck on the surface of the desk. He did all this at a leisurely pace; his gaze did not leave the Prefect's face. He exhaled smoke and said to the magistrate, 'Some fruit. And iced sherbet.' He told Prefect Corin, 'While we're waiting, you can tell me about your long walk from—' he glanced at the tablet '—Aeolis. A party of palmers has gone missing somewhere around there, I believe. Perhaps you know something. Meanwhile, Nym will talk with the boy, and we'll see if the stories are the same. What could be simpler?'

Prefect Corin said, 'The boy must stay with me. He is in my charge.'

'Oh, I think he will be safe with Nym, don't you?'

'I have my instructions,' Prefect Corin said.

The officer stubbed out his half-smoked cigarette. 'You cleave to them with admirable fidelity. We'll take care of the boy. You'll tell your story to me. He'll tell his to Nym. Then we'll see if the stories are the same. What could be simpler?'

Prefect Corin said, 'You do not know—'

The officer raised an eyebrow.

'He is in my charge,' Prefect Corin said. 'We will go now, I think.'

He started to rise, and for an instant was crowned with a jagged circle of sparks. There was a sudden sharp smell of burnt hair and he fell heavily onto the stool. The little machines calmly circled his head, as if nothing had happened.

'Take the boy away, Nym,' the officer said. 'Find out where he's been and where he's going.'

Prefect Corin turned and gave Yama a dark stare. His shoulders were hunched and his hands were pressed between his knees. A thin line of white char circled his sleek black head, above his eyes and the tops of his tightly folded ears. 'Do what you are told,' he said. 'No more than that.'

The magistrate, Nym, took Yama's arm and steered him around the windows in the air. The machines quit their orbits around Prefect Corin's head and followed the magistrate in a compact cloud. In the hot sunlight outside the dome, Nym looked through Yama's satchel and took out the sheathed knife.

'That was a gift from my father,' Yama said. He half-hoped that the knife would do something to the magistrate, but it remained inert. Yama added, 'My father is the Aedile of Aeolis, and he told me to take good care of it.'

'I'm not going to steal it, boy.' The magistrate pulled the blade halfway out of its sheath. 'Nicely balanced. Loyal, too.' He dropped it into Yama's satchel. 'It tried to bite me, but I know something about machines. You use it to cut firewood, I suppose. Sit down. There. Wait for me. Don't move. Try to leave, and the machines will knock you down, like they did with your master. Try to use your weapon and they'll boil you down to a grease spot. I'll come back and we'll have a little talk, you and me.'

Yama looked up at the magistrate. He tried not to blink when the machines settled in a close orbit around his head. 'When you fetch refreshments for my master, remember that I would like sherbet, too.'

'Oh yes, we'll have a nice talk, you and me. Your master doesn't have a pass for you, and I'll bet you don't have a permit for your knife, either. Think about that.'

Yama waited until Nym had gone down the stairway, then told the machines to leave him alone. They wanted to know where they should go, so he asked them if they could cross the river, and when they said that they could he told them to go directly across the river and to wait there.

The machines gathered into a line and flew straight out over the edge of the wall, disappearing into the blue sky above the crowded roofs of the stilt shanties and the masts of the ships anchored at the floating docks. Yama went down the stairs and walked boldly past the soldiers. None of them spared him more than a glance, and he walked out of the shadow of the gate into the busy street beyond the wall.

16 ~ The Cateran

At first the landlord of the inn did not want to rent a room to Yama. The inn was full, he said, on account of the Water Market. But when Yama showed him the two gold rials, the man chuckled and said that he might be able to make a special arrangement. Perhaps twice the usual tariff, to take account of the inconvenience, and if Yama would like to eat while waiting for the room to be made up . . .? The landlord was a fat young man with smooth brown skin and short, spiky white hair, and a brisk, direct manner. He took one of the coins and said that he'd bring change in the morning, seeing as the money changers were closed up for the day.

Yama sat in a corner of the taproom, and presently a pot boy brought him a plate of shrimp boiled in their shells and stir-fried okra and peppers, with chili and peanut sauce and flat discs of unleavened bread and a beaker of thin rice beer. Yama ate hungrily. He had walked until the sun had fallen below the roofs of the city, and although he had passed numerous stalls and street vendors he had not been able to buy any food or drink – he had not realized that there were men whose business was to change coins like his into smaller denominations. The landlord would change the coin tomorrow, and Yama would begin to search for his bloodline. But now he was content to sit with a full stomach, his head pleasantly lightened by the beer, and watch the inn's customers.

They seemed to fall into two distinct groups. There were ordinary working men of several bloodlines, dressed in homespun and clogs, who stood at the counter drinking quietly, and there was a party of men and a single red-haired woman eating at a long table under the stained glass window which displayed the inn's sign of two crossed axes. They made a lot of noise, playing elaborate toasting games and calling from one end of the table to the other. Yama thought that they must be soldiers, caterans or some other kind of irregulars, for they all wore bits of armour, mostly metal or resin chestplates painted with various devices, and wrist guards and greaves. Many were scarred, or had missing fingers. One big, barechested man had a silver patch over one eye; another had only one arm, although he ate as quickly and as dextrously as his companions. The red-haired woman seemed to be one of them, rather than a concubine they had picked up; she wore a sleeveless leather tunic and a short leather skirt that left her legs mostly bare.

The landlord seemed to know the caterans, and when he was not busy he sat with them, laughing at their jokes and pouring wine or beer for those nearest him. He whispered something in the one-eyed man's ear and they both laughed, and when the landlord went off to serve one of the other customers, the one-eyed man grinned across the room at Yama.

Presently, the pot boy told Yama that his room was ready and led him around the counter and through a small hot kitchen into a courtyard lit by electric floodlights hung from a central pole. There were whitewashed stables on two sides and a wide square gate shaded by an avocado tree in which green parrots squawked and rustled. The room was in the eaves above one of the stable blocks. It was long and low and dark, with a single window at its end looking out over the street and a tumble of roofs falling towards the Great River. The pot boy lit a fish-oil lantern and uncovered a pitcher of hot water, turned down the blanket and fussed with the bolster on the bed, and then hesitated, clearly reluctant to leave.

'I do not have any small coins,' Yama said, 'but tomorrow I will give you something for your trouble.'

The boy went to the door and looked outside, then closed it and turned to Yama. 'I don't know you, master,' he said, 'but I think I should tell you this, or it'll be on my conscience. You shouldn't stay here tonight.'

'I paid for the room with honest money left on account,' Yama said.

The boy nodded. He wore a clean, much-darned shirt and a pair of breeches. He was half Yama's height and slightly built, with black hair slicked back from a sharp, narrow face. His eyes were large, with golden irises that gleamed in the candlelight. He said, 'I saw the coin you left on trust. I won't ask where you got it, but I reckon it could buy this whole place. My master is not a bad man, but he's not a good man either, if you take my meaning, and there's plenty better that would be tempted by something like that.'

'I will be careful,' Yama said. The truth was that he was tired, and a little dizzy from the beer.

'If there's trouble, you can climb out the window onto the roof,' the boy said. 'On the far side there's a vine that's grown up to the top of the wall. It's an easy climb down. I've done it many times.'

After the boy left, Yama bolted the door and leaned at the open window and gazed out at the vista of roofs and river under the darkening sky, listening to the evening sounds of the city. There was a continual distant roar, the blended noise of millions of people going about their business, and closer at hand the sounds of the neighbourhood: a hawker's cry; a pop ballad playing on a tape recorder; someone hammering metal with quick sure strokes; a woman calling to her children. Yama felt an immense peacefulness and an intense awareness that he was there, alone in that particular place and time with his whole life spread before him, a sheaf of wonderful possibilities.

He took off his shirt and washed his face and arms, then pulled off his boots and washed his feet. The bed had a lumpy mattress stuffed with straw, but the sheets were freshly laundered and the wool blanket was clean. This was probably the pot boy's room, he thought, which was why the boy wanted him to leave.

He intended to rest for a few minutes before getting up to close the shutters, but when he woke it was much later. The cold light of the Galaxy lay on the floor; something made a scratching sound in the rafters above the bed. A mouse or a gecko, Yama thought sleepily, but then he felt a feathery touch in his mind and knew that a machine had flown into the room through the window he had carelessly left open.

Yama wondered sleepily if the machine had woken him, but then there was a metallic clatter outside the door. He sat up, groping for the lantern. Someone pushed at the door and Yama, still stupid with sleep, called out.

The door flew open with a tremendous crash, sending the broken bolt flying across the room. A man stood silhouetted in the broken frame. Yama rolled onto the floor, reaching for his satchel, and something hit the bed. Wood splintered and straw flew into the air. Yama rolled again, dragging his satchel with him. He cut his hand getting his knife out but hardly noticed. The curved blade shone with a fierce blue light and spat fat blue sparks from its point.

The man turned from the bed, a shadow in the blue half-light. He had broken the frame and slashed the mattress to ribbons with the long, broad blade of his sword. Yama threw the pitcher of water at him and he ducked and said, 'Give it up, boy, and maybe you'll live.'

Yama hesitated, and the man struck at him with a sudden fury. Yama ducked and heard the air part above his head, and slashed at the man's legs with the knife, so that he had to step back. The knife howled and Yama felt a sudden coldness in the muscles of his arm.

'You fight like a woman,' the man said. Knife-light flashed on something on his intent face.

Then he drove forward again, and Yama stopped thinking. Reflexes, inculcated in the long hours in the gymnasium under Sergeant Rhodean's stern instruction, took over. Yama's knife was better suited to close fighting than the man's long blade, but the man had the advantage of reach and weight. Yama managed to parry a series of savage, hacking strokes – fountains of sparks spurted at each blow – but the force of the blows numbed his wrist, and then the man's longer blade slid past the guard of Yama's knife and nicked his forearm. The wound was not painful, but it bled copiously and weakened Yama's grip on his knife.

Yama knocked the chair over and, in the moment it took the man to kick it out of the way, managed to get out of the corner into which he had been forced. But the man was still between Yama and the door. In a moment he pressed his attack again, and Yama was driven back against the wall. The knife's blue light blazed and something white and bone-thin stood between Yama and the man, but the man laughed and said, 'I know that trick,' and kicked out, catching Yama's elbow with the toe of his boot. The blow numbed Yama's arm and he dropped the knife. The phantom vanished with a sharp snap.

The man raised his sword for the killing blow. For a moment, it was as if he and Yama stood in a tableau pose. Then the man grunted and let out a long sighing breath that stank of onions and wine fumes, and fell to his knees. He dropped his sword and pawed at his ear, then fell on his face at Yama's feet.

Yama's right arm was numb from elbow to wrist; his left hand was shaking so much that it took him a whole minute to find the lantern and light it with his flint and steel. By its yellow glow he tore strips from the bedsheet and bound the shallow but bloody wound on his forearm and the smaller, self-inflicted gash on his palm. He sat still then, but heard only horses stepping about in the stables below. If anyone had heard the door crash open or the subsequent struggle, which was unlikely given that the other guests would be sleeping on the far side of the courtyard, they were not coming to investigate.

The dead man was the one-eyed cateran who had looked at Yama across the taproom of the inn. Apart from a trickle of dark, venous blood from his right ear he did not appear to be hurt. For a moment, Yama did not understand what had happened. Then the dead man's lips parted and a machine slid out of his mouth and dropped to the floor.

The machine's teardrop shape was covered in blood, and it vibrated with a brisk buzz until it shone silver and clean. Yama held out his left hand and the machine slid up the air and landed lightly on his palm.

'I do not remember asking you for help,' Yama told it, 'but I am grateful.'

The machine had been looking for him; there were many of its kind combing this part of Ys. Yama told it that it should look elsewhere, and that it should broadcast that idea to its fellows, then stepped to the window and held up his hand. The machine rose, circled his head once, and flew straight out into the night.

Yama pulled on his shirt and fastened his boots and set to the distasteful task of searching the dead cateran. The man had no money on him and carried only a dirk with a thin blade and a bone hilt, and a loop of wire with wooden pegs for handles. He supposed that the man would have been paid after he had done his job. The pot boy had been right after all. The landlord wanted both coins.

Yama sheathed his knife and tied the sheath to his belt, then picked up his satchel. He found it suddenly hard to turn his back on the dead man, who seemed to be watching him across the room, so he climbed out of the window sideways.

A stout beam jutted above the window frame; it might once have been a support for a hoist used to lift supplies from the street. Yama grasped the beam with both hands and swung himself once, twice, and on the third swing got his leg over the beam and pulled himself up so that he sat astride it. The wound on his forearm had parted a little, and he retied the bandage. Then it was easy enough to stand on the beam's broad top and pull himself on to the ridge of the roof.

17 ~ The Water Market

The vine was just where the pot boy had said it would be. It was very
large and very old – perhaps it had been planted when the inn had been
built – and Yama climbed down its stout leafy branches as easily as down
a ladder. He knew that he should run, but he also knew that Telmon
would not have run. It was a matter of honour to get the coin back, and
there in the darkness of the narrow alley at the back of the inn Yama
remembered the landlord's duplicitous smile and felt a slow flush of
anger.

He was groping his way towards the orange lamplight at the end of
the alley when he heard footsteps behind him. For a moment he feared
that the cateran's body had been found, and that his friends were
searching for his killer. But no cry had been raised, and surely the city
was not so wicked that murder would go unremarked. He forced himself
not to look back, but walked around the corner and drew his knife and
waited in the shadows by the inn's gate, under the wide canopy of the
avocado tree.

When the pot boy came out of the alley, Yama pushed him against
the wall and held the knife at his throat. 'I don't mean any harm!' the
boy squealed. Above them, a parrot echoed his frightened cry, modulat-
ing it into a screeching cackle.

Yama took away the knife. The thought came to him that if the one-
eyed cateran had crept into the room to cut his throat or use the
strangling wire, instead of bursting in with his sword swinging wildly,
he, and not the cateran, would now be dead.

'He came for you,' the pot boy said. 'I saw him.'

'He is dead.' Yama sheathed his knife. 'I should have listened to you.
As it is, I have killed a man, and your master still has my coin.'

The pot boy fussily straightened his ragged jerkin. He had regained his dignity. He looked up at Yama boldly and said, 'You could call the magistrates.'

'I do not want to get you into trouble, but perhaps you could show me where your master sleeps. If I get back the coin, half of it is yours.'

The boy said, 'Pandaras, at your service, master. For a tenth of it, I'll skewer his heart for you. He beats me, and cheats his customers, and cheats his provisioners and wine merchants, too. You are a brave man, master, but a poor judge of inns. You're on the run, aren't you? That's why you won't call on the magistrates.'

'It is not the magistrates I fear most,' Yama said, thinking of Prefect Corin.

Pandaras nodded. 'Families can be worse than any lock-up, as I know too well.'

'As a matter of fact, I have come here to search for my family.'

'I thought you were from the wrong side of the walls – no one born in the city would openly carry a knife as old and as valuable as yours. I'll bet that dead man in your room was more interested in the knife than your coins. I may not be much more than a street urchin, but I know my way around. If hunting down your family is what you want, why then I can help you in a hundred different ways. I'll be glad to be quit of this place. It never was much of a job anyway, and I'm getting too old for it.'

Yama thought that this pitch was little more than a gentler form of robbery, but said that for the moment he would be glad of the boy's help.

'My master sleeps as soundly as a sated seal,' Pandaras said. 'He won't wake until you put your blade to his throat.'

Pandaras let Yama into the inn through the kitchen door and led him upstairs. He put a finger to his black lips before delicately unlatching a door. Yama's knife emitted a faint blue glow and he held it up like a candle as he stepped into the stuffy room.

The landlord snored under a disarrayed sheet on a huge canopied bed that took up most of the space; there was no other furniture. Yama shook him awake, and the man pushed Yama's hand away and sat up. The sheet slipped down his smooth naked chest to the mound of his belly. When Yama aimed the point of the knife at his face, the man smiled and said, 'Go ahead and kill me. If you don't, I'll probably set the magistrates on you.'

'Then you will have to explain that one of your guests was attacked in his room. There is a dead man up there, by the way.'

The landlord gave Yama a sly look. The knife's blue glow was liquidly reflected in his round, black eyes and glimmered in his spiky white hair. He said, 'Of course there is, or you wouldn't be here. Cyg wasn't working for me, and you can't prove different.'

'Then how did you know his name?'

The landlord's shrug was like a mountain moving. 'Everyone knows Cyg.'

'Then everyone will probably know about the bargain he made with you. Give me my coin and I will leave at once.'

'And if I don't, what will you do? If you kill me you won't find it. Why don't we sit down over a glass of brandy and talk about this sensibly? I could make use of a sharp young cock like you. There are ways to make that coin multiply, and I know most of them.'

'I have heard that you cheat your customers,' Yama said. 'Those who cheat are always afraid that they will be cheated in turn, so I would guess that the only place you could have hidden my coin is somewhere in this room. Probably under your pillow.'

The landlord lunged forward then, and something struck at Yama's knife. The room filled with white light and the landlord screamed.

Afterwards, the landlord huddled against the headboard of his bed and wouldn't look at Yama or the knife. His hand was bleeding badly, for although he had wrapped his sheet around it before grabbing at the knife, the blade had cut him badly. But he took no notice of his wound, or Yama's questions. He was staring at something which had vanished as quickly as it had appeared, and would only say, over and over, 'It had no eyes. Hair like cobwebs, and no eyes.'

Yama searched beneath the bolster and the mattress, and then, remembering the place where he had hidden his map in his own room in the peel-house, rapped the floor with the hilt of his knife until he found the loose board under which the landlord had hidden the gold rial. He had to show the landlord his knife and threaten the return of the apparition to make the man roll onto his belly, so that he could gag him and tie his thumbs together with strips torn from the bedsheet.

'I am only taking back what is mine,' Yama said. 'I do not think you have earned any payment for hospitality. The fool you sent to rob me is dead. Be grateful you are not.'

Pandaras was waiting outside the gate. 'We'll get some breakfast by the fishing docks,' he said. 'The boats go out before first light and the stalls open early.'

Yama showed Pandaras the gold rial. His hand shook. Although he had felt quite calm while looking for the coin, he was now filled with an excess of nervous energy. He laughed and said, 'I have no coin small enough to pay for breakfast.'

Pandaras reached inside his ragged shirt and lifted out two worn iron pennies hung on a string looped around his neck. He winked. 'I'll pay, master, and then you can pay me.'

'As long as you stop calling me master. You are hardly younger than I am.'

'Oh, in many ways I'm much older,' Pandaras said. 'Forgive me, but you're obviously of noble birth. Such folk live longer than most; relatively speaking, you're hardly weaned from the wet nurse's teat.' He squinted up at Yama as they passed through the orange glow of a sodium vapour lamp. 'Your bloodline isn't one I know, but there are many strange folk downriver of Ys, and many more in her streets. Everything may be found here, it's said, but even if you lived a thousand years and spent all your time searching you'd never find it all. Even if you came to the end of your searching so much would have changed that it would be time to start all over again.'

Yama smiled at the boy's babble. 'It is the truth about my bloodline I have come to discover,' he said, 'and fortunately I think I know where to find it.'

As they descended towards the waterfront, down narrow streets that were sometimes so steep that they were little more than flights of shallow steps, with every house leaning on the shoulder of its neighbour, Yama told Pandaras something of the circumstances of his birth, of what he thought Dr Dismas had discovered, and of his journey to Ys. 'I know the Department of Apothecaries and Chirurgeons,' Pandaras said. 'It's no grand place, but stuck as an afterthought on the lower levels of the Palace of the Memory of the People.'

'Then I must go there after all,' Yama said. 'I thought I had escaped it.'

'The place you want is on the roof,' Pandaras said. 'You won't have to go inside, if that's what's worrying you.'

The sky was beginning to brighten when Yama and Pandaras reached the wide road by the old waterfront. A brace of camels padded past, loaded with bundles of cloth and led by a sleepy boy, and a few merchants were rolling up the shutters of their stalls or lighting cooking fires. On the long piers which ran out to the river's edge between shacks raised on a forest of stilts above the wide mud flats, fishermen were coiling ropes and taking down nets from drying poles and folding them in elaborate pleats.

For the first time, Yama noticed the extent of the riverside shanty town. The shacks crowded all the way to the edge of the floating docks, half a league distant, and ran along the river edge for as far as the eye could see. They were built mostly of plastic sheeting dulled by smoke and weather towards a universal grey, and roofed with tarpaper or sagging canvas. Channels brimming with thick brown water ran between mudbanks under the tangle of stilts and props. Tethered chickens pecked amongst threadbare grass on drier pieces of ground. Already, people were astir, washing clothes or washing themselves, tending tiny cooking fires, exchanging gossip. Naked children of a decad or more different blood-lines chased each other along swaybacked rope walkways.

Pandaras explained that the shanty towns were the home of refugees from the war. 'Argosies go downriver loaded with soldiers, and return with these unfortunates. They are brought here before they can be turned by the heretics.'

'Why do they live in such squalor?'

'They know no better, master. They are unchanged savages.'

'They must have been hunters once, or fishermen or farmers. Is there no room for them in the city? I think that it is much smaller than it once was.'

'Some of them may go to the empty quarters, I suppose, but most would be killed by bandits, and besides, the empty quarters are no good for agriculture. Wherever you dig there are stones, and stones beneath the stones. The Department of Indigenous Affairs likes to keep them in one place, where they can be watched. They get dole food, and a place to live.'

'I suppose many become beggars.'

Pandaras shook his head vigorously. 'No, no. They would be killed by the professional beggars if they tried. They are nothing, master. They are not even human beings. See how they live!'

In the shadows beneath the nearest of the shacks, beside a green, stagnant pool, two naked men were pulling pale guts from the belly of a small cayman. A boy was pissing into the water on the other side of the pool, and a woman was dipping water into a plastic bowl. On a platform above, a woman with a naked baby on her arm was crumbling grey lumps of edible plastic into a blackened wok hung over a tiny fire. Beside her, a child of indeterminate age and sex was listlessly sorting through wilted cabbage leaves.

Yama said, 'It seems to me that they are an army drawn up at the edge of the city.'

'They are nothing, master. We are the strength of the city, as you will see.'

Pandaras chose a stall by one of the wide causeways that ran out to the pontoon docks, and hungrily devoured a shrimp omelette and finished Yama's leavings while Yama warmed his hands around his bowl of tea. In the growing light Yama could see, three or four leagues downriver, the wall where he and Prefect Corin had been taken yesterday, a black line rising above red tile roofs like the back of a sleeping dragon. He wondered if the magistrates' screens could be turned in this direction. No, they had set machines to look for him, but he had dealt with them. For now he was safe.

Pandaras called out for more tea, and told Yama that there was an hour at least before the money changers opened.

Yama said, 'I will make good my debt to you, do not worry. Where will you go?'

'Perhaps with you, master,' Pandaras said, grinning. 'I'll help you find your family. You do not know where you were born, and wish to find it, while I know my birthplace all too well, and want to escape it.'

The boy had small, sharp teeth all exactly the same size. Yama noticed that his black, pointed fingernails were more like claws, and that his hands, with leathery pads on their palms and hooked thumbs stuck stiffly halfway up the wrists, resembled an animal's paws. He had seen many of Pandaras's bloodline yesterday, portering and leading draft animals and carrying out a hundred other kinds of menial jobs. The strength of the city.

Yama asked about the caterans who had been eating in the taproom of the inn, but Pandaras shrugged. 'I don't know them. They arrived only an hour before you, and they'll leave this morning for the Water Market by the Black Temple, looking for people who want to employ them. I thought that you might be one of them, until you showed my master the coin.'

'Perhaps I am one, but do not yet know it,' Yama said, thinking of his vow. He knew that he was still too young to join the army in the usual way, but his age would be no bar to becoming an irregular. Prefect Corin might think him young, but he had already killed a man in close combat, and had had more adventures in the past two decades than most people could expect in a lifetime. He said, 'Before we go anywhere else, take me to the Water Market, Pandaras. I want to see how it is done.'

'If you join up then I'll go with you, and be your squire. You've enough money to buy a good rifle, or better still, a pistol, and you'll need armour, too. I'll polish it bright between battles, and keep your devices clean—'

Yama laughed. 'Hush! You build a whole fantasy on a single whim. I only want to find out about the caterans; I do not yet want to become one. After I know more about where I come from, then, yes, I intend to enlist and help win the war. My brother was killed fighting the heretics. I have made a vow to fight in his place.'

Pandaras drained his cup of tea and spat fragments of bark onto the ground. 'We'll do the first before the Castellan of the Twelve Devotions sounds its noon gun,' he said, 'and the second before the Galaxy rises. With my help, anything is possible. But you must forgive my prattle. My people love to talk and to tell stories, and invent tall tales most of all. No doubt you see us as labourers little better than beasts of burden. And that is indeed how we earn our bread and beer, but although we may be poor in the things of the world, we are rich in the things of imagination. Our stories and songs are told and sung by every bloodline, and a few of us even gain brief fame as jongleurs to the great houses and the rich merchants, or as singers and musicians and storytellers of cassette recordings.'

Yama said, 'It would seem that with all their talents, your people deserve a better station than they have.'

'Ah, but we do not live long enough to profit from them. No more than twenty years is the usual; twenty-five is almost unheard of. You're surprised, but that's how it is. It is our curse and our gift. The swiftest stream polishes the pebbles smoothest, as my grandfather had it, and so with us. We live brief but intense lives, for from the pace of our living comes our songs and stories.'

Yama said, 'Then may I ask how old you are?'

Pandaras showed his sharp teeth. 'You think me your age, I'd guess, but I've no more than four years, and in another I'll marry. That is, if I don't go off adventuring with you.'

'If you could finish my search in a day, I would be the happiest man on Confluence, but I think it will take longer than that.'

'A white boat and a shining woman, and a picture of one of your ancestors made before the building of Confluence. What could be more distinctive? I'll make a song of it soon enough. Besides, you said that you know to begin your search in the records of the Department of Apothecaries and Chirurgeons.'

'If Dr Dismas did not lie. He lied about much else.'

The sky above the crowded rooftops was blue now, and traffic was thickening along the road. Fishing boats were moving out past the ends of the piers of the floating docks, their russet and tan sails bellying in the wind and white birds flying in their wake as they breasted the swell of the morning tide. As he walked beside Pandaras, Yama thought of the hundred leagues of docks, of the thousands of boats of the vast fishing fleets which put out every day to feed the myriad mouths of the city, and began to understand the true extent of Ys.

How could he ever expect to find out about his birth, or of the history of any one man, in such a mutable throng? And yet, he thought, Dr Dismas had found out something in the records of his department, and he did not doubt that he could find it too, and perhaps more. Freshly escaped from his adventure with the cateran and from the fusty fate the Aedile and Prefect Corin had wished upon him, Yama felt his heart rise. It did not occur to him that he might fail in his self-appointed quest. He was, as Pandaras had pointed out, still very young, and had yet to fail in anything important.

The first money changer refused Yama's rials after a mere glance. The second, whose office was in a tiny basement with a packed dirt floor and flaking pink plaster walls, spent a long time looking at the coins under a magnifying screen, then scraped a fleck from one coin and tried to dissolve it in a minim of aqua regia. The money changer was a small, scrawny old man almost lost in the folds of his black silk robe. He clucked to himself when the fleck of gold refused to dissolve even when he heated the watchglass, then motioned to his impassive bodyguard, who fetched out tea bowls and a battered aluminium pot, and resumed his position at the foot of the steps up to the street.

Pandaras haggled for an hour with the money changer, over several pots of tea and a plate of tiny honeycakes so piercingly sweet that they made Yama's teeth ache. Yama felt cramped and anxious in the dank little basement, with the tramp of feet going to and fro overhead and the bodyguard blocking most of the sunlight that spilled down the stair, and was relieved when at last Pandaras announced that the deal was done.

'We'll starve in a month, but this old man has a stone for a heart,' he said, staring boldly at the money changer.

'You are quite welcome to take your custom elsewhere,' the money changer said, thrusting his sharp face from the fold of black silk over his head and giving Pandaras a fierce, hawkish look. 'I'd say your coins were stolen, and any price I give you would be fair enough. As it is, I risk ruining my reputation on your behalf.'

'You'll not need to work again for a year,' Pandaras retorted. Despite the money changer's impatience, he insisted on counting the slew of silver and iron coins twice over. The iron pennies were pierced – for stringing around the neck, Pandaras said. He demonstrated the trick with his share before shaking hands with the money changer, who suddenly smiled and wished them every blessing of the Preservers.

The street was bright and hot after the money changer's basement. The road was busier than ever, and the traffic crowding its wide asphalt pavement moved at walking pace. The air was filled with the noise of hooves and wheels, the shouts and curses of drivers, the cries of hawkers and merchants, the silver notes of whistles and the brassy clangour of bells. Small boys darted amongst the legs of beasts and men, collecting the dung of horses, oxen and camels, which they would shape into patties and dry on walls for fuel for cooking fires. There were beggars and thieves, skyclad mendicants and palmers, jugglers and contortionists, mountebanks and magicians, and a thousand other wonders, so many that as he walked along amongst the throng Yama soon stopped noticing any but the most outrageous, for else he would have gone mad with wonder.

A black dome had been raised up amongst the masts of the ships and the flat roofs of the godowns at the edge of the river, and Yama pointed to it. 'That was not there when we first came here this morning,' he said.

'A voidship,' Pandaras said casually, and expressed surprise when Yama insisted that they go and look at it. He said, 'It's just a lighter for a voidship really. The ship to which it belongs is too big to make riverfall and hangs beyond the edge of Confluence. It has been there a full year now, unloading its ores. The lighter will have put in at the docks for fresh food. It's nothing special.'

In any case, they could not get close to the lighter; the dock was closed off and guarded by a squad of soldiers armed with fusiliers more suited to demolishing a citadel than keeping away sightseers. Yama looked up at the lighter's smooth black flank, which curved up to a blunt silver cap that shone with white fire in the sunlight, and wondered at what other suns it had seen. He could have stood there all day, filled with an undefined longing, but Pandaras took his arm and steered him away.

'It's dangerous to linger,' the boy said. 'The star-sailors steal children, it's said, because they cannot engender their own. If you see one, you'll understand. Most do not even look like men.'

As they walked on, Yama asked if Pandaras knew of the ship of the Ancients of Days.

Pandaras touched his fist to his throat. 'My grandfather said that he saw two of them walking through the streets of our quarter late one night, but everyone in Ys alive at that time claims as much.' He touched his fist to his throat and added, 'My grandfather said that they glowed the way the river water sometimes glows on summer nights, and that they stepped into the air and walked away above the rooftops. He made a song about it, but when he submitted it to the legates he was arrested for heresy, and he died under the question.'

The sun had climbed halfway to zenith by the time Yama and Pandaras reached the Black Temple and the Water Market. The Black Temple had once been extensive, built on its own island around a protrusion or plug of keelrock in a wide deep bay, but it had been devastated in the wars of the Age of Insurrection and had not been rebuilt, and now the falling level of the Great River had left it stranded in a shallow muddy lagoon fringed with palm trees. The outline of the temple's inner walls and a row of half-melted pillars stood amongst outcrops of keelrock and groves of flame trees; the three black circles of the temple's shrines glittered amongst grassy swales where the narthex had once stood. Nothing could destroy the shrines, not even the energies deployed in the battle which had won back Ys from the Insurrectionists, for they were only partly of the world of material existence. Services were still held at the Black Temple every New Year, Pandaras said, and Yama noticed the heaps of fresh flowers and offerings of fruits before the shrines. Although most of the avatars had disappeared in the Age of Insurrection, and the last had been silenced by the heretics, people still came to petition them.

At the mouth of the bay which surrounded the temple's small island, beyond wrinkled mudflats where flocks of white ibis stalked on delicate legs, on rafts and pontoons and barges, the Water Market was in full swing. The standards of a hundred condottieri flew from poles, and there were a dozen exhibition duels under way, each at the centre of a ring of spectators. There were stalls selling every kind of weapon, armourers sweating naked by their forges as they repaired or reforged pieces, provisioners extolling the virtue of their preserved fare. A merchant blew up a water bottle and jumped up and down on it to demonstrate its durability. Newly indentured convicts sat in sullen groups on benches behind the auction block, most sporting fresh mutilations. Galleys, pinnaces and picket boats stood offshore, their masts hung with bright flags that flapped in the strong, hot breeze.

Yama eagerly drank in the bustle and the noise, the exotic costumes of the caterans and the mundane dove-grey uniforms of regular soldiers mingled together, the ringing sound of the weapons of the duellists, and the smell of hot metal and plastic from the forges of the armourers. He wanted to see everything the city had to offer, to search its great temples and the meanest of its alleys and courts for any sign of his bloodline.

As he followed Pandaras along a rickety gangway between two rafts, someone stepped out of the crowd and hailed him. His heart turned over. It was the red-haired woman who last night had sat eating with the man he had killed. When she saw that he had heard her, she shouted again and raised her naked sword above her head.

18 ~ The Thing in the Bottle

'They are yours by right of arms,' Tamora, the red-haired cateran, said. 'The sword is too long for you, but I know an armourer who can shorten and rebalance it so sweetly you'd swear afterwards that's how it was first forged. The corselet and the greaves can be cut down to suit, and you can sell the trimmings. That way it pays for itself. Old armour is expensive because it's the best. Especially plastic armour, because no one knows how to make the stuff any more. You might think my breastplate is new, but that's only because I polished it this morning. It's a thousand years old if it's a day, but even if it's better than most of the clag they make these days, it's still only steel. But, see, these greaves are real old. I could have taken them, but that wouldn't be right. Everyone says we're vagabonds and thieves, but even if we don't belong to any department, we have our traditions. So these are your responsibility now. You won them by right of arms. You can do what you want with them. Throw them in the river if you want, but it would be a fucking shame if you did.'

'She wants you to give them back to her as a reward for giving them to you,' Pandaras said.

'I talk to the master,' Tamora said, 'not his fool.'

Pandaras struck an attitude. 'I am his squire.'

'I was the fool,' Yama said to Tamora, 'and because I was a fool your friend died. That is why I cannot take his things.'

Tamora shrugged. 'Cyg was no friend of mine, and as far as I'm concerned he was the fool, getting himself killed by a scrap of a thing like you. Why, you're so newly hatched you probably still have eggshell stuck to your back.'

Pandaras said, 'If this is to be your career, then you must arm yourself properly, master. As your squire, I strongly suggest it.'

'Squire, is it?' Tamora cracked open another oyster with her strong, ridged fingernails, slurped up the flesh and wiped her mouth with the back of her hand. The cateran's bright red hair, which Yama suspected was dyed, was cut short over her skull, with a long fringe in the back that fell to her shoulders. She wore her steel breastplate over a skirt made of leather strips and a mesh shirt which left her muscular arms bare. There was a tattoo of a bird sitting on a nest of flames on the tawny skin of her upper arm, the flames in red ink, the bird, its wings outstretched as if drying them in the fire which was consuming it, in blue.

They were sitting in the shade of an umbrella at a table by a food stall on the waterfront, near the causeway that led from the shore to the island of the Black Temple. It was sunstruck noon. The owner of the stall was sitting under the awning by the ice-chest, listening with half-closed eyes to a long antiphonal prayer burbling from the cassette recorder under his chair.

Tamora squinted against the silver light that burned off the wet mudflats. She had a small, triangular, feral face, with green eyes and a wide mouth that stretched to the hinges of her jaw. Her eyebrows were a single brick-red rope; now the rope dented in the middle and she said, 'Caterans don't have squires. That's for regular officers, and their squires are appointed from the common ranks. This boy has leeched onto you, Yama. I'll get rid of him if you want.'

Yama said, 'It is just a joke between the two of us.'

'I *am* his squire,' Pandaras insisted. 'My master is of noble birth. He deserves a train of servants, but I'm so good he needs no other.'

Yama laughed.

Tamora squinted at Pandaras. 'You people are all the same to me, like fucking rats running around underfoot, but I could swear you're the pot boy of the crutty inn where I stayed the night.' She told Yama, 'If I was more suspicious, I might suspect a plot.'

'If there was a plot, it was between your friend and the landlord of the inn.'

'Grah. I suspected as much. If I survive my present job, and there's no reason why I shouldn't, then I'll have words with that rogue. More than words, in fact.'

Tamora's usual expression was a sullen, suspicious pout, but when she smiled her face came to life, as if a mask had suddenly dropped, or the sun had come out from behind a cloud. She smiled now, as if at the thought of her revenge. Her upper incisors were long and stout and sharply pointed.

Yama said, 'He did not profit from his treachery.'

Pandaras kicked him under the table and frowned.

Tamora said, 'I'm not after your fucking money, or else I would have taken it already. I have just now taken on a new job, so be quick in making up your mind on how you'll dispose of what is due to you by right of arms. As I said before, you can throw it in the river or leave it for the scavengers if you want, but it's good gear.'

Yama picked up the sword. Its broad blade was iron and had seen a lot of use. Its nicked edge was razor sharp. The hilt was wound with bronze wire; the pommel an unornamented plastic ball, chipped and dented. He held the blade up before his face, then essayed a few passes. The cut on his forearm stickily parted under the crude bandage he had tied and he put the sword down. No one sitting at the tables around the stall had looked at the display, although he had hoped that they would.

He said, 'I have a knife that serves me well enough, and the sword is made for a strong unsubtle man more used to hewing wood than fighting properly. Find a woodsman and give it to him, although I suspect he would rather keep his axe. But I will take the armour. As you say, old armour is the best.'

'Well, at least you know something about weapons,' Tamora said grudgingly. 'Are you here looking for hire? If so, I'll give some advice for free. Come back tomorrow, early. That's when the best jobs are available. Condottieri like a soldier who can rise early.'

'I had thought to watch a duel or two,' Yama said.

'Grah. Exhibition matches between oiled cornfed oafs who wouldn't last a minute in real battle. Do you think we fight with swords against the fucking heretics? The matches draw people who would otherwise not come, that's all. They get drunk with recruiting sergeants and the next day find themselves indentured in the army, with a hangover and the taste of the oath like a copper penny in their mouth.'

'I am not here to join the army. Perhaps I will become a cateran eventually, but not yet.'

'He's looking for his people,' Pandaras said.

It was Yama's turn to kick under the table. It was green-painted tin, with a bamboo and paper umbrella. He said, 'I am looking for certain records in one of the departmental libraries.'

197

Tamora swallowed the last oyster and belched. 'Then sign up with the department. Better still, join the fucking archivists. After ten years' apprenticeship you might just be sent to the Palace of the Memory of the People; more likely you'll be sent to listen to the stories of unchanged toads squatting in some mudhole. But that's a better chance than trying to bribe your way into their confidence. They're a frugal lot, and besides, if any one of them was caught betraying his duty he'd be executed on the spot. The same penalty applies to any who try to bribe them. Those records are all that remains of the dead, kept until they're resurrected at the end of time. It's serious shit to even look at them the wrong way.'

'The Puranas say that the Preservers need no records, for at the end of time an infinite amount of energy becomes available. In the last instant as the Universe falls into itself all is possible, and everyone who ever lived or ever could have lived will live again for ever, in that eternal now. Besides, the records I am looking for are not in the Palace of the Memory of the People, but in the archives of the Department of Apothecaries and Chirurgeons.'

'That's more or less the same place. On the roof rather than inside, that's all.'

'Just as I told you, master,' Pandaras said. 'You don't need her to show you what I already know!'

Tamora ignored him. 'Their records are maintained by archivists, too. Unless you're a sawbones or a sawbones' runner, you can forget about it. It's the same in all the departments. The truth is expensive and difficult to keep pure, and so getting at it without proper authority is dangerous.' Tamora smiled. 'But that doesn't mean that there aren't ways of getting at it.'

Pandaras said, 'She is baiting a hook. Be careful.'

Yama said to Tamora, 'Tell me this. You have fought against the heretics – that is what the tattoo on your arm implies, anyway. In all your travels, have you ever seen any other men and women like me?'

'I fought in two campaigns, and in the last I was so badly wounded that I took a year recovering. When I'm fit I'll go again. It's better pay than bodyguard or pickup work, and more honourable, although honour has little to do with it when you're there. No, I haven't seen anyone like you, but it doesn't signify. There are ten thousand bloodlines on Confluence, not counting all those hill tribes of indigens, who are little more than animals.'

'Then you see how hard I must search,' Yama said.

Tamora smiled. It seemed to split her face in half. 'How much will you pay?'

'Master—'

'All I have. I changed two gold rials for smaller coins this morning. It is yours, if you help me.'

Pandaras whistled and looked up at the blue sky.

'Grah. Against death, that is not so much.'

Yama said, 'Do they guard the records with men, or with machines?'

'Why, mostly machines of course. As I said, the records of any department are important. Even the poorest departments guard their archives carefully – often their archives are all they have left.'

'Well, it might be easier than you suppose.'

Tamora stared at Yama. He met her luminous green gaze and for a long moment the rest of the world melted away. Her pupils were vertical slits edged with closely crowded dots of golden pigment that faded to copper at the periphery. Yama imagined drowning in that green-gold gaze, as a luckless fisherman might drown in the Great River's flood. It was the heart-stopping gaze that a predator turns upon its prey.

Tamora's voice said from far away, 'Before I help you, if I do help you, you must prove yourself.'

Yama said faintly, 'How?'

'Don't trust her,' Pandaras said. 'If she really wanted the job, she'd have asked for all your money. There are plenty like her. If we threw a stone in any direction, we'd hit at least two.'

Tamora said, 'In a way, you owe it to me.'

Yama was still looking into Tamora's gaze. He said, 'Cyg was going to partner you, I think. Now I know why you came here. You were not looking for me, but for a replacement. Well, what would you have me do?'

Tamora pointed over his shoulder. He turned, and saw the black, silver-capped dome of the voidship lighter rising beyond the flame trees of the island of the Black Temple. The cateran said, 'We have to bring back a star-sailor who jumped ship.'

They sold the sword to an armourer for rather more than Yama expected, and left the corselet and the greaves with the same man to be cut down. Tamora insisted that Yama get his wounds treated by one of the leeches who had set up their stalls near the duelling arena, and Yama sat and watched two men fence with chainsaws ('Showboat juggling,' Tamora sneered) while the cut on his forearm was stitched, painted with blue gel and neatly bandaged. The shallow cut on Yama's palm should be left to heal on its own, the leech said, but Tamora made him bandage it anyway, saying that the bandage would help Yama grip his knife. She bought Pandaras a knife with a long thin round blade and a fingerguard chased with a chrysanthemum flower; it was called a kidney puncher.

'Suitable for sneaking up on someone in the dark,' Tamora said. 'If you stand on tiptoe, rat-boy, you should be able to reach someone's vitals with this.'

Pandaras flexed the knife's blade between two clumsy, clawed fingers, licked it with his long, pink tongue, then tucked it in his belt. Yama told him, 'You do not have to follow me. I killed the man who would have helped her, and it is only proper that I should take his place. But there is no need for you to come.'

'Well put,' Tamora said.

Pandaras showed his small sharp teeth. 'Who else would watch your back, master? Besides, I have never been aboard a voidship.'

One of the guards escorted them across the wharf to the voidship lighter. Cables and flexible plastic hoses lay everywhere, like a tangle of basking snakes. Labourers, nearly naked in the hot sunlight, were winching a cavernous pipe towards an opening which had dilated in the lighter's black hull. An ordinary canvas and bamboo gangway angled up to a smaller entrance.

Yama felt a distinct pressure sweep over his skin as, following Tamora up the gangway, he ducked beneath the port's rim. Inside, a passageway sloped away to the left, curving as it rose so that its end could not be seen. Yama supposed that it spiralled around the inside of the hull of the lighter like the track a maggot leaves in a fruit. It was circular in cross-section, and lit by a soft directionless red light that seemed to hang in the air like smoke. Although the lighter's black hull radiated the day's heat, inside it was as chilly as the mountain garden of the curators of the City of the Dead.

A guard waited inside. He was a short, thickset man with a bland face and a broad, humped back. His head was shaven, and ugly red scars criss-crossed his scalp. He wore a many-pocketed waistcoat and loose-fitting trousers, and did not appear to be armed. He told them to keep to the middle of the passageway, not to touch anything, and not to talk to any voices which might challenge them.

'I've been here before,' Tamora said. She seemed subdued in the red light and the chill air of the passageway.

'I remember you,' the guard said, 'and I remember a man with only one eye, but I do not remember your companions.'

'My original partner ran into something unexpected. But I'm here, as I said I would be, and I vouch for these two. Lead on. This place is like a tomb.'

'It is older than any tomb,' the guard said.

They climbed around two turns of the passageway. Groups of coloured lights were set at random in the black stuff which sheathed the walls and ceiling and floor. The floor gave softly beneath Yama's boots, and there was a faint vibration in the red-lit air, so low-pitched that he felt it more in his bones than in his ears.

The guard stopped and pressed his palm against the wall, and the black stuff puckered and pulled back with a grating noise. Ordinary light flooded through the orifice, which opened onto a room no more than twenty paces across and ringed round with a narrow window that looked out across the roofs of the city in one direction and the glittering expanse of the Great River in the other. Irregular clusters of coloured lights depended from the ceiling like stalactites in a cave, and a thick-walled glass bottle hung from the ceiling in the middle of the clusters of lights, containing some kind of red and white blossom in turgid liquid.

Yama whispered to Tamora, 'Where is the captain?'

He had read several of the old romances in the library of the peel-house, and expected a tall man in a crisp, archaic uniform, with sharp, bright eyes focused on the vast distances between stars, and skin tanned black with the fierce light of alien suns.

Pandaras snickered, but fell silent when the guard looked at him.

The guard said, 'There is no captain except when the crew meld, but the pilot of this vessel will talk with you.'

Tamora said, 'The same one I talked with two days ago?'

'Does it matter?' the guard said. He pulled a golden circlet from one of his pockets and set it on his scarred scalp. At once, his body stiffened. His eyes blinked, each to a different rhythm, and his mouth opened and closed.

Tamora stepped up to him and said, 'Do you know who I am?'

The guard's mouth hung open. Spittle looped between his lips. His tongue writhed behind his teeth like a wounded snake and his breath came out as a hiss that slowly shaped itself into a word.

'Yessss.'

Pandaras nudged Yama and indicated the bottled blossom with a crooked thumb. 'There's the star-sailor,' he said. 'It's talking through the guard.'

Yama looked more closely at the thing inside the bottle. What he had thought were fleshy petals of some exotic flower were the lobes of a mantle that bunched around a core woven of pink and grey filaments. Feathery gills rich with red blood waved slowly to and fro in the thick liquid in which they were suspended. It was a little like a squid, but instead of tentacles it had white, many-branching fibres that disappeared into the base of its bottle.

Pandaras whispered, 'Nothing but a nervous system. That's why it needs puppets.'

The guard jerked his head around and stared at Yama and Pandaras. His eyes were no longer blinking at different rates, but the pupil of the left eye was much bigger than that of the right. Speaking with great effort, as if forcing the words around pebbles lodged in his throat, he said, 'You told me you would bring only one other.'

Tamora said, 'The taller one, yes. But he has brought his . . . servant.'

Pandaras stepped forward and bowed low from the waist. 'I am Yama's squire. He is a perfect master of fighting. Only this night past he killed a man, an experienced fighter better armed than he, who thought to rob him while he slept.'

The star-sailor said through its puppet, 'I have not seen the bloodline for a long time, but you have chosen well. He has abilities you will find useful.'

Yama stared at the thing in the bottle, shocked to the core.

Tamora said, 'Is that so?'

'I scanned all of you when you stepped aboard. This one—' the guard slammed his chest with his open hand '—will see to the contract, following local custom. It will be best to return with the whole body, but if it is badly damaged then you must bring a sample of tissue. A piece the size of your smallest finger will be sufficient. You remember what I told you.'

Yama said, 'Wait. You know my bloodline?'

Tamora ignored him. She closed her eyes and recited, ' "It will be lying close to the spine. The host must be mutilated to obliterate all trace of occupation. Burn it if possible." ' She opened her eyes. 'Suppose we're caught? What do we tell the magistrates?'

'If you are caught by your quarry, you will not live to tell the magistrates anything.'

'He'll know you sent us.'

'And we will send others, if you fail. I trust you will not.'

'You know my bloodline,' Yama said. 'How do you know my bloodline?'

Pandaras said, 'We aren't the first to try this, are we?'

'There was one attempt before,' Tamora said. 'It failed. That is why we're being so well paid.'

The guard said, 'If you succeed.'

'Grah. You say I have a miracle worker with me. Of course we'll succeed.'

The guard was groping for the circlet on his head. Yama said quickly, 'No! I want you to tell me how you know my bloodline!'

The guard's head jerked around. 'We thought you all dead,' he said, and pulled the circlet from his scalp. He fell to his knees and retched up a mouthful of yellow bile which was absorbed by the black floor, then got to his feet and wiped his mouth on the sleeve of his tunic. He said in his own voice, 'Was it agreed?'

Tamora said, 'You'll make the contract, and we put our thumbs to it.'

'Outside,' the guard said.

Yama said, 'He knew who I was! I must talk with him!'

The guard got between Yama and the bottled star-sailor. He said, 'Perhaps when you return.'

'We should get started straight away,' Tamora said. 'It's a long haul to the estate.'

The door ground open. Yama looked at the star-sailor in its bottle, and said, 'I will return, and with many questions.'

19 ~ Iachimo

When the giant guard went past the other side of the gate for the third time, Tamora said, 'Every four hundred heartbeats. You could boil an egg by him.'

She lay beside Yama and Pandaras under a clump of thorny bushes in the shadows beyond the fierce white glare of a battery of electric arc lamps that crackled at the top of the wall. The gate was a square lattice of steel bars set in a high wall of fused rock, polished as smoothly as black glass. The wall stretched away into the darkness on either side, separated from the dry scrub by a wide swathe of barren sandy soil.

Yama said, 'I still think we should go over the wall somewhere else. The rest of the perimeter cannot be as heavily guarded as the gate.'

'The gate is heavily guarded because it's the weakest part of the wall,' Tamora said. 'That's why we're going in through it. The guard is a man. Doesn't look it, but he is. He decides who to let in and who to keep out. Elsewhere, the guards will be machines or dogs. They'll kill without thinking and do it so quick you won't know it until you find yourself in the hands of the Preservers. Listen. After the guard goes past again, I'll climb the wall, kill him, and open the gates to let you in.'

'If he raises the alarm—'

'He won't have time for that,' Tamora said, and showed her teeth.

'Those won't do any good against armour,' Pandaras said.

'They'll snap off your head if you don't swallow your tongue. Be quiet. This is warrior work.'

They were all tired and on edge. It had been a long journey from the waterfront. Although they had travelled most of the distance in a public calash, they had had to walk the final three leagues. The merchant's estate was at the top of one of a straggling range of hills that, linked by steep scrub-covered ridges, rose like worn teeth at the edge of the city's wide basin. An age ago, the hills had been part of the city. As Yama, Tamora and Pandaras had climbed through dry, fragrant pine woods, they had stumbled upon an ancient paved street and the remains of the buildings which had once lined it. They had rested there until just after sunset. Yama and Pandaras had eaten the raisin cakes they had bought hours before, while Tamora had prowled impatiently amongst the ruins, wolfing strips of dried meat and snicking off the fluffy seeding heads of fireweed with her rapier.

The merchant who owned the estate was a star-sailor who had jumped ship the last time it had lain off the edge of Confluence, over forty years ago. He had amassed his wealth by surreptitious deployment of technologies whose use was forbidden outside the voidships. For that alone, quite apart from the crime of desertion, he had been sentenced to death by his crewmates, but they had no jurisdiction outside their ship and, because of the same laws which the merchant had violated, could not use their powers to capture him.

Tamora was the second cateran hired to carry out the sentence. The first had not returned, and was presumed to have been killed by the merchant's guards. Yama thought that this put them at a disadvantage, since the merchant would be expecting another attack, but Tamora said it made no difference.

'He has been expecting this ever since his old ship returned. That's why he has retreated to this estate, which has better defences than the compound he maintains in the city. We're lucky there aren't patrols outside the walls.'

In fact, Yama had already asked several machines to ignore them as they had toiled up the hill through the pine woods, but he did not point this out. There was an advantage in being able to do something no one suspected was possible. He already owed his life to this ability, and it was to his benefit to have Tamora believe that he had killed the cateran by force of arms rather than by lucky sleight of hand.

Now, crouched between Tamora and Pandaras in the dry brush, Yama could faintly sense other machines beyond the high black wall, but they were too far away to count, let alone influence. He was dry-mouthed, and his hands had a persistent uncontrollable tremor. All his adventures with Telmon had been childhood games without risk, inadequate preparation for the real thing. His suggestion to try another part of the wall was made as much from the need to delay the inevitable as to present an alternative strategy.

Pandaras said, 'I have an idea. Master, lend me your satchel, and that book you were reading.'

Tamora said fiercely, 'Do as I say. No more, no less.'

'I can have the guard open the gates for me,' Pandaras said. 'Or would you rather break your teeth on steel bars?'

'If you insist that we have to go through the gate,' Yama told Tamora, as he emptied out his satchel, 'at least we should listen to his idea.'

'Grah. Insist? I *tell* you what to do, and you do it. This is not a democracy. Wait!'

But Pandaras stood up and, with Yama's satchel slung around his neck, stepped out into the middle of the asphalt road which ran through the gateway. Tamora hissed in frustration as the boy walked into the glare of the arc lights, and Yama told her, 'He is cleverer than you think.'

'He'll be dead in a moment, clever or not.'

Pandaras banged on the gate. A bell trilled in the distance and dogs barked closer at hand. Yama said, 'Did you know there were dogs?'

'Grah. Dogs are nothing. It is easy to kill dogs.'

Yama was not so sure. Any one of the watchdogs of the peel-house could bring down an ox by clamping its powerful jaws on the windpipe of its victim and strangling it – and to judge by the volume and ferocity of the barking there were at least a dozen dogs beyond the gate.

The guard appeared on the other side of the gate. In his augmented armour, painted scarlet as if dipped in fresh blood, he was more than twice Pandaras's height. His eyes were red embers that glowed in the shadow beneath the bill of his flared helmet. Energy pistols mounted on his shoulders trained their muzzles on Pandaras and the guard's amplified bass voice boomed and echoed in the gateway.

Pandaras stood his ground. He held up the satchel and opened it and showed it to the guard, then took out the book and flipped through its pages in an exaggerated pantomime. The guard reached through the gate's steel lattice, his arm extending more than a man's arm should reach, but Pandaras danced backwards and put the book back in the satchel and folded his arms and shook his head from side to side.

The guard conferred with himself in a booming mutter of subsonics; then the red dots of his eyes brightened and a bar of intense red light swept up and down Pandaras. The red light winked out and with a clang

206

the gate sprang open a fraction. Pandaras slipped through the gap. The gate slammed shut behind him and he followed the monstrously tall guard into the shadows beyond.

'He's brave, your fool,' Tamora remarked, 'but he's even more of a fool than I thought possible.'

'Let us wait and see,' Yama said, although he did not really believe that the pot boy could do anything against the armoured giant. He was as astonished as Tamora when, a few minutes later, the dogs began to bark again, the gate clanged open, and Pandaras appeared in the gap and beckoned to them.

The giant guard sprawled on his belly in the roadway a little way beyond the gate. His helmet was turned to one side, and one of his arms was twisted behind him, as if he was trying to reach something on his back. Yama knew that the guard was dead, but he could feel a glimmer of machine intelligence in the man's skull, as if something still lived there, gazing with furious impotence through its host's dead eyes.

Pandaras returned Yama's satchel with a flourish, and Yama stuffed his belongings into it. Tamora kicked the guard's scarlet cuirass, then turned on Pandaras.

'Tell me how you did it later,' she said. 'Now we must silence the dogs. You're lucky they weren't set on you.'

Pandaras calmly stared up at her. 'A harmless messenger like me?'

'Don't be so fucking cute.'

'Let me deal with the dogs,' Yama said.

'Be quick,' Pandaras said. 'Before I killed him, the guard sent for someone to escort me to the house.'

The dogs were baying loudly, and other dogs answered them from distant parts of the grounds. Yama found the kennel to the left of the gate, cut into the base of the wall. Several dogs thrust their snouts through the kennel's barred door with such ferocity that their skull caps and the machines embedded in their shoulders struck sparks from the iron bars. They howled and whined and snapped in a ferocious tumult, and it took Yama several minutes to calm them down to a point where he could ask them to speak with their fellows and assure them that nothing was wrong.

'Go to sleep,' he told the dogs, once they had passed on the message, and then he ran back to the road.

Tamora and Pandaras had rolled the guard under the partial cover of a stand of moonflower bushes beside the road. Tamora had stripped the guard's heavy pistols from their shoulder mountings. She handed one to Yama and showed him how to press two contact plates together to make it fire.

'I should have one of those,' Pandaras said. 'Right of arms, and all that.'

Tamora showed her teeth. 'You killed a man in full powered armour twice your height and armed with both of these pistols. I'd say you are dangerous enough with that kidney puncher I chose for you. Follow me, if you can!'

She threw herself into the bushes, and Yama and Pandaras ran after her, thrashing through drooping branches laden with white, waxy blossoms. Tamora and Pandaras quickly outpaced Yama, but Pandaras could not sustain his initial burst of speed and Yama soon caught up with him. The boy was leaning against the trunk of a cork oak, watching the dark stretch of grass beyond while he tried to get his breath back.

'She has the blood rage,' Pandaras said, when he could speak again. 'No sense in chasing after her.'

Yama saw a string of lights burning far off through a screen of trees on the far side of the wide lawn. He began to walk in that direction, with Pandaras trotting at his side.

Yama said, 'Will you tell me how you killed the guard? I might need the trick myself.'

'How did you calm the watchdogs?'

'Do you always answer a question with a question?'

'We say that what you know makes you what you are. So you should never be free with what you know, or strangers will take pieces of you until nothing is left.'

'Nothing is free in this city, it seems.'

'Only the Preservers know everything, master. Everyone else must pay or trade for information. How did you calm the dogs?'

'We have similar dogs at home. I know how to talk to them.'

'Perhaps you'll teach me that trick when we have time.'

'I am not sure if that is possible, Pandaras, but I suppose that I can try. How did you get through the gate and kill the guard?'

'I showed him your book. I saw you reading in it when we rested in the ruins. It's very old, and therefore very valuable. My former master—' Pandaras spat on the clipped grass '—and that stupid cateran you killed

208

would have taken the gold rials and left the book, but my mother's family deals in books, and I know a little about them. Enough to know that it is worth more than the money. I talked with someone through the guard, and they let me in. The rich often collect books. There is power in them.'

'Because of the knowledge they contain.'

'You're catching on. As for killing the guard, it was no trick. I'll tell you how I did it now, master, and you must tell me something later. The guard seemed a giant, but he was an ordinary man inside that armour. Without power, he could not move a step; with it, he could sling a horse over his shoulders and still run as fast as a deer. I jumped onto his back, where he couldn't reach me, and pulled the cable that connected the power supply to the muscles in his armour. Then I stuck my knife in the gap where the cable went in, and pierced his spinal cord. A trick one of my stepbrothers taught me. The family of my mother's third husband work in a foundry that refurbishes armour. I helped out there when I was a kit. You get to know the weak points that way – they're where mending is most needed. Do we have to go so fast?'

'Where is the house, Pandaras?'

'This man is rich, but he is not one of the old trading families, who have estates upriver of the city. So he has a compound by the docks where he does his business, and this estate in the hills on the edge of the city. That is why the wall is so high and strong, and why there are many guards. They all fear bands of robbers out here, and arm their men as if to fight off a cohort.'

Yama nodded. 'The country beyond is very wild. It used to be part of the city, I think.'

'No one lives there. No one important, anyhow. The robbers come from the city.'

'The law is weaker here, then?'

'Stronger, master, if you fall foul of it. The rich make their own laws. For ordinary people, it's the magistrates who decide right and wrong. Isn't that how it was where you come from?'

Yama thought of the Aedile, and of the militia. He said, 'More or less. Then the house will be fortified. Sheer force of arms might not be the best way to try and enter it.'

'Fortified and hidden. That's the fashion these days. We could wander around for a day and not find it. Those lights are probably where the servants live, or a compound for other guards.' Pandaras stopped to untangle the unravelling edge of his sleeve from the thorny canes of a bush. 'If you ask me, this crutty greenery is all part of the defences.'

Yama said, 'There is a path through there. Perhaps that will lead to the house.'

'If it was that simple, we'd all be rich, and have big houses of our own, neh? It probably leads to a pit full of caymans or snakes.'

'Well, someone is coming along it, anyway. Here.'

Yama gave the pistol to Pandaras. It was so heavy that the boy needed both hands to hold it. 'Wait,' he said, 'you can't—'

But Yama ran towards the lights and the sound of hooves, carried by a rush of exhilaration. It was better to act than to hide, he thought, and in that moment understood why Tamora had charged off so recklessly. As he ran, he took the book from his satchel; when lights swooped towards him through the dark air, he stopped and held it up. A triplet of machines spun to a halt above his head and bathed him in a flood of white light. Yama squinted through their radiance at the three riders who had pulled up at the edge of the road.

Two guards in plastic armour reined in their prancing mounts and levelled light lances at him. The third was a mild old man on a grey palfrey. He wore a plain black tunic and his long white hair was brushed back from the narrow blade of his face. His skin was yellow and very smooth, stretched tautly over high cheekbones and a tall, ridged brow.

Yama held the book higher. The white-haired man said, 'Why aren't you waiting at the gate?'

'The guard was attacked, and I got scared and ran. Thieves have been after what I carry ever since I have come to this city. Only last night I had to kill a man who wanted to steal from me.'

The white-haired man jogged his palfrey so that it stepped sideways towards Yama, and he leaned down to peer at the book. He said, 'I can certainly see why someone would want to steal this.'

'I have been told that it is very valuable.'

'Indeed.' The white-haired man stared at Yama for a full minute. The two guards watched him, although their lances were still pointed at Yama, who stood quite still in the light of the three machines. At last, the man said, 'Where are you from, boy?'

'Downriver.'

Did he know? And if he knew, how many others?

'You've been amongst the tombs, have you not?'

'You are very wise, dominie.'

It was possible that the Aedile knew. Perhaps that was why he had wanted to bury Yama in a drab clerkship, away from the eyes of the world. And if the Aedile had known, then Prefect Corin had known too.

One of the guards said, 'Take the book and let us deal with him. He won't be missed.'

'I allowed him in,' the white-haired man said. 'Although he should have waited by the gate, I will continue to be responsible for him. Boy, where did you get that book? From one of the old tombs downriver? Did you find anything else there?'

Before Yama could answer, the second guard said, 'He has the pallid look of a tomb-robber.'

The white-haired man held up a hand. His fingers were very long, with nails filed to points and painted black. 'It isn't just the book. I'm interested in the boy too.'

The first guard said, 'He carries a power knife in his satchel.'

'More loot, I expect,' the white-haired man said. 'You won't use it here, will you, boy?'

'I have not come to kill you,' Yama said.

The second guard said, 'He's a little old for you, Iachimo.'

'Be silent,' the white-haired man, Iachimo, said pleasantly, 'or I'll slice out your tongue and eat it in front of you.' He told Yama, 'They obey me because they know I never make an idle threat. I wish it were otherwise, but you cannot buy loyalty. You must win it by fear or by love. I find fear to be more effective.'

The second guard said, 'We should check the gate.'

Iachimo said, 'The dogs have not raised any real alarm, and neither has the guard.'

The first guard said, 'But here's this boy wandering the grounds. There might be others.'

'Oh, very well,' Iachimo said, 'but be quick.' He swung down from his palfrey and told Yama, 'You'll come with me, boy.'

As they crossed the road and plunged into a stand of pine trees beyond, Iachimo said, 'Is the book from the City of the Dead? Answer truthfully. I can smell out a lie, and I have little patience for evasion.'

Yama did not doubt it, but he thought to himself that Iachimo was the kind of man who believed too strongly in his cleverness, and so held all others in contempt and did not pay as much attention to them as he should. He said, 'It was not from the City of the Dead, dominie, but a place close by.'

'Hmm. As I remember, the house occupied by the Aedile of Aeolis has an extensive library.' Iachimo turned and looked at Yama and smiled. 'I see I have hit the truth. Well, I doubt that the Aedile will miss it. The library is a depository of all kinds of rubbish, but as the fisherfolk of that region have it, rubies are sometimes engendered in mud by the light of the Eye of the Preservers. Nonsense, of course, but despite that it has a grain of truth. In this case, the fisherfolk are familiar with pearls, which are produced by certain shellfish when they are irritated by a speck of grit, and secrete layers of slime to enclose the irritation. This slime hardens, and becomes the black or red pearls so eagerly sought by gentlemen and ladies of high breeding, who do not know of the base origin of their beloved jewels. Your book is a pearl, without doubt. I knew it as soon as I saw it, although I do not think it was you who held it up at the gate.'

'It was my friend. But he got scared and ran off.'

'The guards will catch him. Or the dogs, if he is unlucky.'

'He's only a pot boy from one of the inns by the waterfront. I struck up a friendship with him.'

'From which he hoped to profit, I expect,' Iachimo said, and then stopped and turned to look back at the way they had come.

A moment later, a thread of white light lanced through the darkness, illuminating a distant line of trees. Yama felt the ground tremble beneath his feet; a noise like thunder rolled through the grounds.

Iachimo grasped Yama's shoulders and pushed him forward. 'One of the weapons mounted by the gatekeeper, unless I am mistaken. And I am never mistaken. Your friend has been found, I believe. Do not think of running, boy, or you'll suffer the same fate.'

Yama did not resist. Both Tamora and Pandaras were armed with the pistols taken from the gatekeeper, and Iachimo did not yet know that the gatekeeper was dead. Besides, he was being taken to the very place the others were looking for.

Yama and Iachimo descended into a narrow defile between steep rock walls studded with ferns and orchids. Another white flash lit the crack of sky above. Pebbles rattled down the walls in the aftershock. Iachimo tightened his grip on Yama's shoulder and pushed him on. 'This matter is consuming more time than I like,' he said.

'Are you in charge of the guards? They do not seem to be doing a very good job.'

'I am in charge of the entire household. And do not think I turned out for you, boy. It was the book. But I admit you are a curiosity. There could be some advantage here.'

Yama said boldly, 'What do you know about my bloodline? You recognized it, and that was why I was not killed.'

'You know less than I, I think. I wonder if you even know your parents.'

'Only that my mother is dead.'

A silver lady in a white boat. The old Constable, Thaw, had said that he had plucked Yama from her dead breast, but as a young boy Yama had dreamed that she had only been profoundly asleep, and was searching for him in the wilderness of tombs around Aeolis. Sometimes he had searched for her there – as he was searching still.

Iachimo said, 'Oh, she's dead all right. Dead ages past. You're probably first generation, revived from a stored template.'

The narrow defile opened out into a courtyard dimly lit by a scattering of floating lanterns, tiny as fireflies, that drifted in the black air. Its tiled floor was crowded with grey, life-sized statues of men and animals in a variety of contorted poses. Iachimo pushed Yama forward. Horribly, the statues stirred and trembled, sending up ripples of grey dust and a dry scent of electricity. Some opened their eyes, but the orbs they rolled towards Yama were like dry, white marbles.

Iachimo said in Yama's ear, 'There's worse that can happen to you than being returned to storage. Do we understand each other?'

Yama thought of his knife. It occurred to him that there were situations in which it might be more merciful to use it against himself rather than his enemies. He said, 'You are taking me to your master.'

'He wants only to see the book. You will be a surprise gift. We'll see what shakes out, and afterwards we'll talk.'

Iachimo smiled at Yama, but it was merely a movement of certain muscles in his narrow, high-browed face. He was lost in his own thoughts, Yama saw, a man so clever that he schemed as naturally as other men breathed.

Yama said, 'How do you know about my bloodline?'

'My master's bloodline is long-lived, and he is one of the oldest. He has taught me much about the history of the world. I know that he will be interested in you. Of course, he may want you killed, but I will try to prevent it. And so you owe me your life twice over. Think of that, when you talk with him. We can do things for each other, you and I.'

Yama remembered that the pilot of the voidship lighter had said that it knew his bloodline, and understood that he was a prize which Iachimo would offer to his master in the hope of advancement or reward. He said, 'It seems to me that this is a very one-sided bargain. What will I gain?'

'Your life, to begin with. My master may want to kill you at once, or use you and then kill you, but I can help you, and you can help me. Damn these things!'

Iachimo was standing beside the statue of a naked boy – or perhaps it had once been a living boy, encased or transformed in some way – and the statue had managed to grasp the hem of his tunic. Iachimo tugged impatiently, then broke off the statue's fingers, one by one. They made a dry snapping sound, and fell to dust when they struck the floor.

Iachimo brushed his hands together briskly and said, 'My master has revived certain technologies long thought forgotten. It is the basis of his fortune and his power. You understand why you will be of considerable interest to him.'

Yama realized that this was a question, but he did not know how to begin to answer it. Instead, he said, 'It is a very old edition of the Puranas.'

'Oh, the book. Like you, it is not an original, but it is not far removed. You have read it?'

'Yes.'

'Don't tell my master that. Tell him you stole it, nothing more. Lie if you must; otherwise he may well have you killed on the spot, and that is something that will be difficult for me to prevent. He controls the guards here. Let us go. He is waiting.'

On the far side of the courtyard was an arched doorway and a broad flight of marble steps that led down towards a pool of warm white light. Iachimo's long, pointed nails dug into Yama's shoulder, pricking his skin through his shirt.

'Stand straight,' Iachimo said. 'Use your backbone as it was intended.

Remember that you were made in the image of the Preservers, and forget that your ancestors were animals that went about on all fours. Good. Now walk forward, and do not stare at anything. Most especially, do not stare at my master. He is more sensitive than he might appear. He has not always been as he is now.'

20 ~ The Hollow Man

Even before Yama reached the bottom of the stairs, he knew that there was a large number of machines ahead of him, but the size of the room was still surprising. Golden pillars twisted into fantastic shapes marched away across an emerald green lawn, lending perspective to a space perhaps a thousand paces long and three hundred wide. The lawn was studded with islands of couches upholstered in brilliant silks, and fountains and dwarf fruit trees and statues – these last merely of red sandstone or marble, not petrified flesh. Displays of exotic flowers perfumed the air. Constellations of brilliant white lights floated in the air beneath a high glass ceiling. Above the glass was not air but water – schools of golden and black carp lazily swam through illuminated currents, and pads of water lilies hung above them like the silhouettes of clouds.

Thousands of tiny machines crawled amongst the closely trimmed blades of grass or spun through the bright air like silver beetles or dragonflies with mica wings, their thoughts a single rising harmonic in Yama's head. Men in scarlet and white uniforms and silver helmets stood in alcoves carved into the marble walls. They were unnaturally still and, like the fallen guard at the gate, emitted faint glimmers of machine intelligence, as if machines inhabited their skulls.

As Yama walked across the lawn, with Iachimo following close behind, he heard music in the distance: the chiming runs of a tambura like silver laughter over the solemn pulse of a tabla. A light sculpture twisted in the air like a writhing column of brightly coloured scarves seen through a heat haze.

The two musicians sat in a nest of embroidered silk cushions to one side of a huge couch on which lay the fattest man Yama had ever seen. He was naked except for a loincloth, and as hairless as a seal. A gold circlet crowned his shaven head. The thick folds of his belly spilled his flanks and draped his swollen thighs. His black skin shone with oils and unguents; the light of the sculpture slid over it in greasy rainbows. He was propped on his side amongst cushions and bolsters, and pawed in a distracted fashion at a naked woman who was feeding him pastries from a pile stacked high on a silver salver. Without doubt, this was the master of the house, the merchant, the rogue star-sailor.

Yama halted a few paces from him and bowed from the waist, but the merchant did not acknowledge him. Yama stood and sweated, with Iachimo beside him, while the musicians played through the variations of their raga and the merchant ate a dozen pastries one after the other and stroked the gleaming pillows of the woman's large breasts with swollen, ring-encrusted fingers. Like her master, the woman was quite without hair. The petals of her labia were pierced with rings; from one of these rings a fine gold chain ran to a bracelet on the merchant's wrist.

When the concluding chimes of the tambura had died away, the merchant closed his eyes and sighed deeply, then waved at the musicians in dismissal. 'Drink,' he said in a high, wheezing voice. The woman jumped up and poured red wine into a bowl which she held to the merchant's lips. He slobbered at the wine horribly and it spilled over his chin and chest onto the grassy floor. Yama saw now that the cushions of the couch were stained with old spillages and littered with crumbs and half-eaten crusts; underlying the rich scents of spikenard and jasmine and the sweet smoke of candles which floated in a bowl of water was a stale reek of old sweat and spoiled food.

The merchant belched and glanced at Yama. His cheeks were so puffed with fat that they pushed his mouth into a squashed rosebud, and his eyes peered above their ramparts like sentries, darting here and there as if expecting a sudden attack from any quarter. He said petulantly, 'What's this, Iachimo? A little old for your tastes, isn't he?'

Iachimo inclined his head. 'Very amusing, master, but you know that I would never trouble you with my bed companions. Perhaps you might look more closely. I believe that you will find he is a rare type, one not seen on Confluence for many an age.'

The merchant waved a doughy paw in front of his face, as if trying to swat a fly. 'You are always playing games, Iachimo. It will be your downfall. Tell me and have done with it.'

'I believe that he is one of the Builders,' Iachimo said.

The merchant laughed – a series of grunts that convulsed his vast, gleaming body as a storm tosses the surface of the river. At last he said, 'Your inventive mind never ceases to amaze me, Iachimo. I'll grant he has the somatype, but this is some river-rat a mountebank has surgically altered, no doubt inspired by some old carving or slate. You've been had.'

'He came here of his own accord. He brought a book of great antiquity. I have it here.'

The merchant took the copy of the Puranas from Iachimo and pawed through it, grunting to himself, before casually tossing it aside. It landed face down and splayed open amongst the cushions on which the merchant sprawled. Yama made a move to retrieve it, but Iachimo caught his arm.

'I've seen better,' the merchant said. 'If this fake says he brought you an original of the Puranas, then that too will be a fake. I'm no longer interested. Take this creature away, Iachimo, and its book. Dispose of it in the usual way, and dispose of its companion, too, once you've caught it. Or do I have to take charge of the guards and do that myself?'

'It won't be necessary, master. The other boy is certainly no more than a river-rat. He won't be missed. But this one is something rarer.' Iachimo prodded Yama in the small of the back with a fingernail as sharply pointed as a stiletto and whispered, 'Show him what you can do.'

'I do not understand what you want of me.'

'Oh, you understand,' Iachimo hissed. 'I know what you can do with machines. You got past the gatekeeper, so you know something of your inheritance.'

The merchant said, 'I'm in an indulgent mood, Iachimo. Here's your test. I'm going to order my soldiers to kill you, boy. Do you understand? Stop them, and we'll talk some more. Otherwise I'm rid of a fraud.'

Four of the guards started forward from their niches. Yama stepped back involuntarily as the guards, their faces expressionless beneath the bills of their silver helmets, raised their gleaming falchions and marched stiffly across the lawn towards him, two on the right, two on the left.

Iachimo said in a wheedling tone, 'Master, surely this isn't necessary.'

'Let me have my fun,' the merchant said. 'What is he to you, eh?'

Yama put his hand inside his satchel and found the hilt of his knife, but the guards were almost upon him and he knew that he could not fight four at once. He felt a tingling expansion and shouted at the top of his voice. 'Stop! Stop now!'

The guards froze in midstep, then, moving as one, knelt and laid down their falchions, and bent until their silver helmets touched the grass.

The merchant reared up and squealed, 'What is this? Do you betray me, Iachimo?'

'Quite the reverse, master. I'll kill him in a moment, if you give the word. But you see that he is no mountebank's fake.'

The merchant glared at Yama. There was a high whine, like a bee trapped in a bottle, and a machine dropped through the air and hovered in front of Yama's face. Red light flashed in the backs of his eyes. He asked the machine to go away, but the red light flashed again, filling his vision. He could see nothing but the red light and held himself still, although panic trembled in his breast like a trapped dove. He could feel every corner of the machine's small bright mind, but by a sudden inversion, as if a flower had suddenly dwindled down to the seed from which it had sprung, it was closed to him.

Somewhere beyond the red light, the merchant said, 'Recently born. No revenant. Where is he from, Iachimo?'

'Downriver,' Iachimo said, close by Yama's ear. 'Not far downriver, though. There's a small town called Aeolis amongst the old tombs. The book at least comes from there.'

The merchant said, 'The City of the Dead. There are older tombs elsewhere on Confluence, but I suppose you aren't to know that. Boy, stop trying to control my machines. I have told them to ignore you, and fortunately for you, you don't know the extent of your abilities. Fortunate for you, too, Iachimo. You risked a great deal bringing him here. I'll not forget that.'

Iachimo said, 'I am yours to punish or reward, master. As always. But be assured that this boy does not understand what he is. Otherwise I would not have been able to capture him.'

'He's done enough damage. I have reviewed the security systems, something you haven't troubled to do. He blinded the watchdogs and the machines patrolling the grounds, which is why he and his friend could wander the grounds with impunity. I have restored them. He has killed the gatekeeper too, and his friend is armed. Wait – there are two of them, both armed, and loose in the grounds. The security system was told to ignore them, but I'm tracking them now. You have let things get out of hand, Iachimo.'

'I had no reason to believe the security system was not operating correctly, master, but it proves my point. Here is a rare treasure.'

Yama turned his head back and forth, but could see nothing but red mist. There was a splinter of pain in each of his eyes. He said, 'Am I blinded?' and his voice was smaller and weaker than he would have liked.

'I suppose it isn't necessary,' the merchant said, and the red mist was gone.

Yama knuckled his stinging eyes, blinking hard in the sudden bright light. Two of the guards stood at attention behind the merchant's couch, their red and white uniforms gleaming, their falchions held before their faces as if at parade.

The merchant said, 'Don't mind my toys. They won't harm you as long as you're sensible.' His voice was silkily unctuous now. 'Drink, eat. I have nothing but the best. The best vintages, the finest meats, the tenderest vegetables.'

'Some wine, perhaps. Thank you.'

The naked woman poured wine as rich and red as fresh blood into a gold beaker and handed it to Yama, then poured another bowl for the merchant, who slobbered it down before Yama could do more than sip his. He expected some rare vintage, and was disappointed to discover that it was no better than the ordinary wine of the peel-house's cellars.

The merchant smacked his lips and said, 'Do you know what I am? And do stop trying to take control of my servants. You will give me a headache.'

Yama had been trying to persuade one of the machines which illuminated the room to fly down and settle above his head, but despite his sense of expansion, as if his thoughts had become larger than his skull, he might as well have tried to order an ossifrage to quit its icy perch in the high foothills of the Rim Mountains. He stared at the gold circlet on the merchant's fleshy, hairless pate, and said, 'You are really one of those things which crew the voidships. I suppose that you stole the body.'

'As a matter of fact I had it grown. Do you like it?'

Yama took another sip of wine. He felt calmer now. He said, 'I am amazed by it.'

'You have been raised to be polite. That's good. It will make things easier, eh, Iachimo?'

'I'm sure he could stand a little more polishing, master.'

'I've yet to find a body that can withstand my appetites,' the merchant told Yama, 'but that's of little consequence, because there are always more bodies. This is my – what is it, Iachimo? The tenth?'

'The ninth, master.'

'Well, there will soon be need for a tenth, and there will be more, an endless chain. How old are you, boy? No more than twenty, I'd guess. This body is half that age.'

The merchant pawed at the breasts of the woman. She was feeding him sugared almonds, popping them into his mouth each time it opened. He chewed the almonds mechanically, and a long string of pulp and saliva drooled unheeded down his chin.

He said, 'I've been male and female in my time, too. Mostly male, given the current state of civilization, but now that I've made my fortune and have no need to leave my estate, perhaps I'll be female next time. Are there others like you?'

'That is what I want to discover,' Yama said. 'You know of my bloodline. You know more than me, it seems. You called me a builder. A builder of what?'

But he already knew. He had read in the Puranas, and he remembered the man in the picture slate which Osric and Beatrice had shown him.

Iachimo said, ' "And the Preservers raised up a man and set on his brow their mark, and raised up a woman of the same kind, and set on her brow the same mark. From the white clay of the middle region did they shape this race, and quickened them with their marks. And those of this race were the servants of the Preservers. And in their myriads this race shaped the world after the ideas of the Preservers." There's more, but you get the general idea. Those are your people, boy. So long dead that almost no one remembers—'

Suddenly, the room brightened: white light flashed beyond the lake which hung above the long room. Rafts of waterlily pads swung wildly on clashing waves and there was a deep, heavy muffled sound, as if a massive door had slammed in the keel of the world.

The merchant said, 'No hope there, boy. You put some of my guards to sleep, but they're all under my control again, and almost have your two friends. Iachimo, you did not say that one of them was a cateran.'

'There was another boy, master. I knew of no other.'

The merchant closed his eyes. For a moment, Yama felt that a thousand intelligences lived in his head. Then the feeling was gone and the merchant said, 'She has killed several guards, but one caught a glimpse of her. She's of the Fierce People, and she's armed with one of the gatekeeper's pistols.'

'There are still many guards, master, and many machines. Besides, the lake will absorb any blast from the pistol.'

The merchant pulled the woman close to him. 'He's an assassin's tool, you idiot! Why else would a cateran come here? You know I have been expecting this ever since my old ship returned through the manifold.'

'There was the man who broke into the godown,' Iachimo said, 'but we dealt with him easily enough.'

'It was just the beginning. They won't rest—'

There was another flash of white light. A portion of water above the glass ceiling seethed into a spreading cloud of white bubbles, and the glass rang like a cracked bell.

The merchant closed his eyes briefly, then relaxed and drew the naked woman closer. 'Well, it doesn't matter now. There's a weapon in his satchel, Iachimo. Take it out and give it to me.'

The white-haired man lifted out the sheathed knife and said, 'It is only a knife, master.'

'I know what it is. Bring it here.'

Iachimo offered the sheathed knife, hilt first. Yama implored it to manifest the horrible shape which had frightened Lob and the landlord of *The Crossed Axes*, but he was at the centre of a vast muffling silence. The merchant squinted at the knife's goatskin sheath, and then the woman drew it and plunged it into Iachimo's belly.

Iachimo grunted and fell to his knees. The knife flashed blue fire and the woman screamed and dropped it and clutched her smoking hand. The knife embedded itself point first in the grass, sizzling faintly and emitting a drizzle of fat blue motes. Iachimo was holding his belly with both hands. There was blood all over his fingers and the front of his black tunic.

The merchant looked at the woman and she fell silent in mid-scream. He said to Yama, 'So die all those who think to betray me. Now, boy, you'll answer all my questions truthfully, or you'll join your two friends. Yes, they have been captured. Not dead, not yet. We'll talk, you and I, and decide their fate.'

Iachimo, kneeling over the knife and a pool of his own blood, said

222

something about a circle, and then the guards seized him and jerked him upright and cut his throat and lifted him away from the merchant, all in one quick motion. They dropped the body onto the neatly trimmed grass beneath the light sculpture and returned to their position behind the merchant's couch.

'You're trouble, boy,' the merchant said. The woman tremblingly placed the mouthpiece of a clay pipe between his rosebud lips and lit the scrap of resin in its bowl. He drew a long breath and said, dribbling smoke with the words, 'Your people were the first. The rest came later, but you were the first. I had never thought to see your kind again, but this is an age of wonders. Listen to me, boy, or I'll have you killed too. You see how easy it is.'

Yama was holding the wine goblet so tightly that he had reopened the wound in his palm. He threw it away and said as boldly as he could, 'Will you spare my friends?'

'They came to kill me, didn't they? Sent by my crewmates, who are jealous of me.'

Yama could not deny it. He stared in stubborn silence at the merchant, who calmly drew on his pipe and contemplated the wreathes of smoke he breathed out. At last, the merchant said, 'The woman is a cateran, and their loyalty is easily bought. I might have a use for her. The boy is no different from a million other river-rats in Ys. I could kill him and it would be as if he had never been born. I see that you want him to live. You are very sentimental. Well then. You must prove your worth to me, and perhaps the boy will live. Do you know exactly what you are?'

Yama said, 'You say that I am of the bloodline of the Builders, and I have seen an ancient picture showing one of my kind before the world was made. But I also have been told that I might be a child of the Ancients of Days.'

'Hmm. It's possible they had something to do with it. In their brief time here they meddled in much that didn't concern them. They didn't achieve anything of consequence, of course. For all that they might have appeared as gods to the degenerate population of Confluence, they predated the Preservers by several million years. Their kind were the ancestors of the Preservers, but with about as much relation to them as the brainless plankton grazers which were the ancestors of my own bloodline have to me. It is only because the Ancients of Days were timeshifted while travelling to our neighbouring galaxy and back at close

223

to the speed of light that they appeared so late, like an actor delayed by circumstance who incontinently rushes on stage to deliver his lines and finds that he has interrupted the closing soliloquy instead of beginning the second act. We are in the end times, young builder. This whole grand glorious foolish experiment has all but run its course. The silly little war downriver begun by the Ancients of Days is only a footnote.'

The merchant seemed exhausted by this speech, and drank more wine before he continued. 'Do you know, I haven't thought about this for a long time. Iachimo was a very clever man, but not a brave one. He was doomed to a servant's role, and resented it. I thought at first you were some scheme of his, and I haven't fully dismissed the thought from my mind. I do not believe that it was through simple carelessness that he allowed the cateran to roam free, or that you were allowed to carry a knife into my presence.'

'I have never seen him before tonight. I am not the servant of any man.'

The merchant said, 'Don't be a fool. Like most here, your bloodline was created as servants to the immediate will of the Preservers.'

'We all serve the Preservers as we can,' Yama said.

'You've been in the hands of a priest,' the merchant said. His gaze was shrewd. 'You parrot his pious phrases, but do you really believe them?'

Yama could not answer. His faith was never something he had questioned, but now he saw that by disobeying the wishes of his father he had rebelled against his place in the social hierarchy, and had not that hierarchy proceeded from the Preservers? So the priests taught, but now Yama was unsure. For the priests also taught that the Preservers wanted their creations to advance from a low to a high condition, and how could that happen if society was fixed, eternal and unchanging?

The merchant belched. 'You are just a curiosity, boy. A revenant. An afterthought or an accident – it's all the same. But you might be useful, even so. You and I might do great things together. You asked why I am here. It is because I have remembered what all others of my kind have long forgotten. They are lost in ascetic contemplation of the mathematics of the manifolds and the secrets of the beginning and end of the cosmos, but I have remembered the pleasures of the real world, of appetite and sex and all the rest of the messy wonderful business of life. They would say that mathematics is the reality underlying everything; I say that it is an abstraction of the real world, a ghost.' He belched again. 'There is my riposte to algebra.'

Yama made a wild intuitive leap. He said, 'You met the Ancients of Days, didn't you?'

'My ship hailed theirs, as it fell through the void towards the Eye of the Preservers. They had seen the Eye's construction by ancient light while hundreds of thousands of years out, and were amazed to discover that organic intelligent life still existed. We merged our mindscapes and talked long there, and I followed them out into the world. And here I am. It is remarkably easy to make a fortune in these benighted times, but I'm finding that merely satisfying sensual appetites is not enough. If you're truly a Builder, and I am not quite convinced that you are, then perhaps you can help me. I have plans.'

'I believe that I am no man's servant. I cannot serve you as Iachimo did.'

The merchant laughed. 'I would hope not. You will have to unlearn your arrogance to begin with; then I will see what I can make of you. I can teach you many things, boy. I can realize your potential. There are many like Iachimo in the world, intelligent and learned and quite without the daring to act on their convictions. There is no end to natural followers like him. You are something more. I must think hard about it, and so will you. But you will serve, or you will die, and so will your friends.'

The twisting scarves of colour in the light sculpture ran together into a steely grey and widened into a kind of window, showing Tamora and Pandaras kneeling inside tiny cages suspended in dark air.

For a moment, Yama's breath caught in his throat. He said, 'Let them go, and I will serve you as I can.'

The merchant shifted his immense oiled bulk. 'I think not. I'll give you a taste of their fate while I decide how I can make use of you. When you can make that promise from your heart, then we can talk again.'

The two guards turned towards Yama, who stared in sudden panic into their blank, blind faces. His panic inflated into something immense, a great wild bird he had loosed, its wings beating at the edges of his sight. In desperation, quite without hope, his mind threw out an immense imploring scream for help.

The merchant pawed at his head and far down the room something struck the glass ceiling with a tremendous bang. For a moment, all was still. Then a line of spray sheeted down, and the glass around it gave with a loud splintering crash. The spray became a widening waterfall that poured down and rebounded from the floor and sent a tawny wave flooding down the length of the room, knocking over pillars and statues and sweeping tables and couches before it.

The merchant's couch lurched into the air. The woman gave a guttural cry of alarm, and clung to her master's flesh as a shipwrecked sailor clings to a bit of flotsam. Yama dashed forward through surging water (for a moment, Iachimo's corpse clutched at his ankles; then it was swept away), made a desperate leap and caught hold of one end of the rising couch. His weight rocked it on its long axis, so violently that for one moment he hung straight down, the next tipped forward and fell across the merchant's legs.

The merchant roared and his woman clawed at Yama with sudden fury, her long nails opening his forehead so that blood poured into his eyes. The couch turned in a dizzy circle above the guards as they struggled to stay upright in the seething flood. The merchant caught at Yama's hands, but his grasp was feeble, and Yama, half-blinded, grabbed the golden circlet around the man's fleshy scalp and pulled with all his strength.

For a moment, he feared that the circlet would not give way. Then it snapped in half and unravelled like a ribbon. All the lights went out. The couch tipped and Yama and the merchant and the woman fell into the wash of the flood. Yama went under and got a mouthful of muddy water and came up spitting and gasping.

The guards had fallen; so had all the machines.

Yama asked a question, and after a moment points of intense white light flared down the length of the room, burning through the swirling brown flood. Yama wiped blood from his eyes. The current swirled around his waist. He was clutching a tangle of golden filaments tipped with stringy fragments of flesh.

At the far end of the huge room, something floated a handspan above the water, turning slowly end for end. It was as big as Yama's head, and black, and decorated all over with spikes of varying lengths and thickness, some like rose thorns, others long and finely tapered and questing this way and that with blind intelligence. The thing radiated a black icy menace, a negation not only of life, but of the reality of the world. For a moment, Yama was transfixed; then the machine rose straight up, smashing through the ceiling. Yama felt it rise higher and higher, and for a moment felt all the machines in Ys turn towards it – but it was gone.

The merchant sprawled across the fallen couch like a beached grampus. A ragged wound crowned his head, streaming blood; he snorted a jelly of blood and mucus through his nose. The woman lay beneath him, entirely submerged. Her head was twisted back, and her eyes looked up through the swirling water. Up and down the length of the room, the guards were dead, too.

Yama held the frayed remnants of the circlet before the merchant's eyes, and said, 'Iachimo told me about this with his last breath, but I had already guessed its secret. I saw something like it on the lighter.'

'The Preservers have gone away,' the merchant whispered.

The floodwaters were receding, running away into deeper levels of the sunken house. Yama knelt by the couch and said, 'Why am I here?'

The merchant drew a breath. Blood ran from his nostrils and his mouth. He said wetly, 'Serve no one.'

'If the Preservers are gone, why was I brought back?'

The merchant tried to say something, but only blew a bubble of blood. Yama left him there and went to find Tamora and Pandaras.

21 ~ The Fierce People

Tamora came back to the campfire at a loping run. She was grinning broadly and there was blood around her mouth. She threw a brace of coneys at Yama's feet and said proudly, 'This is how we live, when we can. We are the Fierce People, the Memsh Tek!'

Pandaras said, 'Not all of us can live on meat alone.'

'Your kind have to exist on leaves and the filth swept into street gutters,' Tamora said, 'and that is why they are so weak. Meat and blood are what warriors need, so be glad that I give you fine fresh guts. They will make you strong.'

She slit the bellies of the conies with her sharp thumbnail, crammed the steaming, rich red livers into her mouth and gulped them down. Then she pulled the furry skins from the gutted bodies, as someone might strip gloves from their hands, and set about dismembering them with teeth and nails.

She had attacked the merchant's carcass with the same butcher's skill, using a falchion taken from one of the dead guards to fillet it from neck to buttocks and expose the thing which had burrowed into the fatty flesh like a hagfish. It was not much like the bottled creature Yama had seen on the lighter. Its mantle was shrunken, and white fibres had knitted around its host's spinal column like cords of fungus in rotten wood.

Tamora kept most of the coney meat for herself and ate it raw, but she allowed Yama and Pandaras to cook the haunches over the embers of the fire. The unsalted meat was half-burned and half-raw, but Yama and Pandaras hungrily stripped it from the bones.

'Burnt meat is bad for the digestion,' Tamora said, grinning at them across the embers of the fire. She wore only her leather skirt. Her two pairs of breasts were little more than enlarged nipples, like tarnished coins set on her narrow ribcage. In addition to the bird burning in a nest of fire on her upper arm, inverted triangles were tattooed in black ink on her shoulders. There was a bandage around her waist; she had been seared by backflash from a guard's pistol shot. She took a swallow of brandy and passed the bottle to Yama. He had bought the brandy in a bottleshop and used a little to preserve the filaments Tamora had flensed from the merchant's body and placed in a beautiful miniature flask, cut from a single crystal of rose quartz, which Yama had found in the wreckage left by the flood when he had been searching for his copy of the Puranas.

Yama drank and passed the bottle to Pandaras, who was cracking coney bones between his sharp teeth.

'Drink,' Tamora said. 'We fought a great battle today.'

Pandaras spat a bit of gristle into the fire. He had already made it clear how unhappy he was to be in the Fierce People's tract of wild country, and he sat with his kidney puncher laid across his lap and his mobile ears pricked. He said, 'I'd rather keep my wits about me.'

Tamora laughed. 'No one would mistake you for a coney. You're about the right size, but you can't run fast enough to make the hunt interesting.'

Pandaras took the smallest possible sip from the brandy bottle and passed it back to Yama. He told Tamora, 'You certainly ran when the soldiers came.'

'Grah. I was trying to catch up with you to make sure you went the right way.'

'Enough stuff to set a man up for life,' Pandaras said, 'and we had to leave it for the city militia to loot.'

'I'm a cateran, not a robber. We have done what we contracted to do. Be happy.' Tamora grinned. Her pink tongue lolled amongst her big, sharp teeth. 'Eat burnt bones. Drink. Sleep. We are safe here, and tomorrow we are paid.'

Yama realized that she was drunk. The bottle of brandy had been the smallest he could buy, but it was still big enough, as Pandaras put it, to drown a baby. They had needed only a few minims to fill the crystal flask, and Tamora had drunk about half of what was left.

'Safe?' Pandaras retorted. 'In the middle of any number of packs of bloodthirsty howlers like you? I won't sleep at all tonight.'

'I will sing a great song of our triumph, and you will listen. Pass that bottle, Yama. It is not your child.'

Yama took a burning swallow of brandy, handed the bottle over, and walked out of the firelight to the crest of the ridge. The sandy hills where the Fierce People maintained their hunting grounds looked out across the wide basin of the city towards the Great River. The misty light of the Arm of the Warrior was rising above the farside horizon. It was past midnight. The city was mostly dark, but many campfires flickered amongst the scrub and clumps of crown ferns, pines and eucalyptus of the Fierce People's hunting grounds, and from every quarter came the sound of distant voices raised in song.

Yama sat on the dry grass and listened to the night music of the Fierce People. The feral machine still haunted him, like a ringing in the ears or the afterimage of a searingly bright light. And beyond this psychic echo he could feel the ebb and flow of the myriad machines in the city, like the flexing of a great net. They had also been disturbed by the feral machine, and the ripples of alarm caused by the disturbance were still spreading, leaping from cluster to cluster of machines along the docks, running out towards the vast bulk of the Palace of the Memory of the People, clashing at the bases of the high towers and racing up their lengths out of the atmosphere.

Yama still did not know how he had called down the feral machine, and although it had saved him he feared that he might call it again by accident, and feared too that he had exposed himself to discovery by the network of machines which served the magistrates, or by Prefect Corin, who must surely still be searching for him. The descent of the feral machine was the most terrifying and the most shameful of his adventures. He had been paralysed with fear when confronted with it, and even now he felt that it had marked him in some obscure way, for some small part of him yearned for it, and what it could tell him. It could be watching him still; it could return at any time, and he did not know what he would do if it did.

The merchant — Yama still found it difficult to think of him as the parasitic bundle of nerve fibres burrowed deep within that tremendously fat body — had said that he was a Builder, a member of the first bloodline of Ys. The pilot of the voidship had said something similar, and the slate that Beatrice and Osric had shown him had suggested the same thing. His people had walked Confluence in its first days, sculpting the world under the direct instruction of the Preservers, and had died out or ascended ages past, so long ago that most had forgotten them. And yet he was here, and he still did not know why; nor did he know the full extent of his powers.

The merchant had hinted that he knew what Yama was capable of, but he might have been lying to serve his own ends, and besides, he was dead. Perhaps the other star-sailors knew – Iachimo had said that they were very long-lived – or perhaps, as Yama had hoped even before he had set out from Aeolis, there were records somewhere in Ys that would explain everything, or at least lead him to others of his kind. He still did not know how he had been brought into the world, or why he had been found floating on the river on the breast of a dead woman who might have been his mother or nurse or something else entirely, but surely he had been born to serve the Preservers in some fashion. After the Preservers had fallen into the event horizon of the Eye, they could still watch the world they had made, for nothing fell faster than light, but they could no longer act upon it. But perhaps their reach was long – perhaps they had ordained his birth, here in what the merchant had called the end times, long before they had withdrawn from the Universe. Perhaps, as Derev believed, many of Yama's kind now walked the world, as they had at its beginning. But for what purpose? All through his childhood he had prayed for a revelation, a sign, a hint, and had received nothing. Perhaps he should expect nothing else. Perhaps the shape of his life was the sign he sought, if only he could understand it.

But he could not believe he was the servant of the feral machines. That was the worst thought of all.

Yama sat on a hummock of dry grass, with the noise of crickets everywhere in the darkness around him, and leafed through his copy of the Puranas. The book had dried out well, although one corner of its front cover was faintly but indelibly stained with the merchant's blood. The pages held a faint light, and the glyphs stood out like shadows against this soft effulgence. Yama found the sura which Iachimo had quoted, and read it from beginning to end.

The world first showed itself as a golden embryo of sound. As soon as the thoughts of the Preservers turned to the creation of the world, the long vowel which described the form of the world vibrated in the pure realm of thought, and re-echoed on itself. From the knots in the play of vibrations, the crude matter of the world curdled. In the beginning, it was no more than a sphere of air and water with a little mud at the centre.

And the Preservers raised up a man and set on his brow their mark, and raised up a woman of the same kind, and set on her brow the same mark. From the white clay of the middle region did they shape this race, and quickened them with their marks. And those of this race were the servants of the Preservers. And in their myriads this race shaped the world after the ideas of the Preservers.

Yama read on, although the next sura was merely an exhaustive description of the dimensions and composition of the world, and he knew that there was no other mention of the Builders, nor of their fate. This was towards the end of the Puranas. The world and everything in it was an afterthought at the end of the history of the Galaxy, created in the last moment before the Preservers fell into the Eye and were known no more in the Universe. Nothing had been written about the ten thousand bloodlines of Confluence in the Puranas; if there had been, then there would have never been a beginning to the endless disputations amongst priests and philosophers about the reason for the world's creation.

Tamora said, 'Reading, is it? There's nothing in books you can't learn better in the world, nothing but fantastic rubbish about monsters and the like. You'll rot your mind and your eyes, reading too much in books.'

'Well, I met a real monster today.'

'And he's dead, the fucker, and we have a piece of him in brandy as proof. So much for him.'

Yama had not told Tamora and Pandaras about the feral machine. Tamora had boasted that one of her pistol shots had weakened the ceiling and so caused the flood which had saved them, and Yama had not corrected her error. He felt a rekindling of shame at this deception, and said weakly, 'I suppose the merchant was a kind of monster. He tried to flee from his true self, and let a little hungry part of himself rule his life. He was all appetite and nothing else. I think he would have eaten the whole world, if he could.'

'You want to be a soldier. Here's some advice. Don't think about what you have to do and don't think about it when it's done.'

'And can you forget it so easily?'

'Of course not. But I try. We were captured, your rat-boy and me, and thrown into cages, but you had it worse, I think. The merchant was trying to bend you towards his will. The words of his kind are like thorns, and some of them are still in your flesh. But they'll wither, and you'll forget them.'

Yama smiled and said, 'Perhaps it would be no bad thing, to be the ruler of the world.'

Tamora sat down close beside him. She was a shadow in the darkness. She said, 'You would destroy the civil service and rule instead? How would that change the world for the better?'

Yama could feel her heat. She gave off a strong scent compounded of fresh blood and sweat and a sharp musk. He said, 'Of course not. But the merchant told me something about my bloodline. I may be alone in the world. I may be a mistake thrown up at the end of things. Or I may be something else. Something *intended*.'

'The fat fuck was lying. How better to get you to follow him than by saying that you are the only one of your kind, and he knows all about you?'

'I am not sure that he was lying, Tamora. At least, I think he was telling part of the truth.'

'I haven't forgotten what you want, and I was a long time hunting coneys because I really went to ask around. Listen. I have a way of getting at what you want. There is a job for a couple of caterans. Some little pissant department needs someone to organize a defence of its territory inside the Palace of the Memory of the People. There are many disputes between departments, and the powerful grow strong at the expense of the weak. That's the way of the world, but I don't mind defending the weak if I get paid for it.'

'Then perhaps maybe they are stronger than you after all.'

'Grah. Listen. When a litter is born here, the babies are exposed on a hillside for a day. Any that are weak die, or are taken by birds or foxes. We're the Fierce People, see? We keep our bloodline strong. The wogs and wetbacks and snakes and the rest of the garbage down there in the city, they're what we prey on. They need us, not the other way around.' Tamora spat sideways. Yes, she had drunk a lot of brandy. She said, 'There's prey, and there's hunters. You have to decide which you are. You don't know, now is the time you find out. Are you for it?'

'It seems like a good plan.'

'Somewhere or other you've picked up the habit of not speaking plain. You mean yes, then say it.'

'Yes. Yes, I will do it. If it means getting into the Palace of the Memory of the People.'

'Then you got to pay me, because I found it for you, and I'll do the work.'

'I know something about fighting.'

Tamora spat again. 'Listen, this is a dangerous job. This little department is certain to be attacked and they don't have a security office or they wouldn't be hiring someone from outside. They're bound to lose, see, but if it's done right then only their thralls will get killed. We can probably escape, or at worse lose our bond when we're ransomed, but I won't deny there's a chance we'll get killed, too. You still want it?'

'It is a way in.'

'Exactly. This department used to deal in prognostication, but it is much debased. There are only a couple of seers left, but it is highly placed in the Palace of the Memory of the People, and other more powerful departments want to displace it. It needs us to train its thralls so they can put up some kind of defence, but there will be time for you to search for whatever it is you're looking for. We will agree payment now. You'll pay any expenses out of your share of the fees for killing the merchant and for this new job, and I keep my half of both fees, and half again of anything that's left of yours.'

'Is that a fair price?'

'Grah. You're supposed to bargain, you idiot! It is twice what the risk is worth.'

'I will pay it anyway. If I find out what I want to know, I will have no need of money.'

'If you want to join the army as an officer, you'll need plenty, more than you're carrying around now. You'll have to buy the rest of your own armour, and mounts, and weaponry. And if you're looking for information, there will be bribes to be paid. I'll take a quarter of your fees, bargaining against myself like a fool, and share expenses with you. You'll need the rest, believe me.'

'You are a good person, Tamora, although I would like you better if you were more tolerant. No one bloodline should raise itself above any other.'

234

'I'll do well enough out of this, believe me. One other thing. We won't tell the rat-boy about this. We do this without him.'

'Are you scared of him because he killed the gatekeeper?'

'If I was scared of any of his kind, I would never dare spit in the gutter again, for fear of hitting one in the eye. Let him come if he must, but I won't pretend I like it, and any money he wants comes from you, not me.'

'He is like me, Tamora. He wants to be other than his fate.'

'Then he's certainly as big a fool as you.' Tamora handed Yama the brandy bottle. It was almost empty. 'Drink. Then you will listen to me sing our victory song. The rat-boy is scared to sit with my brothers and sisters, but I know you won't be.'

Although Yama tried not to show it, he was intimidated by the proud, fierce people who sat around the campfire: an even decad of Tamora's kin, heavily muscled men and women marked on their shoulders by identical tattoos of inverted triangles. Most intimidating of all was a straight-backed matriarch with a white mane and a lacework of fine scars across her naked torso, who watched Yama with red-backed eyes from the other side of the fire while Tamora sang.

Tamora's victory song was a discordant open-throated ululation that rose and twisted like a sharp silver wire into the black air above the flames of the campfire. When it was done, she took a long swig from a wine skin while the men and women murmured and nodded and showed their fangs in quick snarling smiles, although one complained loudly that the song had been less about Tamora and more about this whey-skinned stranger.

'That is because it was his adventure,' Tamora said.

'Then let him sing for himself,' the man grumbled.

The matriarch asked Tamora about Yama, saying that she had not seen his kind before.

'He's from downriver, grandmother.'

'That would explain it. I'm told that there are many strange peoples downriver, although I myself have never troubled to go and see, and now I am too old to have to bother. Talk with me, boy. Tell me how your people came into the world.'

'That is a mystery, even to myself. I have read something in the

Puranas about my people, and I have seen a picture of one in an old slate, but that is all I know.'

'Then your people are very strange indeed,' the matriarch said. 'Every bloodline has its story and its mysteries and its three names. The Preservers chose to raise up each bloodline in their image for a particular reason, and the stories explain why. You won't find your real story in that book you carry. That's about older mysteries, and not about this world at all.' She cuffed one of the women and snatched a wine skin from her. 'They keep this from me,' she told Yama, 'because they're frightened I'll disgrace myself if I get drunk.'

'Nothing could make you drunk, grandmother,' one of the men said. 'That's why we ration your drinking, or you'd poison yourself trying.'

The matriarch spat into the fire. 'A mouthful of this rotgut will poison me. Can no one afford proper booze? In the old days we would have used this to fuel our lamps.'

Yama still had the brandy bottle, with a couple of fingers of clear, apricot-scented liquor at its bottom. 'Here, grandmother,' he said, and handed it to the matriarch.

The old woman drained the bottle and licked her lips in appreciation. 'Do you know how we came into the world, boy? I'll tell you.'

Several of the people around the fire groaned, and the matriarch said sharply, 'It'll do you good to hear it again. You young people don't know the stories as well as you should. Listen, then.

'After the world was made, some of the Preservers set animals down on its surface, and kindled intelligence in them. There are a people descended from coyotes, for instance, whose ancestors were taught by the Preservers to bury their dead. This odd habit brought about a change in the coyotes, for they learned to sit up so they could sit beside the graves and mourn their dead properly. But sitting on cold stone wore away their bushy tails, and after many generations they began standing upright because the stone was uncomfortable to their naked arses. When that happened, their forepaws lengthened into human hands, and their sharp muzzles shortened bit by bit until they became human faces. That's one story, and there are as many stories as there are bloodlines descended from the different kinds of animals which were taught to become human. But our own people had a different origin.

'Two of the Preservers fell into an argument about the right way to make human people. The Preservers do not have sexes as we understand them, nor do they marry, but it is easier to follow the story if we think of them as wife and husband. One, Enki, was the Preserver who had charge of the world's water, and so his work was hard, for in those early times all there was of the world was the Great River, running from nowhere to nowhere. He complained of his hard work to his wife, Ninmah, who was the Preserver of earth, and she suggested that they create a race of marionettes or puppets who would do the work for them. And this they did, using the small amount of white silt that was suspended in the Great River. I see that you know this part of the story.'

'Someone told me a little of it today. It is to be found in the Puranas.'

'What I tell you is truer, for it has been told from mouth to ear for ten thousand generations, and so its words still live, and have not become dead things squashed flat on plastic or pulped wood. Well then, after this race was produced from the mud of the river, there was a great celebration because the Preservers no longer needed to work on their creation. Much beer was consumed, and Ninmah became especially light-headed. She called to Enki, saying, "How good or bad is a human body? I could reshape it in any way I please, but could you find tasks for it?" Enki responded to this challenge, and so Ninmah made a barren woman, and a eunuch, and several other cripples.

'But Enki found tasks for them all. The barren woman he made into a concubine; the eunuch he made into a civil servant, and so on. Then in the same playful spirit he challenged Ninmah. He would do the shaping of different races, and she the placing. She agreed, and Enki first made a man whose making was already remote from him, and so the first old man appeared before Ninmah. She offered the old man bread, but he was too feeble to reach for it, and when she thrust the bread into his mouth, he could not chew it for he had no teeth, and so Ninmah could find no use for this unfortunate. Then Enki made many other cripples and monsters, and Ninmah could find no use for them, either.

'The pair fell into a drunken sleep, and when they wakened all was in uproar, for the cripples Enki had made were spreading through the world. Enki and Ninmah were summoned before the other Preservers to explain themselves, and to escape punishment Enki and Ninmah together made a final race, who would hunt the lame and the old, and so make the races of the world stronger by consuming their weak members.

'And so we came into the world, and it is said that we have a quick and cruel temper, because Enki and Ninmah suffered dreadfully from

237

the effects of drinking too much beer when they made us, and that was passed to us as a potmaker leaves her thumbprint in the clay.'

'I have heard only the beginning of this story,' Yama said, 'and I am glad that now I have heard the end of it.'

'Now you must tell a story,' one of the men said loudly. It was the one who had complained before. He was smaller than the others, but still a head taller than Yama. He wore black leather trousers and a black leather jacket studded with copper nails.

'Be quiet, Gorgo,' the matriarch said. 'This young man is our guest.'

Gorgo looked across the fire at Yama, and Yama met his truculent, challenging gaze. Neither was willing to look away, but then a branch snapped in the fire and sent burning fragments flying into Gorgo's lap. He cursed and brushed at the sparks while the others laughed.

Gorgo glowered and said, 'We have heard his boasts echoed in Tamora's song. I simply wonder if he has the heart to speak for himself. He owes that courtesy, I think.'

'You're a great one for knowing what's owed,' someone said.

Gorgo turned on the man. 'I only press for payment when it's needed, as you well know. How much poorer you would be if I didn't find you work! You are all in my debt.'

The matriarch said, 'That is not to be spoken of. Are we not the Fierce People, whose honour is as renowned as our strength and our temper?'

Gorgo said, 'Some people need reminding about honour.'

One of the women said, 'We fight. You get the rewards.'

'Then don't ask me for work,' Gorgo said petulantly. 'Find your own. I force no one, as is well known, but so many ask for my help that I scarcely have time to sleep or catch my food. But here is our guest. Let's not forget him. We hear great things of him from Tamora. Hush, and let him speak for himself.'

Yama thought that Gorgo could speak sweetly when he chose, but the honey of his words disguised his envy and suspicion. Clearly, Gorgo thought that Yama's was one of the trash or vermin bloodlines.

Yama said, 'I will tell a story, although I am afraid that it might bore you. It is about how my life was saved by one of the indigens.'

Gorgo grumbled that this didn't sound like a true story at all. 'Tell something of your people instead,' he said. 'Please do not tell me that such a fine hero as yourself, if we are to believe the words of our sister here, is so ashamed of his own people that he has to make up stories of sub-human creatures which do not carry the blessing of the Preservers.'

Yama smiled. This at least was easy to counter. 'I wish I knew such stories, but I was raised as an orphan.'

'Perhaps your people were ashamed of you,' Gorgo said, but he was the only one to laugh at his sally.

'Tell your story,' Tamora said, 'and don't let Gorgo interrupt you. He is jealous, because he hasn't any stories of his own.'

When Yama began, he realised that he had drunk more than he intended, but he could not back out now. He described how he had been kidnapped and taken to the pinnace, and how he had escaped (making no mention of the ghostly ship) and cast himself upon a banyan island far from shore.

'I found one of the indigenous fisherfolk stuck fast in a trap left by one of the people of the city which my father administers. The people of the city once hunted the fisherfolk, but my father put a stop to it. The unfortunate fisherman had become entangled in a trap made of strong, sticky threads of the kind used to snare bats which skim the surface of the water for fish. I could not free him without becoming caught fast myself, so I set a trap of my own and waited. When the hunter came to collect his prey, as a spider sidles down to claim a fly caught in its web, it was the hunter who became the prey. I took the spray which dissolves the trap's glue, and the fisherman and I made our escape and left the foolish hunter to the torments of those small, voracious hunters who outnumber their prey, mosquitoes and blackflies. In turn, the fisherman fed me and took me back to the shore of the Great River. And so we saved each other.'

'A tall tale,' Gorgo said, meeting Yama's gaze again.

'It is true I missed out much, but if I told everything then we would be up all night. I will say one more thing. If not for the fisherman's kindness, I would not be here, so I have learnt never to rush to judge any man, no matter how worthless he might appear.'

Gorgo said, 'He asks us to admire his reflection in his tales. Let me tell you that what I see is a fool. Any sensible man would have devoured the fisherman and taken his coracle and escaped with a full belly.'

'I simply told you what happened,' Yama said, meeting the man's yellow gaze. 'Anything you see in my words is what you have placed there. If you had tried to steal the hunter's prey, you would have been stuck there too, and been butchered and devoured along with the fisherman.'

Gorgo jumped up. 'I think I know something about hunting, and I do know that you are not as clever as you imagine yourself to be. You side with prey, and so you're no hunter at all.'

Yama stood too, for he would not look up from a lesser to a higher position when he replied to Gorgo's insult. Perhaps he would not have done it if he had been less drunk, but he felt the sting of wounded pride. Besides, he did not think that Gorgo was a threat. He was a man who used words as others use weapons. He was taller and heavier than Yama, and armed with a strong jaw and sharp teeth, but Sergeant Rhodean had taught Yama several ways by which such differences could be turned to an advantage.

'I described what happened, no more and no less,' Yama said. 'I hope I do not need to prove the truth of my words.'

Tamora grabbed Yama's hand and said, 'Don't mind Gorgo. He has always wanted to fuck me, and I've always refused. He's quick to anger, and jealous.'

Gorgo laughed. 'I think you have me wrong, sister. It is not your delusion I object to, but his. Remember what you owe me before you insult me again.'

'You will both sit down,' the matriarch said. 'Yama is our guest, Gorgo. You dishonour all of us. Sit down. Drink. We all lose our temper, and the less we make of it the better.'

'You all owe me,' Gorgo said, 'one way or another.' He glared at the circle of people, then spat into the fire and turned and stalked away into the night.

There was an awkward pause. Yama sat down and apologized, saying that he had drunk too much and lost his judgment.

'We've all slapped Gorgo around one time or another,' one of the women said. 'He grows angry if his advances are ignored.'

'He is more angry than fierce,' someone said, and the rest laughed.

'He's a fucking disgrace,' Tamora said. 'A sneak and a coward. He never hunts, but feeds off the quarry of us all. He shot a man with an arbalest instead of fighting fair—'

'Enough,' the matriarch said. 'We do not speak of others to their backs.'

'I'd speak to his face,' Tamora said, 'if he'd ever look me in the eye.'

'If we say no more about this,' Yama said, 'I promise to say no more about myself.'

There were more drinking games, and more songs, and at last Yama begged to be released, for although Tamora's people seemed to need little sleep, he was exhausted by his adventures. He found his way back to his own campfire by the faint light of the Arm of the Warrior, falling several times but feeling no hurt. Pandaras was curled up near the warm ashes, his kidney puncher gripped in both hands. Yama lay down a little way off, on the ridge which overlooked the dark city. He did not remember wrapping himself in his blanket, or falling asleep, but he woke when Tamora pulled the blanket away from him. Her naked body glimmered in the near dark. He did not resist when she started to undo the laces of his shirt, or when she covered his mouth with hers.

22 ~ The Country of the Mind

The next morning, Pandaras watched with unconcealed amusement as Tamora swabbed the scratches on Yama's flanks and the sore places on his shoulders and neck where she had nipped him. Pandaras sleeked back his hair with wrists wet by his own saliva, slapped dust from his ragged jerkin, and announced that he was ready to go.

'We can buy breakfast on the way to the docks. With all the money we have earned, there's no reason to live like unchanged rustics.'

'You slept soundly last night,' Yama said.

'I was not sleeping at all. When I had not fainted away with fright I was listening to every sound in the night, imagining that some hungry meat-eater was creeping up on me. My people have lived in the city for ever. We were not made for the countryside.'

Yama held up his shirt. It was stained with silt from the flood which had fallen through the ceiling of the merchant's house, and flecked with chaff where he and Tamora had used it as a pillow. He said, 'I should wash out my clothes. This will make no impression on our new employers.'

Pandaras looked up. 'Are we away then? We'll collect our reward, and go to our new employer in the Palace of the Memory of the People, and find your family, all before the mountains eat the sun. We could already be there, master, if you had not slept so late.'

'Not so quickly,' Yama said, smiling at Pandaras's eagerness.

'I'll be an old man before long, and no use to you at all. At least let me wash your clothes. It will take but a minute, and I am, after all, your squire.'

Tamora scratched at reddened skin at the edge of the bandage around her waist. 'Grah. Some squire you'd make,' she said, 'with straws in your hair and dirt on your snout. Come with me, Yama. There's a washing place further up.'

Pandaras flourished his kidney puncher and struck an attitude and smiled at Yama, seeking his approval. He had an appetite for drama, as if all the world were a stage, and he was the central player. He said, 'I will guard your satchel, master, but do not leave me alone for long. I can fight off two or three of these ravenous savages, but not an entire tribe.'

A series of pools in natural limestone basins stepped away down the slope of the hill, with water rising from hot springs near the crest and falling from one pool to the next. Each pool was slightly cooler than the one above. Yama sat with Tamora in the shallow end of the hottest pool he could bear and scrubbed his shirt and trousers with white sand. He spread them out to dry on a flat rock already warm from the sun, and then allowed Tamora to wash his back. Little fish striped with silver and black darted around his legs in the clear hot water, nipping at the dirt between his toes. Other people were using pools higher up, calling cheerfully to each other under the blue sky.

Tamora explained that the water came from the Rim Mountains. 'Everyone in the city who can afford it uses mountain water; only beggars and refugees drink from the river.'

'Then they must be the holiest people in Ys, for the water of the Great River is sacred.'

'Grah, holiness does not cleanse the river of all the shit put into it. Most bathe in it only once a year, on the high day celebrated by their bloodline. Otherwise those who can avoid it, which is why water is brought into the city. One of the underground rivers which transports the mountain water passes close by. It's why we have our hunting grounds here. There are waterholes where animals come to drink and where the hunting is good, and at this place we have hidden machines to heat the water.'

'It is a wonderful place,' Yama said. 'Look, a hawk!'

Tamora lifted the thong around Yama's neck and fingered the coin which hung from it. 'What's this? A keepsake?'

'Someone gave it to me. Before I left Aeolis.'

'You find them everywhere, if you bother to dig for a few minutes. We used to play with them when we were children. This is less worn than most, though. Who gave it to you? A sweetheart, perhaps?'

Derev. This was the second time Yama had betrayed her trust. Although he did not know if he would ever see Derev again, and although he had been drunk, he felt suddenly ashamed that he had allowed Tamora to take him.

Tamora's breath feathered his cheek. It had a minty tang from the leaf she had plucked from a bush and folded inside her mouth between her teeth and her cheek. She fingered the line of Yama's jaw and said, 'There's hair coming in here.'

'There is a glass blade in my satchel. I should have brought it to shave. Or perhaps I will grow a beard.'

'It was your first time, wasn't it? Don't be ashamed. Everyone must have a first time.'

'No. I mean, no, it was not the first time.'

Telmon's high, excited voice as he threw open the door of the brothel's warm, scented, lamp-lit parlour. The women turning to them like exotic orchids unfolding. Yama had gone with Telmon because he had been asked, because he had been curious, because Telmon had been about to leave for the war. Afterwards, he had suspected that Derev had known all about it, and if she had not condoned it, then perhaps at least she had understood. That was why Yama had been so fervent with his promises on the night before he left Aeolis, and yet how easily he had broken them. He felt a sudden desolation. How could he even think of being a hero?

Tamora said, 'It was your first time with one of the Fierce People. That should burn away the memory of all others.' She nipped his shoulder. 'You have a soft skin, and it tastes of salt.'

'I sweat everywhere, except the palms of my hands and the soles of my feet.'

'Really? How strange. But I like the taste. That's why I bit you last night.'

'I heal quickly.'

Tamora said, 'Yama, listen to me. It won't happen again. Not while we're working together. No, stay still. I can't clean your back if you turn around. We celebrated together last night, and that was good. But I won't let it interfere with my work. If you don't like that, and think yourself used, then find another cateran. There are plenty here, and plenty more at the Water Market. You have enough money to hire the best.'

'I was at least as drunk as you were.'

'Drunker, I'd say. I hope you didn't fuck me just because you were drunk.'

244

Yama blushed. 'I meant that I lost any inhibitions I might otherwise have had. Tamora—'

'Don't start on any sweet talk. And don't tell me about any sweetheart you might have left at home, either, or about how sorry you are. That's there. This is here. We're battle companions. We fucked. End of that part of the story.'

'Are all your people so direct?'

'We speak as we find. Not to do so is a weakness. I like you, and I enjoyed last night. We're lucky, because some bloodlines are only on heat once a year – imagine how miserable they must be – and besides, there's no danger of us making babies together. That's what happens when my people fuck, unless the woman is already pregnant. I'm not ready for that, not yet. In a few years I'll find some men to run with and we'll raise a family, but not yet. A lot of us choose the metic way for that reason.'

Yama was interested. He said, 'Can you not use prophylactics?'

Tamora laughed. 'You haven't seen the cock of one of our men! There are spines to hold it in place. Put a rubber on that? Grah! There's a herb some women boil into a tea and drink to stop their courses, but it doesn't work most of the time.'

'Women of your people are stronger than men.'

'It's generally true of all bloodlines, even when it doesn't seem so. We're more honest about it, perhaps. Now you clean my back, and I'll go use the shittery, and then we'll find the rat-boy. If we're lucky, he's run back to where he belongs.'

As they went back down the hill, along the path that wandered between stands of sage and tall sawgrasses, Yama saw someone dressed in black watching them from the shade at the edge of a grove of live oaks. He thought it might have been Gorgo, but whoever it was stepped back into the shadows and was gone before Yama could point him out to Tamora.

The city was still disturbed by Yama's drawing down of the feral machine. Magistrates and their attendant clouds of machines were patrolling the streets, and although Yama asked the machines to ignore him and his companions, he was fearful that he would miss one until it was too late, or that Prefect Corin would lunge out of the crowds towards him. He kept turning this way and that until Tamora told him to stop it, or they'd be arrested for sure. Little groups of soldiers lounged at every major intersection. They were the city militia, armed with fusils and carbines, and dressed in loose red trousers and plastic cuirasses as slick and cloudily transparent as ice. They watched the crowds with hard, insolent eyes, but they did not challenge anyone. They did not dare, Pandaras said, and Yama asked how that could be, if they had the authority of the Preservers.

'There are many more of us than there are of them,' Pandaras said, and made the sign Yama had noticed before, touching his fist to his throat.

The boy did not seem scared of the soldiers, but instead openly displayed a smouldering contempt, and Yama noticed that many of the other people made the same sign when they went by a group of soldiers. Some even spat or shouted a curse, safe in the anonymity of the crowd.

Pandaras said, 'With the war downriver, there are even fewer soldiers in the city, and they must keep the peace by terror. That's why they're hated. See that cock there?'

Yama looked up. An officer in gold-tinted body armour stood on a metal disc that floated in the air above the dusty crowns of the ginkgoes which lined one side of the broad, brawling avenue.

'He could level a city block with one shot, if he had a mind to,' Pandaras said. 'But he wouldn't unless he had no other choice, because there'd be riots and even more of the city would be burned. If someone stole a pistol and tried to use it against soldiers or magistrates, then he might do it.'

'It seems an excessive punishment.'

Tamora said, 'Energy weapons are prohibited, worse luck. *I'd* like one right now. Clear a way through these herds of grazers in a blink.'

'One of my uncles on my mother's side of the family was caught up in a tax protest a few years back,' Pandaras said. 'It was in a part of the city a few leagues upriver. A merchant bought up a block and levelled it to make a park, and the legates decided that every tradesman living round about should pay more tax. The park made the area more attractive, neh? The legates said that more people would come because of the open space, and spend more in the shops round about. So the tradesmen got together and declared a tax strike in protest. The legates called up the magistrates, and they came and blockaded the area. Set their machines spinning in the air to make a picket line, so no one could get in or out. It lasted a hundred days, and at the end they said people inside the picket line were eating each other. The food ran out, and there was no way to get more in. A few tried to dig tunnels, but the magistrates sent in machines and killed them.'

Yama said, 'Why did they not give up the strike?'

'They did, after twenty days. They would have held out longer, but there were children, and there were people who didn't live there at all but happened to be passing through when the blockade went up. So they presented a petition of surrender, but the magistrates kept the siege going as punishment. That kind of thing is supposed to make the rest of us too frightened to spit unless we get permission.'

Tamora said, 'There's no other way. There are too many people living in the city, and most are fools or grazers. An argument between neighbours can turn into a feud between bloodlines, with thousands killed. Instead, the magistrates or the militia kill two or three, or even a hundred if necessary, and the matter is settled before it spreads. There are a dozen bloodlines they could get rid of and no one would notice.'

'We're the strength of Ys,' Pandaras said defiantly, and for once Tamora didn't answer back.

They reached the docks late in the afternoon. The same stocky, shaven-headed guard met them in the shadow of the lighter. He looked at the brandy-filled flask and the strings of nerve tissue that floated inside and said that he had already heard that the merchant was dead.

Tamora said, 'Then we'll just take our money and go.'

Yama said to the guard, 'You said you would need to test what we brought.'

The guard said, 'The whole city knows that he was killed last night. To be frank, we would have preferred less attention drawn to it, but we are happy that the task was done. Do not worry. We will pay you.'

'Then let's do it now,' Tamora said, 'and we'll be on our way.'

Yama said quickly, 'But we have made an agreement. I would have it seen through to the letter. Your master wanted to test what we brought, and I would have it done no other way, to prove that we are honest.'

The guard stared hard at Yama, then said, 'I would not insult you by failing to carry out everything we agreed. Come with me.'

As they followed the guard up the gangway, Tamora caught Yama's arm and whispered fiercely, 'This is a foolish risk. We do the job, we take the money, we go. Who cares what they think of us? Complications are dangerous, especially with the star-sailors, and we have an appointment at the Water Market.'

'I have my reasons,' Yama said stubbornly. 'You and Pandaras can wait on the dock, or go on to the Water Market, just as you please.'

He had thought it over as they had walked through the streets of the city to the wharf where the voidship lighter was moored. The star-sailor who piloted the lighter had said that it knew something of Yama's bloodline, and even if it was only one tenth of what the merchant had claimed to know, it was still worth learning. Yama was prepared to pay for the knowledge, and he thought that he knew a sure way of getting at it if the star-sailor refused to tell him anything.

Inside the ship, in the round room at the top of the spiral corridor, the guard uncapped the crystal flask and poured its contents onto the black floor, which quickly absorbed the brandy and the strings of nervous tissue. He set the gold circlet on his scarred, shaven scalp and jerked to attention. His mouth worked, and he said in a voice not his own, 'This one will pay you. What else do you want of me?'

Yama addressed the fleshy blossom which floated inside its bottle. 'I talked with your crewmate before he died. He said that he knew something of my bloodline.'

The star-sailor said through its human mouthpiece, 'No doubt he said many things to save his life.'

'This was when he had me prisoner, and my friends, too.'

'Then perhaps he was boasting. You must understand that he was mad. He had corrupted himself with the desires of the flesh.'

'I remember you said that I had abilities that might be useful.'

'I was mistaken. They have proved ... inconvenient. You have no control over what you can do.'

Tamora said, 'We should leave this. Yama, I'll help you find out what you want to know, but in the Palace of the Memory of the People, not here. We made a deal.'

Yama said stubbornly, 'I have not forgotten. The few questions I want to ask will not end my quest, but they may aid it.' He turned back to the thing in the bottle. 'I will waive my part of the fee for the murder of your crewmate if you will help me understand what he told me.'

Tamora said, 'Don't listen to him, dominie! He hasn't the right to make that bargain!'

The guard's mouth opened and closed. His chin was slick with saliva. He said, 'He was driven mad by the desires of the flesh. I, however, am not mad. I have nothing to say to you unless you can prove that you know what you are. Return then, and we can talk.'

'If I knew that, I would have nothing to ask you.'

Tamora grabbed Yama's arm. 'You're risking everything, you fool. Come on!'

Yama tried to free himself, but Tamora's grip was unyielding and her sharp nails dug into his flesh until blood ran. He stepped in close, thinking to throw her from his hip, but she knew that trick and butted him on the bridge of his nose with her forehead. A blinding spike of pain shot through his head and tears sprang to his eyes. Tamora twisted his arm up behind his back and started to drag him across the room to the dilated doorway, but Pandaras wrapped himself around her legs and fastened his sharp teeth on her thigh. Tamora howled and Yama pulled free and flung himself at the guard, ripping the gold circlet from the man's head and jamming it on his own.

White light.

White noise.

Something was in his head. It fled even as he noticed it and he turned in a direction he had not seen before and flew after it. It was a woman, a naked, graceful woman with pale skin and long black hair that fanned out behind her as she soared through clashing currents of light. Even as she fled, she kept looking back over her bare shoulder. Her eyes blazed with a desperate light.

Yama followed with mounting exhilaration. He seemed to be connected to her through a kind of cord that was growing shorter and stronger, and he twisted and turned after his quarry without thought as they plunged together through interlaced strands of light.

Others were pacing them on either side, and beyond these unseen presences Yama could feel a vast congregation, mostly in clusters as distant and faint as the halo stars. They were the crews of the voidships, meeting together in this country of the mind, in which they swam as easily as fish in the river. Whenever Yama turned his attention to one or another of these clusters, he felt an airy expansion and a fleeting glimpse of the combined light of other minds, as if through a window whose shutters are flung back to greet the rising sun. In every case the minds he touched with his mind recoiled; the shutters slammed; the light faded.

In his desperate chase after the woman through the country of the mind, Yama left behind a growing wake of confused and scandalized inhabitants. They called on something, a guardian or watchdog, and it rose towards Yama like a pressure wave, angling through unseen dimensions like a pike gliding effortlessly through water towards a duckling paddling on the surface. Yama doubled and redoubled his effort to catch the woman, and was almost on her when white light blinded him and white noise roared in his ears and a black floor flew up and struck him with all the weight of the world.

23 ~ The Temple of the Black Well

When Yama woke, the first thing he saw was Pandaras sitting cross-legged by the foot of the bed, sewing up a rip in his second-best shirt. Yama was naked under the scratchy starched sheet, and clammy with old sweat. His head ached, and some time ago a small animal seemed to have crept into the dry cavern of his mouth and died there. Perhaps it was a cousin of the bright green gecko which clung upside down in a patch of sunlight on the far wall, its scarlet throat pulsing. This was a small room, with ochre plaster walls painted with twining patterns of blue vines, and dusty rafters under a slanted ceiling. Afternoon light fell through the two tall windows, and with it the noise and dust and smells of a busy street.

Pandaras helped him up, fussing with the bolster, and brought him a beaker of water. 'It has salt and sugar in it, master. Drink. It will make you stronger.'

Yama obeyed the boy. It seemed that he had been asleep for a night and most of the day that followed. Pandaras and Tamora had brought him here from the docks.

'She has gone out to talk with the man we should have met yesterday. And we didn't get paid by the star-sailor, so she's angry with you.'

'I remember that you tried to help me.' Yama discovered that at some time he had bitten his tongue and the insides of his cheeks. He said, 'You killed the guard with that kidney puncher she gave you.'

'That was before, master. At the gate of the merchant's estate. After that there was the voidship lighter, when you snatched the circlet from the guard and put it on your head.'

'The merchant was wearing the circlet. It was how he controlled his household. But I broke it when I took it away from him.'

'This was in the voidship lighter. Please try and remember, master!

You put the circlet on your head and straightaway you collapsed with foam on your lips and your eyes rolled right back. One of my half-sisters has the falling sickness, and that's what it looked like.'

'A woman. I saw a woman. But she fled from me.'

Pandaras pressed on with his story. 'I snatched the circlet from your head, but you didn't wake. More guards came, and they marched us off the lighter. The first guard, the one you took the circlet from, he and Tamora had an argument about the fee. I thought she might kill him, but he and his fellows drew their pistols, and there was no argument after that. We took some of your money to pay for the room, and for the palanquin that carried you here. I hope we did right.'

'Tamora must be angry with you, too.'

'She doesn't take any account of me, which is just as well. I bit her pretty badly when she tried to stop you taking the circlet, but she bandaged up her legs and said nothing of it. Wouldn't admit I could hurt her, neh? And now I'm not frightened of her because I know I can hurt her, and I'll do it again if I have to. I didn't want to fight with her, master, but she shouldn't have tried to stop you. She didn't have the right.'

Yama closed his eyes. Clusters of lights hanging from the ceiling of the round room at the top of the voidship lighter. The thing in the bottle, with rose-red gills and a lily-white mantle folded around a thick braid of naked nerve tissue. 'I remember,' he said. 'I tried to find out about my bloodline. The country of the mind—'

Pandaras nodded eagerly. 'You took the circlet from the guard and put it on your own head.'

'Perhaps it would have been better if Tamora had stopped me. She was worried that I would no longer have any need of her.'

Pandaras took the empty beaker from Yama and said, 'Well, and do you need her, master? You stood face to face with that thing and talked to it direct. Did it tell you what you wanted to know?'

It seemed like a dream, fading even as Yama tried to remember its details. The woman fleeing, the faint stars of other minds. Yama said, 'I saw something wonderful, but I did not learn anything about myself, except that the people who crew the voidships are scared of me.'

'You scared me too, master. I thought you had gone into the place where they live and left your body behind. I'll have some food sent up. You haven't eaten in two days.'

'You have been good to me, Pandaras.'

'Why, it's a fine novelty to order people about in a place like this. A while ago it was me running at any cock's shout, and I haven't forgotten what it was like.'

'It was not that long ago. A few days.'

'Longer for me than for you. Rest, master. I'll be back soon.'

But Pandaras was gone a long time. The room was hot and close, and Yama wrapped the sheet around himself and sat at one of the windows, where there was a little breeze. He felt weak, but rested and alert. The bandage was gone from the wound on his forearm and the flesh had knitted about the puckers made by the black crosses of the stitches; the self-inflicted wound on his palm was no more than a faint silvery line. All the bruises and small cuts from his recent adventures were healed, too, and someone, presumably Pandaras, had shaved him while he had been sleeping.

The inn stood on a broad avenue divided down the centre by a line of palm trees. The crowds which jostled along the dusty white thoroughfare contained more people than Yama had ever seen in his life, thousands of people of a hundred different bloodlines. There were hawkers and skyclad mendicants, parties of palmers, priests, officials hurrying along in groups of two or three, scribes, musicians, tumblers, whores and mountebanks. An acrobat walked above the heads of the crowd on a wire strung from one side of the avenue to the other. Vendors fried plantains and yams on heated iron plates, or roasted nuts in huge copper basins set over oil burners. Ragged boys ran amongst the people, selling flavoured ice, twists of licorice, boiled sweets, roast nuts, cigarettes, plastic trinkets representing one or another of the long-lost aspects of the Preservers, and medals stamped with the likenesses of official heroes of the war against the heretics. Beggars exhibited a hundred different kinds of mutilation and deformity. Messengers on nimble genets or black plumaged ratites rode at full tilt through the crowds. A few important personages walked under silk canopies held up by dragomen, or were carried on litters or palanquins. A party of solemn giants walked waist high amidst the throng as if wading in a stream. Directly across the avenue, people gathered at a stone altar, burning incense cones bought from a priest, muttering prayers and wafting the smoke towards themselves. A procession of ordinands in red robes, their freshly shaven heads gleaming with oil, wound in a long straggling line behind men banging tambours.

In the distance, the sound of braying, discordant trumpets rang above the noise of the crowded avenue, and presently the procession heralded by the trumpeters hove into view. It was a huge cart pulled by a team of a hundred sweating, half-naked men, with priests swinging fuming censers on either side. It was painted scarlet and gold and bedecked with garlands of flowers, and amidst the heaps of flowers stood a screen, its black oval framed by ornate golden scrollwork. The cart stopped almost directly opposite Yama's window, and people gathered on the rooftops and threw down bucketfuls of water on the men who pulled it, and dropped more garlands of flowers onto the cart and around the men and the attendant priests in a soft, multicoloured snowstorm. Yama leaned out further to get a better view, and at that moment heard a noise in the room behind him and turned, thinking it was Pandaras.

A patch of ochre plaster on the wall opposite the window was cracked in a spiderweb pattern, and in the centre of the web stood an arbalest bolt.

The bolt was as long as Yama's forearm, with a shaft of dense, hard wood and red flight feathers. From the downward pointing angle at which the bolt had embedded itself in the plaster, it must have been fired from one of the flat roofs on the other side of the avenue, for all of them were higher than the window. Yama crouched down and scanned the rooftops, but there were hundreds of people crowded along their edges, scattering flowers and pitching silvery twists of water at the cart. He tried to find a machine which might have been watching, but it seemed that there were no magistrates here.

Still crouching, Yama closed and bolted the heavy slatted shutters of both windows, then pulled the arbalest bolt from the wall.

A few minutes later, Pandaras returned ahead of a pot boy who set a tray covered in a white cloth on the low, round table which, apart from the bed and the chair in which Yama sat, were the only pieces of furniture in the room. Pandaras dismissed the pot boy and whipped away the tray's cover like a conjuror, revealing a platter of fruit and cold meat, and a sweating earthenware pitcher of white wine. He poured wine into two cups, and handed one to Yama. 'I'm sorry it took so long, master. There's a festival. We had to pay double rates just to get the room.'

The wine was cold, and as thickly sweet as syrup. Yama said, 'I saw the procession go by.'

'There's always some procession here. It's in the nature of the place. Eat, master. You must break your fast before you go anywhere.'

Yama took the slice of green melon Pandaras held out. 'Where are we?'

Pandaras bit into his own melon slice. 'Why, it's the quarter that runs between the river and the Palace of the Memory of the People.'

'I think we should go and find Tamora. Where are my clothes?'

'Your trousers are under the mattress, to keep them pressed. I am mending one of your shirts; the other is in your pack. Master, you should eat, and then rest.'

'I do not think so,' Yama said, and showed Pandaras the arbalest bolt.

The landlady called to Yama and Pandaras as they pushed through the hot, crowded taproom of the inn. She was a plump, broad-beamed, brown-skinned woman, her long black hair shiny with grease and braided into a thick rope. She was sweating heavily into her purple and gold sarong, and she waved a fretted palm leaf to and fro as she explained that a message had been left for them.

'I have it here,' she said, rummaging through the drawer of her desk. 'Please be patient, sirs. It is a very busy day today. Is this it? No. Wait, here it is.'

Yama took the scrap of stiff paper. It had been folded four times and tucked into itself, and sealed with a splash of wax. Yama turned it over and over, and asked Pandaras, 'Can Tamora read and write?'

'She put her thumb to the contract, master, so I'd guess she has as much reading as I have, which is to say none.'

The landlady said helpfully, 'There are scribes on every corner. The seal is one of theirs.'

'Do you know which one?'

'There are very many. I suppose I could have one of my boys . . .' The landlady patted her brow with a square of yellow cloth that reeked of peppermint oil. Her eyes were made up with blue paint and gold leaf and her eyebrows had been twisted and stiffened with wax to form long tapering points, giving the effect of a butterfly perched on her face. She added, 'That is, when we are less busy. It is a festival day, you see.'

Yama said, 'I saw the cart go by.'

'The cart? Oh, the shrine. No, no, that is nothing to do with the festival. It passes up and down the street every day, except on its feast day, of course, when it is presented at the Great River. But that is a hundred days off, and just a local affair. People have come here from all over Ys for the festival, and from downriver, too. A very busy time, although of course there are not so many people as there once were. Fewer travel, you see, because of the war. That is why I was able to find you a room at short notice.'

'She moved two palmers into the stables, and charges us twice what they paid,' Pandaras remarked.

'And now they are paying less than they would have,' the landlady said, 'so it all evens out. I hope that the message is not bad news, sirs. The room is yours as long as you want it.' Despite her claim to be busy, it seemed that she had plenty of time to stick her nose in other people's business.

Yama held up the folded paper and said, 'Who brought this?'

'I didn't see. One of my boys gave it to me. I could find him, I suppose, although it's all a muddle today—'

'Because of the festival.' Yama snapped the wax seal and unfolded the paper.

The message was brief, and written in neatly aligned glyphs with firm and decisive downstrokes and fine feathering on the upstrokes. Most likely it had been set down by a scribe, unless Tamora had spent as long as Yama learning the finer nuances of penmanship.

I have gone on. The man you want is at the Temple of the Black Well.

Pandaras said, 'What does it say?'

Yama read the message to Pandaras, and the landlady said, 'That's not too far from here. Go down the passage at the left side of the inn and strike towards the Palace. I could get you a link boy if you'd like to wait . . .'

But Yama and Pandaras were already pushing their way through the crowded room towards the open door and the sunlit avenue beyond.

The narrow streets that tangled behind the inn were cooler and less crowded than the avenue. They were paved with ancient, uneven brick courses, and naked children played in the streams of dirty water that ran down the central gutters. The houses were flat-roofed and none were more than two storeys high, with small shuttered windows and walls covered in thick yellow or orange plaster, walls that were crumbling and much-patched. Many had workshops on the ground floor, open to the street, and Yama and Pandaras passed a hundred tableaus of industry, most to do with the manufacture of the religious mementoes which were displayed in shops which stood at every corner of every street, although none of the shops seemed to be open.

It was a secretive, suspicious place, Yama thought, noting that people stopped what they were doing and openly stared as he and Pandaras went past. But he liked the serendipitous geography, so that a narrow street might suddenly open onto a beautiful square with a white fountain splashing in its centre, and liked the small neighbourhood shrines set into the walls of the houses, with browning wreaths of flowers and pyramids of ash before a flyspotted circle of black glass that poorly mimicked the dark transparency of true shrines.

The domes and pinnacles and towers of temples and shrines reared up amongst the crowded flat roofs of the ordinary houses like ships foundering in the scruffy pack ice of the frozen wilderness at the head of the Great River hundreds of leagues upstream. And beyond all these houses and temples and shrines, the black mountain of the Palace of the Memory of the People climbed terrace by terrace towards its distant peak, with the setting sun making the sky red behind it.

Pandaras explained that this part of the city was given over to the business of worship of the Preservers and of the governance of Ys. Civil service departments displaced from the interior of the Palace of the Memory of the People occupied lesser buildings on its outskirts, and a thousand cults flourished openly or skulked in secret underground chambers.

'At night it can be a dangerous place for strangers,' Pandaras said.

'I have my knife. And you have yours.'

'You should have worn your armour. We collected it from the Water Market, cut down neatly and polished up as good as new.'

Yama had found it when he had taken his shirt from the satchel. He said, 'It would attract attention. Someone might take a fancy to it. Already I feel as if I am a procession, the way people turn to stare.'

'They might want our blood. Or want to scoop out our brains and put them in tanks, all alive-o like the star-sailors.'

Yama laughed at these fantasies.

Pandaras said darkly, 'This is a place of good and evil, master. It is the New Quarter, built on a bloody battleground. You are a singular person. Don't forget it. You would be a great prize for a blood sacrifice.'

'New? It seems to me very old.'

'That's because nothing here has been rebuilt since the Age of Insurrection. The rest of the city is far older, but people are always knocking down old buildings and putting up new ones. The Hierarchs built the Palace of the Memory of the People where the last battle between machines was fought, and the bones and casings of all the dead were tipped into great pits and the ground around about was flattened and these houses were built.'

'I know there was a battle fought near Ys, but I thought it was much further upriver.' Yama remembered now that the Temple of the Black Well had something to do with that last battle, although he could not quite remember what it was.

Pandaras said, 'They built the houses over the battleground, and nothing's changed since, except for the building of shrines and temples.'

'I had thought the houses were built around them.'

'Houses have to be knocked down each time a new temple is built. It's a dangerous business. There are old poisons in the ground, and old weapons too, and sometimes the weapons discharge when they are uncovered. There's a department which does nothing but search by divination for old weapons, and make them safe when they're found. And some parts of the quarter are haunted, too. It's why the people are so strange hereabouts, neh? The ghosts get inside their heads, and infect them with ideas from ages past.'

Yama said, 'I have never seen a ghost.' The aspects which haunted the City of the Dead did not count, for they were merely semi-intelligent projections. And while the Amnan claimed that the blue lights sometimes seen floating amongst the ruins below the peel-house were wights, the eidolons of the restless dead, Zakiel said that they were no more than wisps of burning marsh gas.

Pandaras said, 'These are machine ghosts mostly, but some were human, once, and they say that those are the worst. That's why they make so many icons hereabouts, master. If you were to look inside one of these houses, you'd find layer upon layer of them on the walls.'

'To keep out the ghosts.'

'They don't usually work. That's what I heard, anyway.'

258

'Look there. Is that our temple?'

It reared up a few streets ahead, a giant cube built of huge, roughly hewn stone blocks stained black with soot, and topped by an onion dome lapped in scuffed gilt tiles.

Pandaras squinted at it, then said, 'No, ours has a rounder roof, with a hole in the top of it.'

'Of course! Where the machine fell!'

The Temple of the Black Well had been built long after the feral machine's fiery fall, but its dome had been left symbolically uncompleted, with the aperture at its apex directly above the deep hole made when the machine had struck the surface of the world and melted a passage in the rock all the way down to the keel. Yama had been told the story by the aspect of a leather merchant who had had his tannery near the site of the temple's construction. Mysyme, that had been the merchant's name. He had had two wives and six beautiful daughters, and had done much charitable work amongst the orphaned river rats of the docks. Mysyme was dead an age past, and Yama had lost interest in the limited responses of his aspect years ago, but now he remembered them all over again. Mysyme's father had seen the fall of the machine, and had told his son that when it hit, a plume of melted rock had been thrown higher than the atmosphere, while the smoke of secondary fires had darkened the sky above Ys for a decad.

'It's a little to the left,' Pandaras said, 'and maybe ten minutes' walk. That place with the gold roof is a tomb of a warrior-saint. It's solid all the way through except for a secret chamber.'

'You are a walking education, Pandaras.'

'I have an uncle who used to live here, and one time I stayed with him. He was on my mother's side, and this was when my father ran off and my mother went looking for him. She was a year at it, and never found him. And a year is a long time for my people. So she came back and married another man, and when that didn't work out she married my stepfather. I don't get on with him, and that's why I took the job of pot boy, because it came with a room. And then you came along, and here we are.' Pandaras grinned. 'For a long time after I left this part of the city, I thought maybe I was haunted. I'd wake up and think I'd been hearing voices, voices that had been telling me things in my sleep. But I haven't heard them since I met up with you, master. Maybe your bloodline is a cure for ghosts.'

'All my bloodline are ghosts, from the little I have learned,' Yama said.

The Temple of the Black Well stood at the centre of a wide, quiet plaza of mossy cobbles. It had been built in the shape of a cross, with a long atrium and short apses; its dome, covered in gold leaf that shone with the last light of the sun, capped the point where the apses intersected the atrium. The temple was clad in lustrous black stone, although here and there parts of the cladding had fallen away to reveal the greyish limestone beneath. Yama and Pandaras walked all the way around the temple and saw no one, and then climbed the long flight of shallow steps and went through the tall narthex.

It was dark inside, but a thick slanted column of reddish light fell through the open apex of the dome at the far end of a long atrium flanked by colonnades. Yama walked towards the light. There was no sign of Tamora or her mysterious contact; the whole temple seemed deserted. The pillars of the colonnades were intricately carved and the ruined mosaics of the floor sketched the outlines of heroic figures. The temple had been splendid once, Yama thought, but now it had the air of a place that was no longer cared for. He thought it an odd choice for a rendezvous – far better for an ambush.

Pandaras clearly felt the same thing, for his sleek head continually turned this way and that as they went down the atrium. The reddish light, alive with swirling motes of dust, fell on a waist-high wall of undressed stone which ringed a wide hole that plunged down into darkness. It was the well, the shaft the fallen machine had melted. The wide coping on top of the wall was covered in the ashy remnants of incense cones, and here and there were offerings of fruit and flowers. A few joss sticks jammed into cracks in the wall sent up curls of sweet-smelling smoke, but the flowers were shrivelled and brown, and the little piles of fruit were spotted with decay.

'Not many come here,' Pandaras said. 'The ghost of the machine is powerful, and quick to anger.'

Yama gripped the edge of the coping and looked into the depths of the well. A faint draught of cold, stale air blew up around him from the lightless depths. The walls of the shaft were long glassy flows of once-melted rock, veined with impurities, dwindling away to a vanishing point small as the end of his thumb. It was impossible to tell how deep the well really was, and in a spirit of enquiry Yama dropped a softening pomegranate into the black air.

'That isn't a good idea,' Pandaras said uneasily.

'I do not think a piece of fruit would wake this particular machine. It fell a long way as I recall – at least, it was two days in falling, and appeared in the sky as a star clothed in burning hair. When it struck the ground, the blow knocked down thousands of houses and caused a wave in the river that washed away much of the city on the far shore. And then the sky turned black with smoke from all the fires.'

'There might be other things down there,' Pandaras said. 'Bats, for instance. I have a particular loathing of bats.'

Yama said, 'I should have thrown a coin. I might have heard it hit.'

But a small part of his mind insisted that the fruit was still falling through black air towards the bottom, two leagues or more to the keel. He and Pandaras walked around the well, but apart from the smoking joss sticks there was no sign that Tamora or anyone else had been there recently, and the hushed air was beginning to feel oppressive, as if it held a note endlessly drawn out just beyond the range of hearing.

Pandaras said, 'We should go on, master. She isn't here.' He added hopefully, 'Perhaps she has run off and left us.'

'She made a contract with me. I should think that is a serious thing for someone who lives from one job to the next. We will wait a little longer.' He took out the paper and read it again. '"The man you want . . ." I wonder what she meant.'

'It'll be dark soon.'

Yama smiled, and said, 'I believe that you are scared of this place.'

'You might not believe in ghosts, master, but there are many who do – most of the people in the city, I reckon.'

'I might have more cause to believe in ghosts, because I was brought up in the middle of the City of the Dead, but I do not. Just because a lot of people believe in ghosts does not make them real. I might believe that the Preservers have incarnated themselves in river turtles, and I might persuade a million people to believe it, too, but that does not make it true.'

'You shouldn't make jokes like that,' Pandaras said. 'Especially not here.'

'Surely the Preservers will forgive a small joke.'

'There's many who would take offence on their account,' Pandaras said stubbornly. He had a deep streak of superstition, despite his worldly-wise air. Yama had seen the care with which he washed himself in a ritual pattern after eating and upon waking, the way he crossed his fingers when walking past a shrine – a superstition he shared with the citizens of Aeolis, who believed that it disguised the fact that you had come to a shrine without an offering – and his devotion at prayer. Like the Amnan, who could not or would not read the Puranas and so only knew them secondhand through the preaching of priests and iconoclasts, Pandaras and the countless millions of ordinary folk of Ys believed that the Preservers had undergone a transubstantiation, disappearing not into the Eye but dispersing themselves into every particle of the world which they had made, so that they were everywhere at once, immortal, invisible and, despite their limitless power, quick to judge and requiring constant placation. It was not surprising, then, that Pandaras believed in ghosts and other revenants.

Pandaras said, 'Ghosts are more like ideas than you might think. The more people believe in them, the more powerful they become. Listen! What was that?'

'I heard nothing,' Yama said, but even as he said it there was a faint brief rumble, as if the temple, with all its massy stones, had briefly stirred and then settled again. It seemed to come from the well, and Yama leaned over and peered into its depths. The wind which blew out of the darkness seemed to be blowing a little more strongly, and it held a faint tang, like heated metal.

'Come away,' Pandaras pleaded uneasily. He was shifting his weight from foot to foot, as if ready to run.

'We will look in the apses. If anything was going to happen, Pandaras, it would have happened by now.'

'If it does happen, it'll be all the worse for waiting.'

'You go left and I will go right, and if we find nothing I promise we will go straight out of this place.'

'I'll come with you, master, if you don't mind. I've no liking for being left alone in this hecatomb.'

The archway which led into the apse to the right of the well was curtained by falls of fine black plastic mesh. Beyond was a high square space lit by shafts of dim light striking through knotholes that pierced the thick walls just beneath the vaulted roof. There was a shrine set in the centre of the space, a glossy black circle like a giant's coin or eyeglass stood on its side.

Statues three times the height of a man stood in recesses all around the four walls, although they were not statues of men, and nor were they carved from stone, but were made of the same slick, translucent stuff as ancient armour. Yama could dimly see shapes and catenaries inside their chests and limbs.

Pandaras went up to a statue and knocked his knuckles against its shin: it rang with a dull note. 'There's a story that these things fought against the Insurrectionists.'

'More likely they were made in the likeness of great generals,' Yama said, looking up at their grim visages.

'Don't worry,' a woman's voice said. 'They've been asleep so long they've forgotten how to wake.'

24 ~ The Woman in White

Yama turned, and streamers of blazing white light suddenly raced through the shrine's black disc. He raised an arm to shade his eyes, but the white light had already faded into a swirling play of soft colours.

Pandaras's clenched paw fluttered under his open mouth. He said, 'Master, this is some horrid trick.'

Cautiously, Yama stepped through polychromatic light and touched the shrine's slick, cold surface. He was possessed by the mad idea that he could slip into it as easily as slipping into the cool water of the river.

Like a reflection, a hand rose through swirling colours to meet his own. For a moment he thought that he felt its touch, like a glove slipping around his skin, and he recoiled in shock.

Laughter, like the chiming of small silver bells. Streaks and swirls and dabs of a hundred colours collapsed into themselves, and a woman was framed in the disc of the shrine. Pandaras shouted and ran, flinging himself in a furious panic through the black mesh curtains which divided the apse from the main part of the temple.

Yama knelt before the shrine, fearful and amazed. 'Lady . . . what do you want from me?'

'Oh do get up. I can't talk to the top of your head.'

Yama obeyed. He supposed that the woman was one of the avatars of the Preservers, who, as was written in the Puranas, stood between the quotidian world and the glory of their masters, facing both ways at once. She was tall and slender, with a commanding, imperious gaze, and wore a white one-piece garment which clung to her limbs and body. Her skin was the colour of newly forged bronze, and her long black hair was caught in a kind of net at her right shoulder. A green garden receded behind her: smooth lawns and a maze of high, trimmed hedges. A stone fountain sent a muscular jet of water high into the sunlit air.

'Who are you, domina? Do you live in this shrine?'

'I don't know where I live, these days. I'm scattered, I suppose you could say. But this is one of the places where I can look out at the world. It's like a window. You live in a house made of rooms. Where I live is mostly windows, looking out to different places. You drew me to this window and I looked out and found you.'

'Drew you? Domina, I did not mean to.'

'You wear the key around your neck. You have discovered that, at least.'

Yama lifted out the coin which hung on the thong around his neck, the coin which the anchorite had given him the spring night when Dr Dismas had returned to Ys, and everything had changed. Yama had gone out to hunt frogs, and caught something far stranger. The coin was warm, but perhaps only because it had lain next to his skin.

The woman in the shrine said, 'It works by light, and briefly talked with this transceiver. I heard it, and came here. Don't be afraid. Do you like where I live?'

Yama said, with reflexive politeness, 'I have never seen a garden like yours.'

'Of course you haven't. It is from some long-vanished world, perhaps even from Earth. Do you wish me to change it? I could live anywhere, you know. Or at least anywhere on file that hasn't been corrupted. The servers are very old, and there's much that has been corrupted. Atoms migrate; cosmic rays and neutrinos corrupt the lattices ... Anyway, I like gardens. It stirs something in my memory. My original ruled many worlds once, and surely some of those possessed gardens. It's possible she owned a garden just like this, once upon a time. But I've forgotten such a lot, and I was never really whole in the first place. There are peacocks. Do you know peacocks? No, I suppose not. Perhaps there are autochthonous creatures like peacocks somewhere on Confluence, but I don't have the files to hand. If we talk long enough perhaps one will come past. They are birds. The cocks have huge fan-shaped tails, with eyes in them.'

Yama was suddenly overwhelmed by the image of an electric blue long-necked bird with concentric arcs of fiery eyes peering over its tiny head. He turned away, the heels of his palms pressed into his eye sockets, but the vision still beat inside his head.

'Wait,' the woman said. Was there a note of uncertainty in her voice? 'I didn't mean . . . The gain is difficult to control . . .'

The sheaves of burning eyes vanished; there was only ordinary bloodwarm darkness behind his eyelids. Cautiously, Yama turned back to the shrine.

'It isn't real,' the woman said. She stepped up to the inner surface of the shrine and pressed her hands against it and peered between them as if trying to see through the window of a lighted room into a dark landscape. Her palms were dyed red. Paeolin. She said, 'That it isn't real is the important thing to remember. But isn't everything an illusion? We're all waves, and even the waves are really half-glimpsed strings folded deeply into themselves.'

She seemed to be talking to herself, but then she smiled at Yama. Or no, her eyes were not quite focused on him, but at a point a little to one side of the top of his head.

Yama said, prompted by a flicker of suspicion, 'Excuse me, domina, but are you really an avatar? I have never seen one before.'

'I'm no fragment of a god, Yamamanama. The clade of my original ruled a million planetary systems, once upon a time, but she never claimed to be a god. None of the transcendents ever claimed that, only their enemies.'

Fear and amazement collapsed into relief. Yama laughed and said, 'An aspect. You are an aspect. Or a ghost.'

'A ghost in the machine. Yes, that's one way of looking at it. Why not? Even when my original walked the surface of this strange habitat she was a copy of a memory, and I suppose that would make me a kind of a ghost of a ghost. But you're a ghost, too. You shouldn't be here, not at this time. You're either too young, or too old, a hundred thousand years either way . . . Do you know why you are here?'

'I wish with all my heart to find out,' Yama said, 'but I do not believe in ghosts.'

'We have spoken before.' The woman tilted her head with a curiously coquettish gesture, and smiled. 'You don't remember, do you?' she said. 'Well, you were very young, and that foolish man with you hid your face in a fold of his robes. I think he must have done something to the shrine, afterwards, because that window has been closed to me ever since, like so many others. There is much old damage in the system from the war between the machines. I could only glimpse you now and then as you grew up. How I wish I could have spoken to you! How I wish I could have helped you! I am so happy to meet you again, but you should not be here, in this strange and terrible city. You should be on your way downriver, to the war.'

'What do you know about me? Please, domina, will you tell me what you know?'

'There are gates. Manifolds held open by the negative gravity of strange matter. They run in every direction, even into the past, all the way back to when they were created. I think that is where you come from. That, or the voidships. Perhaps your parents were passengers or stowaways on a voidship, time-shifted by the velocity of some long voyage. We did not learn where the voidships went. There was not enough time to learn a tenth of what we wanted to know. In any case, you come from the deep past of this strange world, Yamamanama, but although I have searched the records, I do not know who sent you, or why. Does it matter? You are here, and there is much to be done.'

Yama could not believe her. For if he had been sent here from the deep past when his people, the Builders, had been constructing the world according to the desires of the Preservers, then he could never find his family or any others like him. He would be quite alone, and that was unthinkable.

He said, 'I was found on the river. I was a baby, lying on the breast of a dead woman in a white boat.' He suddenly felt that his heart might burst with longing. 'Please tell me! Tell me why I am here!'

The woman in the shrine lifted her hands, wrists cocked in an elegant shrug. She said, 'I'm a stranger here. My original walked out into your world and died there, but not before she started to change it. And before she died part of her came here, and here I am still. I sometimes wonder if you're part of what she did after she left me here. Would that make you my son, if it were true?'

Yama said, 'I am looking for answers, not more riddles.'

'Let me give an example. You see the statues? You think them monuments to dead heroes, but the truth is simpler than any story.'

'Then they are not statues?'

'Not at all. They are soldiers. They were garrisoned here after the main part of the temple was built, to guard against what the foolish little priests of the temple call the Thing Below. I suppose that when the apses were remodelled many years later it was easier to incorporate the soldiers into the architecture than to move them. Most of their kind have been smelted down, and small pieces of armour have been cast from their remains, so in a sense they still defend the populace. But the soldiers around us are the reality, and the human soldiers who wear reforged scraps of the integuments of their brothers are but the shadows of that reality, as I am a shadow of the one for whom I speak. Unlike the soldiers, she is quite vanished from this world, and only I remain.'

Yama looked up at the nearest of the figures. It stared above his head at one of its fellows on the opposite side of the square apse, but Yama fancied that he saw its eyes flicker towards him for an instant. They were red, and held a faint glow that he knew had not been there before.

He said, 'Am I then a shadow too? I am searching for others like me. Can I find them?'

'I would be amazed and delighted if you did, but they are all long dead. I think that you will be sufficient, Yamamanama. Already you have discovered that you can control the machines which maintain this habitat. There is much more I can teach you.'

'My bloodline was made by the Preservers to build the world, and then they went away. That much I have learnt, at least. I will discover more in the Palace of the Memory of the People.'

'They were taken back,' the woman said. 'You might say that if I am a shadow of what I was, then your kind were a shadow of what you call the Preservers and what I suppose I could call my children, although they are as remote from me as I am from the plains apes which walked out of Afrique and set fire to the Galaxy.'

Someone had recently said something similar to Yama. Who? Trying to remember, he said automatically, 'All are shadows of the Preservers.'

'Not quite all. There are many different kinds of men on this strange world – I suppose I must call it a world – and each has been reworked until it retains only a shadow of its animal ancestors. Most, but not all, have been salted with a fragment of inheritable material derived from the Preservers. The dominant races of this habitat are from many different places and many different times, but they all are marked by this attribute, and all believe that they can evolve to a higher state. Indeed, many seem to have evolved out of existence, but it is not clear if they have transcended or merely become extinct. But the primitive races, which resemble men but are little better than animals, are not marked, and have never advanced from their original state. There is much I still do not understand about this world, but that much I do know.'

'If you can help me understand where I came from, perhaps I can help you.'

The woman smiled. 'You try to bargain with me. But I have already told you where you came from, Yamamanama, and I have already helped you. I have sung many songs of praise in your honour. I have told many of your coming. I have raised up a champion to fight for you. You should be with him now, sailing downriver to the war.'

Yama remembered the young warlord's story. He said, 'With Enobarbus?'

'The soldier too. But I meant Dr Dismas. He found me long ago, long before I spoke with Enobarbus. You should be with them now. With their help, and especially with mine, you could save the world.'

Yama laughed. 'Lady, I will do what I can against the heretics, but I do not think I can do more than any other man.'

'*Against* the heretics? Don't be silly. I have not been able to speak to you, but I have watched you. I heard your prayers, after your brother's death. I know how desperately you wish to become a hero and avenge him. Ah, but I can make you more than that.'

After the news of Telmon's death, Yama had prayed all night before the shrine in the temple. The Aedile had sent two soldiers to watch over him, but they had fallen asleep, and in the quiet hour before dawn Yama had asked for a sign that he would lead a great victory in Telmon's name. He had thought then that he wanted to redeem his brother's death, but he understood now that his prayers had been prompted by mere selfishness. He had wanted a shape to his own life, to know its beginning and to be given a destiny. He realized that perhaps his prayer had been answered after all, but not in the way he had hoped.

'You must take up your inheritance,' the woman said. 'I can help you. Together we can complete the changes my original began. I think you have already begun to explore what you can do. There is much more, if you will let me teach you.'

'If you had listened to me, domina, you would know that I pledged to save the world, not change it.'

Did her gaze darken? For a moment, it seemed to Yama that her strange beauty was merely a mask or film covering something horrible.

She said, 'If you want to save the world, it must be changed. Change is fundamental to life. The world will be changed whichever side wins the war, but only one side can ensure that stasis is not enforced again. Stasis preserves dead things, but it suffocates life. A faction of the servants of this world realized that long ago. But they failed, and those which survived were thrown into exile. Now they are our servants, and together we will succeed where they alone did not.'

Yama remembered the cold black presence of the feral machine he had inadvertently called down at the merchant's house, and it took all his will not to run from the woman, as Pandaras had run at first sight. He knew now which side this avatar was on, and where Enobarbus and Dr Dismas would have taken him if he had not escaped. Dr Dismas had lied about everything. He was a spy for the heretics, and Enobarbus was not a champion against them, but a warlord secretly fighting on their side. He had not escaped when his ship had been sunk, but had been captured by the heretics and made into one of them. Or perhaps he had been granted safe passage because he already was one of them – for had he not spoken of a vision which had spoken to him from the shrine of the temple of his people? Yama knew now who had spoken to the young soldier, and knew what course he had been set upon. Not against the heretics, but for them. What a fool he had been to believe otherwise!

He said, 'The world cannot be saved by contesting the will of those who made it. I will fight the heretics, not serve them.'

Silver bells, ringing in the air all around. 'You are still so young, Yamamanama! You still cling to the beliefs of your childhood! But you will change your mind. Dr Dismas has promised that he has already sown the seeds of change. Look on this, Yamamanama. All this can be ours!'

The shrine flashed edge to edge with white light. Yama closed his eyes, but the white light was inside his head, too. Something long and narrow floated in it, like a needle in milk. It was his map. No, it was the world.

Half was green and blue and white, with the Great River running along one side and the ranges of the Rim Mountains on the other, and the icecap of the Endpoint shining in the sunlight; half was tawny desert, splotched and gouged with angry black and red scars and craters, the river dry, the icecap gone.

It floated before Yama, serene and lovely, for a long moment. And then it was gone, and the woman smiled at him from the window of the shrine, with the green lawn and the high hedges of the garden receding behind her.

'Together we will do great things,' she said. 'We will remake the world, and everyone in it, as a start.'

Yama said steadfastly, 'You are an aspect of one of the Ancients of Days. You raised up the heretics against the will of the Preservers. You are my enemy.'

'I am no enemy of yours, Yamamanama. How could an enemy speak from a shrine?'

'The heretics silenced the last avatars of the Preservers. Why shouldn't something else take their place? Why do you tempt me with foolish visions? No one can rule the world.'

The woman smiled. 'No one does, and there is its problem. Any advanced organism must have a dominating principle, or else its different parts will war against each other, and it will be paralysed by inaction. As with organisms, so with worlds. You have so many doubts. I understand. Hush! Not another word! Someone comes. We'll talk again. If not here, then at one of the other transceivers that are still functioning. There are many on the far shore.'

'If I talk with you again, it will be because I have found some way of destroying you.'

She smiled. 'I think you will change your mind about that.'

'Never!'

'Oh, but I think that you will. Already it has begun. Until then.'

And then she was gone, and with her the light. Once more, Yama could see through the darkly transparent disc of the shrine. On the far side of the apse, the curtain of black mesh stirred as someone pushed it aside.

25 ~ The Assassin

It was not Pandaras, nor even Tamora, but a barechested giant of a man in black leather trews. His skin was the colour of rust and his face was masked with an oval of soft black moleskin. He carried a naked falchion, and there was a percussion pistol tucked into his waistband. His muscular arms were bound tightly with leather thongs; plastic vambraces, mottled with extreme age, were laced around his forearms.

As soon as he saw Yama, the man quickly advanced around the shrine. Yama stepped backwards and drew his long knife. It ran with blue fire, as if dipped in flaming brandy.

The man smiled. His mouth was red and wet inside the slit in his black mask. The pointed teeth of a small fierce animal made a radiating pattern around the mask's mouth slit and little bones made a zig-zag pattern around the eyeholes, exaggerating their size. The man's rust-coloured skin shone as if oiled, and a spiral pattern of welts was raised on the skin of his chest. Yama thought of the friendly people who had colonized the abandoned tombs at the edge of Ys. This was one of their sons, corrupted by the city. Or perhaps he had left his people because he was already corrupted.

'Who sent you?' Yama said. He was aware that one of the statues was only a few paces from his back. Remembering what Sergeant Rhodean had taught him, he carefully watched as the man moved towards him, looking for weaknesses he might exploit if it came to a fight.

'Put up that silly pricking blade, and I'll tell you,' the man said. His voice was deep and slow, and set up echoes in the vaulted roof of the apse. 'I was asked to kill you slowly, but I promise to make it quick if you don't struggle.'

'It was Gorgo. He hired you at the Water Market.'

The man's eyes widened slightly under the mask and Yama knew that he had guessed right, or had struck close to the truth.

He said, 'Or you are a friend of Gorgo, or someone who owes him a favour. In any case, it is not an honourable act.'

The man said, 'Honour has nothing to it.'

Yama's fingers sweated on the hilt of the knife and the skin and muscles of his forearm tingled as if held close to a fire, although the knife blade gave off no heat. Pandaras had not known to leave the knife in sunlight while I was ill, he thought. Now it takes the energy it needs from me, and I must strike soon.

He said, 'Did Gorgo tell you who I killed? He cannot have forgotten, because it was only two nights ago. It was a rich and powerful merchant, with many guards. I was his prisoner, and my knife was taken from me, but he is dead and I stand here before you. Go now, and I will spare you.'

He was calling out to any machine for help, but there were none close by. He could only feel their distant, directionless swarm, as a man hears the many voices of a city as an unmodulated roar.

The assassin said, 'You think to keep me talking, that I may spare you or help will come. Those are foolish hopes. Put up your knife and it'll be a quick dispatch. You have my word.'

'And perhaps you talk because you do not have the stomach for it.'

The assassin laughed, a rumble like rocks moving over each other in his belly. 'It's the other way around. I was paid to kill you as slowly as possible, and to withhold the name of my client until the last possible moment. You won't put away your silly little blade? You choose a slow death, then.'

Yama saw that the assassin favoured his right arm; if he ran to the left, the man must turn before striking. In that instant Yama might have a chance at a successful blow. Although the shrine was dark and fading sunlight had climbed halfway up the walls, laying a bronze sheen on the cloudily opaque torsoes of the gigantic soldiers, everything in the square apse shone with an intense particularity. Yama had never felt more alive than now, at the moment before his certain death.

He yelled and ran, striking at the man's masked face. His opponent whirled with amazing speed and parried automatically with such force that Yama was barely able to fend off the blow. The knife screamed and spat a stream of sparks, and notched the assassin's sword.

The assassin did not press his advantage, but stared distractedly at something above Yama's head. Yama struck again, lunging with the point of his knife; Sergeant Rhodean had taught him that the advantage of a shorter blade is the precision with which it can be directed. The assassin parried with the same casual, brutal force as before and stepped back, pulling the percussion pistol from his waistband.

Suddenly, dust boiled around them in a dry, choking cloud. Chips of stone rained down like hail, ringing on the stone flags of the floor. In the midst of this, Yama lunged again. It was a slight, glancing blow that barely grazed the assassin's chest, but the knife flashed and there was a terrific flash of blue light that knocked the man down. Yama's arm was instantly numbed from wrist to shoulder. As he shifted the knife to his left hand, the assassin got to his feet and raised the percussion pistol.

The man's mouth was working inside the mask's slit, and his eyes were wide. He fired and fired again at something behind Yama. The pistol failed on the third shot and the assassin threw it hard over Yama's head and ran, just as Pandaras had run when the woman had appeared in the shrine.

Yama chased after the assassin, his blood singing in his head, but the man plunged through the curtain of black mesh and Yama stopped short, fearing an ambush on the other side. He turned and looked up at the soldier which had stepped from its niche, and asked it to go back to sleep until it was needed again. The soldier, its eyes glowing bright red in its impassive face, struck its chestplate with a mailed fist, and the apse rang like a bell with the sound.

26 ~ The Thing Below

A long way down the shadow-filled atrium, in the glow of a palm-oil lantern which had been lowered on a chain from the lofty ceiling, two men bent over something. Yama ran forward with his knife raised, but they were only priests tending to Pandaras. The boy lay sprawled on the mosaic floor, alive but unconscious. Yama knelt and touched his face. His eyes opened, but he seemed unable to speak. There was a bloody gash on his temple; it seemed to be his only wound.

Yama sheathed his knife and looked up at the two priests. They wore homespun robes and had broad, wide-browed faces and tangled manes of white hair: the same bloodline as Enobarbus. Although Yama had guessed that this was the place where the young warlord had received his vision, he still felt a small shock of recognition.

He asked the priests if they had seen who had wounded his friend, and they looked at each other before one volunteered that a man had just now run past, but they had already discovered this poor boy. Yama smiled to think of the spectacle the masked assassin must have made, running through the temple with a sword in his hand and blood running down his bare chest. Gorgo must be nearby – if he had sent the assassin, surely he would want to witness what he had paid for – and he would have seen the rout of his hireling.

The priests looked at each other again and the one who had spoken before said, 'I am Antros, and this is my brother, Balcus. We are keepers of the temple. There is a place to wash your friend's wound, and to tend to your own wounds, too. Follow me.'

Yama's right arm had recovered most of its strength, although it now tingled as if it had been stung by a horde of ants. He gathered up Pandaras and followed the old priest. The boy's skin was hot and his heartbeat was light and rapid, but Yama had no way of knowing whether or not this was normal.

Beyond the colonnade on the left-hand side of the atrium was a little grotto carved into the thick stone of the temple's outer wall. Water trickled into a shallow stone trough from a plastic spout set in the centre of a swirl of red mosaic. Yama helped Pandaras kneel, and bathed the shallow wound on his temple. Blood which had matted the boy's sleek hair fluttered into the clear cold water, but the bleeding had already stopped and the edges of the wound were clean.

'You will have a headache,' Yama told Pandaras, 'but nothing worse. I think he struck you with the edge of his vambrace, or with his pistol, rather than with his falchion. You should have stayed with me, Pandaras.'

Pandaras was still unable to speak, but he clumsily caught Yama's hand and squeezed it.

The old priest, Antros, insisted on cleaning the shallow cuts on Yama's back. As he worked, he said, 'We heard two pistol shots. You are lucky that he missed you, although I would guess that he did not miss you by much, and you were hurt by stone splinters knocked from the wall.'

'Fortunately, he was not aiming at me,' Yama said.

Antros said, 'This was a fine place once. The pillars were painted azure and gold, and beeswax candles as tall as a man scented the air with their perfume. Our temple was filled with mendicants and palmers from every town and city along the length of the river. That was long before my time, of course, but I do remember when an avatar of the Preservers still appeared in the shrine.'

'Was this avatar a woman, dressed in white?'

'It was neither man nor woman, and neither young nor old.' The old priest smiled in recollection. 'How I miss its wild laughter – it was filled with fierce joy, and yet it was a gentle creature. But it is gone. They have all gone. Men still come to pray at the shrine, of course, but although the Preservers hear every prayer, men have fallen so far from grace that there are no longer answers to their questions. Few come here now, and even fewer to bare themselves humbly before their creators. Most who come do so to ask the one below to curse their enemies, but there are not even very many of them.'

'I suppose that most people fear this place.'

'Just so, although we do have problems with cultists from time to time, for they are attracted by the same thing which the ordinary folk fear. My brother and I come here each evening to light the lamps, but otherwise the temple is not much used, even by our own bloodline. Of course, we have our high day when the atrium is decorated with palm fronds and wreaths of ivy and there is a solemn procession to aspurge every corner and to propitiate the Thing Below. But otherwise, as I have said, most people keep away. You are a stranger here. A palmer, perhaps. I am sorry that you and your friend were attacked. No doubt a footpad followed you, and saw his chance.'

Yama asked Antros if the Thing Below was the machine which had fallen in the final battle at the end of the Age of Insurrection.

'Indeed. You must not suppose it was destroyed. Rather, it was entombed alive in rock made molten by its fall. It stirs, sometimes. In fact, it has been very restless recently. Listen! Do you hear it?'

Yama nodded. He had supposed that the high singing in his head was his own blood rushing through his veins with the excitement of his brief skirmish.

'It is the second time in as many days,' Antros said. 'Most of our bloodline are soldiers, and part of our duty is to guard the well and the thing entombed at its bottom. But many have gone downriver to fight in the war, and many of those have been killed there.'

'I met one,' Yama said. He did not need to ask when the machine had begun to be restless, and felt a chill in his blood. He had called for help in the merchant's house, and the feral machine which had answered his call was not the only one to have heard him. What else? What else might he have inadvertently awakened?

Out in the atrium, someone suddenly started to shout, raising overlapping echoes. The old priest looked alarmed, but Yama said, 'Do not be afraid, dominie. I know that voice.'

Tamora had returned to the inn, she said, and had had to threaten the painted witch who ran it to find out where Yama and Pandaras had gone. 'Then I realised what the game was, and came straightaway.'

'It was Gorgo,' Yama said, as he tied the laces of his torn, blood-stained shirt. 'I appear to have a knack of making enemies.'

'I hope you gouged out his eyes before you killed him,' Tamora said.

'I have not seen him. But someone shot an arbalest bolt at me earlier, and I remember that you said Gorgo had killed someone with an arbalest.

He missed, and then he sent another man to kill me. Fortunately, I had some help, and was able to scare off the assassin.'

'I will have his eyes,' Tamora said with venomous passion, 'if I ever see him again! His balls and his eyes! He is a disgrace to the Fierce People!'

'He must be very jealous, to want to kill me because of you.'

Tamora laughed, and said, 'O Yama, at last you show some human weakness, even if it is only conceit about your cockmanship. The truth is, I owe Gorgo money. He's not one for fighting, but for making deals. He finds work for others, and takes a cut of the fees for his trouble. And he loans money, too. I borrowed from him to buy new armour and this sword after I was wounded in the war last year. I lost my kit then, you see. I was working on commission to pay off the debt and the interest. I got enough to live on, and he took the rest.'

'Then the job I did with you—'

'Yes, yes,' Tamora said impatiently. 'On Gorgo's commission. He didn't really expect me to succeed, but he was still angry when I told him that we'd killed the merchant and hadn't been able to collect the fee.'

'And that is why you agreed to help me.'

'Not exactly. Yama, we don't have time for this.'

'I need to know, Tamora.'

Yama understood now why Tamora had embarked on such a risky enterprise, but he still did not understand why Gorgo wanted him dead.

Tamora hung her head for a moment, then said with a mixture of vulnerability and defiance, 'I suppose it's only fair. The star-sailor job would have paid well, but we lost the fee because you went crazy and grabbed that circlet. And I still owe Gorgo, and I was going off to work for you, as he saw it. I said he should wait and I'd pay back everything, but he's greedy. He wants the liver and the lights as well as the meat and bones.'

Yama nodded. 'He decided to kill me and steal the money I have.'

'He said that he would rob you, not kill you. He said it was only fair, because you'd lost him the fee for killing the merchant. I didn't know he'd try and kill you. I swear it.'

'I believe you,' Yama said. 'And I know that Gorgo found someone else to help you with the job in the Palace of the Memory of the People. He wanted me out of the way.'

'A man with red skin and welts on his chest. I told Gorgo that I was going to work with you, Yama, and no other, but Gorgo said the man would be waiting for me at the Palace gate. I went there, but I couldn't find the man and I went back to the inn and found that you had come here.'

'Well, the man you were waiting for was here. It was he who tried to kill me.'

'I was going to tell you everything,' Tamora said. 'I decided something, while I was waiting. Hear me out. I made an agreement with you, and I will stick with it. Fuck Gorgo. When the job is finished I'll find him and kill him.'

'Then you will work for me, and not Gorgo?'

'Isn't that what I said?' Tamora said impatiently. 'But there isn't time to stand and talk a moment longer, not now! You've been lying around in bed, and then fooling about in this mausoleum, and meanwhile I have been busy. We have already missed one appointment, and we must not miss the second, or the contract will be voided. Can you ride?'

'A little.'

'That had better mean you can ride like the wind.' Tamora seemed to notice Pandaras for the first time. 'What happened to the rat-boy?'

'A blow to the head. Luckily, the assassin Gorgo hired had some scruples.'

'Maybe it'll have knocked some of his airs out and let some sense in. I suppose you still want to bring him? Well, I'll carry him for you. Why are you staring at me? Do you call off our contract after all this?'

'I have already woken things best left sleeping. If I go on, what else might I do?'

Tamora said briskly, 'Would you emasculate yourself, then? If you don't know who you are and where you came from, then you can't know what you can become. Come with me, or not. I'm taking the job anyway, because I'll get paid for it with you or without you. And when I've finished there, I'll kill Gorgo.'

She slung Pandaras over her shoulder and walked away with a quick, lithe step, as if the boy weighed nothing at all. After a moment, Yama followed.

It was dusk. Warm lights glowed in windows of the houses around the mossy plaza. Two horses were tethered to a pole topped by a smoky, guttering cresset. Tamora and Yama lifted Pandaras on to the withers of her mount, and then she vaulted easily into the saddle behind him. She leaned down and told Yama, 'I had to pay the painted witch a fortune for the hire of these. Don't stand and gape. Already it may be too late.'

The horses were harnessed cavalry fashion, with light saddles and high stirrups. Yama had just grasped the horn of his mount's saddle and fitted his left foot in the stirrup, ready to swing himself up, when the ground shook. The horse jinked and as Yama tried to check it, he saw a beam of light shoot up through the aperture of the domed roof of the Black Temple.

The light was as red as burning sulphur, with flecks of violet and vermilion whirling in it like sparks flying up a chimney. It burned high into the sky, so bright that it washed the temple and the square in bloody light.

Yama realized at once what was happening, and knew that he must confront what he had wakened. He was horribly afraid of it, but if he did not face it then he would always be afraid.

He threw the reins of his mount to Tamora and ran up the steps into the temple. As he entered the long atrium, the floor groaned and heaved, like an animal tormented by biting flies. Yama fell headlong, picked himself up, and ran on towards the column of red light that burned up from the well and filled the temple with its fierce glare.

The temple was restless. The stone of its walls squealed and howled; dust and small fragments rained down from the ceiling. Several of the pillars on either side had cracked from top to bottom; one had collapsed across the floor, its heavy stone discs spilled like a stack of giant's coins. The intricate mosaics of the floor were fractured, heaved apart in uneven ripples. A long ragged crack ran back from the well, and the two old priests stood either side of it, silhouetted in the furnace light. Balcus had drawn his sword and held it above his head in pitiful defiance; Antros knelt with the heels of his hands pressed to his eyes, chanting over and over an incantation or prayer.

The language was a private dialect of the priests' bloodline, but its rhythm struck deep in Yama. He fell to his knees beside the old priest and began to chant too.

It was not a prayer, but a set of instructions to the guards of the temple.

He was repeating it for a third time when the black mesh curtain which divided the right-hand apse from the atrium was struck aside. Two, four, five of the giant soldiers marched out. The red light gleamed like fresh blood on their transparent carapaces.

The two old priests immediately threw themselves full-length on the floor, but Yama watched with rapt fascination. The five soldiers were the only survivors of the long sleep of the temple's guards. One dragged a stiff leg, and another was blind and moved haltingly under the instructions of the others, but none of them had forgotten their duty. They took up position, forming a five-pointed star around the well, threw open their chest-plates and drew out bulbous silver tubes as long as Yama was tall. Yama supposed that the soldiers would discharge their weapons into the well, but instead they aimed at the coping and floor around it and fired as one.

One of the weapons exploded, blowing the upper part of its owner to flinders; from the others, violet threads as intensely bright as the sun raked stone until it ran like water into the well. Heat and light beat at Yama's skin; the atrium filled with the acrid stench of burning stone. The floor heaved again, a rolling ripple that snapped mosaics and paving slabs like a whip and threw Yama and the priests backwards.

And the Thing Below rose up from the white-hot annulus around its pit.

It was brother to the feral machine that Yama had inadvertently drawn down at the merchant's house, although it was very much larger. It barely cleared the sides of the well — black, spherical, and bristling with mobile spines. It had grown misshapen during its long confinement, like a spoiled orange that flattens under its own weight.

The giant soldiers played violet fire across the machine, but it took no notice of them. It hung in the midst of its column of red light and looked directly into Yama's head. *You have called me. I am here. Now come with me, and serve.*

Pain struck through Yama's skull like an iron wedge. His sight was filled with red and black lightnings. Blind, burning inside and out, he gave the soldiers a final order.

They moved as one, and then Yama could see again. The four soldiers were clinging to the machine as men cling to a bit of flotsam from a wreck. They were shearing away the machine's spines with the blades of their hands.

The spines were what enabled the machine to bend the gravity field of the world to its will. It spun and jerked, like a hyrax attacked by dire wolves, but it was too late. It fell like a stone into the well, and the temple shuddered again. There was a long roaring sound, and the column of red light flickered and then went out.

27 ~ The Palace of the Memory of the People

Yama and the two priests helped each other through the smoky wreckage of the temple. A great cheer went up when they emerged into the twilight, scorched, blinking, coughing on fumes and covered in soot. The people who lived in the houses around and about the temple had run out of their homes convinced that the last day of the world was at hand, and now they knew that they were saved. Men of the priests' bloodline ran up and helped them away; Tamora urged her horse up the shallow steps, leading Yama's mount by its reins.

Yama fought through the crowd. 'It is gone!' he shouted to her. 'I woke the soldiers and I defeated it!'

'We may be too late!' Tamora shouted back. 'If you're done here, follow me!'

By the time Yama had climbed into the saddle of his horse, she was already galloping away across the square. He whooped and gave chase. His horse was a lean, sure-footed gelding, and needed little guidance as he raced Tamora through the narrow streets. The rush of warm evening air stung his scorched skin but cleared his head. His long hair, uncut since he had left Aeolis, streamed out behind him.

A bell began to toll, and Tamora looked back and yelled, 'The gate! Ten minutes before it closes!'

She lashed the flanks of her mount with her reins, and it laid back its ears and raised its tail and doubled its speed. Yama shouted encouraging words in the ear of his own horse, and it took heart and gave chase. A minute later, they shot out of the end of the narrow street and began to plough through crowds that clogged a wide avenue beneath globes of blue fire floating high in the air.

They were petitioners, penitents and palmers trying to gain entrance to the Palace of the Memory of the People, their numbers swelled by those panicked by earth tremors and strange lights. Tamora laid about her with bunched reins, and people pressed back into each other as she forced a way through, with Yama close behind. The tolling of the bell shivered the air, drowning the screams and shouts of the crowd.

When Tamora and Yama reached the end of the avenue, they found a picket line of machines spinning in the air, burning with fierce radiance like a cord of tiny suns. Overhead, more machines flitted through the dusk like fireflies. They filled Yama's head with their drowsy hum, as if he had plunged head-first into a hive of bees. Robed and hooded magistrates stood behind the glare of the picket line. Beyond them the avenue opened out into a square so huge it could easily have contained the little city of Aeolis. At the far side of the square a high smooth cliff of keelrock curved away to the left and right, punctuated by a gateway that was guarded by a decad of soldiers in silvery armour who stood on floating discs high in the blue-lit air.

The black mountain of the Palace of the Memory of the People loomed above all of this, studded with lights and blotting out the sky. Its peaks vanished into a wreath of clouds. Yama stared up at it. He had come so far in a handful of days, from the little citadel of the peel-house of the Aedile of Aeolis to this, the greatest citadel of all, which the preterites claimed was older than the world itself. He had learned that his bloodline was older than the world, and that he could bend to his will the machines which maintained the world. He had learned that the heretics considered him a great prize, and had resolved to fight against them with all his might — and he had confronted and defeated one of their dark angels.

He had left behind his childhood. Ahead lay the long struggle by which he would define himself. Perhaps it would end in death; certainly, countless men had already died in the war, and many more would die before the heretics were defeated. But at this moment, although he was exhausted and bruised, his clothes scorched and tattered, he felt more alive than ever before. Somewhere in the great citadel that reared above him, in the stacks of its ten thousand libraries, in the labyrinths of the hundreds of temples and shrines and departments, must be the secret of his origin. He did not doubt it. The woman in the shrine had said that he had come from the deep past, but she was his enemy, and surely she had been lying. He would prove her wrong. He would find the secrets that Dr Dismas had uncovered and discover where his bloodline still lived, and learn from them how to use his powers against the heretics.

Tamora caught the bridle of Yama's horse and shouted that they would do better to return tomorrow. 'The gates are about to close!'

'No! We must go now! It is my destiny!'

Pandaras raised his head and said weakly, 'My master wills it.'

Tamora grinned, showing the rack of her sharp white teeth, and held up something that flashed with red light. The picket line of incandescent machines spun apart before her. People started towards the gap and magistrates moved forward, lashing out with their quirts, driving those at the front into those pressing forward from behind. In the midst of the mêlée, a fat woman reclining on a pallet born by four oiled, nearly naked men suddenly clutched at the swell of her bosom. Under her plump hands, a vivid red stain spread over her white dress. She slumped sideways and the pallet tipped and foundered, sending a wave of confusion spreading out through the close-packed people.

Yama did not understand what had happened until a man right by his horse's flank flew forward and folded over and fell under the feet of his neighbours. Yama glimpsed the red fletching of the bolt in the dead man's back, and then the crowd closed over him.

Tamora had drawn her sword and was brandishing it about her as she forced a way through the crowd. Yama kicked at hands which tried to grasp the bridle of his plunging mount, and fought through the tumult to her side.

'Gorgo!' he shouted at Tamora. 'Gorgo! He is here!'

But Tamora did not hear him. She was leaning against Pandaras and shouting at the magistrates who barred her way. Yama reached for her shoulder and something went past his ear with a wicked crack, and when he jerked around to see where it had come from another bolt smashed the head of a man who had been trying to catch hold of the bridle of his horse.

Yama lashed out in panic and anger then. Red and black lightning filled his head. And suddenly he saw the square from a thousand points of view that all converged on a figure on a flat roof above the crowded avenue. Gorgo screamed and raised the arbalest in front of his face as hundreds of tiny machines smashed into him, riddling his torso and arms and legs. He must have died in an instant, but his body did not fall.

Instead, it rose into the air, the sole of one boot brushing the parapet as it drifted out above the packed heads of the crowd.

Yama came to himself and saw that Tamora had forced her way through the line of magistrates. He galloped after her. On the far side of the vast square, the great iron gates of the Palace of the Memory of the People were closing. The bell fell silent, and there was a shocking moment of silence. Then people felt drops of blood falling on them and looked up and saw Gorgo's riddled body sustained high above, head bowed and arms flung wide, the arbalest dangling by its strap against his ruined chest.

A woman screamed and the crowd began to yell again, ten thousand voices shouting against each other. The discs which bore the soldiers swooped towards the crowd as Yama and Tamora raced their horses across the square and plunged through the gates into the darkness beyond.